TURPINES STORY

EARLY ENGLISH TEXT SOCIETY
No. 322
2004

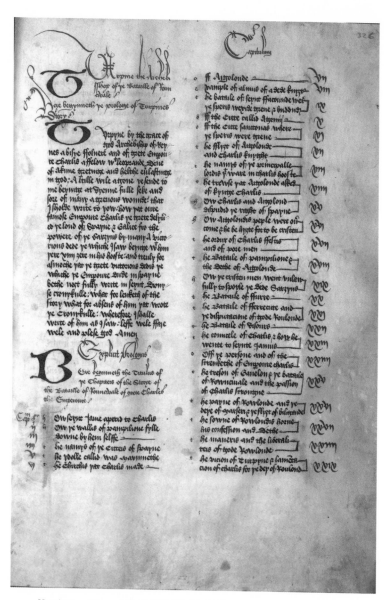

Huntington Library MS HM 28,561 fol. 326ʳ. Reproduced by permission of The Huntington Library, San Marino, California.

TURPINES STORY

A MIDDLE ENGLISH TRANSLATION OF THE *PSEUDO-TURPIN CHRONICLE*

EDITED BY

STEPHEN H. A. SHEPHERD

Published for
THE EARLY ENGLISH TEXT SOCIETY
by the
OXFORD UNIVERSITY PRESS
2004

OXFORD

UNIVERSITY PRESS

Great Clarendon Street, Oxford OX2 6DP

Oxford University Press is a department of the University of Oxford.
It furthers the University's objective of excellence in research, scholarship,
and education by publishing worldwide in

Oxford New York

Auckland Bangkok Buenos Aires Cape Town Chennai
Dar es Salaam Delhi Hong Kong Istanbul Karachi Kolkata
Kuala Lumpur Madrid Melbourne Mexico City Mumbai Nairobi
São Paulo Shanghai Singapore Taipei Tokyo Toronto

Oxford is a registered trade mark of Oxford University Press
in the UK and in certain other countries

Published in the United States
by Oxford University Press Inc., New York

British Library Cataloguing in Publication Data

Data available

Library of Congress Cataloging in Publication Data

Data applied for

ISBN 0-19-722325-7

1 3 5 7 9 10 8 6 4 2

Typeset by Anne Joshua, Oxford
Printed in Great Britain
on acid-free paper by
Print Wright Ltd., Ipswich

For Douglas Gray

PREFACE

Near the time I had anticipated completing this volume, I was able to identify the original owners of the manuscript that includes *Turpines Story*. The discovery compelled me into a re-examination of the text and its provenance which, with further delays brought on by other projects, ended up taking several years. I am grateful to all who have supported and assisted this project for their great patience, in particular Mr. Ronald Waldron, Professor Hoyt N. Duggan, Professor Ralph Hanna, and Dr. H. L. Spencer, also my departmental Chair, Dennis Foster, and Deans Jasper Neel, and U. Narayan Bhat at Southern Methodist University.

I am also grateful to the Henry E. Huntington Library in San Marino, California, for providing me with a W. M. Keck Visiting Fellowship which enabled me to transcribe the manuscript at first hand and begin researching its provenance. During that time my friend Hoku Janbazian and her family were extremely generous in hosting me at their home in nearby Monrovia. Billie Stoval of the Interlibrary Loan department at Fondren Library, SMU, was relentless in procuring a variety of books and articles, as well as images of early books and manuscripts, without which I would have made little progress in subsequent research. Two M.A. candidates in my department, Claudia Hinz and the late Tiberiu Rus, worked very carefully on preliminary drafts of the Glossary. Professor Jeanne Krochalis provided me with some useful leads for contextualizing *Turpines Story* based on her work with the *Pilgrim's Guide to Santiago de Compostela*, and Professor P. J. C. Field provided invaluable advice on navigating and interpreting fifteenth-century English genealogical and governmental records. Professor John Baker, Dr. A. I. Doyle, and Mr. Malcolm Underwood each kindly answered some crucial manuscript questions, and their contributions are detailed in footnotes in the Introduction.

All this support notwithstanding, my dear wife Shelli's care and encouragement have been the key to this project's realization.

CONTENTS

ILLUSTRATIONS

ABBREVIATIONS

The primary texts most frequently referred to are represented by the following sigla:

AN   *The Anglo-Norman 'Pseudo-Turpin Chronicle' of William de Briane*, ed. Ian Short, Anglo-Norman Text Society, 25 (Oxford, 1973)

Ir   *Gabháltas Serluis Mhóir, The Conquests of Charlemagne*, ed. Douglas Hyde, Irish Texts Society, 19 (London, 1917)

Johannes   *The Old French Johannes Translation of the 'Pseudo-Turpin Chronicle'*, ed. R. N. Walpole, 2 vols [as Critical Edition and Supplement] (Berkeley and Los Angeles, 1976)

Tr   Dublin, Trinity College MS 667, Latin text of the *Pseudo-Turpin Chronicle*

WPs-T   *Ystorya de Carolo Magno o Lyfr Coch Hergest*, ed. Stephen J. Williams (Cardiff, 1930, revised 1968)

The following are the principal abbreviations used:

EETS, os, es   Early English Text Society, Original Series, Extra Series
ME   Middle English
MED   Middle English Dictionary
MS(S)   manuscript(s)
OED   Oxford English Dictionary
om.   omitted
LALME   McIntosh *et al.*, *A Linguistic Atlas of Late Medieval English*, 4 vols.
RMLWL   Revised Medieval Latin Word-List from British and Irish Sources

INTRODUCTION

MANUSCRIPT

I. GENERAL DESCRIPTION

The following description is intended to supplement and provide corrections to the detailed account in C. W. Dutschke, *et al.*, *Guide to Medieval and Renaissance Manuscripts in the Huntington Library*.[1]

San Marino, California, Huntington Library MS HM 28,561

The manuscript (sometimes referred to as 'The Burghley *Polychronicon*')[2] comprises 337 parchment leaves, size 380 mm by 277 mm; written space is typically 264 mm by 176 mm in two columns. The collation is i parchment flyleaf, $1-4^8$, 5^8 (plus a 9th folio, f. 40), $6-24^8$, (thereafter three quires missing), $25-39^8$, 40^8 (wants the 8th folio, after f. 320), 41^8 (wants the 7th and 8th folios after f. 325), 42^8, 43^{10} (wants three folios after f. 337, with the 8th folio now used as the rear pastedown, pricked and ruled as the rest of the gathering, with a matching stub between ff. 333 and 334). Through quire 33, medieval quire signatures +, a–x, aa–hh survive; Dutschke surmizes 'the "x" on quire 23; presumably "y" on quire 24; "z", tironian 7, and "cum" symbol possibly on the 3 missing quires'. Foliation is modern, in pencil. The binding is substantial fifteenth-century work: it comprises 'three layers of leather over bevelled [oak] boards; [the outer] two layers once dyed pink or red, now faded.' There is 'evidence of two fore-edge straps closing on pins on the back cover; of the original ten brass bosses, three are missing';[3] the manuscript is sewn onto seven thongs, each inserted into its own channel in the boards. The front flyleaf and rear pastedown are contemporary with the manuscript and contain evidence of various owners: see *Later Owners* below.

---

[1] Two vols (San Marino, California, 1989), II, 683–7; all further references to Dutschke are to this guide.

[2] *Olim* Marquess of Exeter, Burghley House, Stamford, Lincs.: see *Later Owners*, below, p. xxxi.

[3] Dutschke, vol. II, p. 686.

1. ff. $1^{ra}-5^{vb}$: John Trevisa's English translation of Pseudo-William of Ockham, *Dialogus inter militem et clericum*.

2. ff. $5^{vb}-20^{vb}$: John Trevisa's English translation of Richard Fitz-ralph, *Defensio curatorum*.

3. ff. $21^{ra}-23^{va}$: An English translation, perhaps by John Trevisa, of Pseudo-Methodius, *The Beginning of the World and the End of Worlds*.[4]

4. ff. $24^{ra}-32^{rb}$: Alphabetical subject index to the *Polychronicon* in Latin.

5. ff. $32^{rb}-40^{vb}$: Alphabetical subject index to the *Polychronicon* in English.

6. ff. $41^{ra}-42^{rb}$: John Trevisa's *Dialogue between a Lord and a Clerk upon Translation*, preface to his translation of the *Polychronicon*.

7. f. $42^{rb}-42^{vb}$: John Trevisa's *Epistle* to Thomas IV, Lord Berkeley, further prefatory matter to his translation of the *Polychronicon*.[5]

8. ff. $43^{ra}-319^{va}$: John Trevisa's English translation of Ranulph Higden's *Polychronicon*.[6]

9. ff. $320^{ra}-325^{rb}$: Latin documents pertaining to the kings of England, with a Lancastrian bias (the latest date mentioned in these documents is 1447–*ad annum regni regis Henrici sexti xxv^m* (f. 323va)): i. verses on the kings of England from Alfred to Henry VI (ff. $320^{ra}-320^{vb}$); ii. details of the deposition of Richard II, his renunciation of the throne,[7] and Henry of Lancaster's

---

[4] Items 1, 2, and 3 edited by A. J. Perry, *Dialogus inter Militem et Clericum, Richard FitzRalph's Sermon: 'Defensio Curatorum,' and Methodius: Þe Bygynnyng of Þe World and Þe Ende of Worldes' by John Trevisa*, EETS os 167. Perry, not having had access to HM 28,561, argues (pp. cxi–cxv) that the translation of Methodius is not by Trevisa. Even with the additional support of the Huntington manuscript, however, the Trevisan status of the translation remains in question, as it is otherwise found in only one other manuscript, London, British Library MS Harley 1900, where it appears to have been added into the manuscript on erased leaves; that manuscript may, according to Ronald Waldron, have served as an exemplar for HM 28,561: see notes 45 and 109 below.

[5] Items 6 and 7 edited by Ronald Waldron, 'Trevisa's Original Prefaces on Translation: a Critical Edition', in *Medieval English Studies Presented to George Kane*, ed. E. D. Kennedy, *et al.*, (Woodbridge, Suffolk, 1988), pp. 285–299.

[6] *Polychronicon Ranulphi Higden monachi Cestrensis*, ed. C. Babington and R. Lumby, 9 vols, Rolls Series 41 (London, 1865–86). All further references to the *Polychronicon*, both in Latin and in Trevisa's translation, are to this edition.

[7] The text of Richard's renunciation is based on that of the 'Record and Process' found in the parliament roll of 1 Henry IV (see Richard Blyke and John Stachey, *Rotuli Parliamentorum*, 6 vols (London, 1767–77), III, 415^a). It is also nearly identical to a Latin document edited by G. O. Sayles as 'Appendix A' to his article 'The Deposition of Richard II: Three Lancastrian Narratives', *Bulletin of the Institute of Historical Research*, 54 (1981), 256–267.

accession (ff. 320vb–321va); iii. highlights of the reign of Henry IV
(ff. 321va–322rb); iv. highlights of the reign of Henry V (ff. 322rb–
323vb); v. coronations (at Westminster and St. Denis), marriage,
and genealogical claim to the thrones of Britain and France, not, as
Dutschke says, of Edward IV, but of Henry VI (ff. 323rb–325rb). As
a supplement to the fifth item, a genealogical table in the second
column of f. 323^{v} shows Edward III's claim to the sovereignty of
France; and another table (f. 324^{v}) shows the descent of Henry VI
from St Louis. The latter appears to derive from a pictorial
genealogy commissioned around 1423 by John, Duke of Bedford,
as part of his propaganda campaign in France to bolster Henry VI's
claim to the French throne, and is identical in text and layout to the
table found in Cambridge, University Library MS Ll. v. 20, f. 34^{r}
(produced in 1444).[8] A famously ornate version of this pictorial
genealogy, rendered on the frame of a large illuminated fleur-de-lys,
with miniature portraits, appears in London, British Library MS
Royal 15 E. vi, f. 3^{r}, the oft-cited collection of romances and
chivalric works in French commissioned by John Talbot, Earl of
Shrewsbury, as a gift for Margaret of Anjou, probably on the
occasion of her marriage to Henry VI in 1445.[9] This item is
possibly a later addition to the manuscript; see p. xviii below.

10. ff. 326ra–337vb: *Turpines Story*, ending imperfectly in the twenty-
fifth of thirty-five chapters, as projected in the table of chapters
(see n. to l. 16); a unique text.[10] Possibly another later addition; see
p. xviii.

---

[8] See J. W. McKenna, 'Henry VI of England and the Dual Monarchy: Aspects of Royal
Political Propaganda, 1422–1432', *Journal of the Warburg and Courtauld Institutes*, 28
(1965), 145–162 (152–153, and Plate 28b).

[9] See B. J. H. Rowe, 'King Henry VI's Claim to France in Picture and Poem', *The
Library* 4th series, 13 (1933), 77–88 (78, 80–83); see also McKenna, 'Royal Political
Propaganda', pp. 152–153, and Plate 27. For a colour plate, see *The Oxford Illustrated
History of Britain* (Oxford, 1984), ed. Kenneth O. Morgan, facing p. 193.

[10] On the choice of *Turpines Story* as the name of this text, see the Commentary, n. to
l. 1. The text is also described in Ralph Hanna III, *A Handlist of Manuscripts containing
Middle English Prose in the Henry E. Huntington Library*, The Index of Middle English
Prose: Handlist I (Woodbridge, Suffolk, 1984), pp. ix–x, 44; and listed briefly by Edward
Donald Kennedy, 'Chronicles, Other than Genealogical . . .' in *A Manual of the Writings in
Middle English 1050–1500, Volume 8: Chronicles and Other Historical Writing*, ed. Edward
Donald Kennedy (New Haven, 1989), p. 2672 (item 39). The missing leaves of the quire
could have provided enough space for the remaining chapters: see Stephen H. A.
Shepherd, 'The Middle English *Pseudo-Turpin Chronicle*', *Medium Ævum*, 65 (1996),
19–34, 29, n.6.

There are five scribes, all using variations on Secretary hands consistent with the third quarter of the fifteenth century.[11] Scribes i and ii write, in sometimes rapidly intervening stints,[12] ff. 1–319^v (items 1–8, all the Trevisan material; 40 lines to the column); According to M. B. Parkes, scribe i writes in a 'late *Anglicana Formata* of idiosyncratic type with Secretary forms' and scribe ii writes in a standard Secretary hand. Scribe iii writes ff. 320–337^v (item 9, all the Latin documents concerning the kings of England and Lancastrian succession; 39 lines to the column), using a 'late *Anglicana Formata* with some ornate secretary forms'; at the end of this material the scribe provides a numerical cipher, with arabic numerals, possibly for his name: *7.8.4.13.5*). Scribe iv writes the main text of item 10 (*Turpines Story*; 42 lines to the column), using an 'excellent Secretary hand [which is] English . . . but [which] shows Burgundian influence';[13] and scribe v (not remarked in previous descriptions of the manuscript) rubricates all the chapter headings in item 10, using an unevenly but appropriately engrossed Secretary hand.[14]

The decoration of the manuscript is of special interest. The impression is of a project of considerable ambition gone awry. Within the 'Trevisan' part of the manuscript (items 1–8), decoration, when complete, is impressive, but is often found in various stages of incompletion,[15] and is absent altogether after f. 138. At its most

---

[11] The dating of all these hands was supported by Dr. A. I. Doyle, private correspondence, 3 November, 1997; cf. Ronald Waldron, 'The Manuscripts of Trevisa's Translation of the *Polychronicon*: Towards a New Edition', *Modern Language Notes*, 51 (1990), 281–317 (p. 309, n. 29, referring to the *Polychronicon* section of the manuscript only).

[12] Scribe i writes the following stints: ff. 1–78ra, l. 5; f. 78va l. 11–end of column; ff. 81ra–82rb, l. 4; f. 87rb, l. 31–87va, l. 23; f. 100va, ll. 1–29; ff. 101va, l. 1–102va, l. 11; f. 104rb, l. 20–end of f. 104^r; f. 105ra, l. 1–105va, entire column ; fols. 109ra–111vb; all of f. 123^r. Scribe ii writes the following stints: f. 78ra, l. 5–78va, l. 10; ff. 78vb, l.1–80vb; ff. 82rb, l. 4–87rb, l. 31; ff. 87va, l. 23–all of 100^r; ff. 100va, l. 29–all of 101^r; ff. 102ra, l. 11–104rb, l. 20; all of f. 104^v; ff. 105vb–all of 108^v; ff. 112ra–all of 122^v; ff. 123va–all of 319^v (this tabulation follows Dutschke, vol. II, p. 686).

[13] M. B. Parkes, note in the Huntington Library's 'Information File' for HM 28, 561.

[14] That scribe v is not simply scribe iv adopting a different style is evident in his spelling; see *Dialect*, below.

[15] 'Stages of the unfinished decoration are apparent on ff. 26^v, 27^v, and 28^v with the outline of the border decoration and of the initials, to which gesso has been applied; on ff. 25^r, 26^r, 27^r, and 28^r the gold has been added; on ff. 83^r, 85^r, 87^r (for example) the first base of colour is present; on ff. 81^r and 82^r the ink sprays and the outlining of the bar border were completed, but colours still lack final modelling and highlighting. In quires 10, . . . 16, . . . and 18–41 . . . spaces were reserved for the initials indicated by guide letters' (Dutschke, II. 686).

elaborate, as on ff. 1^r and 88^r, the decoration involves full bar-frame
borders 'composed of narrow gold and colour strips with acanthus
leaves and ink sprays ending in green leaves, flowers and gold motifs
. . . with five- or four-line particoloured pink and green initials,
infilled with acanthus leaves and set on cusped gold grounds.'[16]
Additionally, the borders on ff. 1^r and 88^r are testaments to pride
in patronage, integrating coats of arms;[17] but even in the arms on f. 88^r
there are signs of an abortive project, where the second quartering,
which should contain *three lions rampant argent*, shows the unfinished
argent silhouettes of two lions so oversized as to permit beneath them
only the head of the third lion (also rendered in silhouette, but
fainter). It seems possible to infer that the error was noted and halted
before it went any further, but the opportunity to fix it did not come.
On the style of the decoration in this part of the manuscript, Kathleen
L. Scott notes that the borders ' . . . are probably not London work,
but I [cannot] offer any evidence except that there are many unusual
or unusually rendered motifs (e.g., f. 50^r, the half-moon shapes and
"wiggly" crowns; 58^r, oddly formed leaf; frequent occurrence of gold
balls turned into daisy flowers). The work is done by a person who
knew current styles and shop work but seems to be out of touch with
more disciplined renderings of it. It [is] a sort of "dialect style." '[18]

Decoration is absent altogether in the Latin texts of item 9, though
spaces for two-, three-, and four-line initials are reserved, with guide
letters. The four-line spaces begin on f. 323rb and appear only within
the treatment of Henry VI. The decoration of *Turpines Story* (item
10) is, like that of the Trevisan material, unfinished, but its style is
different and less ambitious. Spaces for two-, three-, and four-line
initials are reserved at the begining of each chapter, with guide letters.
Four large plain blue initials have been filled in, as the first three large
initials on the first page (f. 326ra, beginning of quire 42; first title line
and ll. 1 and 16 of this edition) and as the first large initial of the first
folio of quire 43 (f. 334rb; not noted in Dutschke; l. 819 of this
edition). Guide letters also appear for one-line initials to each of the
items in the *Titulus* at the beginning of the text (l. 18). The
rubrication is complete, and pervasive in a manner not matched

---

[16] Dutschke, II. 686.
[17] The armorials appear to be original insofar as they do not show signs of being
palimpsests and there has been no obvious attempt to erase or otherwise obscure them. For
further details, see *The Identity of the Original Owners*, below.
[18] Kathleen L. Scott, note in HM 28, 561 Information File.

anywhere else in the manuscript. Rubricated titles on the first page intrude into the margin in such a way as to suggest there was no plan for elaborate foliated borders. Two of the four blue initials are erroneous (*Bere* for *Here*, f. 326ra; *Whenne* for *Thenne*, f. 334rb).

A clear implication of the differences in contents, scripts, number of lines to the column, and decoration between the Trevisan, Latin, and 'Turpinian' material is that the latter two items are not original to the plan of the first eight. These items indeed, if not later additions, would make HM 28,561 the only major Trevisa manuscript containing additional works not attributed to him. There are, however, a few reasons for entertaining the proposition that all the items were in fact assembled under the ægis of a single patron—see *Date and Possible Circumstances of Assembly*, below, p. xxv.

2. THE IDENTITY OF THE ORIGINAL OWNERS

f. 1^r: detail   f. 88^r: detail

Reproduced by permission of the Huntington Library.

The arms on f. 1^r are those of MULL (alias Mill or Myll)[19] of Harescombe, Gloucestershire. The arms on f. 88^r are those of Mull of Harescombe quartering ROUS, also of Harescombe; the union of these arms occurred with the marriage, before 1395, of Thomas Mull of Traymill, Devon, to Julian, daughter and sole heir of Thomas Rous

---

[19] *Mull* has been selected as the representative spelling because it most likely reflects the fifteenth-century Gloucestershire pronunciation of the name (showing characteristic South-West Midlands *u* for OE *ȳ*); and it is the spelling used at that time in letters of the Berkeleys of Berkeley Castle when writing about this family (see below, pp. xxiii–xxv). All three spellings, however, are found in other contemporary records.

of Harescombe.[20] The quartering of these arms signifies the son and heir of this marriage, Thomas Mull the younger (b. 1400, d. 1460). On the basis of this identification, and other aspects of the manuscript and of the younger Thomas's life, to be outlined below, he was the commissioner of the manuscript (all further references to Thomas are to the younger unless otherwise noted).

Upon his death, Thomas was seised of the manors of Harescombe and Duntisbourne Rous in Gloucestershire; Alansmore, Avenbury, and Tregeit in Herefordshire; and Berton Mill in Devon. He owned more than 350 acres of additional land in those counties and received rents from Abbey Dore in the march of Wales in adjoining Herefordshire.[21] He inherited most or all of these estates and incomes upon the death of his father in 1422, and, from then until his death appears gradually to have increased his and his family's local prominence. At times he participated in matters of national import. He served on many royal commissions in Gloucestershire from 1437 through 1459 and was a Gloucestershire Justice of the Peace from 1437 to 1458 (he was also a lawyer);[22] he was Sheriff of Hereford for 1435–6 and 1445–6, and a member of parliament for Gloucestershire in the parliaments of 1435, 1439–40, and 1449(l).[23] Between 1435 and 1459 Thomas is recorded as in the service of Humphrey Stafford, Duke of Buckingham, as one of his estate stewards for Gloucestershire, Hampshire, and Wiltshire, and an itinerant justice in his Welsh Marcher lordships.[24] He was also a neighbour to the Staffords, as the Harescombe lands adjoined those of Haresfield, which had been

---

[20] The arms of Mull are *ermine a mill-rind sable* and those of Rous are *per pale azure and gules three lions rampant argent*. For Mull, see *Papworth's Ordinary*, pp. 955–56 and for Rous see Chesshyre and Woodcock, *Dictionary of British Arms, Medieval Ordinary, Vol. 1* (London, 1992), p. 280. The use of the mill-rind (the x-shaped hub of a millstone) is a canting device, punning on the family name. For pedigrees of Mull and Rous—with corrections and additions to the Herald's visitation of 1569 as published by the Harleian Society—and a brief history of these families' activities in and around Harescomb—see Rev. J. Melland Hall, 'Harescombe: Fragments of Local History', *Transactions of the Bristol and Gloucestershire Archaeological Society* 10 (1885–86), 67–132, 85–7, 124–30.

[21] *Calendar of the Patent Rolls, I Edward IV–7 Edward IV (1461–1467)*, pp. 72, 388, 424, 462.

[22] See Josiah C. Wedgwood, *History of Parliament: Biographies of the Members of the Commons House 1439–1509 (London, 1936)*, p. 595, and *Calendar of the Patent Rolls, 31 Henry VI–40 Henry VI (1452–1461)*, pp. 557–60, 666.

[23] Wedgwood, *Biographies*, p. 595.

[24] See Carole Rawcliffe, *The Staffords, Earls of Stafford and Dukes of Buckingham 1394–1521* (Cambridge, 1978), pp. 210, 224, 234.

held by Humphrey Stafford's parents since 1421, and by Humphrey himself from 1458.[25]

The peak of the Mull family's prominence appears to have occurred in the last two decades of Thomas's life. One indication of this comes from the reredos of the Boteler Chapel (now known as the War Memorial Chapel of St. Edmund and St. Edward) in the north-east corner of the ambulatory at Gloucester Cathedral. Reginald Boteler (alias Reynold Boulers) was Abbot of St. Peter's, Gloucester, from 1437–1450 and apparently commissioned the reredos. In two rows at the top of the reredos are painted the arms of saints, kings, and nationally, as well as locally, prominent families. The arms of Mull of Harescombe appear in the fourth bay from the left in the top row. Other arms include those of Stafford, Beauchamp, and Despenser, and, representing more local families, Boteler, Tracy (Thomas had married a Margery Tracy), Langley, Whittington, and Berkeley.[26] Thomas had two sons who rose to some prominence in this period. His second son, Hugh (b. 1425, d. 1490), was a Justice of the Peace for Gloucestershire from 1456 to 1458 and member of parliament for Shoreham (Sussex) in 1459 and Gatton (Surrey) in 1460–61; he was also a lawyer, and, after the accession of Edward IV, a conspicuous Lancastrian rebel.[27] This is the same Hugh Mull who in 1468 was imprisoned in the Tower for his part in the notorious 'Cornelius' plot, in which letters from Margaret of Anjou concerning her plans to restore Henry VI by invasion from France were to be circulated amongst some of her supporters based in London.[28] Thomas's first son, William, improved his family's prospects by marrying Frances, coheir of the prominent Gloucestershire family of

[25] *A History of the County of Gloucester*, ed. C. R. Elrington and N. M. Herbert, 10 (Oxford, 1972), p. 191.

[26] 'Notes by Canon Bazeley on the Boteler Chapel of Gloucester Cathedral', *Transactions of the Bristol and Gloucestershire Archaeological Society*, 36 (1913), 33–36. The precise date at which the reredos was installed is not known.

[27] Wedgwood, *Biographies*, pp. 594–5.

[28] See Michael Hicks, *Richard III and His Rivals: Magnates and Their Motives in The War of The Roses* (London, 1991), pp. 424, 428–9. It is assumed that Sir Thomas Malory was also a part of this plot (see P. J. C. Field, *The Life and Times of Sir Thomas Malory* (Cambridge, 1993), pp. 137–3). A Mercers Company cartulary uncovered by Anne F. Sutton shows Malory imprisoned at Newgate, 20 April, 1469, suggesting a non-political—or additional—charge: see Anne F. Sutton, 'Malory in Newgate: A New Document', *The Library*, Seventh Series, 1 (2000), 243–62). Later, Hugh 'supported the Readeption, and was specifically exempted from pardon in South Wales with the duke of Exeter, the Earl of Pembroke and Thomas ap Harry, May 1471. Nevertheless he was pardoned at last, 14 April 1475' (Wedgwood, *Biographies*, p. 594).

Winchcombe (William, like his father, could thus have been able to impale his wife's arms with his own—a sign that HM 28,561 was not commissioned by him).[29] William had achieved the rank of knight by 7 December 1460,[30] and died, within a year of his father,[31] fighting for the Lancastrian cause at the Battle of Towton ('Palm Sunday Field', 29 March 1461). In the first Parliament of Edward IV, William was posthumously attainted as a rebel; all his property was seized by the crown, and the family disinherited.[32]

Thomas himself must have been a staunch Lancastrian. He is recorded as a Lancastrian 'party' member for the parliament of 1449,[33] and in 1459 as a commissioner of array, along with his son Hugh (and others), to raise men 'to resist the rebellion of Richard, Duke of York . . .'.[34] His service with Humphrey Stafford might also presuppose a Lancastrian leaning.

Apart from the record of his fatal service at Towton, little detail survives concerning William's Lancastrian sympathies. William is recorded as having been appointed Escheator for Gloucestershire and the adjacent march of Wales from 7 November 1459 to 7 November 1460 and, in that capacity, as having taken into keeping for the Crown the manor of Painswick, formerly in the possession of John Talbot, second Earl of Shrewsbury. Talbot, like Humphrey Stafford, had been killed as a defender of King Henry at the 10 July battle with the Yorkists at Northampton in 1460. The Painswick estate was within

---

[29] See Hall, 'Harescombe', p. 128. The Winchcombe arms are *Ermine two annulets interlaced azure, on a bend gules three escallops argent.*

[30] *Calendar of the Fine Rolls* for 39 Henry VI (1460), December 1.

[31] Thomas is not recorded as holding any offices after 21 December, 1459. See *Calendar of the Patent Rolls, 31 Henry VI–39 Henry VI (1452–1461),* pp. 557–60. That his son William is not styled a knight in records before December 1, 1460 (see previous n.) might suggest that Thomas was dead by this date and that William now had enough combined income to qualify for knighthood; on the implications of this for arriving at some sense of Thomas's annual income, see n. 46 below. An unproved copy of Thomas's will, which mentions no books, is dated March 12, 1460: see Mary A. Rudd, 'Abstracts of Deeds relating to Chalford and Colcombe', *Transactions of the Bristol and Gloucestershire Archaeological Society,* 51 (1929), 211–214 (p. 214).

[32] For the Act of Attainder (December 16, 1461), see *Rotuli Parliamentorum,* (London, 1767) V, 476–83. Unlike his elder brother, Hugh Mull does not appear to have been attainted—perhaps this was because the attainder of William meant that by default Hugh had no significant property. He seems, moreover, to have been a good enough lawyer to know how to obtain pardons for himself where others could not: see P. J. C. Field, *Life and Times,* pp. 137–143.

[33] Josiah C. Wedgwood, *History of Parliament: Register of the Ministers and of the Members of both Houses, 1439–1509* (London, 1938), p. 106.

[34] *Calendar of The Patent Rolls, 31 Henry VI–39 Henry VI (1452–1461),* pp. 557–60.

three miles of Harescombe and was handed over to Talbot's mother Margaret in December.[35]

In the years after 1461, Edward IV established a conciliatory policy toward many of those attainted,[36] but the Mull family did not regain their forfeited possessions, and their appeals for restitution into the reign of Henry VII achieved very little.[37] The Mulls were clearly lesser gentry, and the apparent vehemence with which retribution was exacted upon them suggests that their importance was estimated according to their conduct and not their wealth. William's duties at Painswick could have been merely official, but there is evidence of his brother's and his father's longstanding support of the Talbots in an infamous local litigation. It is in connection with this litigation that HM 28,561, probably produced 1460–61 (see *Date* below) and thus itself a product of Thomas's heyday, perhaps reveals more about Mull's interests and ambitions than any other extant record. The litigation is known to historians of the Wars of the Roses as 'the great Berkeley law suit'. J. R. Lander provides a convenient summary of a somewhat complex history:

In a litigious age the great Berkeley law suit, or rather series of law suits, stands paramount. It was undoubtedly the longest family squabble in the whole course of English legal history . . . . The disputes originated in conflicting entails of certain parts of the Berkeley estates made between 1332 and the end of the fourteenth century. Thomas IV, Lord Berkeley, who died in 1417, failed adequately to shatter these when making his own property dispositions. . . . Lord Thomas divided his lands between his daughter [Elizabeth] and his nephew [James], the heir general and the heir male, in a way which ignored the still unbroken fourteeth-century entails which covered part of them, thus leaving wide open a path to bitter disputes and nearly two centuries of field days for the legal profession. . . . [Elizabeth] died in 1422, passing on her claims to three co-heiresses, her three daughters, Margaret, the second wife of the famous

---

[35] *Calendar of the Fine Rolls* for 39 Henry VI (1460), December 1.

[36] See J. R. Lander, 'Attainder and forfeiture, 1453 to 1509', in J. R. Lander, *Crown and Nobility 1450–1509* (Montreal, 1976), 127–58 (pp. 133–7).

[37] See Hall, 'Harescombe', pp. 86–7. Edward Mull, grandson of Sir William, is styled 'lord of Harescombe' upon the institution of Sir William Nicholson, Chaplain, to the chapel of Harescombe on 27 May, 1512, but there is no material evidence of the family's having regained its full holdings or status (see Hall, 'Harescombe', p. 95). William Mull's widow Frances was, however, permitted to hold the family's estates in Avenbury, Alansmore, and Tregeit for life; upon her death they were to revert to Thomas Herbert the elder, one of the esquires of the body to Edward IV and the king's appointed holder of most of the other Mull estates (see the entries in the *Calendar of The Patent Rolls* for 1461–1467 as identified in n. 21 above; see also pp. 197 and 205).

warrior, John Talbot, first earl of Shrewsbury; Eleanor, married in succession to
Thomas, Lord Roos of Hamlake and Edmund Beaufort, duke of Somerset; and
Elizabeth, married to George Neville, Lord Latimer. . . . [O]nly Margaret and
her descendants continued the fight . . . . [I]t was 'dirty fighting' from beginning
to end — legal actions, bribery of the great with influence at court, violent
attacks on property and mayhem on tenants. Margaret, countess of Shrewsbury
. . . captured [Isabel,] Lady Berkeley, the wife of James IV, Lord Berkeley, and
imprisoned her in Gloucester Castle. During her imprisonment she died and the
Berkeleys alleged that she was murdered.[38]

Harescombe is but eleven miles from Berkeley, home of the great
Trevisan translations, and a site of literary patronage which, as Ralph
Hanna has argued, encouraged others to engage in similar patronage
at both a national level and at the level of local acquaintance in 'what
one might consider a manorial or country-house culture'.[39] Thomas
Mull would have been very young if he knew Trevisa's original
patron, Thomas IV, Lord Berkeley (d. 1417), but he must have been
familiar with his nephew and heir male, James (d. 1462), at least from
local repute, and perhaps also from their presence at the same
parliaments (though in different Houses). Explicit evidence of the
interaction of the two families around the time HM 28,561 was
produced points to hostilities. In a letter of 1449 written to James
Berkeley, his wife, Isabel, acting as his legal representative in London,
warns him 'bee well ware of . . . Thom Mull and your false Counsell;
keep well your place, the Erle of Shroesbury lyeth right nye you, and
shapeth all the wyles that hee can to distrusse you and yours . . .'.[40]
Isabel's warnings were no exaggeration, for when she died in
Gloucester Castle (27 September, 1452),[41] Thomas Mull was a Justice

---

[38] 'Family, "Friends" and Politics in Fifteenth-Century England', in *Kings and Nobles
in the Later Middle Ages*, ed. Ralph A. Griffiths and James Sherborne (New York, 1986),
pp. 27–40 (pp. 29–30). For other accounts of the great Berkeley law suit, sometimes also
called the 'Berkeley-Lisle dispute', see Hicks, *Richard III and His Rivals*, pp. 17, 26, 50;
and John Watts, *Henry VI and The Politics of Kingship* (Cambridge, 1996), p. 176.

[39] Ralph Hanna III, 'Sir Thomas Berkeley and His Patronage,' *Speculum* 64 (1989),
878–916 (p. 906).

[40] *The Berkeley Manuscripts*, ed. John Maclean, 3 vols (London, 1883–85), II (*The Lives
of the Berkeleys by John Smyth, of Nibley*), 63. A legal manuscript written in Mull's own hand
may survive. London, British Library, MS Harley 5159, contains yearbooks of Henry VI, in
French, for 1424–26, 1431–32, 1435–37, 1440–42, and 1456–57. Sections of this large
manuscript are often signed, *quod T Mulle, Mulle, quod Mulle T*, etc. Unfortunately, the
hand does not match any found in HM 28,561 and the contents do not appear to refer to its
author's own legal activities (Professor John Baker of St. Catharine's College, Cambridge
kindly drew attention to this manuscript in private correspondence, 17 July, 1999).

[41] See *The Complete Peerage of England Scotland Ireland Great Britain and the United
Kingdom*, ed. Vicary Gibbs, *et. al.*, 12 vols (London, 1910–1959), II, 132.

of the Peace for Gloucestershire, and may have had some jurisdiction over her imprisonment.[42]

In 1469, with the feud between the Berkeleys and the Talbots passed to the next generation, William Berkeley (now Lord Berkeley) writes to Thomas Talbot, then Viscount Lisle,

I marveill greatly of thy strange and lewd writinge, made I suppose by thy false untrue Counsell that thou hast with thee, Hugh Mull, and Holt: As for Hugh Mull it is not unknown to all the worshipfull men of this Relme, how hee is attaint of falseness and rasing of the king's records. . . .[43]

Clearly the evidence of the Mull family's involvement in the Berkeleys' affairs points to a dangerously litigious relationship. Perhaps the relationship extended to Thomas Mull's decision to commission his manuscript. One cannot be certain about the extent to which the manuscript was intended for public viewing (presumably this would occur at the manor house at Harescombe), but its inclusion of armorials is consistent with Mull's desire for public identification as evident in the Mull arms on the reredos of the Boteler Chapel at Gloucester.

Perhaps Mull intended the Berkeleys of Berkeley Castle, through the interactions of a 'manorial or country-house culture', to become aware of his commission of the manuscript. Perhaps he intended for them to see in the manuscript a symbol of the appropriation of their heritage which was the goal of the lawsuit; and perhaps he intended the Berkeleys to be demoralized by the evident determination of his antagonism. If Mull's employers, the Talbots, had been made aware of the manuscript's commission, they may have been flattered by their employee's emulation of their own interests in literary patronage. Hanna has noted that one fairly prolific route by which Berkeley's patronage of English translation extended beyond Lord Thomas himself was through the influence of his daughter Elizabeth Berkeley-Beauchamp and her household, in the first quarter of the fifteenth century.[44] From this perspective, Thomas Mull's association with Elizabeth's daughter, Margaret, Countess of Shrewsbury,

---

[42] For a full list of the Gloucestershire Comission for the Peace for that year, which included not just Mull but also John Talbot, son of the Earl of Shrewsbury, see the *Calendar of the Patent Rolls* (1452–1461), p. 666.

[43] *The Berkeley Manuscripts*, II, 110.

[44] Hanna, 'Sir Thomas Berkeley', pp. 901–6. See also Margaret Connolly, *John Shirley: Book Production and the Noble Household in Fifteenth-Century England* (Aldershot, 1998), pp. 114–16 (under 'The Beauchamp books').

suggests that he may have intended his manuscript to stand in his employer's eyes as an extra-legal commitment (no doubt with a view to seeking preferment) to preserving the literary heritage sustained by Elizabeth's branch of the family.

These possibilities give additional (if not ironic) weight to Hanna's proposition that 'Berkeley influence [in the patronage of English translation] may, in some quarters, have had considerable staying-power' beyond Lord Thomas's lifetime.[45] By the time of Mull's commission, the esteem in which patronage of English translation was held appears to have been strong enough—at least within the Berkeley milieu— to be implicated in a politics of identity, supporting a claim of hereditary entitlement among the nobility and social preferment among the gentry.

For further consideration of the possible implications of Mull's patronage, see the next section (3), and *Contextualizing 'Turpines Story'* (4), below.

3. DATE AND POSSIBLE CIRCUMSTANCES OF ASSEMBLY

It seems likely that the deaths and attainders of Thomas Mull and his eldest son Sir William in 1460–61 provide, on political and financial grounds, a *terminus ad quem* for the Trevisan elements of the manuscript, and may account for their incomplete decoration. Presumably work on the manuscript would have ceased as soon as it became clear that the patron, or his heir, or both, were dead, and that, because of the posthumous attainder against them, their estate would not exist to pay for remaining work.[46] Thomas Mull may never

---

[45] Hanna, 'Sir Thomas Berkeley', p. 905. It may also be supposed that, despite their proximity to Berkeley, the Mulls probably had to get their copy texts for the Trevisan material elsewhere, perhaps from someone within the Talbot/Beauchamp (or possibly Stafford) affinity. Ronald Waldron has established that the *Polychronicon* of HM 28,561, like its closest relative and possible exemplar, London, British Library, MS Harley 1900, is unlikely to derive immediately from a text sourced at Berkeley Castle: see Waldron, 'The Manuscripts of Trevisa's Translation of the *Polychronicon*', pp. 281–317. Like Harley 1900, however, as Waldron also notes, the dialect of the *Polychronicon* in HM 28,561 retains a south-western character; see p. xlviii below.

[46] A contemporary model for the kind of payment-in-process proposed here is available in the records of Sir John Paston's dealings in 1468 with the main scribe of his 'Grete Boke', William Ebesham, who records partial payments from Paston and outlines the cost of work yet to be done; see G. A. Lester, *Sir John Paston's 'Grete Boke'* (Woodbridge, Suffolk, 1984), pp. 36–43. Ebesham charged 2*d* for one leaf of single-column prose: the 'Grete Boke' (now London, British Library MS Lansdowne 285) is a less ostentatious book than HM 28,561, rather similar in size and decorative scope to the Winchester Malory (see Carol Meale, 'Manuscripts, Readers and Patrons in Fifteenth-Century England: Sir Thomas Malory and Arthurian Romance,' in *Arthurian Literature IV*, ed. Richard

have seen his book, let alone read it. One aspect of the decoration which may support this proposition is the unfinished but also faulty rendering of the armorial on f. 88^r. Even if the decoration had been stopped by Thomas Mull before 1460 simply because of financial constraint, one wonders if he would have been willing to settle for a faulty blazon on what was the premier, and otherwise complete, display page for the manuscript. It also seems possible that the Lancastrian material in Latin could have been included in the manuscript to suit Mull's interests; clearly, as history, it is suitable company for the *Polychronicon*, and even provides a kind of updated epitome of English history since the closing date of the *Polychronicon* in 1387. As Lancastrian history in particular, it would have served the Mulls' political enthusiasms well; even the pictorial genealogy of Henry VI, which has its origins around 1423 as propaganda for use in France, belongs to a cluster of Lancastrian symbols which 'seem to have been adopted and sophisticated by the participants in the party struggles which characterized the middle decades of the fifteenth century.'[47] Further, if the pictorial genealogy was comissioned by Mull, then it may have been intended in part as a tribute to his employer, the Earl of Shrewsbury, who had commissioned a *de luxe* version of the genealogy about fifteen years earlier for Margaret of Anjou (see above, p. xv).

Circumstantial evidence suggests that it may be premature also to assume that *Turpines Story* does not owe its existence to Thomas Mull's patronage. There is nothing compelling on palaeographical or lexical[48] grounds to suggest a date inconsistent with 1460–61. Like

---

Barber (Cambridge, 1985), 93–126 (pp. 114–16)). Using Ebesham's rates as a rough yet conservative guide, Mull would have had to pay at least £3 for just the basic copying of the Trevisan portion of the manuscript, excluding rubrics and decoration. The significance of such expenditure for Mull is difficult to gauge. According to a statute of 18 Henry VI (1439) as a Justice of the Peace, he would have had to hold lands to the annual value of £20: see Terrick V. H. FitzHugh, *The Dictionary of Genealogy* (Sherborne, Dorset, 1985), under 'Justices of the Peace'. That Mull had income to spare is suggested by a Patent Roll record of 1462 which reports that before his death, Thomas granted his son William the manors of Avensbury and Alansmore, rendering William £10 annually: see *Calendar of the Patent Rolls* (1461–1467), p. 72.

[47] McKenna, 'Royal Political Propaganda,' p. 162,

[48] A number of words in *Turpines Story* are not recorded before the second quarter of the fifteenth century (MED earliest dates are cited): (*a*)*poynment* (1427: ll. 610, 612, 616, 773), *beuteus* (a. 1438: l. 111), *gurgulione* (?1440: l. 860), (*h*)*eritaunce* (c. 1450: ll. 555, 582), *inperscrutable* (c. 1450: l. 707), *regulere* (of canons, 1440: l. 627); and cf. the notes to ll. 4, 180, and 535. Antedatings in *Turpines Story*, assuming a *terminus ad quem* of 1460–61, are largely attributable to variations between established English forms, or anglicizing of the

the Latin material, the quality of parchment, the quality and style of script, and the dimensions of the bicolumnar body of text (including ample margins), are consistent with the Trevisan portion of the manuscript. Indeed, the dimensions of the written space, the space between columns, and the location of the colums on the page are virtually identical across the manuscript, giving the impression of a quite deliberate consistency. The quires comprising *Turpines Story*, as well as the Latin material, show no signs of wear on their faces or edges, or signs of re-sewing consistent with prior unbound circulation. The decoration, like that of the Trevisan section, has been started but then abandoned. The content of *Turpines Story* is itself a natural complement to the *Polychronicon* and the text 'may well have been added in response to Higden's own recommendation . . . (as translated by Trevisa)':[49]

. . . who þat woll se more of Charlis lif mot loke of . . . Turpyn þe archebisshopis bokis.[50]

There may even have been a Lancastrian interest behind adding *Turpines Story* because it glorifies Charlemagne.[51] A Ballade by John Lydgate, presented to the young king on the occasion of his French coronation in 1431, cites Charles the Great as one of the king's worthy ancestors. And at roughly the same time as HM 28,561 was being produced, a pageant symbolically established Queen Margaret as the Tenth Worthy, the fourth Christian among the group and a peer of Charlemagne.[52] Finally, several features of *Turpines Story*: aspects of its dialect, a couple of evidently deliberate and eccentric deviations from its Latin source, and perhaps some suggestions of its proximity to the translator's draft, all show the signs of a work which could well have been commissioned by Thomas Mull himself.[53]

Latin source from which *Turpines Story* is translated: *lymfatted* (OED 1610: l. 1068); *rynedide* 'rinded' (OED 1552: l. 434); see also the n. to l. 535, and cf. *calor* (OED 1599: l. 836) quoted in the text as a Latin word in need of translation. On the Latin source, see '*Turpines Story* as a Translation' below, pp. xxxviii–xliii. For the immediate sources of the words cited, see the notes in the Commentary.

[49] Shepherd, 'Middle English *Pseudo-Turpin*', p. 20.

[50] Quoted from MS HM 28,561, f. 221vb (= *Polychronicon* ,VI, 265).

[51] *The Minor Poems of John Lydgate* II (Secular Poems) ed. H. N. MacCracken, EETS OS 192 (1934), p. 625, l. 13.

[52] See B. P. Wolffe, *Henry VI* (London, 1981), p. 306. Cf. also the extensive Carolingian content of the well known manuscript of romances and other chivalric materials given by John Talbot to Margaret of Anjou, probably on the occasion of her marriage: see below, p. lii.

[53] See *Contextualizing 'Turpines Story' : Patronage*, below.

If the entire manuscript was compiled at the behest of Mull, then its component parts, presumably having been contracted out separately, would appear to have been rounded up when notice, either of the patron's death, or his attainder was received. It is possible that the manuscript was retrieved by William Mull after the death of his father; with the simultaneous violent deaths of his family's principal noble employers, Humphrey Stafford and John Talbot, the effect on the Mulls' political and financial security must have been catastrophic. Perhaps the binding had already been paid for, but it is just as likely that it was made for a later owner. Kathleen Scott's remark about the 'dialect style' of decoration in the Trevisan portion of the manuscript suggests regional production, and A. I. Doyle argues that 'it would be wrong to suppose that by . . . the second or third decade of the fifteenth century, English books of the highest quality were produced only in the metropolis.' When considering two manuscripts of this period made for Thomas Lord Berkeley, apparently of local manufacture, and other manuscripts with similar traits, Doyle wonders "if the manuscripts of this group are not Bristol products, as the most obvious regional centre for a book-trade.'[54]

4. LATER OWNERS

Technically speaking, the second owner of the manuscript would have been Edward IV, who on 9 May, 1461, commissioned his Esquire of the Body, Thomas Herbert '. . . to take into the King's hands all the possessions late of William Mille, knight, deceased, rebel . . .'.[55] A little over a year later Herbert was granted most of the Mull estates 'with all woods, mills, fisheries, knights' fees, wards,

---

[54] A. I. Doyle, 'English books In and Out of Court from Edward III to Henry VII', in *English Court Culture in the Later Middle Ages*, ed. V. J. Scattergood and J. W. Sherborne (New York, 1983), 163–81 (172–3). If they are local products, the two manuscripts known to have been comissioned for Berkeley, Oxford, Bodleian Library, MS Bodley 953 (containing Rolle's Psalter) and MS Digby 233 (containing Trevisa's translation of Giles of Rome's *De Regimine Principium* and Walton's translation of Vegetius, *De Re Militari*), both with south-western dialect characteristics, demonstrate a very high quality of production, superior in every way to that of HM 28,561. They suggest that HM 28, 561 fell well within the capabilities of local producers. For comparative illustrations, see O. Pächt and J. J. G Alexander, *Illuminated Manuscripts in the Bodleian Library*, III (Oxford, 1973), 63, no. 701, plates lxx–lxxi, and p. 72, no. 815, plate lxx: cf. Dutschke, vol. II, plate 127.

[55] *Calendar of the Patent Rolls, 1461–1467*, p. 30. For further details about Herbert, see Wedgwood, *Biographies*, pp. 443–4.

marriages, reliefs, escheats, courts, views of frankpledge, and other appurtenances, to hold by fealty only'.[56] Whether Herbert, or his successors to the Mull estate[57] ever materially came into possession of the manuscript is unknown. If he did, the likelihood is that he would have sold it quickly, as there were no guarantees that the privations of attainder were permanent.[58]

What is more certain is that, before the end of the fifteenth century, the manuscript found its way to a small area in south Lincolnshire extending from Moulton, fifteen miles southwest, to Burghley House, one mile south of Stamford, where it stayed until 1959. A number of personal names appear in the margins and on the flyleaves in fifteenth- and sixteenth-century hands. Two groups of names are especially revealing. On the rear pastedown, in a large fifteenth-century hand are three trial notations: 'þ^{is} boke longyth to Rycharde Welby gentyllman', 'þ^{is} boke longyth to Rychard Welby', 'Welby Rycharde'; and, on f. 255^r, in lead, appears 'Welby Willm'. On the front flyleaf, verso, appear seven Latin entries detailing marriages and births from 1503 to 1514 in a family named Hornby.

A Richard Welby (1415–65) of Moulton, Lincolnshire, is recorded as Member of Parliament for Lincolnshire for 1450–51 and Justice of the Peace for Holland 1444–65. Like Thomas Mull he was a lawyer, and he served on the same Lancastrian commission of array as Mull in December 1459.[59] The *Chronicle of the Abbey of Croyland* says that in this period Welby's family were 'the principal inhabitants of Multon, a family highly ennobled and of gentle blood . . . and to whom the people of those parts were not in the habit of offering opposition'.[60] Richard had seven sons, the fifth of whom was named

---

[56] Grant dated 12 July 1462: *Calendar of the Patent Rolls, 1461–1467*, p. 72.

[57] Upon his death, the properties passed to his son Thomas the younger, who died without issue. The properties were transferred to Sir Richard Beauchamp by 1475 (*Calendar of the Patent Rolls, 1467–1477*, p. 454). Records of subsequent holders of the property before 1509 are obscure: see Hall, 'Harescombe', pp. 87, 95.

[58] It is conceivable that the manuscript came into the hands of Hugh Mull, perhaps by subterfuge, if he alone knew of its whereabouts while under construction. However, the tumultuous circumstances of his life over the next fourteen years (see p. xx above) and its attendant rigours of mobility and insolvency would make this circumstance seem unlikely.

[59] Wedgwood, *Biographies*, pp. 927. Unless otherwise noted, all subsequent details about the Welby family derive from pp. 927–8 of this volume. On the commission of array shared with Thomas Mull, see above, p. xxi.

[60] Henry T. Riley, ed., *Ingulph's Chronicle of the Abbey of Croyland with the Continuations by Peter of Blois and Anonymous Writers* (London, 1854), p. 507 (continuation for 1485).

William (d. 1519);[61] the signature of 'Willm' on f 255^r, made in lead with very large otiose strokes, could be that of a youth. Given his death date, Richard would have had to have acquired the manuscript not long after the 1461 attainder.[62] That the Welby family was from the other side of the country suggests that the manuscript probably reached them by way of London.

Richard's first son was also named Richard (born 1440), and so he cannot be ruled out as the first Welby to own the manuscript. He was Member of Parliament for Lincolnshire for 1472–75 and 1483–85; he was Justice of the Peace for Holland more or less continuously from 1466 until his death in 1487; he was Sheriff of Lincolnshire c. 1471; and from 1478 he was made receiver general for the Honour of Richmond estates in Lincolnshire, a position he held until his death.[63]

Since the Welby signatures appear on the rear pastedown, it is reasonable to assume that the binding was in place, giving the likely *terminus ante quem* for its construction as 1465, if the signature is the elder Richard's, or 1487 if it is the younger's. The elder is more likely to be the purchaser of the manuscript. His acquaintance with Thomas Mull is possible, for their common service on the December 1459 commission of array could point, at least, to shared Lancastrian sympathies, though Richard did retain his place on the bench after 1461.

The entries on the front flyleaf, verso, concern the Hornby family of Deeping, Lincolnshire, six miles east of Stamford, and were written by Henry Hornby (d. 1518).[64] By 1499 Henry was Dean of

---

[61] *Lincolnshire Pedigrees*, Publications of the Harleian Society 52 (1904), pp. 1055–7. According to this pedigree, William had a son, Henry, born 1501 (d. 1536), who married an unnamed daughter of David Sysell (i.e. Cecil) of Stamford, grandfather of William, Lord Burghley. On Welby's duties as receiver, see B. P. Wolffe, 'The Management of English Royal Estates under the Yorkist Kings', *English Historical Review*, 71 (1956), 1–27 (7–9).

[62] Welby's will survives, in English, but mentions no books: see *Lincoln Diocese Documents*, ed. Andrew Clark, EETS 149 (1914), 119–125.

[63] The Honour of Richmond, a valuable collection of estates centred in Yorkshire but extending into several other counties, had from the Conquest until 1399 been claimed by the Dukes of Brittany. In 1342 it was granted by Edward III to his son, John of Gaunt, who surrendered it in 1372, when it was granted to John de Montfort, Duke of Brittany. In 1399 it was seized by Henry IV who then granted it to Ralph, fourth Baron Neville of Raby. From 1414 to 1435 it was conferred upon John, duke of Bedford; in 1452 it was conferred upon Edmund Tudor, and in 1485, with the accession of Edmund's son, Henry VII, it merged with the crown. On Welby's retention of his position under Henry VII, see B. P. Wolffe, 'Henry VII's Land Revenues', p. 234.

[64] Hornby does not name himself in his notes, but refers to *Georgus filius meus . . . . Henricus filius meus . . . . Nicholaus filius . . . .* The names of the children correspond to

Chapel to Lady Margaret Beaufort, and he was her chancellor from 1504 to 1509, serving, among other places, at her favoured manor of Collyweston, just four miles south-west of Stamford.[65] He was also an academic, having been credited with contributing in 1489 to the creation of a new office for the feast of the Name of Jesus; he founded a school at Boston, and was Master of Peterhouse from 1501 to 1518 and Master of Tattershall College from 1502 to 1508.[66] He was clearly no stranger to books, and presumably would have had access to many different sources and resources for acquiring them. There is some evidence to suggest an indirect connection with the Welbys by way of Lady Margaret Beaufort,[67] but the most that can be said with confidence is that Hornby probably acquired the manuscript from within the immediate environs of Stamford.

It is also likely that William Cecil, Lord Burghley (1520–1598) acquired the manuscript in or around Stamford. He may have indulged in the collecting of *Polychronicons*.[68] Notes in his hand appear in the margins of ff. 287^r, 299^v, and 319^r. The manuscript was kept, presumably since William Cecil's lifetime, at Burghley House,

those given in his will (Prerogative Court of Canterbury, 6 Ayloffe, proved 16 March 1518). Mr. Malcolm Underwood of St John's College, Cambridge, kindly made this identification in private correspondence, 20 July 1999.

[65] Michael K. Jones and Malcolm G. Underwood, *The King's Mother: Lady Margaret Beaufort, Countess of Richmond and Derby* (Cambridge, 1992), pp. 153–4.

[66] *The King's Mother*, pp. 168, 276. Tattershall College, 35 miles northeast of Stamford, was founded by Ralph, fourth Baron Cromwell, Lord High Treasurer, near the time of his death in 1456. The College, a grammar school, was intended to bring together priests and local secular clerks and choristers. After Cromwell's death one of his executors, William Waynflete, Bishop of Winchester, was responsible for much of the development of the college, though he also took advantage of revenues from Cromwell's legacy in endowing his own foundation, Magdalen College, Oxford. See Virginia Davis, *William Waynflete: Bishop and Educationalist* (Woodbridge, Suffolk, 1993), pp. 77–9, 138–51. For details of Lady Margaret's administration of the College and of Hornby's career there, see Malcolm G. Underwood, 'The Lady Margaret and Her Cambridge Connections', *Sixteenth-Century Journal*, 13 (1982) 67–82 (p. 72).

[67] In 1487, the year of the younger Richard Welby's death, Lady Margaret Beaufort was granted by the crown the Honour of Richmond estates in Lincolnshire, situated mainly in the Fens around Boston; these were the same estates for which Welby had been receiver general (see *The King's Mother*, p. 103; cf. n. 66 above).

[68] Three *Polychronicons* are listed in a 1687 sale catalogue advertising books from Cecil's library: see W. W. Greg, 'Books and Bookmen in the Correspondence of Archbishop Parker', *The Library*, 4th series, 16 (1935–36), 243–79 (275–6). Burghley was known for his avid acquisition of books and manuscripts from early adulthood, and appears to have assembled a library in excess of a thousand volumes. In addition to Greg's article, see B. W. Beckingsale, *Burghley: Tudor Statesman* (London, 1967), 249–50; J. A. van Dorsten, 'Mr. Secretary Cecil, Patron of Letters', *English Studies*, 50 (1969), 545–53; and Michael A. R. Graves, *Burghley* (London, 1998), p. 209.

Stamford, until it was sold to Frank Hammond Booksellers of Birmingham at Christie's on 15 July, 1959. Hammond sold the manuscript in 1965 to J. Howell Books in San Francisco, who sold it to the Huntington Library in the same year.[69]

Evidence of other owners between Hornby and Cecil is less secure but still informative. Latin notations on ff. 210^v and 213^v in a late fifteenth-century or early sixteenth-century hand, concerning Peterborough and Croyland abbeys, suggest a local interest consistent with the region of the known later owners. Two different mid to late sixteenth-century Secretary hands on the rear pastedown name 'Robard Smythe' who was 'marryed the .xix. daye of Octobar anno 1500/30/7,' and 'Johnn Hornywold the sone off Richard Hornywold'. The 'Hornywold' hand also writes 'The Kyng off mery England.' Smythe and the Hornywolds remain to be identified, but the name Hornywold is likely to be a variant of Hornighold (alias Horniwale, Horniold), the name of a village in Leicestershire just fifteen miles south-west of Stamford—a further indication that the manuscript circulated in this restricted area. A few pen trials in French also appear, perhaps written by the 'Hornywold' scribe, though rendered in a more formal style closer to that of an engrossing Elizabethan Secretary hand.[70] That the manuscript remained in learned and bibliophilic circles is suggested by the longest of these trials—

A Paris sur petit pont geline de feur*re*

—seemingly a verbatim transcription of a line either from Rabelais's *Pantagruel*, first published in 1532, or a song by Jannequin (though both appear to be recalling a conventional cry of Paris merchants).[71] The earliest known untranslated quotation of Rabelais in an English context occurs in *A Dictionarie French and English*, by Claude de Sainliens (alias Claudius Holyband), published in 1593.[72]

[69] Dutschke, II. 687. The manuscript had gone missing for a long time at Burghley House and was unavailable to Perry for his edition of Trevisan texts; see Perry, *Dialogus*, pp. xxv–xxvii.

[70] Cf. Anthony G. Petti, *English Literary Hands from Chaucer to Dryden* (London, 1977), plate 21 (hand dated 1574), p. 17.

[71] See *Oeuvres de François Rabelais*, ed. Abel Lefranc et. al., 6 vols. (Paris, 1912–1931), IV, ll. 77–78 (pp. 151–2) and n. 67.

[72] Huntington Brown, *Rabelais in English Literature* (New York, 1967), pp. 41–2.

CONTEXTUALIZING *TURPINES STORY*

I. SOME ENGLISH CONTEXTS

As a major component of the 'Matter of France' in Britain, the place of the *Pseudo-Turpin Chronicle* generally has been well documented and need not be repeated here.[73] Less discussed is the degree to which the work was abstracted into non-legendary and non-historiographical literatures in England. In this respect two trends deserve consideration for their potential influence on *Turpines Story*, however circumstantial the evidence for that influence may be. As noted above (p. xxvii), Higden explicitly acknowledges the *Pseudo-Turpin* as an authority on Charlemagne, and the placing of *Turpines Story* in a *Polychronicon* manuscript suggests that it was seen as an appropriate complement.[74] But Higden also makes five substantial references to the *Chronicle* itself within the *Polychronicon*: 1) on the origin of *Franci* as the name for Frenchmen (I, 272–274; corresponding to a passage in chapter XXX of the standard Latin version of the *Pseudo-Turpin*[75]— now missing in *Turpines Story*). 2) on the idol of Muhammad (VI, 40–42; corresponding to *Pseudo-Turpin* chapter IV = *Turpines Story*, ll. 214–38). 3) on the story of Charles and the paupers (VI, 251–253; corresponding to *Pseudo-Turpin* chapter XIII = *Turpines Story*,

---

[73] For an introductory survey of the primary texts (including the English 'Charlemagne romances') and related scholarship, as well as lists (and references to lists) of known *Pseudo-Turpin* manuscripts of Insular provenance, see Shepherd, 'Middle English *Pseudo-Turpin*', section III. To the lists of manuscripts of Insular provenance containing versions of the *Pseudo-Turpin* should be added Gloucester Cathedral MS 1 (probably produced at the monastery at Reading or its cell at Leominster, containing material mostly related to miracles of St James, with excerpts from *Pseudo-Turpin* chapters 1, 2, 5, 7, 21, 22, and 25). See *The Pilgrim's Guide: A Critical Edition*, ed. Alison Stones and Jeanne Krochalis, 2 vols (London, 1998), I. 230–1. The most complete critical bibliography is by Susan E Farrier, *The Medieval Charlemagne Legend: An Annotated Bibliography* (New York, 1993).

[74] Other manuscripts which combine a Latin *Pseudo-Turpin* with a Latin *Polychronicon* are London, British Library MS Royal 13 D.i and Cambridge, University Library MS Dd. i.17, possibly a copy. On the former, see *The Pseudo-Turpin*, ed. H. M. Smyser (Cambridge, Massachusetts, 1937), p. 53; on the latter, see André de Mandach, *La Geste de Charlemagne et de Roland* (Paris, 1961), p. 368; Anne Middleton, 'The Audience and Public of *Piers Plowman*', in *Middle English Alliterative Poetry and Its Literary Background*, ed. David Lawton (Cambridge, 1982), 101–123 (p. 106); and Julia Crick, *Historia Regum Britanniæ of Geoffrey of Monmouth*, vol. 3, *A Summary Catalogue of the Manuscripts* (Cambridge, 1989), 180–3.

[75] *Historia Karoli Magni et Rotholandi, ou Chronique du Pseudo-Turpin*, ed. C. Meredith-Jones (Paris, 1936), p. 219, l. xxiii–p. 221, l. iv. For the conventions adopted by the present edition for citing Meredith-Jones and other selected versions of the *Pseudo-Turpin*, see the headnote to the Commentary, p. 37.

ll. 616–48). 4) on the description of Charles (VI, 252–254; corresponding to the beginning of *Pseudo-Turpin* chapter XX (175, vii—177, iv) = *Turpines Story*, ll. 1057–87). 5) on Turpin's vision concerning the dead Emperor's salvation (VI, 264–266; corresponding to *Pseudo-Turpin* chapter XXXII (229, xv—231, iv) —now missing in *Turpines Story*). All of these are translated by Trevisa, mostly without comment, but the third clearly drew his ire and he could not resist a rebuke:

De libro Turpini. In a day whan trewes was i-graunted [in] eiþer side, Aigolandus, a strong prince of Spayne, come to Charles to be cristned, and sigh al þat were at þe bord realliche i-cloþed and likyngliche i-fedde, and sigh afer þrittene pore men sitte on þe grounde and have foule mete and symple wiþ oute eny bord, and he axede what þey were. Me answerde hym and seide: 'þese þrittene beeþ Goddes messangers, and prayeþ for us, and bringeþ to us mynde of þe nombre of Cristes disciples.' 'As I see,' quod Aigolandus, 'ʒoure lawe is nouʒt riʒtful þat suffreþ Goddes messangers be þus evel bylad; he serveþ evel his lord þat so fongeþ his servauntes;' and so he was lewedliche offended, and despised cristenynge and wente hoom aʒen; but Charles worschipped afterward pore men þe more. Trevisa. Aigolandus was a lewed goost, and lewedliche i-meved as þe devel hym tauʒte, and blende hym þat he kouþe nouʒt i-knowe þat men schulde be i-served as here astaat axeþ. (VI, 251–253)

Higden seems to offer this striking story primarily as a measure of Charles's admirable capacity for self-correction,[76] but it also implicitly carries the force of a censorious *exemplum* on the high demands of Christian charity. It was in this latter sense especially that the episode was used by other English writers. Thomas Brinton, Bishop of Rochester, employs the episode in two sermons written c. 1376–1377. In one case his purpose is to demonstrate, as does the *Pseudo-Turpin* in a portion of its conclusion to the episode, the truth of James 2:26: [*est*] *fides sine operibus mortua*[77] (cf. the standard Latin *Pseudo-*

---

[76] On the probable origins of this episode as found in the *Pseudo-Turpin*, see the Commentary, n. to l. 614.

[77] Thomas Brinton, 'De Sancta Maria Magdalena' (Sermon77) in *The Sermons of Thomas Brinton, Bishop of Rochester (1373–1389)*, ed. Sister Mary Aquinas Devlin, 2 vols, Camden Series 75–6 (London, 1954), II. 351. All further references to Brinton are to this edition. To judge from his wording, Brinton's source for the episode is probably the work of another Englishman, the popular *Summa prædicantium* of John Bromyard (d.c. 1390). There is no modern edition of this work, and all further references to the *Summa prædicantium* will be to the two-volume 1586 Venice edition. The story of Charles and the paupers appears under *Eleemosyna*, section 29 (vol. 1, chapter III, f. 230^{ra-va}). Of Charles's mistreatment of the paupers, Bromyard concludes, 'Tales immisericordes dupliciter peccant, primo, quia infideles (ut dictum est) scandalizant, & in spirituali morte detinent, secundo, quia illos, a quibus talia subtrahunt subsidia, corporaliter occidunt.'

Turpin, 139, xxiv–xxvi); in the other, to show that the rich and the poor should serve one another in humility and faith respectively, such that they may become, as Psalm 48 says, *simul in unum dives et pauper*.[78] The latter interpretation favours an ecumenical, even egalitarian approach of a kind which is likely to have irritated Trevisa; perhaps, indeed, Trevisa's reaction to Higden comes as much from his resistance to the prevalence of a personally distasteful interpretation as it does to the interpretation itself.

The kinds of variant positions evident between Brinton and Trevisa appear to be accommodated without opposition, if not difficulty, by William Langland. In B Passus XII, Ymaginatif lectures Will on the salvific advantage of learning: ' . . .he þat knoweþ clergie kan sonner arise/Out of synne and be saaf, þou3 he synne ofte,/If hym likeþ and lest, þan any lewed [sooþly]'.[79] Ymaginatif provides the example of the thief, one alien to Christ's teaching, who yielded to Christ on Good Friday and was saved, but who then received a relatively low station in heaven (' . . .þou3 þat þeef hadde hevene he hadde noon hei3 blisse,/As Seint Iohan and oþere Seintes þat deserued hadde bettre' (XII, 196–197)). Following this come eight lines which support the example with a graphic analogy highly reminiscent of the *Pseudo-Turpin* episode:

> Ri3t as som man yeue me mete and [sette me amydde þe floor];
> [I] hadde mete moore þan ynou3, ac no3t so muche worshipe
> As þo þat seten at þe syde table or wiþ the souereynes of þe halle,
> But as a beggere bordlees by myself on þe grounde.
> So it fareþ by þat felon þat a good friday was saued;
> He sit neiþer wiþ Seint Iohan, Symond ne Iude,
> Ne wiþ maydenes ne with martires [ne wiþ mylde] wydewes,
> But by hymself as a soleyn, and serued on [þe] erþe. (XII, 198–205)[80]

---

[78] Brinton, 'Simul in vnum diues et pauper' (Sermon 44), I, 196. For a translation of this sermon, see Jeanne Krochalis and Edward Peters, *The World of 'Piers Plowman'* (Philadelphia, 1975), pp. 115–24.

[79] *Piers Plowman: The B Version*, ed. George Kane and E. Talbot Donaldson (London, 1975), Passus XII, ll. 171–2. All further quotations from *Piers Plowman* are from this edition.

[80] Langland may have the same source in mind in the next passus, where Will dreams that he and Patience are 'seten bi ourselue at [a] side borde' (XIII, 36) and witness a distinction between the rich spiritual food that they are offered and the rich bodily food unrepentantly consumed by a doctor of divinity, and concludes, '"Ac þis goddes gloton . . . wiþ hise grete chekes/Haþ no pite on vs pouere; he parfourneþ yuele/That he precheþ [and] preueþ no3t [com]pacience" . . .' (XIII, 78–80).

Derek Pearsall notes that the scriptural basis for the 'well established doctrine that there are degrees of bliss in heaven' is John 14:2 ('In my Father's house are many mansions'),[81] but there is perhaps something more to be said about Ymaginatif's choice of the potentially allusive 'beggere bordlees' side of the analogy. If one assumes, with due caution, that the passage from the *Pseudo-Turpin* is Langland's source, whether seen by him directly or in some encylopaedic collection, then Langland has augmented it by adding to the original lesson on the proper treatment of the poor (as alarmingly emphasized by the righteous—and right—outrage of a heathen), a lesson on relative merit in salvation.[82] Langland still has Trajan, his nominal righteous heathen from Passus XI, on his mind at this point, when Ymaginatif says, 'And riȝt as Troianus þe trewe knyȝt [tilde] noȝt depe in helle / That oure lord ne hadde hym liȝtly out, so leue I [by] þe þef in heuene' (XII, 210–211). Not much later, Ymaginatif, in his Latin quotation of I Pet. 4:18, implies that Trajan himself now occupies a similar position in heaven:

> . . . '*Saluabitur vix Iustus in die Iudicij;*
> *Ergo saluabitur*', quod he and seide na moore latyn.
> 'Troianus was a trewe knyght and took neuere cristendom
> And he is saaf, seiþ þe book, and his soule in heuene'.
> (XII, 281–284)

It does not pay to dwell on this evidence as it cannot be proved that the *Pseudo-Turpin* is the source; but if that text is the source, it is not inconceivable that Langland would have wished, with his lines about the 'beggere bordlees', allusively to reinforce not just the view that there are ranks of salvation, but also that the (lower) ranks can admit those worthies that Christian tradition, not God, would mistakenly exclude.

Perhaps out of an awareness of the kind of contention open moralizing about the episode could generate, *Turpines Story* concludes with firm, almost dismissive, abruptness: '[w]an Charlis perseyuyd þat Aigalonde wolde noȝt be baptizide for he saw how vngodely þe pore peple of God was itretid, he lete ordeyne þat alle þe pore peple þat ware in þe hooste shode be honestly cloþid, and fro

---

[81] *Piers Plowman: The C-Text*, ed. Derek Pearsall (Exeter, 1994), p. 241, n. to XIV, 135). The parables of Luke 14:7–24 could provide another scriptural basis for the passage.

[82] Cf. Langland's more conventional treatment of the topic of faith without good works (citing Jas. 2:26), I, 179–99.

þensforth þey had sufficiently mette and drinke ryȝt inow' (ll. 644–48). All of the versions of the *Pseudo-Turpin* which are closest to *Turpines Story* retain the moralizing conclusion,[83] and so its absence here is probably original. *Turpines Story* elsewhere makes substantial and apparently original omissions of moralizing material, and so the omission in this case probably has systematic motives beyond topical diplomacy (see '*Turpines Story*' *as a Translation*, below, especially pp. xl–xli). Nevertheless, the currency of the episode as evidenced by its appearance in Brinton, Higden, Trevisa, Bromyard (see n. 77 above), and possibly Langland, is enough to give one pause in rejecting the idea that the translator was not influenced by a literary milieu.

One might also pause in the same way when considering the treatment in *Turpines Story* of what appears to have been an equally popular episode for Insular collections, the *exemplum* against false executors which comprises the seventh chapter. It is found in Bromyard, Brinton (four times), the Middle English *Dives and Pauper* (written c. 1405–1410), and a fifteenth-century English translation of the *Alphabetum Narratorium*.[84] If the treatment of the episode in *Turpines Story* is influenced by such currency, it comes not from the kinds of interpretation offered in those other texts, which in the main do not vary from the obvious warning of the original. Rather the influence is suggested in the relative confidence and enthusiasm of the translation at this point, as if the story was already familiar to the translator. This is a feature of the passage which has already been examined in some detail[85] and which is documented further in the commentary to ll. 265–304. It seems to follow that (as the several retellings suggest) the episode inherently contains the kinds of didactic, dramatic, and rhetorical elements which would independently attract and inspire medieval writers.[86]

[83] See the Commentary on l. 648.

[84] See *Summa prædicantium*, under *Executor*, section 22, vol. I, chapter VIII, f. 259ra. Brinton, 'Dominica in passione' (Sermon 22), I, 86; 'In die parasceues' (Sermon 39), I, 176; 'De mortuis' (Sermon 62), II, 281; and 'Dominica in passione Domini' (Sermon 103), II, 475 (the references in sermons 39 and 62 are allusive, but the other two sermons contain full paraphrases of the episode); *Dives and Pauper*, ed. Priscilla Heath Barnum, EETS 275 and 280 (London 1976, 1980), vol. I, part 2 (EETS 280), p. 280, l. 45–p. 281, l. 71; *An Alphabet of Tales*, ed. Mary MacLeod Banks, EETS 126 and 127 (1903, 1905), p. 216, l. 16–p. 217, l. 4 (this text also adapts the description of Charlemagne from chapter XX of the *Pseudo-Turpin*, p. 290, ll. 11–31).

[85] Shepherd, 'Middle English *Pseudo-Turpin Chronicle*', pp. 26–7.

[86] Each of the texts cited appears to derive the episode independently: Bromyard's is a brief summary of the episode; Brinton offers a more extensive paraphrase which shows that Bromyard this time is not his source; *Dives and Pauper* offers a paraphrase reasonably close

The kinds of intertextual possibilities suggested above would, from the translator's perspective, have been reflexively allusive; that is, they were derived from, but also presented views about, the very text the translator was working on, and could well have influenced his translation. *Turpines Story* also shows, however, some traces of more direct literate influence. The translator may, for instance, have been familiar with mystery plays (see the note to ll. 88–91), and have enjoyed citing his own Bible references (notes to ll. 115, 502, and 1036–8). As one might expect, he may also have appreciated popular heroic treatments of Charlemagne and his peers (see p. xli below). Other broader influences, concerning the goals of commissioning, or at least copying, the translation, are considered under *Patronage*, below (pp. xlviii–liv).

2. *TURPINES STORY* AS A TRANSLATION

The following main points were put forward in 1996:[87]

[A] *Turpines Story* is a translation of a Latin source (p. 30 and n. 20).

[B] The source belongs to the so-called *C* family of *Pseudo-Turpin* manuscripts. This family appears to have been 'distributed mainly in northern Europe, notably in Britain and Ireland' (p.22 and n. 23). Within this family, five versions, all of them with strong Insular connections, are particularly close to the version represented in *Turpines Story* (p. 22): the Old French *Johannes* translation (*Johannes;* commissioned 1206);[88] the Anglo Norman translation of William de Brianne (*AN;* second decade of the thirteenth century);[89] the medieval Welsh translation (*WPs-T;* made before 1282);[90] *Gabháltas*

---

to the original substance of the *Pseudo-Turpin*, but with significant variation in detail; the *Alphabet of Tales* is closest of all to the original *Pseudo-Turpin* reading.

[87] Shepherd, 'Middle English *Pseudo-Turpin Chronicle*', *Medium Ævum*, 65 (1996), 19–34. Page numbers in parentheses cited in each point refer to this article, to which the reader is directed for elaboration and supporting evidence. For ease of comparison later in this and subsequent sections, each point is labelled alphabetically.

[88] *The Old French Johannes Translation of the 'Pseudo-Turpin Chronicle'*, ed. R. N. Walpole, 2 vols [as Critical Edition and Supplement] (Berkeley and Los Angeles, 1976). All further references to *Johannes* are to this edition.

[89] *The Anglo-Norman 'Pseudo-Turpin Chronicle' of William de Briane*, ed. Ian Short, Anglo-Norman Text Society, 25 (Oxford, 1973). All further references to *AN* are to this edition.

[90] *Ystorya de Carolo Magno o Lyfr Coch Hergest*, ed. Stephen J. Williams (Cardiff, 1930, revised 1968). All further references to *WPs-T* are to this edition.

Serluis Mhóir, a medieval Irish translation (*Ir;* c. 1400);[91] and the unpublished Latin text of Dublin, Trinity College MS 667, pp. 107–130 (*Tr;* copied in the mid fifteenth century).[92] Of these, the closest to *Turpines Story* is *Ir*, followed closely by *Tr* and then, less closely, *WPs-T, AN,* and *Johannes* (pp. 23–24). Even though *Ir* and *Tr* are closest to the source of *Turpines Story*, neither can be said to represent that source absolutely, and exclusive correspondences with the other three texts suggest 'not only a distinctly Insular tradition of *C* texts, but . . . a thriving tradition, one that produced enough different copies introduced over enough time to develop at least one sub-group with its own *sub*-sub-groups' (p.24).

[C] The Middle English translation augments a traditional *C*-family trait of 'resist[ing] criticism of the Christian heroes' (p. 27). Especially notable is the omission in *Turpines Story*, independent of *IrTrWPs-TJohannes*, of an extended moralizing passage which lays blame for the crushing defeat at Roncevaux on Christian warriors who the night before had partaken of Saracen wine and Saracen and Christian women (p. 27). In this respect *Turpines Story* follows the depictions of Roncevaux in the Middle English Charlemagne romances, *Song of Roland* and *Otuel and Roland*, suggesting perhaps a peculiarly English tradition in the representation of the defeat of Charlemagne's greatest warriors (pp. 27–28).

[D] As evidenced by its treatment of the *exemplum* of the false executor, *Turpines Story* reveals a translator enthusiastically engaged with the material (pp. 26–27). This enthusiasm takes on a peculiarly English cast when Milo, father of Roland, is twice (mis)identified as an Englishman; a third occasion which identifies him correctly as a Frenchman suggests that the former two 'errors' were in fact deliberate and that the third 'correct' instance represents an oversight in a plan to anglicize the greatest of French heroes, Roland (pp. 25–26).

Reference to the present edition supplements and in some cases modifies these points, as noted in the following paragraphs.

[A.2] For further evidence of a Latin source, see the notes to ll. 3, 177–8, 263, 337–8, 499, 520, 622, 647, 823, 1068, 1089, and 1150–1;

---

[91] *Gabháltas Serluis Mhóir, The Conquests of Charlemagne*, ed. Douglas Hyde, Irish Texts Society, 19 (London, 1917). All further references to *Ir* are to this edition.

[92] Identified by Mario Esposito, 'Une Version Latine du Roman de *Fierabras*', *Romania*, 62 (1936), 534–541.

see also the listings under section D.2 below. The source manuscript for the translation, or one of that manuscript's sources, was probably written in a cursive script typical of the fourteenth and fifteenth centuries: see the notes to ll. 165, 237–8, 271, 431, 862. The current scribe's Middle English exemplar was also probably written in a cursive script; see the n. to l. 180. The source manuscript, or one of its sources, may have contained additional texts relating to St James, in particular the apocryphal epistle of Pope Leo III, *De Translatione Beati Jacobi*, a common item in *Pseudo-Turpin* manuscripts going back to the earliest known copy, the famous *Codex Calixtinus* (otherwise known as the Compostela *Liber Sancti Jacobi*); see the notes to ll. 80–3 and 89–91.

[B.2] Further evidence for relationships between *IrTrWPs-TJo-hannes* and *Turpines Story* is documented many times throughout the Commentary and supports the order of proximity to the translator's source already proposed. That *Ir* is closest of all versions to *Turpines Story* is reinforced by the findings of the notes to ll. 300, 366, 376, 483–96, and 1064. *Tr*, however, appears to be closer than *Ir* on three occasions, as remarked in the notes to ll. 709, 723, and 1071–6; *Tr* also preserves chapter headings which are closest of all to those in *Turpines Story* (see notes to ll. 265, 529–30, 614, 1000–1, and 1154–5; but *Ir* does not use chapter headings at all). Important evidence that neither *Ir* nor *Tr* reflects the actual source of the Middle English translation emerges at ll. 176–9, 180–6, 186–9, and 995–7. The possibilities of unique correspondences between *Turpines Story* and *AN*, *WPs-T*, and *Johannes* appear, respectively, in the notes to ll. 179, 692, and 704–5. Affinities between *Turpines Story* and non-C-family versions of the *Pseudo-Turpin* are suggested in the notes to ll. 103, 125–6, 170, 190–1, 614, and 692.

[C.2] The omission of the moralizing passage on the 'wine and women' episode is the last of five such omissions, all of them unparalleled in *IrTrWPs-TJohannes*. The first four are made at the ends of contiguous chapters (xv through xviii, which describe Charles's campaign against the Saracen Aigolandus). The second of these omissions concerns the episode of Charles and the paupers, and is described above (pp. xxxvi–xxxvii). For details about the other omissions, see the notes to ll. 603, 648, 680, and 692. Overall the impression is of an attempt, not to strip the *Pseudo-Turpin* wholesale of its didactic import, but to streamline the presentation of this didactic meaning to coincide more appropriately with the military impetus of the narrative. Accounts of the procedures of Charlemagne's campaigns are favoured over their ecclesiastical exegesis.[93] In each case of omission, the translator is careful to leave enough information to render the moral point at least implicit. Elsewhere two moralizing passages, one brief, the other employing military analogies, are left intact in a way which encourages the drawing of moral implications throughout (see ll. 303–6 and 354–69).[94] All of the omitted passages except the third point to failings within the Christian forces. A desire to suppress such indications is evident generally in the translation in several small changes or additions which execrate the heathen: see the notes to ll. 118–19, 201, 260–1, 385, 559–61, 568–72, 578–9, and 1152–3. Small additions reminiscent of vernacular romance are also made which elevate the Christian heroes: Charles slays 'manfully' (l. 347), is a 'gode' king (l. 352), and has a 'tristy' sword (l. 346); Roland is fearlessly pious (ll. 745–6, 750–1, 778–9), 'worthy' (l. 929), and, like Charles, 'gode' (l. 920); the warriors struggling at Roncevaux are repeatedly identified as in the company of the legendary, even proverbial, duo, Roland and Oliver (see the notes ll. 1127, 1133, 1140, and 1141).[95]

---

[93] Omissions of this sort occur not infrequently in independent treatments of the *Chronicle*; consider, for instance, the record of Meredith-Jones's A.1 and B.3 texts in the notes to ll. 680 and 692, respectively. Vincent of Beauvais employs a similar, though more sweeping, pattern of omission in his incorporation of the *Pseudo-Turpin Chronicle* into the encyclopaedic *Speculum historiale* (*c.*1254): although Vincent is no stranger to moralizing passages, his intent here seems primarily historiographical. See the Douai edition of 1624 (*Speculi maioris Vincentii Burgundi . . . Tomus Quartus, qui 'Speculum historiale' inscribitur*), where Vincent's adaptation of the *Pseudo-Turpin* appears on pp. 964–71. On Vincent's pruning of his source, see Ian Short, 'The *Pseudo-Turpin Chronicle:* Some Unnoticed Versions and their Sources', *Medium Ævum*, 38 (1969), 1–22 (p. 10). Another version of the *Pseudo-Turpin* stripped of its explicit moralizing passages—again presumably to serve historiographical interests—is to be found in the *Chronicle* of Hélinand de Froidmont (d. *c.*1227); indeed, Hélinand refuses to relate the matter of the *Pseudo-Turpin* which comes after the war with Aigolandus, claiming that it is *fabulosa, et a doctis reprobata* (*Patrologiæ latina* 212, columns 847–51 (851)).

[94] Consider also signs of a rather terse fatalism on the part of the translator which seem consistent with an understated didacticism: 'manes power faylid' (ll. 193–4); '. . . as many a false execetoure dothe' (l. 276); 'God [is] strenger þan man ' (ll. 744–5). There are also two instances, however, where the translator sees the passage in question as technically or factually (rather than philosophically) instructive: 'Names of þe grete citteis and townnes . . . I reduced to certen numbure . . . in þe whiche þe reder of þis werke sum notable ensample may lerne' (l. 173–6); 'here may ye lerne a shrewde wyle of werre of þe Sarzyns' (ll. 950–1).

[95] By the fifteenth century, 'Roland and Oliver' had become a conventional collocation, which may have been the only source the translator needed; cf., for instance, the Middle English *Richard Coeur de Lyon*, l. 11 (in *Richard Löwenherz*, ed. Karl Brunner (Leipzig,

[D.2] Often the translator's enthusiasm in rendering 'þis matere of cronykullynge', as he uniquely calls it (l. 1097), can be measured in minor rhetorical gestures which aim (not always with success) to clarify, emphasize, or otherwise render certain passages more elegant: see, for instance, the notes to ll. 192–4, 329, 355–6, 389, 414–16, 433–4, 471–3, 497–8, 504–5, 563, 573–4, 611, 618–19, 636–7, 641, 689, 885, 906–7, 929–30, 933–4, 983, 1070, and 1110. In descriptions of battle the translator sometimes inserts motifs not found in the source, that lend an air of practical realism, such as when he observes Roland deflecting an opponent's strokes (see the notes to ll. 759 and 775), or reminds us that, as a giant, Ferrakutte (Ferracutus) is heavy—and so is his fist (see the notes to ll. 921 and 767). During the 'battaile of the visoures' the translator characterizes the Saracens' tactic of smashing cymbals and wearing demonic masks to terrify their enemies' horses as a 'shrewde wyle of werre' and, later, a 'wyly turne of werre'. Then, in a sardonic spirit of revenge, he says of Charles's countermeasure of covering the horses' heads and stopping their ears, 'here was o wyle of werre ayenste here wyle!' (see the notes to ll. 950–1, 961–3, and 970–1).[96] Two passages display what is surely a self-reflexive (one might say Berkeley-Trevisan) admiration for linguistic skill itself. At the moment when Aigalonde (Aigolandus) 'ioyed gretely' upon learning that Charles can speak 'þe Sarȝyns tonge', the translator explains the Saracen's reaction: 'for so he myȝt better denounce and declare his matris by hemselffe þan by anoþer interpretacioune'. This is obvious, perhaps, but said with a high proportion of latinate and romance terms which give the passage an air of multilingual authority (ll. 549–52). Later, during the protracted duel-debate between Roland and Ferrakutte, the seemingly invincible Saracen, mistakenly thinking Roland knows no Spanish, tells him in that language of his one vulnerable point, his navel—and so seals his own death. In handling this moment with a coy application of antistrophe, the translator

1913)); Chaucer's *Book of the Duchess*, l. 1123. Consider also the comment from an anonymous work on the Seven Deadly Sins in Oxford, Balliol College MS 196;462. R.9: 'accidiosus libencius audit frivola de Rodlando et Olivero quam utilem sermonem de deo' (f. 217ʳ). Cf. also B. J. Whiting, *Proverbs, Sentences, and Proverbial Phrases from English Writings Mainly Before 1500* (Cambridge, Massachusetts, 1968), item R179, p. 491. Conventions aside, the rubricator, if not the translator, identifies the work in its titles primarily with the battle of Roncevaux: see the n. to the first title line, and Shepherd, 'Middle English *Pseudo-Turpin Chronicle*', p. 27.

[96] On a similar addition in the alliterative *Siege of Jerusalem*, see the n. to ll. 950–1

reveals again his admiration for translation skills, not to mention his sardonic turn of mind:

this giaunte seid this worde in the Spayennyshe speche, þe whiche þe giaunte went þat Rowlond vndurstode noȝt—but Roulonde vnderstode riȝt wele. (ll. 792–4)[97]

3. DIALECT

If one employs the *LALME* item Questionnaire in seeking out the regional provenance of the scribal language, the profile which emerges resists narrow localization.[98] The text includes forms from a wide range of areas in the midlands and south which yield a profile consistent with the emerging 'standard' literary language of the latter half of the fifteenth century, based in London.[99] A small group of forms, however, presents a sub-profile suggestive of a south-west midlands provenance for at least one stage of copying:

[i] *buthe* 1 'are' (vs. *beth(e)* 34; *ben* 3). *LALME* reports five linguistic profiles containing *buthe*, one in Hampshire, one in Wiltshire, and three in Somerset—certainly southern and western, but not midland. On the other hand, if grouped with close variants *buth, buþ, buþe, buþ^e*, the geographic range extends with 31 more profiles into Gloucestershire (11), Herefordshire (9), and Worcestershire (11); at the same time, even more profiles extend as far south-east as Sussex, but not London (for the profiles, see *LALME* iv. 33, and cf. *LALME* dot map 129 for '*bVth* type, forms with medial *-eu-*, *-u(e)-, -eo-, or -oe-*').[100] *Beth(e)* and *ben* appear in many profiles across the midlands and the south (iv. 32–33). Samuels observes that *beth, buth, ben* are commonly combined in south Worcestershire texts representative of Langland's dialect.[101]

---

[97] For comparison with the Latin, see notes on these lines in the Commentary. Pride in his *métier* notwithstanding, the translator is consistenly prone to errors: see the notes to ll. 3, 185–6, 227, 237–8, 344–5, 413, 450, 512, 545, 582–3, 667–9, 715–16, 799, 836, 862, 964–5, 1093, 1153.

[98] For the Questionnaire, see *LALME* i. 552–8.

[99] On the emerging standard, see M. L. Samuels, 'Some Applications of Middle English Dialectology', *English Studies*, 44 (1963), 81–94; A. O. Sandved, 'Prolegomena to a Renewed Study of the Rise of Standard English', in M. Benskin and M. L. Samuels, eds., *So meny people longages and tonges: Philological Essays in Scots and Medieval English presented to Angus McIntosh* (Edinburgh, 1981), 31–42, and Laura Wright, ed., *The Development of Standard English, 1300–1800: Theories, Descriptions, Conflicts* (Cambridge, 2000).

[100] The dot maps appear in numerical sequence in *LALME* i. 305–551.

[101] M. L. Samuels, 'Langland's Dialect', *Medium Ævum*, 54 (1985), 232–47, pp. 234, 243. Cf. Jeremy Smith, 'The Language', in *Lollard Sermons*, ed. Gloria Cigman, EETS 294 (1989), p. xl.

[ii] [a] addition of unetymological *h-*, and [b] omission of etymological *h-*: [a] *habbeis* 1 'abbeys', *he(e)tte* 2 'ate' (vs. *ette* 1); *here* 1, *heris* 2 'ear, ears'; *herly* 1 'early'; *herthe* 1, *herth(e)ly* 2 'earth, earthly' (vs. *erthe* 5, *erthely* 1); *hesely* 1 'easily'; *hocsyn* 1 'oxen'; *hyueryhorne* 1 'ivory horn'; [b] *alowyde* 1 'hallowed', *arme* 'harm' 1. Jordan observes that 'addition of an ⟨h⟩ . . . points to a slightly aspirated vowel whose appearance is apparently related with silencing [in other words] of old ⟨h⟩'; he also notes that '⟨h⟩ is lacking relatively seldom'.[102] Samuels finds that 'the different areas where this could occur in [fourteenth-century] Middle English are capable of precise delimitation: for the [south-west midlands] it is limited to a patch running from Warwickshire through south Worcestershire to Gloucestershire'.[103] Dot map 1172 shows wide, if relatively rare, distribution of forms across the south for unetymological *h-*, and dot map 1173 shows predictably fewer profiles for loss of etymological *h-*, with some appearing intermittently south and north-east of London but with others tracing a distinct line from Somerset along the south side of the Bristol Channel into south Worcestershire, and ending in west Warwickshire.

Evidence of lost *h-* before *w* is also prevalent in backspelling: *whardis* 1 'wards' (vs. *ward(d)is* 5), *whise* 1 'wise, manner' (vs. *wyse* 4, *wise* 1), *whare/where* 20 'were' (vs. *were*, 71), *whas* 23 'was' (vs. *was* 117), *whaxe* 1 'grow' (vs. *wax-* 4), *whent* 1 'went' (vs. *went(e)* 21), *whey* 6 'way' (vs. *wey* 7). *LALME* identifies this feature in 62 profiles from 23 counties across the south (iv.322); it must be admitted, however, that Gloucestershire, Herefordshire, and Worcestershire together account for ten profiles only (as against, for instance, nine for the single county of Essex) and that this phenomenon is not always accompanied by the converse: namely, addition of unetymological *h-* (cf. dot map 141).[104]

[iii] *þicke* 15, *thicke* 2, *þilke* 4, *þucke* 3, 'the same'. *LALME* reports only one profile for *þicke*, from south-eastern Warwickshire (iv.240); *thicke* is also attested uniquely by a profile from southernmost Staffordshire, close to the border with Worcestershire (iv.239);

---

[102] Richard Jordan, *Handbook of English Grammar: Phonology*, translated and revised by Eugene Joseph Crook (The Hague and Paris, 1974), p. 248.

[103] 'Langland's Dialect', p. 237.

[104] *Turpines Story* also manifests backspelling and lost *h-* forms of 'when': *wan/wanne* 19 'when'; *whan(e)/whanne* 16; *when/whenne* 9. Jeremy Smith states that the mixture of *wanne* and *whanne* in the Lollard sermons of British Library MS Additional 41321 point to a Worcestershire provenance (*Lollard Sermons*, p. xl).

pucke is not reported, but other forms with -*u*- and lacking -*l*-, *puke*, *pukk*, and *pukke*, also apparently rare, are reported in two profiles each from Gloucestershire and Somerset and one each from Kent and Hampshire. *LALME* dot map 1062, grouping forms showing loss of -*l*- (*thik, thek, thok, thuk* types), presents isolated localizations across the south, but with greatest relative density in the south-west midlands. *þilke* is found in 91 profiles for 18 counties across the south (iv.240), though a south-west midlands preponderance also emerges, with 39 profiles from Gloucestershire (17), Worcestershire (12), and Herefordshire (10). John Smyth's observations on the dialect of the Hundred of Berkeley in the early sixteenth century may be of some relevance; he identifies 'certaine words proverbs and phrases of speach,which wee hundreders conceive . . . to bee not only native but confined to the soile, bounds, and territory therof . . . . "Thicke and thucke", for "this and that", rush out of vs at every breath. As, "d'ont thick way; d'ont thuck way" for, "doe it on this way; doe it on that way"'.[105]

[iv] suffixes in -*u*-:

[a] Weak past participle ending in -*ud*(*e*): *i-yeldude* 1, *buddude* 1 (and cf. the weak preterite ending -*ud*(*e*): *askapude, avoydude, buddud, deuydude, grappud, gyrdude, passude, wadude*). This is an extremely limited sample against all other weak past participles in the text which have geographically-widespread -*yd*(*e*), -*id*(*e*), -*ed*(*e*) (see *LALME* dot maps 658–62, 1196). The *LALME* county list (iv.324–325) does not account for the spelling with -*e*, but for -*ud* cites 61 profiles from 15 counties across the south; a south-west midlands preponderance emerges with 22 profiles, from Gloucestershire (6), Herefordshire (5), and especially Worcestershire (11): see dot map 1199, which represents -*ud* almost exclusively, representing only nine more profiles with -*ut*(*e*).

[b] -*us* (post-consonantal plural of nouns): *apostelus* 1, *apostolus* 1, *appostlus* 1, *cubitus* 1, *domus* 1, *disiplus* 1, *Ethiopus* 1, *Galicianus* 1 (vs. *Galiciance* 4), *Galicianus* 1, *kalendus* 1, *idus* 1, *lustus* 1, *mytrus* 1, *Turkus* 1. The usual forms in *Turpines Story* are the very widespread -*ys*, -*is*, -*es* (iv.104–105); -*us* is very widely recorded across the south (iv.105), but, as with -*ud*(*e*), shows a preponderance of forms in the south-west midlands: see dot map 958. The western weighting continues, however, into the north: dot map 642.

[105] *Lives of the Berkeleys*, III. 22–6.

[c] -*ur(e)*, -*ull(e)* in unstressed syllables; -*ur(e)*: *awture* 1, *belefadur*
1, *fadur(e)* 17, *faddur* 1, (*to*)*gadure* 2 (vs. *gader* 1; cf. *gadered* 1,
gaderid(e) 5, *gaderyd* 1), *hyndur* 1, *ordur(e)* 2 (vs. the rubricator's *ordre*
1), *odure* 1 (vs. *oþer* 20), *numbure* 1 (vs. *numbire* 1, *numbre* 1), *profur* 1
(vs. *profered* 1), *raþur* 2 (vs. *raþer*/*rather* 2), *sepulcure*/*sepulture* 2 (vs.
sepulcre 1), *þedur* 1, *togedur* 2, *togedure* 1, *vndur(e)* 11 (cf. *vndurstode* 1
vs. *vnderstode* 1), *wondur* 1 (vs. *wonder* 1; but cf. *wondurfulle* 1,
wondurly 1); -*ull(e)*: *apostulle* 1 (vs. *apostel*- 5, *apostol*- 2), *carebokulle*
1, *cronykulle* 2 (cf. *cronykullynge* 1), *gyrdulle* 1, *ydulle* 2 (vs. *ydol*- 12),
litulle 1 (vs. *litille* 5), *myddulle* 1, *tulle* 2, *vnkulle* 2. In *Turpines Story*
the majority forms, respectively, are -*er* and -*yl(l)e*/-*il(l)e*/-*le*. Jordan
cites -*ur* and -*ul* as distinct west-midland forms, whose area 'includes
. . . Staf., Shrops., Heref., in part Lanc., consequently also Chs.; since
it later also encroaches toward Glouc. . . . Worc. also comes into
consideration'. However, in the fifteenth century, the forms also
spread as far south-east as London.[106] Of the forms listed above,
LALME charts *litulle*, *þedur*, and *togedur(e)*. Only one linguistic
profile, from southernmost Lancashire, represents *litulle* (iv.211).
Forms in -*ill(e)*, by contrast, are widespread, with concentrations in
the south-east midlands and around London (see dot map map 462
and iv.210). *þedur* is attested by 12 profiles from 10 counties (iv.264),
providing weak evidence for localization. *Togedur(e)* is attested by 31
profiles from 14 counties; 16 of these profiles are located in Herefordshire (4), Warwickshire (4), and especially Worcestershire (8),
and forms with -*e* are only recorded in Herefordshire and Worcestershire (iv.269). Dot map 464 shows forms in -*ul* or -*ull(e)* as primarily a
west midlands phenomenon extending southeast to London, with
some isolated occurences near the Wash.

Samuels argues that -*ur*, -*us*, and -*ud* beside -*ir*, -*is*, and -*id* are
variables 'that can be regarded as part of the same Worcestershire
dialect [i.e., that used by Langland]';[107] but for a later text, the late-
fifteenth-century Chetham's Library manuscript of *Ipomadon*, Rhiannon Purdie regards the 'consistent minor variants' -*ur*, -*us*, and -*ud* as
'of dubious significance' in localizing a south-western layer of copying.[108]

[106] Jordan, pp. 138–9.
[107] 'Langland's Dialect', p. 243.
[108] *Ipomadon*, ed. Rhiannon Purdie, EETS 316 (2001), pp. lii–liii.

[v] *dude* 13 'did' (vs. geographically widespread *ded(e)* 29 (see iv.153)): for *dude*, *LALME* (iv.153) reports 134 profiles from 19 counties; a south-west midlands preponderance emerges with 62 profiles, from Gloucestershire (24), Herefordshire (13), western Warwickshire (12), and Worcestershire (13); cf. dot map map 400, and [iv] [a] above.

[vi] *yut* 5, *yutte* 1 (the only forms of 'yet' in the text): *LALME* reports very few profiles with these forms; *yut* is recorded in profiles from Devonshire, Hampshire, Somerset, Warwickshire, Wiltshire, and Worcestershire. Of these, four come from Wiltshire; *yutte* is recorded in just one profile, again from Wiltshire (for both sets of profiles, see iv.73). Even though the forms appear to be more commonly south-western than south-west midland, they exclude all other regions.

[vii] *thousonde* 8, *thousond* 3, *thousounde* 2, *thowsonde* 1: *LALME* (iv. 265–266) records only one profile for *thousonde*, in north-west Worcestershire; for *thousond* one profile each in west Herefordshire, south-east Lancashire, central Staffordshire, central Suffolk, and north Worcestershire; for *thousounde* no examples (but cf. *pousounde* with one profile only, in north-east Gloucestershire); and for *thowsonde*, one profile only in central Suffolk. The representative profiles are few, but the relative numbers of the forms involved suggest a Worcestershire-Gloucestershire weighting.

The numbers of all the examples listed above and their relative proportions against majority forms are in nearly every case very low. The evidence is arguably coherent enough to suggest a layer of copying by a scribe from the south-west midlands, especially when considered against the combinations of forms Samuels cites for evidence of Langland's West Worcestershire dialect–albeit a dialect as much as a century older than the minority profile which emerges from *Turpines Story*.

It is possible that there is no layering. As *LALME* observes, 'the period 1420–1550 is the only one in which writers can be shown to have been replacing their own regional spellings by the more prestigious ones of the emerging standard . . . . the replacements are motivated, not random, and are made from a fairly limited and predictable subset of the language' (i.22; this is category (v) of the "scribal mixtures" distinguished by *LALME*, i.12–13). There is indeed some internal evidence to suggest that this copy is close to the translator's draft, and may have little or no history of circulation and copying underlying the present manuscript (see below, pp. l–li). The south-west midlands sub-profile is also significant in light of the identification of the original owners of at least the Trevisan portion of the manuscript as coming from Harescombe, Gloucestershire, no more than 20 miles south of the Malvern Hills. The three Insular versions of the *Pseudo-Turpin* closest to the source of *Turpines Story*, moreover, have a decidedly western provenance, coming from Wales and Ireland (see above, pp. xxxviii–xxxix).

A systematic study of the dialect of the other Middle English items in the manuscript has yet to be done. However, Ronald Waldron says of its copy of Trevisa's *Polychronicon* that the language 'preserves a distinct South-Western/West-Midland colouring'. On the grounds of 'a close textual and linguistic relationship' Waldron suggests that the Trevisan texts of HM28,561 'could have been copied from [London, British Library MS Harley 1900]' but adds that 'an intermediate between [the two] remains a possibility'.[109] An examination of the texts of Trevisa's introductory *Dialogue* and *Epistle* from this manuscript reveals, again, a linguistically unlocalizable southern text with a handful of forms consistent with the south-west midlands, but even smaller in proportion and of a different kind than those identified above: *buld* 1 'built'; *shuld* 9 'should'; *þeose* 1 'these' (vs. *þes(e)* 7); *Wyrcestur* 1.[110]

4. PATRONAGE

Since its inception, the *Pseudo-Turpin Chronicle* has been used as a medium for a variety of agendas. It was perhaps originally used by interested clerics to advertise the pilgrimage route to Santiago de Compostela. Frederick Barbarossa, concerned to construct parallels between himself and the first Holy Roman Emperor, and engaged in an attempt to canonize Charlemagne, commissioned a *Vita Karoli Magni*, which incorporated the first seven chapters of the *Pseudo-Turpin*.[111] For Nicholas de Senlis, working at the behest of Yolande of

---

[109] 'Caxton and the *Polychronicon*,' in *Middle English Essays in Honour of Norman Blake*, ed. Geoffrey Lester (Sheffield, 1999), 374–94, pp. 388, 378–9.

[110] These texts have been edited by Stephen H. A. Shepherd in *The Idea of the Vernacular: An Anthology of Middle English Literary Theory, 1280–1520*, ed. Jocelyn Wogan-Browne, *et al.* (University Park, Pennsylvania, 1999), pp. 146–56. Editorial normalization of spelling has been removed from the words quoted here.

[111] See Smyser, *The Pseudo-Turpin*, pp. 5–8. Charlemagne was canonized by the anti-pope Paschal III in 1165, but the canonization was never ratified. See *Acta Sanctorum* for

Saint-Pol, it was the vehicle for a polemical introduction of historiography into Old French prose.[112] For William Caxton, who produced *Charles the Grete*, translated from Jean Baignon's *Roman de Fierabras le Geant* (which includes its own translation of the *Pseudo-Turpin*)[113] the purpose, in addition, presumably, to satisfying patrons and perhaps making some money, was 'to gyue to vs ensaumple to lyue in good & vertuous operacions digne & worthy of helth, in folowyng the good and eschewyng the euyl'.[114] And then there were the applications, however free of 'agendas' they may have been, in historical and exemplary manuscript collections of whole texts, in encyclopoedias and florilegia, and in the more 'imaginative' medium of the *chanson de geste* or romance (see above, note 73). Against such a diverse background, one must be careful not to insist upon a single set of motivations behind the production of *Turpines Story*. Some variation on any of the motivations listed above could obtain in any new translation or copying of the *Pseudo-Turpin*. Even a cursory glance at its content reveals the potential for a wide range of receptions: readers might have found it historical, hagiographical, didactic, catechistic, martial, marvellous, humorous, tragic, or any combination of these, and more (the Rude Mechanicals would revel).[115] If, therefore, the possibility of Mull patronage is to be discussed further, the discussion must be understood as compromised, not only by taking the form of a brief and highly speculative

28 January, *De S. Carolo Magno*. His *cultus* did, however, continue at Aachen, and selections from the *Pseudo-Turpin* have found their way into related liturgical materials. See, for instance *Analecta Hymnica*, ed. G. M. Drèves, *et al.*, 55 vols. (Leipzig, 1886–1922), 25, pp. 187–91 and 44, pp. 315–17. None of the source manuscripts there listed are located in Britain.

[112] See Gabriel M. Spiegel, *Romancing the Past: The Rise of Vernacular Prose Historiography in Thirteenth-Century France* (University of California Press, 1993), especially ch. two.

[113] On the relationship between Baignon's text and other versions of the *Pseudo-Turpin*, including that rendered by Vincent de Beauvais in the *Speculum Historiale*, see Short, 'Unnoticed Versions', pp. 9–16.

[114] William Caxton, Introduction to *The Lyf of the Noble and Crysten Prynce Charles the Grete*, ed. Sidney J. Herrtage, EETS ES 36–7 (1880–1), p. 1.

[115] Cf. Smyser, *The Pseudo-Turpin*, p. 8: 'Whether [the author] was always wholly serious . . . or whether he sometimes had his tongue in his cheek, the reader must decide for himself, according to his conception of the Middle Ages'. For discussion of further *Pseudo-Turpin* contexts, see André Moisan, 'L'exploitation de la *Chronique du Pseudo-Turpin*', *Marche Romane*, 31 (1981), 11–41; André Moisan, 'L'exploitation de l'épopée par la *Chronique du Pseudo-Turpin*', *Moyen Age*, 95 (1989) 195–224; and Linda J. Emanuel, 'The *Pseudo-Turpin Chronicle*: Its Influence and Literary Significance, with Special Reference to Medieval French Literature' (doctoral thesis, Pennsylvania State University, 1978).

hypothesis about provenance, but also by representing a narrow conception of 'patronage', for all readers are patrons to some degree of the readings they produce.

If Thomas Mull was responsible for having *Turpines Story* included in his manuscript, then the most satisfying evidence for that commission has been presented above: it is codicological and to a lesser extent dialectal, supported by the western provenance of the closest surviving other versions of the *Pseudo-Turpin* and by the complementary nature of the text to the *Polychronicon* and possibly to the Latin royal pedigrees. If Thomas Mull was further responsible for commissioning the act of translation that produced *Turpines Story*, then the evidence, which is solely internal, must be treated with great caution; one runs the risk of mistaking what may have been brute vicissitudes of translation for an uncommonly subtle scheme. That the surviving copy could have been made from the translator's draft is suggested in a handful of instances documented in the Commentary: see the notes to ll. 209–10, 413, 509, 1073 (and cf. the note to ll. 1134–6). In each note a case is made for the immediate priority of a draft; each case is closely attended by a counter-case for a less arcane origin for the awkward or unusual lection in question. As Ralph Hanna III has observed, the inelegance of some lections in later Middle English prose translations, which has led some scholars mistakenly to argue that the translation is an unrevised draft, can be 'deliberate and purposeful'. To ignore such a purpose 'misrepresents the nature of sophisticated prose translation [of the period]'.[116]

What makes the possibility of an immediately prior draft of *Turpines Story* at all worthy of a second glance are its three nationalistic references to Milo, father of Roland, the first two erroneously proclaiming him an Englishman with details that go beyond the mere mistranslation of his name, and the third correctly making him French (see point D above, p. xxxix). The insistence of the first two references makes the third look like an oversight—and the third restores the name with what is, for this translation, an unusual Francophone patois, as if to suggest that the translator really did know better but had a mission to fulfil (see the note to ll. 486–7. One also wonders whether the oversight was unlikely to be spotted because the patron never got to review the text). The translator could, however, simply have been mistaken to begin

---

[116] Ralph Hanna III, 'Editing Middle English Prose Translations: How Prior Is the Source?' *Text* 4 (1988), 207–16 (p. 209).

with and rendered the third identification correctly without a thought for the first two enthusiastic 'errors'—in which case his draft went uncorrected.

That Thomas Mull could somehow be complicit in the anglicizing of Milo is suggested by his pedigree. Through their Rous heritage, the Mulls were able to claim descent from a famous English Milo: Milo Earl of Hereford (d. 1143).[117] Milo was a very capable warrior who had scored a number of impressive victories against King Stephen in support of the empress Matilda.[118] That was more than three hundred years after Charlemagne, so the implied identification seems as tenuous as it is preposterous. If the tall story is purposeful, however, then its purposes may be compared to those suggested by Caroline D. Eckhardt and Bryan A. Meer for a similar instance in *Castleford's Chronicle*. In that text, Roland is identified as the father of Tristan, even though the reigns of both Arthur and Charlemagne are 'firmly grounded historically'[119] with death-dates of 542 and 815 respectively. The text also advances an unlikely localization of Tristan's activities in Northumbria. If the pseudo-genealogy is deliberate, it might, at the most obvious level, 'in combination with the localization of Tristan in Northumbria, [give] enhanced importance to territories near the chronicler's own homeland . . . territories which can now be spoken of in the same breath as both of those famous warriors' (p. 1094). The pseudo-genealogy also obviously 'reinforces the concept of the intertwined destinies of the French and English nations' (p. 1097). Taken to a postmodern extreme, such an alteration–which for its readership 'must surely have bumped up hard against the predominant sense of "things as they are",' might also be seen as 'a mode of inquiry and an epistemological position that questions prevailing assumptions about order and truth', and might serve as an open signal to knowing readers of 'the awareness that things could be quite different from their usual representation'

---

[117] See Hall, 'Harescombe', p. 112, n. 1; and William Dugdale, *The Baronage of England*, 2 vols. (1675–6), I, p. 537.

[118] On Milo's exploits see *Gesta Stephani*, ed. K. R. Potter (Oxford, 1976), pp. 90–6, 110, 128, 158–60, and R. H. C. Davis, *King Stephen* (third edition, London, 1990), pp. 39–42. Milo's mother, like the mother of Roland, was named Berthe; see *The Complete Peerage*, VI, 451, n. (g).

[119] Caroline D. Eckhardt and Bryan A. Meer, 'Constructing a Medieval Genealogy: Roland the Father of Tristan in "Castelford's Chronicle"', *Modern Language Notes*, 115 (2000), 1085–111 (p. 1087). Further references to this article appear in paretheses in the main text. *Castleford's Chronicle* was written in the North of England about 1327, and is preserved in a fifteenth-century manuscript.

(p. 1098).[120] For the Mulls, a family with clear local, national, and (in the case of Henry VI's claims, international) genealogical agendas, a family identified with 'rasing of the king's records' for its own and its patrons' advantage, and which employed in its armorial a device which played on the family name,[121] such a calculating and provocative adjustment to the text might not have been at all out of the question.

It is likely that such a bogus identification was never fully intended, but that does not diminish the larger implications of Mull patronage. If Thomas Mull did commission *Turpines Story*, then the presence of the text shows him extending the kind of literary patronage significant to those he would wish to impress (namely the descendants of Elizabeth Berkeley-Beauchamp).[122] Of note among surviving manuscripts with Beauchamp or Talbot connections which demonstrate the kind of patronage Mull was likely to emulate are London, British Library manuscripts Additional 24,194 and Royal 15 E.vi. The first is a copy of Trevisa's translation of the *Polychronicon*, produced in London in the first quarter of the fifteenth century and bearing the arms of Thomas Berkeley's son-in-law, Richard Beauchamp, Earl of Warwick, set in full-page borders on ff. 4 and 36.[123] The second manuscript, as mentioned above (p. xv), was commissioned by John Talbot as a gift for Margaret of Anjou, and includes a pictorial genealogy of Henry VI virtually identical in plan (though vastly superior in decorative grandeur) to that found in HM 28,561. Of especial significance in this comparison, Talbot's manuscript also contains a cluster of five Charlemagne romances (150 fols., a third of the manuscript), included no doubt to celebrate the conjoined French sovereign heritage of Margaret's marriage to Henry VI.[124] In the

---

[120] It must be stressed that, as with the misidentification in *Turpines Story*, a simpler explanation is possible, in this case in the form of a pre-existing source or tradition; the romance of *Sir Tristrem*, a northern text contemporary with Castelford, also names Roland as Tristan's father. See Eckhardt and Meer, p. 1089.

[121] See n. 20, above. One might speculate, on the basis of this putative private family meaning, that Roland's comparison of the Resurrection with the motion of a millwheel (ll. 902–4) would have made *Turpines Story* an even more attractive appropriation for this family.

[122] See above, pp. xxii–xxv.

[123] See Margaret Connolly, *John Shirley*, p. 114, and Waldron, 'The Manuscripts of Trevisa's Translation of the *Polychronicon*', pp. 281–317. Waldron suggests (p. 291) that the manuscript (sigil A), unlike HM 28,561, was copied from Manchester, Chetham's Library MS 11,379 (sigil M), itself probably of direct Berkeley provenance.

[124] The Carolingian texts are *Simon de Pouille*, *Aspremont*, *Fierabras*, *Ogier de Dannemarche*, and *Regnault de Montaubain*. The first page of *Simon* (f. 25ʳ) combines an

service of familial self-promotion, the manuscript also includes a version of *Gui de Warewic*, celebrating the exploits of the legendary ancestor of Talbot's wife, Margaret Beauchamp Talbot. As patrons of new works, moreover, Margaret and her father are recorded as having commissioned John Lydgate to compose, respectively, a life of Guy of Warwick and a translation of Lawrence Calot's verse pedigree of Henry VI's claim to the throne of France, the latter probably linked in origin to the pictorial genealogy just mentioned.[125]

The Mulls obviously harboured a vigorous, indeed fatal, dynasticism—they supported the dynastic integrity of the Talbot Earls of Shrewsbury, and of course the Lancastrian sovereigns (including Margaret of Anjou),[126] upon all of whom depended their own heritable integrity—but their manuscript also shows them, if not writing, then at least inscribing with their arms, their identity both as custodians of history and, as noted earlier, as guarantors of a specific dynastic future. In this sense, *Turpines Story*, if it is part of that scheme, is the product of a milieu characterized thus by Paul Strohm:

Even before Henry IV's usurpation, the Lancastrians were displaying an interest in self-transformative practices. John of Gaunt connived to alter chronicle-records by inclusion of the bogus story of ancestor Edmund Crouchback's disparaged claim. Henry IV devised novel coronation ceremonies which portrayed him as God's elect . . . . Henry V reworked existing prophecies on his own behalf, and designed a reburial service for Richard II which portrayed his deposed predecessor as a benign sponsor of his reign.[127]

Strohm refers to royal Lancastrians, but any of those in the Talbot affinity instrumental in the great Berkeley law suit could be said to have been participating in just such 'self-transformative practices'.

Writing of the rise of prose romance in the fifteenth century, and including *Turpines Story* within that group because of its depiction of the decline of Charlemagne's power through familial betrayal, Helen Cooper finds that the new romances strike a different note from their metrical counterparts:

illustration of Charlemagne and four kings with a page border bearing the arms of Margaret of Anjou and John Talbot. For a description of the contents of the manuscript, see Margaret Kekewich, 'Edward IV, William Caxton, and Literary Patronage in Yorkist England', *Modern Language Review*, 66 (1971), 481–487 (485).

[125] See Derek Pearsall, *John Lydgate* (London, 1970), pp. 166–7, and McKenna, 'Royal Political Propaganda', p. 151.

[126] On Hugh Mull's involvement in the 'Cornelius' plot, see p. xx above.

[127] Paul Strohm, 'Counterfeiters, Lollards, and Lancastrian Unease' in *New Medieval Literatures* (Oxford, 1997), 31–58 (p. 44).

The long-established tradition of metrical romances in English had occasionally allowed in ideas of family strife, but their general tenor was much more towards reunion, reconciliation, the due succession of father by heir . . . . The testimony of [the prose romances] indicates that their authors found a new literary form in which to express a more realistic and bleaker view of the world they lived in . . . . The typical metrical romance ends with the succession of the true heir; the disrupted successions of the fifteenth century are much more accurately reflected in the prose romances.[128]

If one leaves aside the question of genre and medium (given the variety of possible receptions the *Pseudo-Turpin* makes available), Cooper's assessment is almost allegorically apposite in the case of *Turpines Story* when seen against the rapacious background of the manuscript book in which the text appears (whether it is an original component or not). If Thomas Mull did indeed commission the translation of *Turpines Story*, then he would have had good reason for seeking the more accurate reflection of political turmoil with which such a new prose form may have been identified; and with this text he may also have been seeking in his own way to contribute to that turmoil.

SELECT BIBILIOGRAPHY

I. PRIMARY UNPRINTED SOURCES

Dublin, Trinity College MS 667
San Marino, California, Huntington Library MS HM 28,561

2. PRIMARY PRINTED SOURCES

A. Relating to the "Pseudo-Turpin Chronicle"

Acta Sanctorum for 28 January, *de S. Carolo Magno*
Acta Sanctorum for 1 November, *de SS. Athanasio et Theodoro*
Analecta Hymnica, ed. G. M. Drèves *et al.*, (55 vols., Leipzig, 1886–1922)
An Alphabet of Tales, ed. Mary MacLeod Banks (2 vols., EETS 126, 127, 1903–1905)
The Anglo-Norman 'Pseudo-Turpin Chronicle' of William de Briane, ed. Ian Short, Anglo-Norman Text Society, 25 (1973)

---

[128] Helen Cooper, 'Counter-Romance: Civil Strife and Father-Killing in the Prose Romances', in *The Long Fifteenth Century: Essays for Douglas Gray*, ed. Helen Cooper and Sally Mapstone (Oxford, 1997), 141–62 (pp. 141–4).

de Beauvais, Vincent, *Speculi maioris Vincentii Burgundi* . . . *Tomus Quartus, qui 'Speculum historiale' inscribitur* (Douai, 1624)

Brinton,Thomas, *The Sermons of Thomas Brinton, Bishop of Rochester (1373–1389)*, ed. Sister Mary Aquinas Devlin, 2 vols, Camden Series 75–6 (London, 1954)

Bromyard, John, *Summa prædicantium* (Venice, 1586)

Cân Rolant: The Medieval Welsh Version of the Song of Roland, ed. Annalee C. Rejhon (Los Angeles, 1984)

Caxton, William, *Charles the Grete*, ed. S. J. Herrtage, 2 vols., EETS, ES, 36, 37, (1880–1881)

Dives and Pauper, ed. Priscilla Heath Barnum, EETS 275, 280 (1976–1980)

Einhard, *The Life of Charlemagne*, in *Two Lives of Charlemagne*, ed. and trans. Lewis Thorpe (London, 1969)

'Firumbras' and 'Otuel and Roland', ed. M. I. O'Sullivan, EETS, 198 (1935)

de Froidmont, Hélinand, *Chronicon*, ed. J. P. Migne, *Patrologia Latina*, 212

Gabháltas Serluis Mhóir, The Conquests of Charlemagne, ed. Douglas Hyde, Irish Texts Society, 19 (1917)

Higden, Ranulph, *Polychronicon Ranulphi Higden monachi cestrensis*, ed. C. Babington and J. R. Lumby, 9 vols., Rolls Series, 41 (London 1865–86)

Historia Karoli Magni et Rotholandi ou Chronique du Pseudo-Turpin, ed. C. Meredith-Jones (Paris, 1936)

Langland, William, *Piers Plowman: The B Version*, ed. George Kane and E. Talbot Donaldson (London, 1975)

Langland, William, *Piers Plowman: The C-Text*, ed. Derek Pearsall (Exeter, 1994)

Malory, Sir Thomas, *The Works of Sir Thomas Malory*, ed. Eugène Vinaver, third edn., revd. by P. J. C. Field, 3 vols. (Oxford, 1990)

The N-Town Play: Cotton MS Vespasian D.8, ed. Stephen Spector, 2 vols, EETS, ss, 11 (1991)

The Old French Johannes Translation of the 'Pseudo-Turpin Chronicle', ed. R. N. Walpole (2 vols., California, 1976)

Der Pseudo-Turpin Harley 273, ed. Rudolf Schmitt (dissertation, Würzburg, 1933)

The Pseudo-Turpin, ed. H. M. Smyser (Cambridge, Massachusetts, 1937)

Richard Löwenherz, ed. Karl Brunner (Leipzig, 1913)

'The Sege off Melayne' and 'The Romance of Duke Rowland and Sir Otuell of Spayne' . . . *Together with a Fragment of 'The Song of Roland'*, ed. S. J. Herrtage, EETS, ES, 35 (1880)

The Siege of Jerusalem, ed. Ralph Hanna and David Lawton, EETS 320 (2003)

'The Taill of Rauf Coilyear' with the Fragments of 'Rouland and Vernagu' and 'Otuel', ed. Sidney J. Herrtage, EETS, ES, 39 (1882)

Trevisa, John, *Dialogus inter Militem et Clericum, Richard FitzRalph's Sermon: 'Defensio Curatorum,' and Methodius: 'Þe Bygynnyng of Þe World and Þe Ende of Worldes' by John Trevisa*, ed. A. J. Perry, EETS, 167 (1925)

Trevisa, John, 'Trevisa's Original Prefaces on Translation: a Critical Edition', ed. Ronald Waldron, in *Medieval English Studies Presented to George Kane*, ed. E. D. Kennedy, *et al.*, (Woodbridge, 1988), pp. 285–99

Ystorya de Carolo Magno o Lyfr Coch Hergest, ed. Stephen J. Williams (Cardiff, 1930, revd. 1968)

B. Relating to the Mull Family and other Contexts for the Provenance of *MS HM 28,561*

'Notes by Canon Bazeley on the Boteler Chapel of Gloucester Cathedral', *Transactions of the Bristol and Gloucestershire Archaeological Society*, 36 (1913), 33–6

Calendar of the Fine Rolls, 22 vols (London, 1911–12)

Calendar of the Patent Rolls, 52 vols (London, 1891–1916)

Hall, Rev. J. Melland, 'Harescombe: Fragments of Local History', *Transactions of the Bristol and Gloucestershire Archaeological Society*, 10 (1885–86), 67–132

Lincoln Diocese Documents, ed. Andrew Clark , EETS 149 (1914)

Lincolnshire Pedigrees, ed. A. R. Maddison, Harleian Society, 4 vols. (London, 1902–06)

Carole Rawcliffe, *The Staffords, Earls of Stafford and Dukes of Buckingham 1394–1521* (Cambridge, 1978)

Rotuli Parliamentorum, ed. Richard Blyke, and John Stachey, 6 vols. (London, 1767–7)

Smyth, John, *The Lives of the Berkeleys*, vols. II and III of *The Berkeley Manuscripts*, ed. John Maclean, 3 vols. (London, 1883–85)

Trevisa, John, 'Dialogue between the Lord and the Clerk on Translation' and 'Epistle to Lord Berkeley', ed. Stephen H. A. Shepherd in *The Idea of the Vernacular: An Anthology of Middle English Literary Theory, 1280–1520*, ed. Jocelyn Wogan-Browne *et al.* (University Park, Pennsylvania, 1999), pp. 146–56

Wedgwood, Josiah C., *History of Parliament: Biographies of the Members of the Commons House, 1439–1509* (London, 1936)

Wedgwood, Josiah C., *History of Parliament: Register of the Ministers and of the Members of both Houses, 1439–1509* (London, 1938)

3. SECONDARY SOURCES

A. Relating to the "Pseudo-Turpin Chronicle"

Alford, John A. 'Piers Plowman': A Glossary of Legal Diction (Woodbridge, 1988)

Bédier, Joseph. Légendes épiques, Recherches sur la formation des chansons de geste, 4 vols. (Paris, 1912–1915)

Brown, Elizabeth A. R., 'Saint-Denis and the Turpin Legend,' in The Codex Calixtinus and The Shrine of St. James, ed. John Williams and Alison Stones (Tübingen, 1992), pp. 51–88

Colley, Scott, 'Richard III and Herod,' Shakespeare Quarterly 37 (1986), 451–8

Cooper, Helen, 'Counter-Romance: Civil Strife and Father-Killing in the Prose Romances', in The Long Fifteenth Century: Essays for Douglas Gray, ed. Helen Cooper and Sally Mapstone (Oxford, 1997), pp. 141–62

Crick, Julia, Historia Regum Britannie of Geoffrey of Monmouth, vol. 3: A Summary Catalogue of the Manuscripts (Cambridge, 1989)

Norman Daniel, 'The Legal and Political Theory of the Crusade,' in A History of The Crusades, ed. Kenneth M. Setton, 6 vols. (Madison, Wisconsin, 1969–89), VI, 3–38

David, Pierre, 'Études sur le livre de saint Jacques attribué au pape Calixte II', Bulletin des Études Portugaises, 10 (1946), 1–41; 11 (1947), 113–85; 12 (1948), 70–223; 13 (1949), 52–104

Eckhardt, Caroline D., and Bryan A. Meer, 'Constructing a Medieval Genealogy: Roland the Father of Tristan in "Castelford's Chronicle"', Modern Language Notes, 115 (2000), 1085–111

Edwards, A. S. G., ed., Middle English Prose: A Critical Guide to Major Authors and Genres (New Brunswick, 1984)

Emanuel, Linda J., 'The Pseudo-Turpin Chronicle: Its Influence and Literary Significance, with Special Reference to Medieval French Literature' (doctoral thesis, Pennsylvania State University, 1978)

Esposito, Mario. 'Une Version Latine du Roman de Fierabras', Romania, 62 (1936), 534–41

Farrier, Susan E., The Medieval Charlemagne Legend: An Annotated Bibliography (New York, 1993)

Fischer, P. Pius. Die französische Uebersetzung des Pseudo-Turpin nach dem Codex Gallicus 52 (München) (Wertheim, 1932)

Foote, Peter G., 'A Note on the Source of the Icelandic Translation of the Pseudo-Turpin Chronicle', Neophilologus, 43 (1959), 137–42

Foote, Peter G., The Pseudo-Turpin Chronicle in Iceland: A Contribution to the Study of the Karlamagnús Saga (London, 1959)

Les Grandes Chroniques de France, ed. J. Viard, 10 vols., Société de l'Histoire de France, 120 (Paris, 1920–53)

Hämel, Adalbert. 'Überlieferung und Bedeutung des Liber Sancti Iacobi und des Pseudo-Turpin', *Sitzungsberichte der Bayerischen Akademie der Wissenschaften, Philologische-historische Klasse*, (1950), Heft 2, 1–75

Hanna, Ralph, 'Editing Middle English Prose Translations: How Prior Is the Source?' *Text*, 4 (1988), 207–16

Kendrick, T. D., *St. James in Spain* (London, 1960)

Kennedy, Edward Donald. 'Chronicles, Other than Genealogical, that Cover World History or the History of Countries Other than England or Scotland', in *A Manual of The Writings in Middle English, Volume 8: Chronicles and Other Historical Writing*, ed. Albert E. Hartung (New Haven, Connecticut, 1989), pp. 2672 and 2887

Krochalis, Jeanne, and Edward Peters, *The World of 'Piers Plowman'* (University of Pennsylvania Press, 1975)

de Mandach, André. *Naissance et Développement de la Chanson de Geste en Europe: I ; La Geste de Charlemagne et de Roland*, Publications Romanes et Françaises, 69 (Geneva and Paris, 1961)

Middleton, Anne, 'The Audience and Public of Piers Plowman', in *Middle English Alliterative Poetry and Its Literary Background*, ed. David Lawton (Cambridge, 1982), 101–23

Moisan, André, 'L'exploitation de la *Chronique du Pseudo-Turpin*', *Marche Romane*, 31 (1981), 11–41

Moisan, André,'L'exploitation de l'épopée par la *Chronique du Pseudo-Turpin*', *Moyen Age*, 95 (1989) 195–224

The Pilgrim's Guide: A Critical Edition, ed. Alison Stones and Jeanne Krochalis, 2 vols (London, 1998)

Rabelais, François, *Œuvres de François Rabelais*, ed. Abel Lefranc *et al.*, 6 vols. (Paris, 1912–31)

Shepherd, Stephen H. A., '"I have gone for thi sak wonderfull wais:" The Middle English Fragment of The *Song of Roland*', *Olifant*, 11 (1986), 219–36

Shepherd, Stephen H. A., '"This Grete Journee:" The *Sege off Melayne*', in *Romance in Medieval England*, ed. Maldwyn Mills (Cambridge, 1991), pp. 113–31

Shepherd, Stephen H. A., 'The Middle English "Pseudo-Turpin Chronicle"', *Medium Ævum*, 65 (1996), 19–34

Shepherd, Stephen H. A., 'Langland's Romances', in *William Langland's 'Piers Plowman': A Book of Essays*, ed. Kathleen Hewett-Smith (Routledge, 2000), pp. 69–81

Short, Ian, 'The *Pseudo-Turpin Chronicle*: Some Unnoticed Versions and their Sources', *Medium Ævum*, 38 (1969), 1–22

Short, Ian, 'A Note on the *Pseudo-Turpin* Translations of Nicolas de Senlis and William de Briane,' *Zeitschrift für romanische Philologie*, 86 (1970), 525–32

Smyser, H. M., 'Charlemagne Legends', in *A Manual of the Writings in Middle English 1050–1500. Fascicule 1: Romances*, ed. J. Burke Severs (New Haven, Connecticut, 1967), pp. 80–100

Spiegel, Gabrielle M., *The Chronicle Tradition of Saint-Denis: A Survey*, Medieval Classics: Texts and Studies, 10 (Leiden, 1979)

Spiegel, Gabrielle M., *Romancing the Past: The Rise of Vernacular Prose Historiography in Thirteenth-Century France* (Los Angeles, 1993)

Spiegel, Gabrielle M., *The Past as Text: The Theory and Practice of Medieval Historiography* (Baltimore, 1997)

Strohm, Paul, 'Counterfeiters, Lollards, and Lancastrian Unease', *New Medieval Literatures* (Oxford, 1997), 31–58

Walpole, R. N., '"Charlemagne and Roland:" ' A Study of the Source of Two Middle English Metrical Romances, "Roland and Vernagu" and "Otuel and Roland" ', *University of California Publications in Modern Philology*, 21 (1944), 385–452

Walpole, R. N., 'The Source manuscript of Charlemagne and Roland and the Auchinleck Bookshop', *Modern Language Notes*, 60 (1945), 22–6

Walpole, R. N., 'Note to the Meredith-Jones Edition of The *Historia Karoli Magni ou Chronique du Pseudo-Turpin*', *Speculum*, 22 (1947), 260–62

B. Relating to the Mull Family and other Contexts for the Provenance of MS HM 28,561

Beckingsale, B. W., *Burghley: Tudor Statesman* (London, 1967)

Boardman, A. W., *The Battle of Towton* (Stroud, 1994)

Brown, Huntington, *Rabelais in English Literature* (New York, 1967)

Connolly, Margaret, *John Shirley: Book Production and the Noble Household in Fifteenth-Century England* (Aldershot, 1998)

Davis, R. H. C., *King Stephen*, 3rd edn. (London, 1990)

Davis, Virginia, *William Waynflete: Bishop and Educationalist* (Woodbridge, Suffolk, 1993)

van Dorsten, J. A., 'Mr. Secretary Cecil, Patron of Letters', *English Studies*, 50 (1969), 545–53

Doyle, A. I., 'English books In and Out of Court from Edward III to Henry VII', in *English Court Culture in the Later Middle Ages*, ed. V. J. Scattergood and J. W. Sherborne (New York, 1983), pp. 163–81

William Dugdale, *The Baronage of England*, 2 vols. (London, 1675–1676)

Field, P. J. C., 'Sir Thomas Malory, M. P.', *Bulletin of the Institute of Historical Research*, 46 (1973), 24–35

Field, P. J. C., *The Life and Times of Sir Thomas Malory* (Cambridge, 1993)

Gesta Stephani, ed. K. R. Potter (Oxford, 1976)

Greg, W. W., 'Books and Bookmen in the Correspondence of Archbishop Parker', *The Library*, 4th series, 16 (1935–6), 243–79

A History of the County of Gloucester, ed. C. R. Elrington and N. M.

Herbert, vol. 10, *Upper Severnside: Westbury and Whitstone hundreds* (Oxford, 1972)

Graves, Michael A. R., *Burghley* (London, 1998)

Hanna, Ralph, 'Sir Thomas Berkeley and His Patronage,' *Speculum*, 64 (1989), 878–916

Hicks, Michael, *Richard III and His Rivals: Magnates and Their Motives in The War of The Roses* (London, 1991)

Ipomadon, ed. Rhiannon Purdie, EETS 316 (2001)

Ingulph's Chronicle of the Abbey of Croyland with the Continuations by Peter of Blois and Anonymous Writers, ed. Henry T. Riley (London, 1854)

Jones, Michael K., and Malcolm G. Underwood, *The King's Mother: Lady Margaret Beaufort, Countess of Richmond and Derby* (Cambridge, 1992)

Richard Jordan, *Handbook of English Grammar: Phonology*, trans. and revd. Eugene Joseph Cook (The Hague and Paris, 1974)

Kekewich, Margaret, 'Edward IV, William Caxton, and Literary Patronage in Yorkist England', *Modern Language Review*, 66 (1971), 481–87

Lander, J. R., 'Attainder and forfeiture, 1453 to 1509', in J. R. Lander, *Crown and Nobility 1450–1509* (Montreal, 1976), 127–58

Lander, J. R., 'Family, "Friends" and Politics in Fifteenth-Century England', in *Kings and Nobles in the Later Middle Ages* ed. Ralph A. Griffiths and James Sherborne (New York, 1986), pp. 27–40

Lester, G. A., *Sir John Paston's 'Grete Boke'* (Woodbridge, 1984)

Lydgate, John, *The Minor Poems of John Lydgate II (Secular Poems)* ed. H. N. MacCracken, EETS, 192 (1934)

McKenna, J. W., 'Henry VI of England and the Dual Monarchy: Aspects of Royal Political Propaganda, 1422–1432', *Journal of the Warburg and Courtauld Institutes*, 28 (1965), 145–62

Meale, Carol, 'Manuscripts, Readers and Patrons in Fifteenth-Century England: Sir Thomas Malory and Arthurian Romance,' in *Arthurian Literature IV*, ed. Richard Barber (Woodbridge, 1985)

The Oxford Illustrated History of Britain, ed. Kenneth O. Morgan (Oxford, 1984)

O. Pächt and J. J. G Alexander, *Illuminated Manuscripts in the Bodleian Library*, 3 vols. (Oxford, 1966–1973)

Pearsall, Derek, *John Lydgate* (London, 1970)

Rowe, B. J. H., 'King Henry VI's Claim to France in Picture and Poem', *The Library* 4th series, 13 (1933), 77–88

Rudd, Mary A., 'Abstracts of Deeds relating to Chalford and Colcombe', *Transactions of the Bristol and Gloucestershire Archaeological Society*, 51 (1929), 211–4

Samuels, M. L., 'Some Applications of Middle English Dialectology', *English Studies*, 44 (1963), 81–94

Samuels, M. L., 'Langland's Dialect', *Medium Ævum*, 54 (1985), 232–47 [with corrigenda, *Medium Ævum*, 55 (1986), 40]

Sandved, A. O., 'Prolegomena to a Renewed Study of the Rise of Standard English' in *So Meny People Longages and Tonges: Philological Essays in Scots and Medieval English presented to Angus McIntosh*, ed. M. Benskin and M. L. Samuels (Edinburgh, 1981), pp. 31–42

Sayles, G. O., 'The Deposition of Richard II: Three Lancastrian Narratives', *Bulletin of the Institute of Historical Research*, 54 (1981), 256–67

Smith, Jeremy, 'The Language', in *Lollard Sermons*, ed. Gloria Cigman, EETS 294 (1989), pp. xxx–xliii

Sutton, Anne F., "Malory in Newgate: A New Document," *The Library*, 7th Series, 1 (2000), 243–62

Underwood, Malcolm G., 'The Lady Margaret and Her Cambridge Connections', *Sixteenth-Century Journal* 13 (1982), 67–82

Waldron, Ronald, 'The Manuscripts of Trevisa's Translation of the *Polychronicon*: Towards a New Edition', *Modern Language Notes*, 51 (1990), 281–317

Waldron, Ronald, 'Caxton and the *Polychronicon*,' in *Middle English Essays in Honour of Norman Blake*, ed. Geoffrey Lester (Sheffield, 1999), pp. 374–94

Watts, John, *Henry VI and The Politics of Kingship* (Cambridge, 1996)

Wolffe, B. P., 'The Management of English Royal Estates under the Yorkist Kings', *English Historical Review*, 71 (1956), 1–27

Wolffe, B. P., 'Henry VII's Land Revenues and Chamber Finance', *English Historical Review*, 79 (1964), 225–54

Wolffe, B. P., *Henry VI* (London, 1981)

Wright, Laura, ed., *The Development of Standard English, 1300–1800: Theories, Descriptions, Conflicts* (Cambridge, 2000)

C. Catalogues and Works of Reference

Catalogue of the Irish Manuscripts in the Library of Trinity College, Dublin, compiled by T. K. Abbott and E. J. Gwynn (Dublin, 1921)

Chesshyre and Woodcock, *Dictionary of British Arms, Medieval Ordinary, Vol.* 1 (London, 1992)

Colker, Marvin L. *Trinity College Dublin Descriptive Catalogue of the Medieval and Renaissance Latin Manuscripts*, 2 vols. (Menston, 1991)

The Complete Peerage of England Scotland Ireland Great Britain and the United Kingdom, ed. Vicary Gibbs, *et al.*, 12 vols. (London, 1910–59)

The Dictionary of National Biography Founded in 1882 by George Smith, ed. Sir Leslie Stephen and Sir Sidney Lee (London, 1921–1922)

Dutschke, C. W. *et al.*, *Guide to Medieval and Renaissance Manuscripts in the Huntington Library*, 2 vols (Huntington Library, San Marino, California, 1989)

FitzHugh, Terrick V. H., *The Dictionary of Genealogy* (Sherborne, 1985)

Flower, Robin. *Catalogue of Irish Manuscripts in the British Museum* (London, 1926)

Hanna, Ralph, *A Handlist of Manuscripts containing Middle English Prose in the Henry E. Huntington Library*, The Index of Middle English Prose: Handlist I (Woodbridge, 1984)

Latham, R. E., *Revised Medieval Latin Word-List from British and Irish Sources* (Oxford, 1965)

McIntosh, Angus, M. L. Samuels, and Michael Benskin., *A Linguistic Atlas of Late Medieval English*, 4 vols. (Aberdeen, 1986)

Middle English Dictionary, ed. H. Kurath, Sherman M. Kuhn, and John Reidy (Ann Arbor, Michigan, 1952-)

The Oxford English Dictionary on Historical Principles, second edition, prepared by J. A. Simpson and E. S. C. Weiner (Oxford, 1989)

M. B. Parkes, *English Cursive Book Hands 1250–1500* (London, 1969)

Papworth, John Woody, *Papworth's Ordinary of British Armorials: An Alphabetical Dictionary of Coats of Arms Belonging to Families in Great Britain and Ireland* (London, 1985)

Petti, Anthony G., *English Literary Hands from Chaucer to Dryden* (London, 1977)

Whiting, B. J., *Proverbs, Sentences, and Proverbial Phrases from English Writings Mainly Before 1500* (Cambridge, Massachusetts, 1968)

EDITORIAL PROCEDURE

Word division has been regularized and capitalization is modern; word-initial *ff* is represented by *F* (or by *f* where capitalization is not consistent with modern practice). In one instance ('Spayne', l. 999) an initial double long *s* is rendered as *S*. The manuscript does not distinguish in form between *ȝ* and *z*, but where *z* is called for, it is substituted. The scribe sometimes uses *vu* as the equivalent of *w* (double-u); in such cases, *w* is substituted. Punctuation is modern, but reflects that used by the scribe where feasible: the scribe's practice is quite careful, using the *punctus elevatus* (:) to signal major pauses, and the *punctus versus* (;) to signal the conclusions of sentences, with the subsequent word very often rendered in the manuscript with an initial capital letter.

Abbreviations are expanded silently as follows: -ꝑ is rendered as -*is*; -⁹ is rendered as -*us*; -*oñ* is rendered as -*oun*; *Iħu* is rendered as *Ihesu*; and *Iħc* as *Ihesus*. Because of their rarity in the manuscript, terminal strokes which might conventionally be considered otiose have been interpreted as meaningful indicators of -*e* where the scribe's usual practice is to add -*e* when writing the word out in full. -*j*- is retained in roman numerals and in words when preceded by *i*; in all other instances, -*i* is substituted.

Emendations are enclosed within square brackets [ ]. Marginal and interlinear corrections are printed in forward and reverse primes ` ´, with details in the apparatus when the insertion is marginal or done by the rubricator. Folio and column breaks are indicated by a vertical line |. Text in bold corresponds to rubrication in the manuscript. Titles and chapter headings are included in the scheme of line numbering. For the conventions adopted by this edition for citing the standard Latin and other selected versions of the *Pseudo-Turpin*, see the headnote to the Commentary, p. 37.

TURPINES STORY

TURPINE THE ARCHEBISSHOP OF
þE BATAILLE OF ROUNCIVALE

Here begynneth þe Prologe of Turpines Story

Tvrpyne, by the grace of God archebiship of Reynes, a bisye foluere
and of grete emperoure Charlis a felow, [to] Leoprande dene of
Akune gretinge and helthe euerlastinge in God. A l[i]tille wile agone
ye sende to me, beyinge at Vyenne fulle seke and sore of many a 5
greuous wounde, that I sholde write to yow how þat oure famose
emperoure Charlis þe Grete delyuered þe lond of Spayne and Galice
fro the powere of þe Sarzyns by many a victorious dede, þe whiche I
saw beynge with him þere .xiiij. ʒere in his hooste. And treuly,
forasmoche þat þe grete victorious dedis þe whiche þe emperoure 10
dude in Spayne bethe noʒt fully write in Seynt Dionyse cronykulle—
what for lenketh of the story, what for absens of him þat wrote þe
cronykulle—wherefore I shalle write of him as I saw. Leffe wele, fare
wele, and plese God. Amen.

Explicit Prologus 15

[H]ere Beginneth the *Titulus* of þe Chapiters of the Storye of
the Bataille of Rouncivale of Grete Charles the Emperoure:

---

3 to] with (*see Commentary*)   4 litlle] ltille   16 Here] Bere   24 *Centred
above the new column, in red*: Capitulum   Off] Ooff

32 knyghtis] knyght   52 Off] Ooff   61 xxvij] xxiiij (for otherwise erroneous
xxviiij)

Explicit Tituli

How Seint Iame apered to King Charles

Capitulum iᵐ

After oure Lord Ihesu Criste had sufferid deþe and paide þe 80
rawnsome for synfulle man by his peynfulle passioun and rose fro
deþe to lyue and at þe laste styede to heuene, þen þe holy appostlus,
after þey had reseyued þe Holy Gost, þey departid hem into diuerse
parties of the worlde to preche oure Lord Cristis lawis. And so it fylle
lot to Seynt Iame þe More, broþer of Seynt Iohan þe Euaungelist, 85
furst to preche þe feythe in Galice to þe Galiciance. And wan he had
conuerted þe Galiciance he came to Ierusalem and þer afterwarde
was martirid by þicke cruelle kynge Horode. Wan he was dede,
Seynt Iamus disiplis toke his body bi ny3t. þey toke also `a´ ship and
putte his body þerine, and bi þe steringe and conueyinge of a gode 90
aungelle þey londid in Galice, and þer beried his body, and preched
þer þe feyþe, and conuerted þe Galiciance to þe lawes of Criste. But
sone after þe disiplus of Seynt Iame | were gone þens, the Galiciance f. 326ᵛᵇ
were peruertide and forsoke þe feyth, and so bode vnto þe tyme of
grete emperoure Charlis. þis grete emperoure Charlis, after he had 95
by many gretefolde laboris, by diuerse climattis and costis of the
worlde, by many auenturus dede, suddued contrius and kyngdomes
as Engelonde, Fraunce, Duchelond, Bakari, Latharinge, Burgayne,
Italie, Britayne, and oþer regions and prouynce, citteis, and townes
withoute numbure fro þe powere and þe right of þe Sarzyns, and 100

broute hem to Cristen feythe, þen he purposide for to haue ceside
and rest and neuer to haue hawntid þe dedis of warre more. But wat?
Sone after þis, Charlis had a visione shewide to him vndur þis forme:
he saw in heuene a wey of sterris þat bygan fro þe Frysonnys See and
105 streyte bytuexe Douchelonde and Italie, Fraunce and Gyane, goynge
euyne by Gaskyne and Nauerne, by Spayne, to Galice were þe body
of þe apostle Seynt Iame was beried and lay vnknowe. This visione
many a tyme, nyght after nyght, saw Kynge Charlis merueylinge
gretely wat it betokenyd. In a nyght, as þis Kynge Charlis musid and
110 stodyed wat þis wey of sterris myght synyfye, he fylle in a slepe; and
as he slepte þere aperid to hym a fulle feyre beuteus man seyinge to
him in þis wyse, 'Sonne, wat doste þou?' He answerid and seyd,
'Sire, who be ȝe?' 'I am', he seid, 'Iamus, the appostle of Criste, þe
sonne of Zebedei, þe broþer of Iohan Euaungeliste, whom oure
115 [Lorde] Criste callid fro fysshinge and made me of his grete merci
and grace apostle and send me to preche Cristis lore and law to
þe peple; whome also Herode, by martirdome of swerde, dude to þe
f. 327ʳᵃ dethe. And [my] body is beryed | in Galice, vnknowen amonge þe
cruelle mysbeleuynge Sarzyns. And þerfore I merveile moche, synes
120 þou haste delyuered so many regiouns, citteis, and cuntries fro þe
hondis and þe power of Sarzynes, whi þou delyuerest nowȝt my lond
fro here powere. Wherefore, I do þe wete þat riȝt as oure Lorde
hathe made þe strengest of alle herthly kynggis, so he hath shosyn þe
for to delyuer my cuntraye of Galice fro þe hondis of þe Moabitis.
125 And afterwarde, for þi labore þou shalte be crownede with þe crowne
of euerlastynge blisse. The whey of sterris þat þou sey in heuene
betokeneth þat [þou] shalte goo fro þat costis of þe Fresoune See
with a grete hooste, by alle þilke cuntreis forsaid, by stronge honde
and bataile to put oute þilke Sarzyns and paynyms and make an opyn
130 and sewere whey to my tumbe and beriell for alle peple þat shalle
come theþer by whey of pylgrymage; and þere they shalle by þe
merci of God haue foreyeuenes of here synnes, tellynge the
mervelous and þe preysinge of God into þe worldis ende. And
therefore, as sone as þou mayste, makeþe redy with þi hooste for to
135 do þis grete werkis of werre. And drede noȝt, for I shalle be þyn
helper in alle þi iorney; and after þi grete labore I shalle gete þe
euerlastynge ioye in þe blisse of heuene, and þyne name shalle be in
worship into þe worldis ende.' Vndure þis forme þe apostelle Seynt

115 Lorde] om. MS; Latin has Dominus (91, x)　　　118 my] many　　　127 þou]
om. MS

Iame aperide to the emperoure Charlis þre tymes. By þe vicioune
and declaracioune of þe same, Charlis whas gretely comforted. He 140
gaderid hym multitude of hoostis for to fy3tte and suddew3 þilke
paynyms, and he | his enterid into Spayne.   f. 327ʳᵇ

How þe walles of Pampilion fille downe by theimsilf

Capitulum ij

The furste citté þat Charlis besegid was Pampylioun, and there þey 145
lay at þe sege þre monthis, for þe citté was so stronge iwallid,
imannyd, and vitailid þat þey my3tte no3t gete hit. Then Charlis
preid to God in þis whise: 'O Lord Ihesu Criste, for whos worship,
loue, and feythe I come for to fy3tte and putt oute of þis lond þis
Sarzyns and mysbeleuynge folke, 3eue me þis towne to þe magni- 150
fiynge of þi name. O Seynt Iame, if it be trewe þat þou aperiste to me
and þou saydust þou wolduste helpe me, let me take þis townne'.
Then, by þe godenes of [God] and þe preyer of Seynt Iame, þe wallis
fylle adoune playne into þe grovnde. þe Sarzyns þat wolde be
cristenyd he kepte alyve, and þo þat wolde no3t he slew. When þe 155
Sarzyns hard how meruelously þe wallis of Pampilioun þat citté fille
downne, þey feryd gretely Kynge Charlis; and euer as he come
toward Galice þey mete hym and worship him and yelde to him
townnes, tribuute, and alle þe cuntré. These Sarzyns merueylid
wondurly þe manlynes, the semelynes, þe comlynes of Charlis and 160
þe Frensch hoost, and þey reseyuyd hem worshipfully and peseably
where-euer þey come, castynge awhey fro hem alle here armore, and
made no recistence. And so Kynge Charlis come to Seynt Iamys
tombe and worshiped him. And fro þens he come to a place þat is
calli[d] Peroune, and þere in see he py3tte his spere, þankeynge God 165
and Seynt Iame þat had conveyd hem þedur and made whey for hem
þat sholde after. The Galicianus þat wolde become Cristen he
baptisid by þe archebisshop Turpyn, and þilke þat wolde no3t be
Cristen, sum he | slowe and sum he kepte presoneris. And fro þens f. 327ᵛᵃ
he went þorow alle Spayne.   170

---

153 God] *om. MS; Latin has* Deo donante *(93, xvii)*   165 callid] callis

The names of þe citees of Spayne

Capitulum iij

Names of þe grete citteis and townnes þat Charlis conquerid in Galicia and Spayne I reduced to certen numbure, nouȝt tellynge þe
175 names of alle but of sum, in þe whiche þe reder of þis werke sum notable ensample may lerne. In Galice he gete .xiiij. notable citteis and townnes, amonge þe whiche on his callid Bracheta, þe whiche is *metropolis*—or 'þe archebisshopis shurche'—of Oure Lady. In Spayne he conquerid .xxxj. citteis and townnes, whos names, for
180 þey bethe hethen, [ben] vnrehersid. But on of hem whas callid Accintina, in þe whiche liethe þe holy confessore Torquatus, sumtyme felow and seruant to Seynt Iame, at whos beriell euer[y] yere *idus Maij*, on þe fest of þe seid confessoure, an olyue tree flowrithe, buddithe, and berithe ripe frute. Another townne is þere
185 þat is callid Bysertim, in þe whiche beth passynge stronge women, þe whiche after þe langage of þe contré bethe callid *Ambices*. And, for to make a shortte processe, Charlis conquerid all Spayne. And sum of þese citteis he gete withoute fyȝtte, and sum with grete batayle, and sum with slyȝe crafte, outetake oo citté of Spayne þat is callid
190 Lucerne, þe whiche he come laste too. Hit was a passinge stronge citté and myȝtly wallid, to þe whiche he leyd a sege the space of .iiij. monthes; but he myȝt noȝt gete hit with no mene of mannes honde no by no dede of armes. But what? Wan Charlis sawȝe þat manes power faylid, he turnyd to God and to Seynt Iame by holy preyer, as
f. 327vb he dud at Pampilioun; and a|none þe wallis fylle downne, and þat
196 citté is a wyldernes into this tyme. In þe myddis of þat citté arose a grete water like a fysshponde, in þe whiche water bethe many horyble grete blake fysshes. Sume of these citteis of Spayne diuerse kynges of Fraunce and also of Almayne had conquerid before þe
200 grete Charlis and iturnyd þe Sarzyns to þe feyth, þe whiche sone after bycome false renegatis and forsoke her feyth into þe tyme of grete Charlis. And after his dethe many kynges and princes fawȝtte in Spayne and beet þe Sarzyns and slowȝ many of hem—as Clodoueus, þe furste Cristen kynge of Fraunce, Clotarius, Dagober-
205 tus, Pipinus, Karolus Martellus, Karolus Caluus, Lodowycus. Summe part of Spayne they conquerid, and sume parte þey leyfte vnconquerid; but þis grete Charlis in his tyme conquerid alle

180 ben] hem (*see Commentary*)   182 euery] euer

Spayne. These beth þe namys of þe citteis and townnus þe whiche
he gete by grete trauayle and sore labore, þe whiche also he cursid—
wherefore neuer man duellid in hem synnes—and beth inhabitte into 210
þis tyme; þat is to sey, Lucerne, Ventosa, Caparra, Adama.

The idol that was called Maumeth

Capitulum iiij

Kynge Charlis dystroyed alle þe ydolis þat he fonde in Spayne,
oute῾take᾽ an ydolle þat was in þe londe of Alandaluffe þat was callid 215
Salamcadis. *Cadis* propurly is callid 'þe place where þe ydoll Salam is
inne': *Salam* in þe tonge of Arabie is callid 'God'. The Sarzyns
tellith þat þere is one þat was callid Mauumeth, þe whiche, himselffe
leuynge, made an image or an ydulle like to himselffe, and [with]
nigromanci and whichecrafte closid in þe ydoll a legioune | of f. 328ʳᵃ
deuelis, þe whiche ydolle is so stronge þat neuer myȝt be broke by 221
þe strenkethe of man. Whan eny Cristen man nyeth þe ydolle, he
parischeth ore dyeth; but whan eny Sarzyne nyeth þe ydolle,
Mawmeth for to worship him or praye to him, he goeth and cometh
hole and sownde. And if eny bride reste ore lyȝtte on þis ydolle, 225
anone he fallith downne dede. There is þ[er] on a brynke by þe see
side an hol[d]e stone .iiij.-square brode in þe hyndure parte; þe stone
is grauyd meruelously with Sarzyns werke, and hit is as hyȝe as a
reuyne flyeth; and euer as þis stone aryseth in heyth he his smaller,
and þe ouer parte of þis stone is .iiij.-square; and aboue on þis stone 230
stondith þis ydolle Mauumeth, of þe best coper shynynge þat myȝt
be had, like to a man. His face is turned into þe soweth. He holdith
in his ryȝt hond a grete key; the whiche key, as þe Sarzyns tellith,
shalle ῾falle᾽ oute of þat ydolleis hond in þicke ȝere þe whiche þere
shalle be bore a kynge in Fraunce þat in þe later dayes shalle 235
conuerte and suddewȝ alle Spayne to Cristis lawes. And anone as þis
Sarzyns se þis key fall oute of Mauumethis hond, þey shalle flyȝe to
castellis and strenkethis and hyde here tresours and richesse.

219 with] *om.* MS   226 þer] þre   227 holde] hole (*Latin has* antiquus
(*103, v*))   þe] of þe

The chirches þat Charles made in Spaine

240 **Capitulum v**

Off þe golde þat Charlis had in Spayne of princis and Spaynelis, furste duellinge þere .iij. ȝere, he made Seynt Iame a feyer chirche and set þerine a bishop and chanonys after þe ordure and þe rewle of Seynt Yseder the bishop and confessoure. He storyd þat churche
245 with bellis, westementis, pallis, bokys, and alle odure ornamentis to |
f. 328ʳᵇ serue God. Of þe resydew of þe golde and syluer þat Charlis had in Spayne, whane he came home he made in Akune a feyer churche in þe worship of Oure Lady. And at a townne þat is callid Biterensis he made a churche in þe worship of Seynt Iame; and anoþer he made at
250 Tolouse in þe worship of Seynt Iame; and anoþer he made in Gaskyne, in a townne þat his callid Axa, in þe whey toward Seynt Iame. Also he made at Parise a churche in worship of Seynt Iame betwexe þe water of Syene and þe Hylle of þe Martiris; and many moo he made in diuerse placis þat I speke not off.

255   **Of Agelonde**

Capitulum vj

After Charlis whas come into Fraunce, a paynym kynge of Affrica þat was callid Aygalond come into Spayne with grete hooste and conqueryd Spayne and alle þe Cristen men þat where in townnes or
260 citteis or holdis þat Charlis lefte to kepe þe londe. He slowȝe hem euery modur-sone and lefte none alyve. Whan Kynge Charlis hard this, he gaderyd hym grete hoostis and many, and grete and stronge, and come ayene into Spayne; and whas with him duke of his hooste Milo of Englond, a worthy warrioure.

265   **Ensample of a false executoure of a ded knighte**

Capitulum vij

Here in þis chapiter ye may see an ensample þat God shewyd of one þat withhylde a dede knyȝtis gode and spende hit in his vse ayens þe ordinaunce of þe dede knyȝt. In a tyme whan Kynge Charlis hooste
270 lay at Bayoun þere whas a knyȝt in þe hooste þat whas callid Rematicus. þis knyȝt whas so seke þat he muste nedis dyȝe. He whas shryue and hoselyde, and disposyd him to þe dethe. þis knyȝt

had a cosyn in þe hooste whome | he preyd þat he wolde selle his   f. 328va
horse þat was worthe an hundred shelingis and yeue it to prestis,
clerkis, and pore men to prey for him. His cosyn seid it shold be   275
do—as many a false execetoure dothe. þis knyȝt dyed. Whan he
whas deed, þis false cosyn, what dude he? He solde þe dede knyȝtis
horse for an hundred shelingys; but he dude noȝt o peny for þe dede
knyȝtis soule, but he spend it in gode metis and drynkis and fresshe
cloþinge. Now, so hit is þat euylle and cruelle dedis God punyschith   280
ryȝtwysely; wherefore, þe .xxx.^{ti} day after þis knyȝtis dethe, he peryd
to his cosyn by nyȝt in a vicioun, and seid to him in þis wyse:
'Forasmoche as I ordynyd my horse and my godys for to be do for
me soule, I woll þat þou knowe God foryaffe me alle my synnes; but
inasmoche þat þou withhylde þo godis and spendiste noȝt hem after   285
my ordinaunce, I haue be þis .xxx.^{ti} dayes in pe`y´nys of purgatorye.
But what shalle come of þis? I do þe to wete, tomorowe þou shallte
be dede and go to þe penys of hell; and I shalle go to þe blisse of
heuene'. Whan þis was done þe dede knyȝt vanshid awhey, and his
slepinge cosyn tremelyd and awoke. On þe morowe þis vntrew   290
excecutoure and cosyn tolde his feleship of þe hooste what his
dreme and what þe dede knyȝt seid to him; and riȝt as alle peple of
þe hooste talked þerof, sodenly in þe eyere aboue þe hooste þere
aperyd many fendis, sume like lyons, sume like beris, sume like
wolffis, and sume like wylde bullis, crieynge and yellinge to grete fere   295
of alle `þe´ hooste. And so, in þe cryis and yellingis, þe fendis toke
this false executoure, bothe `body´ and soule, with hem. | But what   f. 328vb
fille þenne? .iiij. dayes the feleship of þe hooste þey sowȝtte this man,
sume on horse and sume on footte, now by hyllis, now by valeys; but
nowhere þey founde him. .xij. days after, as Charlis hooste went by   300
þe wyldernes and þe hyllis of Naverne, on an hyȝe rocke þey founde
þe body of þis man, alle blacke and alle to-torne—for þere þe
deuyllis lefte it, and þe soule þey bore with hem to helle. And
þereafter Turpynne þe holy bishop seith, 'Know wele, alle ye false
m[e]n þat taketh dede mennys godis and spend not hit after þe dedis   305
laste wille, that ye shalle be þe fendis felowes in helle!'

276 dyed *crossed through ahead of* knyȝt   277 solde] sholde   292 d *in* seid
blurred in the original ink, but clarified in red.   295 u *in* bullis *blurred in the original ink,*
but clarified in red.   305 men] man

The batail of Seint Faucounde, where þe speres waxid grene and budded

Capitulum viij

310 Thenne Kynge Charlis and Milo, duke of his hooste, went forthe
into Spayne for to seke Agalonde, and þei founde him in a lond þat is
callid de Campis, by a feyer reuer þat his callid Ceia, vpon a feyere
mede (where afterward Charlis made a fulle feyere churche in þe
worship of holy martiris Seynt Facounde and Seynt Primitiue, in þe
315 whiche resten þoo holy martiris bodies). In þis medew semelid
Charlis with his hooste, and Aigalond and his hooste. þen Aigalond
send by an herewde to Kynge Charlis vndure þis forme, yeuynge
shoyse were þere shold fy3t .xx. ayenste .xx., ore .xl. ayenste .xl., ore
an .c. ayenste an .c., ore a thousonde ayenste a thousonde. þenne
320 se[n]d Charlis an .c. ayenste an .c., and Charlis kny3ttis slow alle
Aigalondis kny3ttis, þat where Sarzyns. After þen send Aigalond an
.c. ayenste an .c., and alle þey where isleye. The þred tyme send
f. 329ra Aigalond | .ij. þowsonde ayenste .ij. þowsonde, of þe whiche .ij.
þowsonde þat whare in Aigolondis parte, sume where sley and þe
325 remenaunte flew. After þis, þe thride day, Aigalond profered plenare
bataile, and to þis agreed Charlis, on þe morne folowynge. The ny3t
before þe bataile a grete parte of þe Cristen hooste py3tte þeyere
speris in þe grounde in þe vouwarde of þe hooste vpon þe bryncke of
the water of Ceia. But what wonder whas þere? Treuly, on þe morne
330 alle þe speris þat where py3tte soo, þey where ryndyd, buddude, and
grene. And þis where þe speris of hem þat on þe morne in þe
vouwharde were martired for þe feyth. Whane Charlis and his hooste
saw þis meruelous tokyn, merueylinge þey ascryuyde þus to þe grete
godenes of God. þey kytte þere speris by þe grounde, and þe rotis
335 þey where lefte in þe grounde; þere whaxe a grete woode. Many of
[þe] speris where asshe, as it aperith by þe treis þat growithe þere.
But what? A grete wondurfulle þinge to see ore here—but þis whas
ioye to alle soulis of them whos bodyes where martirid on þe morne!
But what more? On þe morne þey had a grete batayle, and a grete
340 slaw3te, insomoche þat þere where on Kynge Charlis parte martirid
for þe feythe and for þe loue of God .xl. thousounde Cristen men—
and amonge þem Duke Milo, a worthi warrioure, a worthi Englysshe
lorde, fadur of þat worshipfull kny3t Rowlond. And in þis batayle,

320 send] seid   333 merueylinge] þey merueylinge   336 þe] om. MS

Charlis steed was sleyne; thenne stoode Charlis on | fotte with few3   f. 329rb
of þat Cristen hooste amyddemonge Aigolondis hooste. He drew3   345
oute his tristy swerde that whas callid Caudiosa and cleue many of þe
Sarzyns atwo, and so he slow3 manfully many a false paynyme.
Whanne hit drew to þe ny3t, Charlis with þo þat where lefte alyue
drew to his loggynge; and so dude Aigolond with his. The morow
after þis bataile come to Charlis oute of þe costis of Italie .iiij. markis   350
with .iiij. thousounde of wele-fytinge men to helpe and socoure þe
gode Kynge Charlis. Whenne Aigalonde harde of þis he toke his
hooste and flew into þe costis of Legionence. And Kynge Charlis
turned home into Fraunce. This bataile morelisithe þe gode archebisshop Turpyne in þis manere: 'Alle Cristen me[n] in þis lyffe bethe   355
in continuale batale of the flesshe, þe worlde, and þe deuyle. Ry3t as
Charlis kny3ttis made redy here armore before þe bataile, so sholle
we arme vs with armore of vertuus ayenste oure gostely enmyes and
vicis; and þerefore whosoeuer wolle arme him with feythe ayenste
heresye, with charité ayenste hatte, with largenes ayenste auarise,   360
with mekenes ayenste pride, with chastité ayenste flessly lustus, with
meke and besy prier ayenste þe fendis temptacions, with silence
ayenste chydinge, and strivis with 'very' obedience ayenste alle the
transgressions of oure Lordis commoundementis, his spere—þat is
to sey, his gode dedis—shalle floure, budde, and waxe grene at þe   365
day of his dethe. And ri3t as Charlis kny3ttis deyde for þe feyth, so
we sholde dy3e for vicis | and liffe with vertuus, þat we haue þe   f. 329va
victorye of oure enemyus, þat we may be rewarded in heuene with
aungelis and seyntis.

A citee þat was called Agenny   370

Capitulum ix

In þis mene tyme Aigalonde had gadered him a grete numbure of
Sarzyns—þat is to sey Mauris, Moabitis, Ethiopus, Parkis, Affricanis, Perses; and Xerephum, kynge of Arabia, Burabell, kynge of
Alexandre, and many oþer kynges—þe Kynge of Bugie, þe Kynge of   375
Agabie, þe Kynge of Barbarie, the Kyng of Cordube—and many
oþer kyngis with Sarzyns, many withoute numbre. With alle þis
grete hooste Aigalonde come into Gaskynne and conquerid a citté

355 men] me   363 very *inserted above* werrey, *which has been crossed through.*

þat whas callid Age[nn]i. Fro þis citté Aigalonde send meissengeris
380 to Kynge Charlis comaundynge him for to come to him peseably
with a fewe feleship of men, behotinge him moche golde and siluer,
with þat þat he wolle become his sugget and abeyȝe to his empere.
But why dude Aigalonde þis? Verely, for he wolde ihaue know
Charlis, þat afterwharde in bataile he myȝt haue isley him. But
385 Charlis perseuyd wele þis foule pride and also þe tresoune. He come
with grete hooste of Cristen peple but foure myle fro þis seid citté,
and þere he lefte his hooste. And with .iij. skore knyȝttis he came to
an hylle where he myȝt see þe citté; and þere he lefte þo .iij. skore
knyȝttis and chaunged his cloþinge and arayede him like a messen-
f. 329ᵛᵇ gere, castynge his shylde vpsodoune on his backe, | leuynge his spere
391 behynde him, as messengeris dothe in tyme of bataile. And [with] o
man alone he came to the citté. Anone, ryght as he whas spyed, þey
send oute men to whete wat he wolde. They seid þey where
'messengeris came fro þe Kynge Charlis to youre kynge, Aigalonde'.
395 þen they where brouȝt into þe citté before Aigalond; and þen þey
seid to Aigalond, 'Charlis send vs to þe, doynge þe to wete þat he is
comynge as þou comoundy[d]e him, with .iij. skore men, to do the
obeysance and serue þe and be þyne, with þat þat þou wolte yeue
him þat þ[at] þou behyȝttiste him. Wherefore come now pesesably
400 with also many men, and speke with him.' Thenne Aigilond armyde
him and seid to hem, 'Turne ayene to Charlis and sey þat I `a´byde
him'. But alle þis tyme knew noȝt Aigalond þat he whas Charlis þat
spake with him. But Charlis knew Aigalond, and behyld fulle wele þe
citté and þe strenkith of þe citté and in whiche parte hit was febelest
405 and myȝt best be wonne; also he toke gode hede of his kyngis
strenkeþis þat where with him. And þen he toke his leue and come
ayene to þe hylle þereas was his thre skore men, and [h]e returnyd to
his hooste. Aigalond þen come after Charlis with .vij. thousond
armyd men for to haue sley him. This treson perseuyd Charlis. He
410 toke his feleship and went into Fraunce and gaderide him a grete
hooste and come ayene to þat citté of Agi[nn]i and leyd þerto a sege;
and þere he lay .vj. monthis. þe .vij. monthe he leyde rounde aboute
f. 330ʳᵃ guwnus and | engynes and alle oþer ordinaunce for to haue ibete

---

379 Agenni] Agemi (*Latin has* urbem . . . Agenni (*115, iv*): *the main scribe uses the m-*
spelling always, but the rubricator's spelling is consistent with the Latin, suggesting a correct
reading in the exemplar)   391 with] *om. MS; Latin has* cum solo milite (*115, xvi*)
393 wolde *struck through ahead of* where   397 comoundyde] comoundynge
399 þat] þow   402 þis] þat þis   407 he] se   411 Aginni] Agimi
413 O Gunneris *crossed through before* engynes (*see Commentary*)

doune þe toune wallis. Whanne Aigalond saw þis grete ordinaunce,
by þe whiche þis toune whas like to be gete and he and his feleship 415
for to be take or be sley, wherefore he and his kyngis [and] alle þo þat
where `of´ worship flow awey by preveis and goutis; and so, by a
reuer þat his callid Guaronam, þey skapide Cha[r]lis hondis. þe day
folouynge, Charlis victoriously gate þe citté, and sum of þe Sarzyns
flow awey by þe ryuere of Guarone, and sum where sley, þe 420
numbure of .x. thousonde.

The citee Sanctonas where speres were grene

Capitulum x

Fro þens Agalond come `to´ a citté icallid Sanctonas, þe whiche þe
Sarzyns hylde, where he taried with his hooste. Kynge Charlis came 425
to þis citté, comoundynge Aigalonde that he sholde yelde him þe
citté. Aigalonde seid þat he wolde noȝt so, but he wolde yeue him
bataile with þis condicione, þat whoso hade þe victory, he sholde
haue þe citté. The day of þe bataile whas syned, and þe nyȝt before
þe bataile, when þe Cristen hooste was departide in diuerse whardis, 430
in a medow betuex a castelle þat his callid [T]alabruge and a toune
by a ryuere þat his named Tharantta, þe Cristen men pyȝtte he[re]
speris in þe grownde, þe whiche on þe morne þey founde grene-
rynedide, flourynge, and buddynge. And þis were þe speris of þem
þat on þe morne sholde be martiride fore Cristis name. On þe 435
morne, þey saw þis meruelouse tokyne, þey þankide God, and kette
here speris and semelid with þe | Sarzyns. By þe grete fyȝtte and at f. 330ʳᵇ
þe begynnynge þe`y´ smote doune and slew many of Sarzyns; but at
þe laste þe Sarzyns had þe ouer hande and slew of [þe] Cristen
hooste .iiij. thousonde—in þe whiche bataile Charlis horse was sley 440
and he himselffe smete doune to þe grounde and almoste steffelde
amonge þe dede men. But Charlis with alle his hert, with alle his
myȝt, turned to God and preide to God to helpe him, to socoure
him, to yeue hym strenketh, for to haue þe victorye and þe felde.
Anone as he hade made þis preier, God sette him on his fette and he 445
`and´ his peple slow, and putte to flyȝtte Aigalonde with his hooste.
þen flew Aigalonde to þe seid citté. [þ]an Charlis pursued vnto þe

416 and] om. MS; Latin has regis et maioribus suis (117, xiv)   418 Charlis] Charis
431 Talabruge] Calabruge (see Commentary)   432 here] he   439 þe] om. MS
443 hepl crossed through before help   447 þan] wan

citté and leyd þerto a sege on þat parte þat was by lond. But þe nyȝt
folouynge Aigalond flow fro þe citté by the watersyde. Þat perseuyd
450 Charlis; he sewyd hem and slow of hem þe Kynge of Arabie and þe
Kynge of Brigie, and with him .iiij. thousonde paynyms.

The fliȝte of Agelonde and Charles kniȝtis

Capitulum xj

Then Aigalonde flowȝ and passyd ouer þe portis of Cisereeus and
455 came to Pampilione; and fro þens he send Kynge Charlis worde þat
þere he wolde abide to yeue him bataile. When Charlis harde þis, he
turnede ayene into Fraunce, and with grete besynes and charge he
send into euery coste of Fraunce to gader strenketh ayenste þe
enemyes of God. He lete crie and ordeyned þat alle þoo þat were
460 bounde to him or eny oþer lorde in Fraunce, þat wolde go with him
f. 330ᵛᵃ into Spayne and fyȝtte ayenste þe | paynenyms and þe enemys of
God, þat þey and alle theyers sholde goo free for euermore. What
more? Þoo also þat were exilid ore banashid, he called hem to
pardone and grace, with þe condicione forseid þat þey sholde goo
465 with him into Spayne. Also, þicke þat were pore, he yaffe hem
richesse; þicke þat were naked, he cloþide hem; þicke þat were at
debate, he pesid hem; þicke þat were disheretide, he restored hem to
þere heretaunce; also alle þicke þat before hade for eny matere be at
debate ore eny trauese, he acordide hem. And alle these he armyd
470 and arayde with armore, euery man after his connynge and his degré.
And þus he gaderid a grete hooste of men of armys, .vj. skore
thousond and .xxx.ᵗⁱ of fyȝttinge men—and footte men were withoute numbure. And alle þese þat Kynge Charlis gaderid to go and
fyȝtte and put vndure footte þe enemys of God, I Turpynne,
475 archebishop, by þe auctorité and power of God, I asoyled hem of
alle here synnys and yaffe hem þe blessynge of God. And with alle
þis worthy hoste Kynge Charlis come into Spayne ayenste Aigalonde.

474 footte] footte of

The names of þe principal lordis þat were with King Charles 480

Capitulum xij

These beth þe names of þe principalle lordis þat ware with Kynge Charlis in þis hooste: I Turpynne, archebishop, þat halpe to gadure þis grete hooste for to fyȝtte ayenste þe Sarzyns and asoylide hem of alle þere synnys, þat also oftetymes fowȝtte ayenste hem myn oune 485 hondis; Rowlond, duke of þe hooste, lorde of Cunomanesis and Blauij, neue to Charlis, þe sonne of | Milo, duke de Angloiris, ibore f. 330ᵛᵇ of Berthe þe suster of Charlis, a grete man and a semely and douȝtty in armys, with .iiij. þousonde wele-fyȝttinge men; Olyuer, duke of þe hoostis, a manfulle knyght and moste eger in bataile—þe Erle of 490 Genebensis—with .iij. þousonde; Arastanus, duke `of´ Brittayne, with .vij. þousonde; Engelerus, duke of Aquitanye, with .iiij. þousonde (alle þese fornamed were expartte of alle dedis of armys, and specialy in archery); Gayferus, kynge of Bedous, with .iij. þousonde; Candebaldus, kynge of Fricie, with .vij. þousonde; 495 Otgerus, kynge of Danys, with .x. þousonde; Constantinus, *Prefectus Romanus*, with .xx. þousonde; and many moo whos names ware vnknowen to me; and Charlis oune hoste were .xl. þousonde of horsemen—but þe foottemen were none numbure. And þese forsaid and forenamyd were famouse men of werre, and redy to fyȝt and 500 dyȝe for defence and mentenaunce of Cristis feythe. And riȝt as oure Lorde Criste with .xij. apostelis and .iij. skore and .xij. disciplis conquerid alle þe worlde to þe feythe, so Kynge Charlis of France and Emperoure of Rome with his hooste conqueride Spayne to þe feyth. 505

The truse þat Aigelond asked of King Charles Emperour

Capitulum xiij

Thenne went forthe Charlis hooste towarde þe coostis of Burdeuce and occupyed and `re´keuerid as moche grownde in lenkethe and brede as a man myȝt go in .ij. days iurnaye; and þe sounde and þe 510 noyse of `þe´ hooste was herde fro hem .xij. myle. Whan þey came `to´ þe hauyne of Cisereos, þen Arnolde de Belandam passid furste

509 re- *inserted below the line (see Commentary)*

oure þe hauyne with his peple and whent towharde Pampilioun; and
f. 331ʳᵃ nexte folowyd hym Estultus, erle, | with his hooste; laste of alle come
515 Kynge Charlis with Roulonde and alle þe oþer hoostis. And þese
peple they rekeuerid alle þe grounde fro þe water of Rune vnto an
hylle þat is thre lekis fro Pampalioun, in þe whey to Seynte Iamus.
And Charlis with his hooste were .viij. dayes passinge ouer þat
hauyne of Cesareos. þenne send Charlis to Aigalonde to Pampilioun
520 in þis forme: þat he shold yelde him þe townne oþer come into þe
felde and yeue him bataile. Aigalonde saw þat þe townne was to feble
to withstonde so stronge an hooste; he chese to come into þe felde to
yeue him bataile, rather þanne cowardly dyȝe in þe citté. þanne send
Aigalond to Kynge Charlis desiringe of him .ij. thynggis: furste, þat
525 alle his hooste myȝt go oute of þe citté and take here grounde and
make hem redy to bataile; and þe secunde, þat he myȝt speke with
Charlis mowthe-by-mowthe, for he desiride gretely to se Kynge
Charlis.

How Charles and Aigelonde disputed þeire righte
530   of Spaigne

Capitulum xiiij

þenne þis treuse was take. þan went oute Aigalonde with his hoostis
fro Pampilioun into þe felde, and þere he lefte hem; and when he
had do so, he toke with him .xl.ᵗⁱ of þe worthiest of his hooste and
535 come to Kynge Charlis were he satte in his trone of astate, .ij. myle
fro þe citté, were Charlis laye with his hoostis. And þenne was
Charlis hoste and Aigalondes hooste in a fulle feire playne place,
faste by Pampilion, .vj. myle of lenkethe; and þe hyȝe wey þat lyethe
f. 331ʳᵇ to Seynt Iamys deseueryde þe .ij. hoostis. þen | seid Charlis to
540 Aigalonde, 'þou artte Aigalonde, þe whiche wrongefully þou haste
take my londe fro me—þat is to say, Spayne and Gaskuyne, þe
whiche I gate by grete power, and made hem suggettis vnto Cristen
lawys; and alle þe kyngis of þese londis ware suggettis and
tribunarius to me. And whanne I was turned home into Fraunce,
545 þou camyste with stronge hond and haste peruertid þese peple and
haste slayne many of hem; and þou haste brende and distroyde þe
lond, with many castellis, townnes, and citteis; and þis is þe cause
why þat I and myne hoostis ben come to gete þis londis ayene.'
When þat Aigalonde harde Kynge Charlis speke þe Sarzyns tonge

(þat sume tyme he lernyd at Tholouse wen he went to scole) he ioyed 550
gretely; for so he my3t better denounce and declare his matris by
hemselffe þan by anoþer interpretacioune. þanne spake Aigalonde to
Kynge Charlis in þis wyse: 'I beseche yow, Charlis, telle me why ye
toke awey þicke londe þat þou, ne þi fadur, ne þi fadris fadur, ne þi
belefadur, hade neuer title þerin bi eritaunce?' þenne seid Kynge 555
Charlis, 'For þis cause: for oure Lorde, Criste Ihesus, maker of
heuene and erthe, hathe chosyn vs þat bethe Cristen peple for to be
principalle of alle peple and to be lordis of alle þe worlde, and that
we shold labore to make alle peple Cristen, wherefore I labored and
made alle Spayne for þe more partte—and þou haste made hem 560
renegatis and false paynyms.' þenne seid Aigalond, 'hit is right a
grete inconuenient þat | oure peple sholde be suggettis to youre f. 331va
peple, synys þat oure god and oure law3e is better þan youre god and
youre law3e. We haue Mauumethe, þe messengere of God send to vs
whos preceptis and comoundmentis we kepe and holde. We haue 565
also goddis almy3tty, the whiche at þe comoundment of Mawmeth
shew vs thinggis for to come; and þese we worshippith, for by þese
we belyuythe and regnythe.' Thenne seid Charlis, 'Aigalond, þou
erriste in þat þou seiste þat youre law3e that Mawmethe yaffe to yow
is more worthy þan oure, for we kepe þe law3e of God almy3tty and 570
his precepttis, and ye kepe þe law3e of a false veynyd dedely man þat
is dampned in helle. And we worship Fadure and Sonne and Holy
Goste in oo godhede, in oo nature, in oo beynge; in him we beleue
and him we worshipe and him we serue. And ye worship þe fende
and false ydolis þat beth deffeth and dome and veyne; in hem ye leue 575
and hem ye worshipe. Oure soulis, for þe feythe and þe law3e þat we
kepe and holde, after þis lyffe shalle go to heuene and haue
euerlastynge blisse; and youre soulis after þis lyffe, for lacke of
Cristen feythe, shalle go to helle. Wherefore, oure law3e is moche
more worthy þan yours. And, forasmoche as ye know no3t, ne wolle 580
know, þe maker of heuene and erthe, ye shulle no3t haue lordship ne
heritaunce, neyþer in heuene neyþer in erthe, but parte youre
possessioune; youre lordship is with þe fendis in helle and youre
god Mawmethe. Wherefore, Aigalonde, chese on of .ij.: take þou
'and' thy peple Cristen feythe and beleue; ore ellis | come to f. 331vb
bataile—and þou shalte dy3e euylle deth.' þenne seid Aigalond, 586
'Nay, I wolle not of þi law3e neyþer þi feyth; but vndure þis forme I

550 wen] weni   565 of Mawmethe shew vs thynggis *subpuncted for omission and*
crossed through in red, ahead of we kepe (*eyeskip error from l. 566*)

shalle fyȝtte with þe and þyne: I for my lawȝe and my feithe and þou
for þi lawȝe and þi feithe, and whoso hathe þe felde and þe victorie,
590 is lawȝe is beste. He shalle haue loude and preysinge, and þat parte
þat is ouercome, euerlastynge shame and repreue. And iff I and my
peple be ouercome, yf I lyue and skape, I wolle be cristenyd.' And
hereto acordide bothe parties.

How þat Aigolondis peple were ouercome and he behyȝtte
595 to be Cristen

Capitulum xv

Anone as þey were apoyntide þus, þey greyþed hem to bataile vndur
þis forme: furste þey send .xx. Cristen knyȝttis ayenste .xx. of þe
Sarzyns. But what? Anone þe Sarzyns where isley eueryshone. þe
600 secunde tyme þey sende an hundrid ayenste an hundrid, and anone
þey were isley. þe .iij.ᵈ tyme þey send an hundrid ayenste an
hundrid—and þen þe Cristen men flow backe; and anone þey
were sley. And þis was þe cause: for þey flow for drede of dethe.
The .iiij. tyme þey send .ij. hundrid ayenste .ij. hundride, and alle þe
605 Sarzyns were isley. At þe laste þey send a thousond ayenste a .mˡ.,
and alle þe Sarzyns were isleyȝe. þenne was treuse ʿtakeʾ on bothe
partie, and Aigalonde come to speke with Kynge Charlis, and he
affermyd þat Cristen mennys lawȝe whas better þanne þe Sarzyns
lawȝe; and so he hyȝtte þat he and his peple on þe morne wolde be
610 cristenyd. And vndur þis poyntment, Aigalonde went to his hooste |
f. 332ʳᵃ and tolde hem þat þe Cristen lawȝ was better þan þe Sarzyns lawȝe,
werefore he and alle his sholde be cristenyd. To þis apoyntment
sume of þe kyngis agreyde, and sum wolde noȝt agree þerto.

The ordre of Charles peple at mete and the pore men
615 **Capitulum xvj**

In þe morne after þis poyntmente vndure trewse, aboute nyne of þe
day, Aigalonde come to Charlis for to haue be cristenyde. And whan
Aigalonde came, Charlis was syttynge at þe mette at a stattly borde
beste besyȝe. He saw also many bordis and diuerse, and diuerse ordis
620 of þem þat ware at þe mette; þan Aigalonde askede of Charlis what

603 of drede *crossed through after* for drede

þey ware at euery borde. Charlis seid, 'þo þat þou seest sitte with
birris ore pulyons of oo coloure, hit bethe bisshoppis, doctoris, and
prestis of oure law3 þat techith vs oure law3e and expouneythe hit,
þat cristen vs, and of oure synnes asoylith vs; and [þo] þat þou seest
sitte in blacke habittis, hit bethe monkis and abbattis, þe whiche 625
euermore prayeth to God for vs; þo þat þou seeste sitte in þat feer
shynnynge habitte, hit ben regulere chanouns, and þey synge and
rede masse, matens, and ouris, and preyeth for alle Cristen peple.'
Amonge oþer sy3ttis, he saw3e .xiij. pore men fulle euylle icloþid
syttinge on þe grounde, withoute borde or cloþe, hauynge a litille 630
mette. þan Aigalonde askede what men þei where. Charlis seid þey
were 'þe messengeris of oure Lorde God, Ihesu Criste, þe whiche,
for loue of Ihesu Criste and þe .xij. apostelis, euery day we fede and
yeue mette'. þan said Aigalonde, 'þese þat sitte aboute þe beth wele
icloþide; þey ette gode | metis and drinke gode drinkis. But þose þat f. 332rb
þou calliste þi goddis messengeris bethe euylle icloþide and fare 636
euylle; þey sitte aferre and litille made of. He seruythe euylle his
lorde þat dothe so litille worship to his seruanttis; and grete
vnreuerence and shame he dothe to his god þat þus dothe to his
meynye. þi law3e þat þou seydiste whas [gode], now þou shewyste to 640
me þe contrary, þat 'it' is false.' And wan Aigalonde hade seid þus,
he toke his leue of Charlis, gretly disklawnder how vngodely Charlis
tretide Goddis messengeris; wherefore he refuside Cristyndome.
[W]an Charlis perseyuyd þat Aigalonde wolde no3t be baptizide
for he saw how vngodely þe pore peple of God was itretid, he lete 645
ordeyne þat alle þe pore peple þat ware in þe hooste shode be
honestly cloþid, and fro þensforth þey had sufficiently mette and
drinke ry3t inow.

The bataille of Pampilion and þe deþe of Aigelonde

Capitulum xvij   650

On þe morow after þis, þe hole hooste of Charlis and of Aigalonde
semelide in the felde iarmyde redy to fy3t vndure þe foreseid
condicione, whos law3e was better. þe numbure of Charlis hooste
þat semelide was an .c.xxx.iiij. þowsonde; þe numbure of Aigalondes

---

624 þo] *om. MS*   630 borde] brode (*Latin has* sine mensa (*137, xvii*))
640 gode] *om. MS; Latin has* . . . quam dicebas bonam esse . . . (*139, ix*). *Cf.* vngodely *in
the next sentence, and see the Commentary on* þe contrary *later in this sentence*   644 Wan]
þan   651 On] Oon

655 hooste were an .c. þowsonde. þe Cristen hooste made .iiij. warddis;
þe Sarzyns made .v. wardis. þe furste warde of þe Sarzyns þat furste
semelid in bataile, þey ware isley; þe secunde warde aperid, and
anone þey ware isley. Wan Aigalonde saw his .ij. wardis and .ij.
f. 332ᵛᵃ parttis of his hooste isley, he onyd togadure alle his | hooste and his
660 peple, and hymselffe whas amyddis hem. Whan this Cristen hooste
saw þis, þey compassyde alle þucke paynyms coste. On þe o parte
whas Arnolde de Bellanda with his retynue, and on anoþer partte
Arastanus, kynge, with his peple; on anoþer partte Gandeobaldus
with his feleship; on anoþer parte whas Kynge Ottogerijus with his
665 meyné; on anoþer part was Kynge Charlis with his grette hooste.
Wan þe hethen hooste was þus besegitte and compasside, the
trompis and trompettis and claryneris blow vp and Charlis lette
crye and bad hem alle, in His name þat þey came fore, to fyȝte
manfully ayenste þe enemyes of God and þe feyth. þan Arnolde de
670 Bellanda furste fylle to fyȝtte, and he and his slew þe Sarzyns boþe
on þe riȝt side and on þe lefte syde—tulle he came to Aigalonde,
whiche was amyddis his hooste; and with him he fauȝtte myȝttly and
slew him with his oune swerde. And wan he was dede, þe Sarzyns
made a grette crie [and] a grette yellynge for þe dethe of Aigalonde;
675 but þe Cristen hooste fylle vpon þe Sarzyns and slewȝ hem euery
modur-sonne, þat none askapid but þe kynge of Sibillie and
Altimaior, kyng of Cordube, þe whiche flew with few of þe Sarzyns.
So moche blode whas shedde of þe Sarzyns þat þe Cristen peple
wadude in þe blode. `And´ Charlis, alle þe Sarzyns þat he founde in
680 þe cittee of Pampilion, he slow.

How þe Cristen men were slaye þat wente by niȝte to spoile þe ded Sarasins

Capitulum xviij

Svme of þe Cristen hooste, þe nyȝt nexte after this bataile, fore
f. 332ᵛᵇ couetouse went to spoyle | þe dede Sarzyns, vnknowynge to Charlis.
686 Wen þey came to þe dede men þey gaderid and charged hem with
golde and syluer and oþer precious þingis and richesse; and when
`þey´ were fulle lade þey turnyd home towarde þe citté. þis dede
covnturwaytide Altumaior, kynge of Cordube, þe whiche hyȝedide

---

674 and] om. MS; Latin has clamor et ululatus (143, iii, n.)   689 Cordube]
Cordubue

himselffe faste by, on þe halkis of þe hylle. He went bytwex hem and 690
þe citté and slew hem, euery man, þat none askapide: þe numbure of
þe Cristen men þat was sley þere, aboute a þousonde.

How Charles faughte with Furre prince of Nauerne

Capitulum xix

In þat oþer day folowinge it was tolde Charlis how one, a Ferre, 695
prince of Nauarne, wolde yeue bataile vpon þe Hylle of Garyzime.
þen Charlis toke his hooste and came to þat Hylle of Garyzyme;
whan þis prince herde this, he disposyde him on þat morne to fyʒtte
with Charlis. þe nyʒt before þe bataile Charlis prayde to God to yeue
him ore shew him sume token of hem þat sholde dyʒe on þe morne 700
in bataile; on þe morne, wan Charlis hooste was armyde and redy to
fyʒtte, þere aperide a rede crosse on þe sholdoris, vpon þe habireiounys, of hem þat sholde be sleye in þat bataile. Anone as Charlis
hade shaw þat merke on þos men, for compacioun þat he hade of
hem, he closid hem vp in his oratorye þat þey sholde not be dede in 705
þe bataile. O, how meruelouse, how incomprehensible, bethe þe
domus of God! O, how onshercheable, | how inpers[c]rutable, bethe þe f. 333ʳᵃ
wey of God! Wat more? Wanne `þe´ bataile was done, and Furre the
prince was sleye with thre thousonde of Nabarris that ware Sarzyns,
thicke þat Charlis had put in his closet was dede: þe numbire of hem 710
was an hundride and fyfty. O, how holy was þe company of þese
knyʒttis of God þe whiche loste not þe crowne of martirdome þow
þey were not martiride wyth swerde! þanne Kynge Charlis toke þe
Hylle of Garizime into his lordship, and þe londe of Nauarne.

The bataille of Ferekot and the disputacion of good 715
Rowlande

Capitulum xx

After þis was done, tydynggis came to Kynge Charlis how Admiraldus, kynge of Babilon, had sende to Vageris a gyaunte of the
kynrade of Golias þat was callid Fereacutus, the whiche came ouʒte 720
of þe coostis of Sirie with .xx. þousonde Turkus for to ʒeue a bataile
to Kynge Charlis. This Ferrakutte drade neyþer spere ne arowe; this

698 to] to to   707 inperscrutable] inperstrutable

had with him a þousonde and fourtty giauntis. Wan Charlis harde
this, anone he with his hooste came to Vageras. þanne this giaunte
725 Ferrakutte came to Charlis and offerid him bataile one-for-one; and
þerto consentid Charlis, and sent forþe kynge of Danys, Ottoger.
Anone as þe giante saw him in þe felde, he came walking softe by
him, and with his riȝtte arme he grappud him with alle his armore
and bare him into the towne, in þe syȝtte of alle þe hooste, as þow he
730 bare a meke shepe. The lenkethe ore þe stature of þis grete giaunte
f. 333ʳᵇ was .xij. cubitus; he hadde a longe face; | his armys and his leggis
ware .iiij. cubitus, and his fyngris were .iiij. spannys longe. After þis
þan se[n]d Charlis to him Reynolde de Alba Spina; and anone he
toke to him Reynolde and bore him into Vageras as he dude þe
735 furste. þan se[n]d Charlis to him Constantone, kynge of Rome, and
Hole, erle; þese þis giaunt toke, one on þe riȝt syde and anoþer on þe
lefte syde, and þus bare hem into þe towne Vageras to þe prisone.
þan se[n]d Charlis .xx. aȝenst þe gyaunte, and alle þese he toke and
put hem into prisone. Wen Charlis saw þis, and alle his hooste, þey
740 merueylid gretely, and Charlis durste send no moo to him. Wan
Rowlonde saw þis, prince of Charlis hooste, þat none in alle þe
hooste durste go to þis gyaunte, he commyttid him hoely to God
with fulle truste in God; he came to his vnkulle Charlis and seid þat
he wolde fyȝtte with thicke Ferakutte, for, he seid, God was strenger
745 þan man—'And for þe feythe of God and for þe defence þerof, I
wolle asaye him.' Charlis was fulle lothe to lete him go, for Rowlonde
was ȝonger, and Charlis louyd him tendurly. At þe laste, by besy
instaunce, þe kynge ȝaue him leue to fyȝtte with him. þan Charlis
preyd to God þat he wolde helpe Rowlonde in fyȝtte with þis gyaunt
750 as he halpe Dauyd aȝenste Golie, of whome þis giaunt came. þan in
þe name of God Rowlonde went to þis giant. Anone as Ferakutte saw
Roulonde in þe place, he toke him with his riȝt honde and sette him
f. 333ᵛᵃ before him on his horse. | Than as þis giaunte was carynge Rowlonde
towarde þe towne of Vageras, Rowlonde confortide him in God and
755 toke his herte to him and his strenkethe; he toke þis Giaunt by þe
chyne and myȝtly he caste him downe of his horse and so fylle to þe
grounde; and anone boþe þey rose and toke þeyer horse. þan drew
oute Rowlonde his gode swerde þat was callid Durendalle; he smote
at þe giaunte, but it blente, and with þat stroke Rowlond smote
760 Ferakuttis horse and slew him downe. þan stode þis giaunte on his

733 send] seid   735 send] seid   738 send] seid   755 & struck through
after þe

feette and Rowlonde on horse. This Ferrakut drew his swerde and
hylde him in his honde, þretinge Rowlonde; þan Rowlonde leyd at þis
giaunte a grete stroke, but he faylyd of Ferakut—but he smote his
swerde oute of his honde. þan was Ferakutte wroþe; he wronge his
fyste togedur and wolde haue ismyte Rowlonde, but as God wold, he 765
faylid of Roulonde and smote his horse on þe hede and slew him—
truly a schrewide fyste and an heuy! þen þey boþe were on fote, and
with stonys and fystis [fauȝtte] alle þat day into nyȝt. Wen it drew to
nyȝt Ferekut asked truse of Rowlonde into þe morow. þan þey
acordide þat on þe morow þey sholde noȝt fyȝte on horse ne with 770
speris, but afotte; and so þey departid and toke þeyer loggynge. þen
on þe morow þey semelyd riȝt herly in the felde after þis
poyntemente ouer nyȝt. Ferekut broute with him a grette swerde,
but it halpe him nouȝt, for Rowlonde had a grete knabbit | longe f. 333vb
staffe, with the whiche he bare of Ferakuttes strokes and bete faste on 775
Ferakutte—but he hurte him noȝt. They fauȝte so longe that this
Giaunte waxide wery and he asked truse of Roulonde that he myȝt
slepe. But wat dude ientille Rowlonde? He toke a stone and leyd [it]
vndur Ferekuttes hede þat he myȝt slepe more hesely. And in this
mene tyme thereas he slepte, þere was none of þe Cristen men durste 780
sley this giaunt; for there was suche a law and an ordinaunce betwexe
the Cristen men and the Sarzyns þat after truse was take betwexe
hem, that yf a Cristen man wronggid a Sarzyne ore a Sarzyne
wronggid a Cristen man, þicke þat dude þe wronge sholde be dede.
When Ferrakutte had refreshed him wele with slepe he wakyd and 785
satte vp. Thanne satte Rowlond by him; and as þey satte togedur
Rowlonde asked Ferrakutte how he was so stronge and so hardy þat
drade neyþer swerde ne spere ne arow ne stone. Thenne seid
Ferrakutte, 'There may no man hurte me ne wounde me with no
manere of wepyn but in my navile.' Whenne Rowlonde had hard þat 790
worde he hylde his pese and turnyd away his here as þow he had
noȝt merked þat worde, for this giaunte seid this worde in the
Spayennyshe speche, þe whiche þe giaunte went þat Rowlond
vndurstode noȝt—but Roulonde vnderstode riȝt wele. þen þis giaunt
behylde faste Roulond and asked him wat was his name, and he 795
answerid him aȝene and to him seid, 'My name is | Roulonde'. He f. 334ra
asked him of wat kynrede he was þat so myȝttely fauȝtte with him—

762 at þis struck through after leyd and before the second instance of at þis
768 fauȝtte] om. MS; Latin has pugnis et lapidibus debellarunt (151, xiv-xv)   Wen]
went   778 it] om. MS

'I founde neuer man þat made me so wery'. þen seid Roulonde, 'I
am a Frenshe man and I am Roulonde, neveye to Kynge Charlis'.
800 þen asked Ferakutte, 'Of wat lawȝe bethe Frenshmen'. þen seid
Roulonde, 'We bethe by þe grete grace of God of Cristis Cristyn
lawȝ, and we obeythe his lawys, and for his lawe and þe feythe of
Criste we fyȝtte'. þen wen þis giauntte herde him name Criste, he
askede, 'what `is´ þicke "Criste" in whome þou beleuyste'? þen seid
805 Roulonde, 'þe Sonne of God þe Fadur of heuene, þe wiche was bore
of a mayde; he dyede on a crosse; he was beride in a sepulcre; he
arose þe þredde day; he styede into heuene and syȝtte in þe riȝtte
syde of his fadur'. þen seid þe giauntte, 'We beleue þat maker of
heuene and of herthe is oo God, but he is neyþer 'fadur' ne 'sonne'
810 ne 'holy goste', for þer is neyþer he þat gete a sonne, ne a sonne þat
was igette; eke þere is oo God and noȝt .iij. "parsonys"'. þen seid
Roulonde, 'In þat þou seyste þere is oo God, þou seyste wele, but
þou seyste þat þer bethe nouȝtte .iij. parsonys, þere þou erriste'. þen
seid Roulonde, 'Yff þou beleue in þe Fadur, beleue in þe Sonne and
815 in þe Holy Goste, for þe Fadur is God, and þese .iij. parsonys bethe
oo God'. þen seid Ferakutte, 'If þe "fadur" bethe God and þe
"sonne" be God and þe "holy goste" be God, þen þere be .iij.
goddis—and þat may noȝt be'.

Here Roulande bringith ensaumple how there may be
820 þre Persones and oon God |

f. 334rb [T]henne seid Roulonde to Ferakutte, 'Nay, but þere bethe .iij.
parsonus and oo God as I seid before, and þerein þree and þree in
oone. And þes .iij. parsonus bethe coeternalle and coequale, and
suche as þe Fadur is, suche is þe Sonne, and suche is þe Holy Goste.
825 In þese parsonys is parsonel propurtté, and [in] þe godhede is vnité;
and in þe maiesté is worshippid equalité. The aungelis in heuene
worship oon in þree and þree in oone. Abraham also sawȝe þree and
worshipid one'. þen seid Ferakutte, 'Shewe me how þat þree bo
oone'. 'I shalle,' quod Roulonde, 'by sample in creaturis. In an harpe
830 wen he sownnythe þere bethe þree: strynggis, crafte, and handdis—
and yutte þese beth but oone in `þe´ harpe ore in harpinge. So in
God is Fadur, Sonne, and Holy Goste—in oo God. And in an
almonde bethe þree: þat is to sey, a rynde, a skale, and a cornell—

821 Thenne] Whenne   825 in] om. MS (see Commentary)

and yut þese bethe but oone almonde. So bethe þree parsonys in
God and oo godhede. And in the sunne beth þree þinggis: þat is to 835
sey, *candor, splendor,* and *calor* – shynynge, lemynge, and hetinge—
and alle bethe oo sunne. Furþermore, in a welle buthe þree
þinggis—and yut is þe welle but oo thynge. And in þiselfe bethe
þree þinggis: þat is to sey, þi body, þi soule, and þi lymmys—and
alle þese bethe oo body and oo man. And so in God is vnité and 840
trinité'. þen seid Ferakutte, 'Now I see how God is oone in þree and
[þree] in oone. But þe fadur gete þe sonne, I fele noȝt'. þen seid
Roulonde, | 'Canste þou beleue þat God made Adam'? 'Yee', seid f. 334ᵛᵃ
Ferakutte. 'þen', seid Roulonde, 'riȝt þen as Adam was not gete of
anoþer and yut he gate sonnys, so þe fadur of heuene was not of 845
anoþer; but he in his eternité gete his euerlastinge Sonne of himselfe
in þe godhede before alle tyme'. þen seid Ferakutte, 'It plesithe me
þat þou seyste, but how was he, þat God vnmade, imade man'?
þenne answeride Roulonde, 'He þat made heuene and erthe and alle
þinge of nout, he made is Sonne man in þe Maideis bely withoute 850
manys seed by his oune godly power'. 'Off þis', quod Ferakutte, 'I
labore to wete how þat a maide myȝtte conseyue withoute feleship or
werke of man'. þen seid Roulonde, 'God þat made Adam withoute
seede of man, euery oþer he made; he made his Sonne man in þe
Ma`ï´ddis wombe withoute þe seede `of´ man; and riȝt as he is gete 855
of God þe fadur withoute man, so he was gete and conceyuyde in þe
Maide withoute man. Such getinge and suche conceyuynge bese-
mythe God'. þen seid Ferakutte, 'I am shamed to here sey þat a
mayde sholde conceyue withoute a man'. þen seid Roulonde, 'He þat
makethe in a bene a gurgulione, a worme in many an herbe, fruȝtte, 860
and trees; wormys growyth withoute seede of male kynde, and also
many fysshis in þe see, and beis withoute þe seed of male or female.
He made a mayde conceyue God and man withoute seede ore
feleship of man. And, as I seide before, he þat made Adam withoute
þe seed of man myȝt lyȝtly make is Sonne man in | þe Maiddis f. 334ᵛᵇ
wombe withoute feleship of man'. þen seid Ferakutte, 'Hit may wele 866
be þat he was bore of a mayde. Sithe he is Goddis sonne, he myȝt
noȝt dyȝe on þe crosse as þou seyduste before; for God dyethe noȝt'.
þen seid Roulonde, 'þou graunttiste þat he was bore o man of a
maide; þen riȝt as he was bore man of a mayde, he myȝt dyȝe as a 870
man, eke he dyed as a man. For euery man þat is bore as a man shalle

---

836 candor] canrdor (*with* r *subpuncted for excision before* d)   842 þree] *om. MS*
867 Sithe] Seithe

dyȝe as a man. And yf þou canste beleue þat `he´ his bore as a man,
þou muste beleue his passioune, for he dyȝed as a man; and also þou
muste beleue his resurreccioune'. 'How sholde I leue his resurrec-
875 cioune?', seid þe giauntte. 'For he,' [seid Roulonde,] 'þat dyed and
rose þe þrede day to lyue.' þen Ferakutte `i´merueylid gretly in þat
worde and seid to Roulonde, 'Why seyste þou to me so many ydulle
wordis? Hit is inposible þat a man `sholde aryse´ fro dethe to lyue'.
þen seid Roulonde, 'Noȝt only Goddis Sonne arose fro dethe to lyue,
880 but also alle þe men and women þat euer ware fro þe begynnynge of
þe worlde into þe worddis endis shalle aryse and pere afore þe hyȝe
trone of God, and reseyue after here deseruynge gode or euylle:
peyne for synne and ioye for gode dedis. Wherefore, God himselffe
þat maketh of a litulle plante [to] growe into an hyȝe tree, and also
885 makethe of a wete corne iburiede in þe erthe `to´ growe in hyȝe and
bryngeth forth fruȝtte, þicke same lorde shalle make alle þo men þat
bethe dede aryse in here oune fleshe and body and soule at þe laste
dredefulle day of dome. Lerne þe nature of a lyone, for yf a lyone þe
f. 335ra þrede | day by his breþinge quekyn and rise to lyue his welpis, no
890 wondur yf þe fadur of heuene þe þredde day arise fro þe dethe to
lyue his Sonne. þou shalte take for none new þinge þat þe Sonne of
God arose fro dethe to lyue. For why? For many þat ware dede afore
the Resurreccioune arose fro dethe to lyue; yf Helias and Heliseus
ware areside fro dethe lyȝttely, moche more raþur the faddur of
895 heuene areside his Sonne. Also, Criste þe fadurs Sonne `of´ heuene
afore his passioune areside many fro dethe; moche more raþur he
himselffe myȝtte arise fro dethe to lyue. þen seid Ferakutte, 'I
perceyue wele wat þou seyste, but how he styede to heuene, as þou
seyest, I can noȝt se it ne belyue it'. þen seid Roulonde, 'He þat
900 lyȝttely descendide fro heuene may lyȝttely ascende to heuene, and
þat lyȝttely arose fro dethe to lyue, he may lyȝttely entre heuene.
Ensample of þis þou mayste see in many thynggis. Furste, in a wele
of a mylle, for þicke part of þe wele þat is now aboue, þicke same is
now benethe. Also þou þiselffe, yf þou come doune an hylle into þe
905 walyȝe, þou maiste ayenewarde ascende oute of þe valyȝe into þe
hylle. þe sonne also, yesturday he arose in þe Este and ascende into
þe Souþe and went doune into þe Weste, and þis day also arose in þe
Este. Therefore, in suche maner wyse þe Sonne `of´ God ascendiþe'.

---

872 he *added to the right of the line*   875 seid Roulonde] *om. MS; Latin has* Quia
inquit Rotolandus, his qui nascitur . . . (*159, x-xi*)   878 sholde aryse *added to the right*
of the line   884 to] *om. MS*   899 he *crossed through after* þat

þen seid Ferakutte vndur þis forme: 'I shalle fyȝtte with þe, þat yf
þis feithe þat þow spekiste of be trew þou shalte ouercome me; and 910
yf it 'be' noȝt trew I shalle ouercome þe; and he þat his ouercome
shalle 'be' in repreue, and he þat ouercome oþer shalle be in loude
and presyinge'. 'I assent', quod Roulonde, 'be it as þou seyste'.
þanne | they arose boþe and made hem redy to fyȝt, and anone f. 335rb
Roulonde smotte at þe giaunte with his grete knabbide staffe, and þe 915
giaunte leyde at Roulonde with his grete gresly swerde; but
Roulonde avoydude þat stroke and bare it of with his staffe, but
þan was his staffe kete atweyne. And þan anone þe giaunte fylle on
Roulonde and leyde on him and þouȝtte so to a sleyne him. þan þe
gode Roulonde knewe wele þat he myȝt neuer askape fro him, for he 920
was so moche and so heuey. To god helpe he with his soule cried, to
Criste Ihesus Mari Sonne, preyinge hem boþe of helpe to helpe him
at þat nede and at þat tyme; and anone, by grace of Criste, he meuyd
þat giauntte and turned him vpriȝt, and with his swerde he prickyde
þe giauntis navylle and he arose and askapide fro him. But wat! þan 925
cried þis giaunte to his god with a loude voyce, seying þus:
'Maumeth, Mavmeth, now socoure me, now helpe me, for now I
dyȝe!' Anone at þis crye þese Sarzyns came and bare him into þe
townne Vageras; and worthy Roulonde came home to Kynge Charlis
his vnkulle hole and sounde, withoute hurtte ore wounde. And anone 930
þe Cristen hooste enteride into þe toune with þe Sarzyns þat bore
Ferakutte with grete crye and power. And þus [þis] giauntte was
sley, þe townne [and] castelle was iyeldude, and Charlis prisoneris
þat Ferakutte toke were delyuered.

The bataille of the visoures 935

Capitulum [xxj]

A litille tyme after þis Ferakutte was isley it was tolde Kynge Charlis
þat Ebrahim, kynge of Sybilie, and Altumaior, kynge of Cordube
[were] abydinge for to | yeue Charlis bataile at Cordube. þe kynge[s] f. 335va
flew before fro þe bataile of Pampilioun. Wen Charlis harde þis he 940
dysposyd him and his peple towarde Cordube; and wen þese kyngis
herde of his comynge þey armyde hem and here hooste and mette
him in þe felde .iij. lekys fro þe townne. There were of þe Sarzyns

---

932 þis] om. MS   933 and] of (see Commentary)   936 xxj] xxij
939 were] om. MS   kynges] kynge (the Latin is plural: qui . . . fugerant (163, xvi))

.ix. þowsonde, and þe Cristen men .vij. þowsonde. þen Charlis
945 departide his hooste a þree warddis, and þe beste fyʒttinge men and
þe strenggeste [he] set hem in þe forewarde; and þe f[o]ttemen he
sette hem in þe myddulle warde; and alle his knyʒttis in þe hyndur
warde. In þis same maner þe Sarzyns departid he[re] peple. Wan alle
ware rayedde Charlis comounddide his forewarde to fyʒtte and ley on
950 þe forewarde of þe paynnyms. But here may ye lerne a shrewde wyle
of werre of þe Sarzyns, for thus þey hade disposide here forewarde:
euery horseman had before hem a fotteman, and eche fotteman hade
a visoure with a longe berdde, iharniyde like þe deuyllis hede, and
euery of þis fottemen hadde a tympane ore a cymballe in his honde;
955 and wen nyʒede þe forewarde of Charlis hooste, þey cried and smote
theyere cymbalis and made a grete horible noyse. Wen þe horse of
Charlis hooste harde þat horible noyse and sawʒe þat cursyd syʒtte of
þe visours, þey waxed woodde for fere and fley abacke insomoche þat
þe horsemen myʒt noʒt make hole wey. Wen þe secunde warde and
f. 335ᵛᵇ þe þred warde of Charlis ooste | sawʒe how þe forewarde flew, þey
961 flew also. Wan Charlis sawʒ þis, he meruelylide þerof whye his peple
flewʒe; but wen he herde of þat wyly turne of werre, he meruelylid
noʒt. þe Sarzyns were ioyfulle þerof, and fayer and softe came after
þe Cristen 'men' to an hylle .ij. myle fro Cordube were Charlis
965 hooste lay. Wen þe Sarzyns hadde aspyed Charlis hooste, þey drew
abacke; for þere Charlis hade pyʒtte his tentes to rest alle nyʒt. þan
on þe morow Charlis hade ordeyned þat his horsemen sholde keuer
alle here horse heddis with lynnyne cloþe þat þey sholde noʒt see þat
curside vysours, and lete stoppe þe horse heris þat þey sholde not
970 here þat horible noyse and crye. Here was o wyle of werre ayenste
here wyle! Wen þe horse hedis were ikeuerede and here heris
istoppid, þey semelyd frely and fouʒtte withoute eny fere; and þe
Cristen men fauʒtte manly into none of þe day and slew a grete parte
of þe Sarzyns. þan alle þe Sarzyns onyde hem togedure. Amydde-
975 monge the Sarzyns hooste was a wayne with .viij. ho[c]syn, and apon
þis wayne was þe Sarzyns banere; þe custume and þe maner of þe
paynnyms was þat þere sholde no man flee fro þe bataile alle þe tyme
þat þe banere stoode. þis custum knew wele Charlis, but wat dude
he? Treuly he, tristinge and callinge after þe helpe of God, enterid in
980 amonge þe Sarzyns and leyde hem doune on euery syde, forte he
came þeras þe banere was; and he smotte doune þe banere staffe with

þe swerde þat was callid Caudiosa, and ouerþrew þe wayne. And alle
the Sarzyns þat saw þis, þey þat were lefte alyue, þey made `a´ grete
crie and flew. And þere was sley þat day .viij. | thousonde Sarzyns, f. 336ʳᵃ
and Ebrahim, kynge of Sibilie. Altumaior, kynge of Cordube, flew 985
into þe townne with .ij. thousonde Sarzyns. þe morow þis Altumaior
was ouercome and yelde himselffe to Charlis, and was baptizide and
yelde þe townne also to Charlis, and hilde of him as for chehoffe
lorde. Wan alle þis was downe, Kynge Charlis deuydude þe londes
and prouynce to hem þat had be with him in his werris and hem þat 990
wolde duelle þere: þe londe of Nauerne and Bace to þe Normans; þe
londe of Castelle to þe Frenshemen; þe londe of Vager and
Ceseraustie to the Grekis and Appuleis þat were in his hooste; and
þe londe of Arogone to þe Pictis; and þe londe of Alandulphe by þe
see syde to þe Almeyns; and þe londe of Burdugalie to þe Danys; and 995
þe Flemyngis þe londe of Galice—fo[r] þe Frenshemen wold not
inhabitte þat londe, for hit was to sharppe a cuntrey for þem þat
ware bredde in Fraunce. And fro þat tyme forthe durste neuer no
man in Spayne profur Charlis bataile.

How þat Charlis wente to Seinte Iames and made ⁣⁣⁣1000
Compostilla a see

Capitulum [xxij]

Wan þis was done Charlis lefte þe grete hooste in Spayne, and `toke´
þe wey to Seynt Iame; and þo he founde, þe trew Cristen men, he
sherished hem and yaffe hem, and þo þat he founde þat were 1005
peruertide renegatis, sume he slew and sume he put to exile into
Fraunce. And þen he helde a counselle in Compostela and ordeyned
bushoppis and prestis in citteis and cuntrayes, and wolde þat þey
sholde abeye þe beshop of Compostela for Seynt Iamys loue. In Sure
he put no [beschope], for he wolde þat þey sholde | [be] sudgettis to f. 336ʳᵇ
Compostle. þen in þat counselle I, Turpyn, archebushop of Reynys, 1011
at þe preyer of Emperoure Charlis, with .ix. oþer bushoppis alowyde
Seynt Iamus churche and þe awture worshipfully, þe kalendus of
Iuly. In þat same counselle Charlis made alle Spayne sudget in
Galice to Compostle, and ordeyned þat euery hosholder in Spayne 1015
and Galice sholde yerely yelde to þat churche .iiij. d., and for þat

995 þe²] þe þe   996 for] fo   1002 xxij] xxiij   1010 beschope] best hope
(*Latin has* præsulem (*171, ii*))   be] *om. MS*

payment þey sholde be free fro alle oþer chargis. And furþermore he
ordeynyd þat Compostela sholde be *Sedes Apostolica*, þat is to say
'Apostelus See', inasmoche as þere lay þe holy body of þe holy
1020 apostulle Seynt Iame. He ordeynyd also þat alle bushopps of Spayne
sholde holde þere þeyere counselle. He ordeynyd also þat þe bushop
of Compostle sholde yeue alle oþer bushoppis here stauys and þeyere
mytrus, þat þe kynggis of Spayne sholde be crownnede þere in þe
worship of Seynt Iame, and, yf so be þat þe feyth of Criste, by eny
1025 heresy ore erroure, began to be hurte ore fayle in eny cittee ore toune
in Spayne, hit sholde be examynyde and reconsiled by the bushope
of Compostle. And ryȝtte as Ephesus, in þe est part of þe worlde, by
Seynt Iohan þe Ewangeliste, Seynt Iamus broþer, was made a see,
ryȝtt so it is conuenient þat in þe weste partte [of] þe worlde, in
1030 Galice, þat þe feythe of Criste be stabylly ikeptte, and þat Compostle
sholde be a see. Forsoþe, þese be þe sees of Cristis herthely
f. 336ᵛᵃ kynddomys: one, | on þe riȝte syde, þis is Epheseus, were Seynt
Iohan þe Euaungeliste satte; and Compostela, þat is on þe lyfte syde
of Cr[i]stis erthely kynddome, were Seynt Iame satte—þe wiche sees
1035 fylle by lotte to þese .ij. sonnys of Zebede. And so was fullid the
askynge of þere moder, meuyde by hem, spekynge to Criste: 'Sey
þou þat my sonnys may sytte, [one] on þe riȝt syde and anoþer on þe
lyfte syde, in þi kyngdome'. In alle þe worlde Cristen men worship
.iij. sees, in Rome, Galice, and Ephesum. For ryȝt as oure Lorde
1040 Criste [ordeynyd] .iij. apostolus for his principalle counceleris, to þe
wiche he shewyde his misterijs and priuiteis, so he ordeynyd þese
þree of þe apostolis principally to be worshipide aboue alle oþer sees.
But yut amonge alle þese þree, þe see of Rome is sheffe and
principalle, þe whiche Petur, prince of þe apostelus, halowyde
1045 with his holy preshinge, his oune blodeshedinge, and with his holy
berynge. Compostela is þe secunde see, for riȝt as Seynt Iame after
Petur was principalle—for he was icallide before oþer, and with his
holy prechinge strenkeþide þe Churche, and by his meruelous
sepulture halouyde Compostela, and yut dothe dayly by many
1050 miraculis—þerefore Compostelanys see is þe secunde. The þredde
is Ephesineis see, for þere Seynt Iohan þe Euaungeliste `prechid´ and
conuertid þe Ephesinis, and þere he dude miraculis and þere he
wrote þe Gospelle þat begynnythe, *In principio erat verbum*, and þere
he was iberyedde. |

1029 of] in   1034 Cristis] crstis   1037 one] *om. MS*   1040 ordeynyd]
om. MS (*see Commentary*)

The discripcion of King Charles persone

Capitulum [xxiij]

Kynge Charlis had aborne here, a rodye face, a semely body and wele
ishape. He hadde a fulle fayer lokynge. He was .viij. fotte longe of þe
lengeste feette, large in þe reynnys, couenabily in þe bellye; he hadde
riȝt grete armys and leggis and beste shappid, and in alle his lymys   1060
moste strenkeste, moste douȝttyeste in dedis of armys, moste of
knyȝttehode and chyualrye. His foredde was a fotte longe; [he] hadde
shynnynge eyen lyke a lyone ore a carebokulle; his browis were a
spanne longe. þere was neuer man þat sawȝe him wroþe but he
feride him. þe gyrdulle þat gyrdude him was .viij. spanne longe to þe   1065
gyrdinge-stede. He hette lyȝtte brede, but of flesshe he wolde heette
a quarter of a shepe, ore .ij. hennus, a gose, a pestelle of porke. He
dranke wynne lymfatted soburly. And he was lyȝtte and stronge, þat
at oo stroke he wolde ismytte a knyȝt iary[m]yde fro þe heed þorow
þe body, and þe horse also, with his swerde þat was callide Caudiosa.   1070
Furþermore, he wolde take .iiij. horse shoys and strecche `hem´
euyne. Also he wolde put his honde on þe grounde and sett þereon a
knyȝtte iarmyd and with on honde lyfte him vp lyȝttely fro þe
grounde to his brest. Furþermore, he was fulle liberalle in his yeftis;
he was moste riȝtfulle and be-avyside in domus and iugementtis; he   1075
was dyscrete in spechis. Also, wile he was in Spayne, .iiij. tymys in
þe yere he weride his croune and bare his septoure in his honde—þat
his to sey, at Cristmas, at Ester, at Wyȝtsounetyde, and at | Seynt
Iamys day. And wan he satte `at´ mette in his trone imperialle a
sparthe or a swerde was holde afore him nakyde and idrawȝe. He   1080
hade euery nyȝt wakynge abouȝtte his bedde .vj. skore knyȝttis of
Cristen feith, of þe wiche .xl. wakyde þe furste part of þe nyȝt, and
.xl. þe secunde parte and .xl. þe þred parte of þe nyȝt: [.x. at his
hede], .x. at his fette, and .x. on þe riȝt sydde and .x. on þe lefte
syde; and euery of hem hade a nakyde swerde idrawe in his riȝt   1085
honde, and a tortes brennynge in his lefte honde. And on þis wise
þey wakyde him tulle it was day. And whoso desirith to here oþer
grete dedis of armys þat he dude—wan he was in exile at Tolowse,
for one Galafrius Almiraldus, þe whiche armyde him riȝt worthyly,

1056 xxiij] xxiiij   1062 he] om. MS   1069 arymyde] arynyde
1073 lyfte] lyȝttely: lyfte (see Commentary)   1079 at added to the right of the line
1084 .x. at his hede] om. MS; Latin has decem scilicet ad caput (177, xix)   1086 and]
and on þis wyse and (dittography of the phrase in the next sentence)

1090 for whos loue he slew a kynge of þe Sarzyns þat [was] callid
Barmatum, þe stronge enemye to Galafri; and how he conqueride
many londdis, prouyns, citteis, and townnus and made suget to God
in Trinité; how many habbeis and churchis [he ordeyned] as he went
þorow þe worlde; and how many relickis and seynttis bodys he
1095 closide in golde and syluer; and how he went to oure Lorddis
sepulcure, and brouȝt oure [Lorddis] crosse—I may not write now,
for in þis matere of cronykullynge þe penne and þe honde wolle
raþer fayle þan þe mater of his story. But sumwat I salle sey shortly
how he came into Fraunce after he hade delyuered Spayne and
1100 Galice fro þe Sarzyns honddis.

The treson of Ganalon and þe batail of Rounsivale

Capitulum xx[iiij]

After þat Charlis, emperoure moste famose, in þat dayes had
f. 337rb iconqueride Spayne to þe worship | of God and of Seynt Iame, as
1105 he came homewarde fro Spayne, he and his hooste were loggide at
Pampilioun. And þa[n] were duellinge at Cesarausta .ij. kynggis of þe
Sarzyns whos namus were Marsirius and Beligandus, his broþer. þes
were send into Spayne of Admiraldus, kynge of Babilone, þe which
were suget to Kynge Charlis; and in alle þinge þey dude him
1110 seruyce—but it was more [for] drede þan for loue. Thoo þese
send Kynge Charlis Ganalion, comoundinge hem to be baptized
and to send him tribute. þen þey send .xxx. horse ilade with golde
and syluer and .xl. horse ilade with riȝt gode swete wynne for his
peple to drinke—and a þousonde of feiere women of Sarzyns. They
1115 yaffe to þis false man Ganolion .xx. horse ilade with golde and syluer,
with this condicioun, þat he sholde betray and take into here honddis
þe myȝttieste of Charlis knyȝttis. He graunted hereto and reseyuyde
here golde. Wen þis traytours couenaunde was made, Ganolioun
came to Kynge Charlis and delyuered his tribute, and seid þat
1120 Marserius was comynge towarde him into Fraunce and wolde
become Cristen, and fro þensforthe wolde holde of him alle Spayne.
The grete and þe worthy warriours, þey toke þe wynne, and the lasse
to`ke´ þe women, to þeyer grete arme. Charlis yaffe credens to

---

1090 was] *om. MS*   1093 he ordeyned] *om. MS (see Commentary)*
1096 Lorddis] *om. MS; Latin has* lignum dominicum *(179, xi; Tr has* lignum dominicum
crucis, *p. 121, col. 2)*   1102 xxiiij] xxv   1106 þan] þat *(Latin has* tunc *(179,
xviii))*   1110 for] *om. MS (see Commentary)*

Ganoliounis wordis and disposyde him to go ouer þe hauyn of
Ciserees and so to passe into Fraunce. But by | the counselle of   f. 337ᵛᵃ
Ganolion, Kynge Charlis comoundide his worþieste princis of his   1126
hooste, Roulonde and Olyuere, and oþer .xx. [þousonde] of þe
Cristen kny3ttis, for to kepe þe rerewarde in Rouncivale, fort Charlis
ware passide þe hauenys of Ciserees. But þe ny3t after þis, many of
þe hooste were dronke of þat wynne and toke many of þucke women   1130
and so were dede. Wat more? Wyle þat Charlis passude ouer þicke
hauyne with .xx. þousonde Cristen men and with Turpyn and
Ganolion, and [with] þicke few Rowlonde and Olyuere kepte þe
rerewarde, herely in þe morowtyde, by þe councelle of Ganalioun,
Marserius and Belicandus with fyfty þousonde of wele-fytinge men   1135
came ou3te of þe wodis and þe hyllis þat had be hydde, by
Ganoliones counselle and ordinaunce, .ij. dayes and .ij. ny3ttes.
And þen þey made .ij. warddis, one of .xx. þousonde and anoþer
of .xxx. þousonde. þe furste warde of .xx. þousonde came after
Roulonde and Olyuere, and fau3tte with hem fro morowtyde into   1140
none of þe day. And oure feliship, Roulonde and Olyuere with here
company, slowe þucke .xx. þousonde Sarzyns eueryshone, and none
of hem askapude. And anone, after þis was done and alle oure
feleship wery of fy3ttinge, came .xxx. þousonde of þe Sarzyns and
slow .xx. þousonde of þe Cristen men, more and lasse, and none   1145
askapide. But sum were sley with speris; and sume were sley with
arowis; and sume were behedide; and sum were | sley with darttis;   f. 337ᵛᵇ
and sume were sley with knyvis; and sume were ibrande; and sume
were honge on trees: and þere alle þe worthy warriers were sley3e,
[oute]take Roulonde and Baldwynne and Turpynne and Coderike   1150
and Ganolion. Baldwynus and Codrike hydde hemselfe in þe wodis
for þe tyme, and so þey askapude. Wen þis bataile was doo, þe
Sarzyns went abacke to here loggynge.

The paine of Rowlande and þe deþe of Marcerie and
fli3te of Bigalande   1155

Capitulum [xxv]

Whanne þis bataile was idoo came Roulonde alone to aspye þe hooste
of þe paynyms were þey were, and as he went he saw3e a blacke

1127 þousonde] om. MS; Latin has viginti . . . milibus (181, xviii-xix)   1133 with] om.
MS   1150 outetake] and take   1156 xxv] xxvj   1157 aspye] aspye were

Sarzyn[e] and wery of fyȝttinge; Roulonde bonde faste him to a tree
1160 and þere he lefte him. And fro þens he went vp an a hylle to wayte
þe hooste [of] Marserie. And wen he saw þat þey were many, he
turnyde ayene to þe wey of Rouncyvale, and he toke his hyuery
horne are a trompe and blewe him as lowde as he myȝt. And at þat
blowynge came to him oute of þe wodis abouȝt an hundride of
1165 Cristen men; and wan he had þis feleship he turned ayene into þe
wode were he bonde þe Sarzyne, and he losyde him and drew his
swerde ouer his hede, and seid to him, 'Yf þow wolte goo with me
and shew me Marseri, þou shalte haue þi lyue, and ellis I shalle slee
þe with þis swerde'—for alle 'þis' tyme Roulonde knew noȝt
1170 Marseri. þe Sarzyne was aferd; he went with Roulonde and shewide
him Marseri aferre vpon a rede horse, and a rounde shylde. þen
Roulonde lete him goo, and he callid to God to helpe him. And
anone. . . .

COMMENTARY

Unless otherwise noted, references to the standard Latin text of the *Pseudo-Turpin* are to the Meredith-Jones edition of the *Codex Calixtinus* (manuscript B.1), incorporating manuscript C.3 variants as reported in Meredith-Jones's notes. All references to this edition (otherwise called 'Meredith-Jones' or the 'standard Latin') are by page and line number. Sometimes reference is made to the edition of H. M. Smyser, *The Pseudo-Turpin* (Cambridge, Massachusetts, 1937); this is an abbreviating version of the chronicle corresponding to Meredith-Jones's A.1. text (Paris, Bibliothèque Nationale, Fonds Latin, MS 17,656). All further references to Smyser, *The Pseudo-Turpin* are to this edition.

The Commentary emphasizes features unique to this text of the *Pseudo-Turpin Chronicle;* the reader is referred to the notes in the editions of Meredith-Jones and Smyser for backgrounds to the common elements of the text.

Ir, Tr, WPs-T, AN, and *Johannes* are the Northern European C-Family versions of the *Pseudo-Turpin* to which the Middle English version is most closely related; for details see the Introduction, pp. xxxviii–xl. For *Ir,* references are to the page numbers for both Hyde's original-language edition and his facing-page translation; for ease of reference, the English translation is quoted unless direct comparisons with the medieval Irish are required. For *Tr,* references are by manuscript page and column number (where the manuscript is paginated in arabic numbers). For *WPs-T,* references are to page and line number in Williams's edition. For *AN,* references are to line numbers in Short's edition. For *Johannes,* references are to chapter and line numbers in Walpole's edition.

'Turpine the Archebisshop of þe Bataille of Rouncivale': the first of two titles which identify the work specifically with the battle of Roncevaux, the climactic, but by no means the final, event described in the chronicle: see also the title given further on, in the heading to the *Titulus,* ll. 16–17. Neither of these titles match those of other versions of the *Pseudo-Turpin* and may be the exclusive work of the rubricator, who supplies one other heading which is more likely to be his than it is the translator's; see the n. to ll. 819–20.

1 'Here begynneth þe Prologe of Turpines Story': 'Turpines Story' is a more conventionally general title than the previous (whence its choice as the title of the present edition); cf. Meredith-Jones, p. 87 (*Historia Turpini*—so *AN,* p. 31); *Tr* uses *Gesta Turpini* (p. 129, top margin); other equally if not

more common titles name Charles only: *Hystoria Karoli Magni* (Meredith-
Jones, p. 130; so *Johannes*, p. 130, *WPs-T*, p. 1; Vincent de Beauvais in
Speculum Maioris, e.g. IV, p. 965; Bromyard, e.g. Sermon 39, p. 176,
Sermon 103, p. 475); *Gesta Karoli* (*Tr*, p. 117, top margin, and p. 130, col. 1;
so Higden in the *Polychronicon*, e.g. I, 272; and Bromyard in *Summa
Prædicantium*, e.g. s.v. *Consilium*, section 39; cf. *Ir*, p. 118). The Prologue
takes the form of a letter written by Turpin to the Dean of Aachen soon
after the death of Charlemagne. Turpin writes from Vienna, where he is
languishing from wounds suffered years earlier in the aftermath of the battle
of Roncevaux. His letter is a complement to chapter xxxiii, now missing
from this manuscript, which letter, attributed to Pope Calixtus, describes
the death and burial of Turpin at Vienna (see Meredith-Jones, Appendix A,
for the full Latin text). Turpin writes to Aachen because that is where
Charlemagne has recently been buried.

3 'to' is the appropriate preposition for an epistolary preface; but 'with' is
consistent with a misreading of the source *Leoprando decano* as ablative (87,
i–ii), perhaps encouraged by a further misreading before those two words of
an abbreviated *consoci*[9] in the translator's exemplar as *consocio*. *Consocius*
properly refers to Turpin's relationship with Charles, not Leoprandus. It is
possible, however, that the error arose from the current scribe's misreading
in his exemplar of *w* in 'fellow' adjacent to *t* in 'to' as an abbreviation for
'with'.

4 'gretinge and helthe euerlastinge': *salutem* (87, iii). In this context 'helthe'
has the sense of 'salvation'; see OED sense 4 and MED sense 3 (a),
especially the example c. 1450 (Capgrave's *Rome* (ed. Mills, 1911), 131).
The Middle English expansion over the Latin may have been made after
the fashion of an epistolary benediction; cf. that used by Margaret Paston in
a letter of 9 July, 1461 to her husband: 'God . . . send yow helthe in body
and sowle and good speed in all your maters' (*Paston Letters and Papers of
the Fifteenth Century*, ed. Norman Davis, 2 vols (Oxford, 1971–76), I,
p. 268).

11 'Seynt Dionyse cronykulle': the reference is more than likely generic, an
evocation of the authority in French royalist history that the Abbey of St
Denis had established for itself since the twelfth century. See Elizabeth A. R.
Brown, 'Saint-Denis and the Turpin Legend,' in *The Codex Calixtinus and
The Shrine of St James*, ed. John Williams and Alison Stones (Tübingen,
1992), pp. 51–88; Gabrielle M. Spiegel, *The Past as Text: The Theory and
Practice of Medieval Historiography* (Baltimore, 1997), especially chapter 5;
and Gabrielle M. Spiegel, *The Chronicle Tradition of Saint-Denis: A Survey*,
Medieval Classics: Texts and Studies, 10 (Leiden, 1979).

12 'absens of him': i.e., his absence amongst Charles's retinue in Spain; . . .
quia idem absens ab Yspania ea ignoravit . . . (87, xv–xvi).

13 'Leffe': *Vivas* (87, xix).

16 'The *Titulus* of þe Chapiters': *Tr* also possesses such a table (p. 107), although there it is written out more economically, without a heading, not as a table with separated listings, and, like the rest of the chronicle, as contiguous bicolumnar text. Such tables are relatively uncommon in *Pseudo-Turpin* manuscripts, and so the provision of one in the Middle English version is especially fortunate, for it permits some account of the contents of the text now missing after fol. 337ᵛ and allows comparisons with other versions which omit certain chapters and appendices. To facilitate such comparisons, the chart below aligns the numbers of the chapters as listed in the Middle English table of contents with those of the Meredith-Jones edition and *Tr*. (Numbers in parentheses refer to the equivalent point in the Meredith-Jones edition; *Tr* almost always uses arabic numbers for chapter headings, and so this practice is reflected in the table).

Meredith-Jones	Turpines Story	Tr
I	I	*Primum*
II	ii	2
III	iii	3
IV	iiii	4
V	v	5
VI	vi	6
VII	vii	7
VIII	viii	8
IX	ix	9
X	x	10
XI	xi	11
	xii (123, ii 'Hæc sunt . . .')	
	xiii (127, ix 'Tunc omnes . . .')	12
XII	xiiii	13
	xv (133, xiv, 'Statim eliguntur')	
XIII	xvi	14
XIV	xvii	15
XV	xviii	16
XVI	xix	17
XVII	xx	18
XVIII	xxi	19
XIX	xxii	20
XX	xxiii	21
XXI	xxiiii	22
XXII	xxv	23
XXIII	xxvi	24
XXIV	xxvii	25

Meredith-Jones	Turpines Story	Tr
XXV	xxviii	26
XXVI	xxix	27
XXVII ———————— xxx		28
XXVIII ———┤		29
XXIX ———————┘ 30		
XXX	[absent]	[absent]
XXXI	[absent]	[absent]
XXXII	xxxi	31
XXXIII	xxxii	32
Appendix A	xxxiii	33 (ends @ M-J 243,viii)
Appendix B	xxxiiii ———————	34 (combines B & C)
Appendix C	xxxiv ————┘	

19–20 'downe by hemselffe': The rubricator mistakenly labels these words as the third chapter and so misnumbers all of the following chapter headings in the table; each number in the table herafter printed within square brackets thus represents the appropriate correction: subtract one from each corrected number to establish the erroneous manuscript reading.

54–6 See the note to l. 1101.

59–76 The remaining chapters described in the *Titulus* have not survived. For guidance on the contents of these chapters, see the last note of the Commentary.

80–3 The references to the Crucifixion, Redemption, Resurrection, Ascension, and Pentecost, while being introductory commonplaces, represent otherwise unrecorded additions to the first sentence of the first chapter proper of the *Pseudo-Turpin* (*Tr* and *Ir* both agree with Meredith-Jones 89, i–iii). Given the context, however, and further references below to James's body having been translated at night with the help of an angel (ll. 89–91), a probable ultimate source for the references is the apocryphal epistle of Pope Leo III, *De Translatione Beati Jacobi*, found in the compilation of Translation texts which comprise Book III of the *Codex Calixtinus* and which appear ahead of its seminal copy of the *Pseudo-Turpin* (which appears as Book IV). The epistle begins:

> *Noscat fraternitas vestra, dilectissimi rectores totius christianitatis, qualiter in Hispania integrum corpus beati Jacobi apostoli translatum est. Post ascensionem Domini nostri Salvatoris ad coelos adventumque Spiritus super discipulos, ab ipsa passione Christi in revolutione anni undecimi, tempore azymorum, beatissimus Jacobus apostolus, perlustratis Judæorum synagogis, Hierosolymis captus ab Abiatar pontifice simul cum Josia suo discipulo, jussu Herodis capite plexus est. Sublaturn est autem corpus illius beatissimi Jacobi apostoli a discipulis suis nocte præ timore Judæorum; qui angelo Domini comitante pervenerunt in Jopem ad littus maris. Ibi vero hæsitantes*

ad invicem quid agere deberent, ecce nutu Dei parata affuit navis. Qui gaudentes intrant in eam, portantes alumnum nostri Redemptoris, erectisque velis simul cum prosperis ventis, cum Magna tranquillitate navigantes super undas maris, collaudantes clementiam nostri Salvatoris, Hyriæ pervenerunt as portum. (*Acta Sanctorum*, for November 1, *de SS. Athanasio et Theodoro*, which quotes from Madrid, Royal Library MS Z-L.1., a copy of the *Codex Calixtinus*.)

The reference in *Turpines Story* to St James as the brother of John the Evangelist, and his distinction from St James the Less, also represent otherwise unrecorded additions. Those references may, however, simply have been derived from ll. 113–14 below. The translator (or an earlier redactor) may have had no direct, or at least recent, acquaintance with such written authorities; see the next note. None of the surviving *C*-family manuscripts of the *Pseudo-Turpin* listed by André de Mandach appear to contain *Translatione* texts (*La Geste de Charlemagne et de Roland*, pp. 385–92).

87 That James converted all of the Galicians is an exaggeration not found in other versions of the *Pseudo-Turpin* (cf. Meredith-Jones 89, iii–vi). The implicit contradiction with the account of the subsequent work of James's disciples at l. 92 seems to have been lost on the translator. '[James] is not credited with wholesale conversions of the people, for most of the Galicians remained obstinately pagan; but the bishoprics of Braga, Lugo, and Astorga are said to have been founded by the apostle, his nominee to the see of Braga being the first bishop in the Iberian peninsula' (T. D. Kendrick, *St James in Spain* (London, 1960), p. 16).

88–91 'martirid by þicke cruelle kynge Horode . . . . þey londid in Galice': the Middle English follows *Tr* and *Ir* exclusively in reporting that James's body was taken at night, that it was placed on a ship, and that his disciples were guided by an angel to Galicia (*Tr* has *discipli eius cum ab Herode [perempto] nocte corpus rapientes nauem ascendunt et angelo duce in Galeciam applicaverunt* (*Tr*, p. 107, col. 2; cf. *Ir*, p. 2)). The source seems likely to be the apocryphal epistle of Pope Leo III, *De Translatione Beati Jacobi;* see the n. to ll. 80–3, where it is evident that the Middle English reception of the source is more fulsome than that of *Ir* and *Tr*, suggesting that the Middle English version may be tied to an older source than that of the Irish texts. The characterization of Herod (Agrippa) as 'cruelle' appears to be an addition unique to the Middle English version but reflects widespread popular tradition (it is also a tradition which often conflates several biblical Herods into one, as could be the case here). For a good summary of the tradition, see Scott Colley, 'Richard III and Herod,' *Shakespeare Quarterly* 37 (1986), 451–8 (451–2). That 'cruelle' alliterates with 'kynge', moreover, suggests that the translator had in mind English mystery plays where

Herod's characterization as a ranting villain is typically reinforced through alliteration.

96 'many gretefolde': the combination of 'grete' and the suffix '-folde' is not recorded in OED or MED; it may represent an emphatic nonce-combination or a scribal transposition of 'grete' and 'many'.

103 In describing the event as a 'visione' the text follows the reading of the *A.1* abbreviated text (*cum per visum nocte intuitus est*, Meredith-Jones 90, n.; cf. Smyser, *The Pseudo-Turpin*, p. 18, n. 1) rather than that of the longer versions which treat the starry way unequivocally as a natural phenomenon (*Statimque intuitus est in celo quendam caminum stellarum incipientem*, 89, xviii–xix; so *Tr* (p. 107, col. 2), *Ir* (p. 4), *AN* (ll. 64–5), and *WPs-T* (p. 1, ll. 20–1); *Johannes* has a preternatural *chemin d'etoiles en semblance de feu* (VI, 5–6)). That the vision was 'shewide' appears to be an addition of the Middle English translation and confirms the translator's sense of 'visione' as a supernatural token (cf. OED sense 1.a *vs.* 2.a).

110–11 '. . . he fylle in a slepe; and as he slepte . . .': *in extasi* (91, vii).

115 'fysshinge': *AN* (l. 80) and *Johannes* (VII, 7) follow the Latin in identifying James's location (*super mare Galileæ*; 91. x) rather than his occupation at the time (after the fashion of the Gospels, Matt. 4:21; Mark 1:19). *Tr* (p. 108, col. 1), *Ir* (pp. 4,5), and *WPs-T* (p. 2, ll. 11–13) mention neither location nor occupation.

116 'apostle': the title is not given in the other versions.

117 'by martirdome of swerde': the Latin has only *gladio* (91, xi).

118–19 'in Galice, vnknowen amonge þe cruelle mysbeleuynge Sarzyns': *in Gallecia, quæ a Sarracenis adhuc turpe opprimitur, incognitum requiescit* (91, xii–xiii). *AN* (l. 81) , *Ir* (p. 5), *WPs-T* (p. 2, ll. 17–19), and *Johannes* (VII, 8–9) translate the Latin more closely and thus describe the nature of James's oppression more than the nature of his oppressors; cf. the paratranslational characterizations of the Saracens at, ll. 201, 260–1, 385, 559–61, 571–2, 578–9, and 1152.

120 'many regiouns, citteis, and cuntries': *urbes tantasque regiones* (91, xv).

120–2 'fro þe hondis and þe power . . . fro here powere': *a Sarracenis* (91, xii).

125–6 'þe crowne of euerlasting blisse': *coronam æternæ* (91, xix; but cf. Meredith-Jones's A.1. reading, *coronam . . . æternæ beatitudinis* (92, n.)); cf. the n. to l. 103.

127–28 'fro þat costis of þe Fresoune See . . . by alle þilke cuntreis forsaid': *ab his horis usque ad Galleciam* (91, xxiii).

130 'tumbe and beriell': *basilicam et sarcofagum* (91, xxii–xxiii). It seems unlikely that the translator would omit reference to the famous edifice at

Santiago; it is probable that the Latin exemplar was defective in a fashion suggested by *Ir*, which has only 'the place where my body was buried' (pp. 4, 5).

133 'into þe worldis ende': cf. the more pedestrian reading of the Latin, . . . *a tempore vero vitæ tuæ usque ad finem præsentis seculi ibunt* (93, ii–iii). The longer reading is also found in *Tr* (p.108, col. 1), *AN* (ll. 93–94), *Johannes* (VII, 19–20), and *WPs-T* (p. 2, l. 29—p. 3, l. 2). Cf. the next note but one.

134–5 Mention of the 'hooste' and 'þis grete werkis of werre' and the injuction to 'drede noȝt' appear to be unique to the Middle English version; *IrTrWPs-TANJohannes* follow the more abstract Latin *nunc autem perge quam cicius poteris, quia ego ero auxiliator tuus in omnibus* (93, ii–iii; cf. *Ir*, p. 5; *AN*, ll. 94–6; *Johannes* VII, 20–1; and *WPs-T*, p. 3, ll. 2–3).

136–8 'and after þi grete labore . . . into þe worldis ende': here are several resonant divergences from the Latin; 'grete' is an elaboration over the Latin (93, iv), and echoes 'grete werkis' (also elaborative) in l. 135 immediately above; 'ioye in þe blisse of heuene' replaces the Latin *coronam a Domino in celestibus* (93, v) and thus echoes the possibly-divergent reading of line 135 (see n.); 'into þe worldis ende' translates *usque ad novissimum diem* (93, v–vi) in a way which reflects (or which perhaps inspired) the embellished reading at l. 133.

139–40 'vicioune and declaracioune': *promissione* (93, viii).

146–7 'iwallid, imannyd, and vitailid': *quia muris inexpugnabilibus munitissima erat* (93, xxii); the attention to the human dimension of the town's invincibility appears unique to the Middle English version.

148–9 'worship, loue, and feythe': *pro cuius fide* (93, xiii). The triplet is not matched in *IrTrWPs-TANJohannes*, though *AN* is close, with . . . *pur la ky amour e pur la ky foy* . . . (l. 105).

149–50 'þis Sarzyns and mysbeleuynge folke': *gentem perfidam* (93, xiv).

152 '. . . and þou saydust þou wolduste helpe me . . .': a somewhat litigious addition over the source, *si verum est quod michi apparuisti* (93, xv–xvi), and not matched in *IrTrWPs-TANJohannes*.

155–7 'When þe Sarzyns hard how meruelously þe wallis of Pampilioun þat citté fille downne . . .': *His auditis mirabilibus* . . . (93, xix—xx).

157 'feryd gretely': *inclinabant* (93, xx).

158 'mete hym and worship him': *mittebant obviam ei tributum* (93, xxi).

159–61 'These Sarzyns merueylid . . . þe Frensch hoost': *Mirabatur gens sarracenica cum videbat gentem gallicam, obtimam scilicet, ac bene indutam, et facie elegantem* (95, i–iii; *Tr* omits *obtimam scilicet, ac* (p. 108, col. 2)). The Middle English translation here values character over appearance, and chooses to single Charles out in this context while still mentioning the

French generally. Perhaps the latter change is influenced by chapter xxiii below, 'The Discripcion of King Charles persone' (ll. 1055–1100).

164 'and worshiped him': another expansion over the Latin (95, iv–v) having the effect of complimenting Charles's character.

165 'Peroune': *Petronum* (95,v). The Middle English translator may just have misread the *t* in the exemplar as an *r*. *AN* also has *Peroun* (l. 120) and *Johannes* has *Perron* (IX, 6). El Padrón, Spain, is the coastal site of the rock upon which, according to legend, the body of St James was first placed after its translation from the Holy Land; see Meredith-Jones, p. 266.

'in see': *in mari* (95, vi).

166–7 'made whey for hem þat sholde after': the Latin ends rather with Charles declaring that *in antea ire non poterat* (95, vii–viii); the Middle English translator, possibly mindful of the great popularity of the pilgrimage route to Compostella, and evidently keen to compliment Charles, may have substituted a less contrite inference. The change may also have been intended to enhance the apostolic dimension of Charles's accomplishment: cf. Acts 19.4.

167–8 'The Galicianus . . . baptisid by þe archebisshop Turpyn': the standard Latin, like *IrTrWPs-TANJohannes*, is more dilatory: *Gallecianos vero, qui post beati Iacobi prædicacionem discipulorumque eius ad perfidam paganorum conversi erant, babtismatis gratia per manus Turpini archiepiscopi regeneravit . . .* (95, viii–x; *AN* retains the illusion of Turpin as narrator by having him refer to himself in the first person, ll. 123–4).

170 'alle Spayne': the Middle English translation agrees with *Tr* (p. 108, col. 2) and *Ir* (pp. 8,9) in not mentioning that Charles passed through Spain *a mari usque ad mare* (Meredith-Jones 95, xiv; so *AN*, l. 129, *Johannes*, IX, 15, and *WPs-T*, p. 5, l. 14); in the portion of the chapter's final sentence that it does retain, however, *Tr* is close to the reading found in Meredith-Jones's A.6. manuscript (94, xi–xii): *Deinde venit per portam Hyspanie.*

174–5 'nou3t tellynge þe names of alle but of sum': the declaration is not matched in the standard Latin or *IrTrWPs-TANJohannes*, though its abbreviating plan is variously supported below; see the notes to ll. 179–80, and 186–7.

175–6 'þe reder of þis werke sum notable ensample may lerne': in introducing the matter of names, the Middle English version appears to be unique beside *IrTrWPs-TANJohannes* for explicitly adducing an exemplary purpose. Note also the adherence to the narratorial persona, something otherwise done only by the *AN* translator, though there to a greater extent (see n. to ll. 167–8).

176 '.xiiij. notable citteis': *Tr*, *Ir*, and *WPs-T* also omit the names of the cities, but none says anything about the number of cities omitted. The standard Latin text does indeed name fourteen cities (95, xv–xix), one of which, as commented upon in the next note, is *Brac(h)ara*. It is possible that the Middle English translator had before him a version of the Latin which, unlike *Tr* or the sources of *Ir* or *WPs-T*, actually listed all fourteen names; for further consideration of this point see the next note. *Notable* here is an addition over the Latin (95, xv–xvi) and reinforces the Middle English translation's apparently original entreaty in the previous sentence for the reader to find a *notable ensample* (see the previous note).

177 'his': it is curious that this form of 'is' mainly occurs in this text in 'that is called / named' phrases: see also ll. 251, 312, 418, 431, but cf. l. 142.

177–8 'Bracheta, þe whiche is *metropolis*—or "þe archebisshopis shurche"—of Oure Lady': the Middle English account of the city has conflated what were originally references to two cities: *Brac(h)ara metropolis, civitas Sanctæ Mariæ* (95, xvii–xviii; 'Braga, the metropolitan see [and] probably Santa Maria Arrifana' (Smyser, *The Pseudo-Turpin*, p. 19, n. 2)). Other translations of the *Ps-T* also misconstrue this pairing: *AN* identifies the two as *Metropot, la cité nostre Dame* (l. 132; and see Short's note thereto, pp. 76–77); *Johannes* has *Bracara, mere des citez* (X, 5); London, British Library, MS Harley 273 has *Brachare, Metropole* (*Der Pseudo-Turpin Harley 273*, ed. Rudolf Schmitt (dissertation, Würzburg, 1933), p. 14, l. 13). Along with a lack of detailed knowledge of Spanish geography, and the not unprecedented misreading of *civitas Sanctæ Mariæ* as an adjectival clause, the Middle English translator's mistake may have been prompted by an understanding of *civitas* as indicating a cathedral town (*RMLWL*, p. 80, s.v. *civ/is*), whence the identification of *Sanctæ Mariæ* as a church—as it were, as *sedes metropolis*. Further, *or* in l. 178 would seem to introduce a clause which is intended to clarify *metropolis*. *Tr* and *Ir* mention no cities at this point.

179 '.xxxj.': even though the standard Latin lists 108 names (and *Johannes* lists 81 (X, 3–32)), the accuracy of the Middle English tally of fourteen in the previous sentence (see note) argues for accuracy in reflecting the contents of the English translator's source; and certainly both tallies taken together suggest a major difference in the Latin source from the versions represented by *Tr, Ir*, and *WPs-T*, all of which name only Lucerna (*Tr*, p. 108, col. 2; *Ir*, pp. 8, 9; *WPs-T*, p. 4, l. 17; cf. the Middle English text below, ll. 180–93). The tally of thirty-one finds its closest match in *AN*, which names twenty-eight (ll. 136–142); the closeness of the count may be more significant if one considers the possibility that some of the cities listed in *AN* have brief descriptions which, in a cursory review, could be mistaken for additional names (e.g., from ll. 137–9: *Carbone un fort chastel . . . Petrosse ou l'em fest le bon argent*). Even so, *AN* alludes to *mout des autres [cités], dount jo ne fas mencioun* (ll. 145–6). The Middle English list cannot, moreover, have been identical to that in *AN* since the equivalent of *Bysertim*, mentioned in the Middle English text below, l. 185, is not mentioned there.

179–80 'for þey bethe hethen, [ben] vnrehersid': like *AN*, *Ir*, and *Tr*, the Middle English translation offers reasons for not listing the names of all of the towns conquered (on those names, see the note to l. 179 above), but the nature of the reasons and the sequence in which they are offered differs somewhat. *Tr* mentions only Spain and refers to the *tedium preferendi barbara nomini* (p. 108, col. 2; in full, the sentence reads *Capitulum de nominibus civitatum quas in Hyspania tunc acquisivit, propter tedium preferendi barbara nomina, pertranseo*). *Ir* is consistent with the translational possibilities of *Tr*, and also only mentions Spain: 'Some of the names of the cities which Charles took in Spain we pass by on account of the difficulty of pronouncing the barbarous names'(pp. 8,9). After this both texts skip to the equivalent of Meredith-Jones 99, xiv–xv (*Omnes præfatas urbes . . .*). *AN*, naming seven conquered towns in Galicia (ll. 131–2), adds that there were '*mout des autres ke moy ne plest nomer, kar ennoy seroyt*' (ll. 133–4); on the names of Spanish towns, the translator declares that he cannot list all '*kar jo nes averoye a peyce acountés totes*' (l. 136).

180 '[ben]': emendation from *hem* to *ben* is strictly conjectural. It is tempting to let *hem* stand, preceded by 'I', thus reflecting the transitive grammar of the reading in *Tr*, where the verb which corresponds to *vnrehersid* is *pertranseo* ('I pass over, ignore'; for the whole Latin sentence, see the next note). However, according to OED, and MED, 'unrehearsed' is only recorded elsewhere in Middle English as a *ppl. a.*, and nowhere else does the Middle English translation present transitive constructions where *hem* is immediately followed by the verb. On palæographical grounds, *ben*, if written in cursive script, seems a likely candidate for having been misread as *hem*. Although *bethe* is the chosen form of the verb just earlier in the sentence, the text does elsewhere use *bethe* and *ben* interchangeably in close proximity: see. ll. 625–7.

181–4 'Accintina, in þe whiche liethe þe holy confessore . . . and berithe ripe frute': the account of the city and the miraculous tomb of Torquatus is omitted in *Tr*, *Ir*, and *WPs-T*, but not *Johannes* (X, 22–5) or *AN* (ll. 141–5); cf. Meredith-Jones, 97, xvii–99, iv. See also the note following.

183–4 'an olyue tree flowrithe, buddithe, and berithe ripe frute': . . . *arbor olivæ divinitus florens maturis fructibus . . . .* (99, ii; om. *Tr*, *Ir*, *WPs-T*). The Middle English account is clearly less explicit about the miraculous nature of the event; cf. *Johannes* X, 23–5; *AN* ll. 143–5.

185–6 'Bysertim, in þe whiche beth passynge stronge women, þe whiche after þe langage of þe contré bethe callid *Ambices*': *Urbs Besertum, in qua milites fortissimi qui vulgo dicuntur Arabites, habentur* (99, iv–v; om. *Tr*, *Ir*, *WPs-T*, and *AN*, but not *Johannes* (X, 26–7)). The Middle English version perhaps derives from a misreading of an abbreviated form of *milites* as *mulieres*.

186–7 'to make a shortte processe, Charlis conquerid all Spayne': this claim to brevity is not matched in *Ir*, *Tr*, or *WPs-T*, or the standard Latin, but cf. *AN: Totes ces cités e mout des autres, dount jo ne fais mencioun, conquist Charles* . . . (ll. 145–6). The claim seems to be an anticipation of the penultimate sentence of the chapter (ll. 207–8) which does translate the Latin (101, x–xi).

189 'sum with sly3e crafte': *cum* . . . *maxima arte* (99, xvi; om. *Ir* and *Tr*).

190–1 'a passinge stronge citté and my3tly wallid': *urbem munitissimam quæ est in valle viridi* (99, xvi; so *Ir* (pp. 8,9), *Tr* (p. 108, col. 2) and *WPs-T* (p. 4, l. 18); *AN* (l. 148) and *Johannes* (XI, 8) mention *Va(a)l Vert*, but not the strength of the city). The Middle English evidently follows the model of Meredith Jones's B.4. text which omits *quæ* . . . *viridi*.

192–3 'he my3t no3t . . . by no dede of armes': the Latin is considerably less emphatic: *capere donec ad ultimum nequivit* (99, xviii). Cf. the note following.

193–4 'Wan Charlis saw3e þat manes power faylid': a touch of fatalism not matched in the standard Latin or *IrTrWPs-TANJohannes*.

194–5 'as he dud at Pampilioun': obvious, perhaps, but left implicit in the standard Latin and *IrTrWPs-TANJohannes* in a way which makes the parallel seem artless.

196 'a wyldernes': *deserta* (99, xxi, n.).

197–8 'like a fysshponde' and 'horyble' are additions to the Latin (99, xxi—101, ii). The first addition conflicts with the impression of this as a 'grete water' but perhaps this is the translator's best effort at conveying the idea that it is a body of water formed in a stream by artificial means. 'Horyble' more directly supports the impression of this as a place out of favour with God; the translator may have had the last sentence of this chapter in mind (ll. 208–11). The possible sources for the Lucerna episode and the true identity of Lucerna have been considered at some length by several scholars: see Walpole's note to *Johannes* X, 12, pp. 187–9.

201 'bycome false renegatis and forsoke her feyth': the Latin account of the pagan relapses is less heated: *postea ad ritum paganorum conversæ sunt* (101, iv; so *Ir*, pp. 8,9; *Tr*, p. 108, col.2; *AN*, ll. 155–6; *WPs-T*, p. 4, l. 26; om. *Johannes*).

204–5 The Middle English translation agrees with *Ir* (pp. 8, 10), *Tr* (p. 108, col. 2), *Johannes* (XI, 19), and *AN* (ll. 161) in omitting *Karlomannus* from the end of the list as it appears in the standard Latin (101, xvii); *WPs-T* omits *Karolus Calvus*, *Ludovicus* and *Karlomannus* (p. 5, l. 2).

209–11 'he cursid—wherefore neuer man duellid in hem synnes—and beth inhabitte into þis tyme': *maledixit, et idcirco sine habitatore permanent usque in hodiernum diem* (101, xii–xiii); the awkward and redundant phrasing could suggest that the scribe was copying from the translator's draft, in which one or the other phrase was subpuncted for excision. One must be cautious with such evidence, however; possibly the translator was concerned with the potential ambiguity of *inhabitte* (MED records only 'inhabitable' as having the negative sense among all 'inhabit-' forms it lists; OED has no example of the sense of 'uninhabited' for related forms before 1614, but does record related forms with the more conventional positive sense as early as c.1374). Addition of *þey* or *þe whiche* between *and* and *beth* would make the reading less awkward, though no less redundant.

211 'Adama': so *Ir* (pp. 10, 11) and *Tr* (p. 108, col. 2); *AN* and *WPs-T*, follow the standard Latin 'Adania' (101, xiii); *Johannes* has both (X, 19; XI, 15).

216 '*Salamcadis* is a corruption of *Sanam Qadis*—Arabic for "Idol of Cadiz"' (Smyser, *The Pseudo-Turpin*, p. 20, n. 1). The story of the statue probably has a basis in Arabian lore and may refer to an actual medieval statue destroyed around 1145: see Meredith-Jones, pp. 291–2.

'Callid' translates *dicitur* (101, xvii) and would seem to have the sense of 'meant to indicate' or 'translated' rather than 'named.'

218–19 'himselffe leuynge': i.e., himself being alive, himself still living; *dum adhuc viveret* (101, xviii). The sense of 'believing' might not, however, be ruled out entirely: cf. the Pseudo-Methodius (preserved in HM 28,561 with *Turpines Story*): 'þe sone of perdicioun schal come, trowynge himself þat he is God' (Trevisa, *Dialogus inter Militem et Clericum . . . and Methodius . . .*, ed. A. J. Perry, pp. 109–10 (the corresponding text appears in HM 28,561 at fol. 25rb)).

219–20 'image or an ydulle': *ydolum* (101, xviii).

'like to himselffe': *in nomine suo* (101, xix).

'[with] nigromanci and whichecrafte': *arte magica* (101, xx).

223 'parischeth ore dyeth': *statim periclitatur* (103, ii).

225 'hole and sownde': *incolumis* (103, iii).

227 '.iiij.-square brode in þe hyndure parte': in the manuscript a *punctus elevatus* has been placed after 'brode', but this conflicts with the phrasing suggested by the Latin, which describes the stone as *deorsum latus et quadratus* (103, vi). In addition, 'hyndure' would seem to derive from a misreading, either in the Latin exemplar or on the part of the English translator, of *deorsum* for *dorsum*. MED records only the sense of 'back part, rear' for *hinder part (adj.¹ 1. (b))*, not 'underside.' One is consequently tempted to replace 'hyndure' with 'undure'— or perhaps 'hundure', given the text's tendency to use initial unetymological *h-* (see the Introduction,

p. xliv). The confused state of the translation may explain the odd placement, first, of the *punctus elevatus*, and second, of 'of' immediately after 'parte' (see apparatus). Perhaps both features represent scribal attempts to make sense of the geometry of the stone: if the stone tapers toward the top, as noted further on (l. 229), then its back cannot be four-square. Cf. Walpole's note to *Johannes* XII, 13, p. 192.

231 'þe best coper shynynge': *de auricalco obtimo* (103, ix).

237–8 'þey shalle flyȝe to castellis and strenkethis and hyde here tresours and richesse': *gazis suis in terra repositis, omnes fugient* (103, vx). The variance of the Middle English translation may derive from a misreading of abbreviated *terra* (*t'ra*) as *castra*, where the source manuscript was written in a current cursive hand with *t* forms in which the shaft barely protrudes above the headstroke, thus closely resembling the script's *c* form (for further such evidence, see the Introduction, p. xl). Such hands are common in England throughout the fourteenth century; see, e.g. Parkes, *English Cursive Book Hands*, plates 1 (ii), 9(i), 11(i).

239 'in Spaine': an addition over the Latin title, which is more accurately translated in the Middle English *Titulus* (l. 23).

242 'he made Seynt Iame a feyer chirche': i.e., the Basilica of St James in Santiago de Compostela.

245 'westementis, pallis': *palliis* (105, i, n.).

247 Before turning to Aachen, the Latin mentions that with the captured treasure Charles *multas ecclesias fecit* (105, iii). In the case of Aachen, the Middle English text agrees against the standard Latin with *Ir* (p. 109, col. 1) and *Tr* (pp. 12, 13) in not mentioning that Charles also established a church of St James there (cf. Meredith-Jones 105, v; so *WPsT* (p. 6, l. 19), *Johannes*, (XIII, 8–9), and *AN* (ll. 195–6)).

253–4 'many moo he made in diuerse placis þat I speke not off': the Middle English translator sustains the chronicle's initial premiss of a first-person narration, where the Latin regresses to the third person: *et abbacias innumeras per mundum fecit* (105, xi).

255 'Agelonde' (*Aigolandus*) probably originates in early tales of Charlemagne's wars in Italy: see Gaston Paris, *Histoire poétique de Charlemagne* (Paris, 1905), pp. 247–9. On his association with Africa, see Meredith-Jones, p. 295.

258 'grete hooste': *suis exercitibus* (105, xiii). The Middle English substitution of *grete* is matched in *Johannes* (XIII, 16) and *WPs-T* (p. 6, l. 27–p. 7, l. 1), and is reminiscent of the reference to innumerable hosts in *Ir* (pp. 12, 13): *AN* (l. 203) follows the Latin.

260–1 'He slowȝe hem euery modur-sone and lefte none alyve': a pejorative touch not matched in the Latin or *IrTrWPs-TANJohannes*, which state that Aigolandus both killed and expelled the Christian custodians (cf. Meredith-Jones, 105, xiv: *eiectis etiam et interfectis*).

262 'grete hoostis and many, and grete and stronge': *cum multis excercitibus* (105, xvi). Both phrases could be said to translate different senses of *multis*.

263 'and whas with him duke of his hooste': the syntax follows that of the Latin: *et erat cum eo dux exercituum* (105, xvii).

264 'Milo of Englond, a worthy warrioure': *Milo de Angleris* (105, xvii–xviii). This first of two consecutive misidentifications of Milo as an Englishman seems to be deliberate, as elsewhere the translator shows that he knows enough to call him 'Milo . . . de Angloiris' (l. 487); for the second misidentification, see ll. 342–3. For a comparative discussion see Shepherd 'Middle English *Pseudo-Turpin Chronicle*', pp. 25–6. If the change is deliberate, it might constitute a reference to the commissioners of the Trevisan portion of the manuscript, the Mulls of Harescombe; see the Introduction, pp. l–lii. The possibility of a straightforward translation error should not, however, be ruled out: the fifteenth-century *Pseudo-Turpin* of London, British Library, MS Harley 108 has *Milo de Anglicis* (see Smyser, *The Pseudo-Turpin*, p. 103, n. to chapter 7, l. 6).

265 'Ensample of a false executoure of a ded knighte': this chapter was one of those most frequently abstracted from the *Pseudo-Turpin* into didactic texts of the later Middle Ages, and is rather conspicuously so abstracted into Insular texts of the fourteenth and fifteenth centuries; see the Introduction, p. xxxvii. It is thus perhaps because of prior familiarity that the translator here attains a confident fluidity and emotive conviction otherwise rare in the text to this point; for further discussion, see Shepherd 'Middle English *Pseudo-Turpin Chronicle*', pp. 26–7, and the notes to this chapter below. The Middle English title given to the chapter agrees with *Tr* alone in mentioning that the *exemplum* concerns a dead knight: *De exemplo elimosinæ mortui militis* (p. 109, col. 2; cf. Meredith Jones, p. 105, heading to chapter VII).

267–9 'Here in þis chapiter . . . of þe dede knyȝt': the standard Latin and *IrTrWPs-TANJohannes* does not mention the knight: *Set quale exemplum Dominus tunc nobis omnibus ostendere dignatus est de his qui mortuorum elemosinas iniuste retinent, nobis est dicendum* (105, xix–xxi). *AN* suggests an affinity with the Middle English reading in saying that the exemplary event was shown *en le oost Charles* (ll. 208–9). The military correpondence notwithstanding, the rest of the Middle English sentence is still quite free in comparison with the Latin, having more an element of précis than general identification of moral subject (cf. Meredith Jones 105, xix–xxi).

271 'Rematicus': *Romaricus* (107, ii).

271–2 'He whas shryue and hoselyde, and disposyd him to þe dethe': *accepta poenitencia et eucarista a sacerdote* (107, ii–iii).

274 'þat was worthe an hundred shelingis': in the standard Latin and *IrTrWPs-TANJohannes* the sum is first given in the next sentence (cf. Meredith-Jones, 107, v–vi).

275–6 'His cosyn seid it shold be do—as many a false execetoure dothe': this jaded monitory observation (offered perhaps from the perspective of a priest or lawyer?) is not made in the standard Latin or *IrTrWPs-TANJohannes* (cf. Meredith-Jones, 107, v).

277 'what dude he?': this rhetorical question, heralding the inevitability of sinful character, is not matched in the standard Latin or *IrTrWPs-TANJohannes* (cf. Meredith-Jones 107, v).

278–9 'but he dude noȝt o peny for þe dede knyȝtis soule': not matched in the standard Latin or *IrTrWPs-TANJohannes* (cf. Meredith-Jones 107, vi–viii).

282 'in a vicioun': *in extasi* (107, ix); cf. the n. to l. 103.

283 'my horse and my godys': *res meas* (107, ix–x).

287 'But what shalle come of þis?': the rhetorical question, with its air of pious foreboding, is not matched in the standard Latin or *IrTrWPs-TANJohannes* (cf. Meredith-Jones 107, xiv).

288–9 'þe blisse of heuene': *in paradiso* (107, xv).

289–90 'his slepinge cosyn': *IrTrWPs-TANJohannes* follow the Latin, *vivusque* (107, xvi); the Middle English account alone emphasizes the kinship between sinner and sinned-against.

290–1 'þis vntrew execcutoure and cosyn': the subject is left grammatically implicit in the Latin (107, xvi–xvii) but, again, the Middle English account (also going against *IrTrWPs-TANJohannes*), stresses the familial nature of the perfidy.

294–5 'sume like lyons, sume like beris, sume like wolffis, and sume like wylde bullis': *quasi rugitus leonum, luporum et vitulorum* (107, xix–xx). A match for 'wylde' seems to be present in the abbreviating version of the *Ps-T*, which has *aliarumque ferarum* in place of *vitulorum* (Meredith-Jones, p. 110, text of manuscript A.1.; Smyser, *The Pseudo-Turpin*, p. 62, ll. 27–8); this reading would seem to agree with *Ir*, which has 'voices of lions or wolves or other brute animals' (pp. 14, 15). The Middle English could represent a combination of these two strains in its source. The presence of the bears is, however, unique to the Middle English.

297 'bothe body and soule': *vivus ac sanus* (107, xxi; so *IrTrWPs-TANJohannes*). The Middle English account draws out the spiritual dimension of the event and presages the important distinction between body and soul made in the penultimate sentence of the chapter.

300 'Charlis hooste': *exercitus noster* (107, xxiv; so *Tr*, p 109, col. 2); *Ir* agrees with the Middle English, having 'hosts of Charles' (pp. 14, 15). *IrTrWPs-TANJohannes* do not have the possessive reference and do not mention Charles.

301 The Middle English agrees with *Tr* (p. 109, col.2), *Ir* (pp. 14, 15), and *AN* (l. 238), in mentioning only Navarre, rather than the *Navarrorum et Alavarum* of the standard Latin (107, xxiv–xxv; so *Johannes* (XV, 10) and *WPs-T* (p. 8, l. 14)). The abbreviated version in Meredith-Jones's A.1. text, however, also omits mention of Álava (p. 110, text of manuscript A.1.; cf. Smyser, *The Pseudo-Turpin*, p. 62, l. 31).

'on an hyȝe rocke': the Latin (109, i–ii), *Ir* (pp. 16, 17), *AN* (ll. 239–40), *Johannes* (XV, 10–12), and *WPs-T* (p. 8, ll. 15–17) all add that the prominence was three leagues from the sea and four days' journey from Bayoun. The Middle English omission probably reflects the realization that the first detail is pointless and the second redundant.

304 'Turpynne þe holy bishop seith': the Middle English text, unlike the Latin (109, iv–v) and *IrTrWPs-TANJohannes*, awkwardly departs from the premise of first-person narration.

306 'þe fendis felowes in helle': *se dampnandos* (109, v).

307–8 'waxid grene and budded': *floruerunt* (109, heading to chapter VIII). On the legend of the flowering lances, see the next note but one.

310 'duke of his hooste': in recalling Milo's rank, the Middle English here agrees only with *AN* (l. 246) and the abbreviated Latin of Meredith-Jones's A.1. text (p. 112; cf. Smyser, *The Pseudo-Turpin* p. 62, chapter VIII, l. 1).

314–15 On the background to legends of the shrines of SS Facundus and Primitivus, see Smyser, *The Pseudo-Turpin*, p. 24, n.1 and p. 26, n.1; Meredith-Jones, pp. 295–296, and Stones and Krochalis, *The Pilgrim's Guide*, II. p. 193, notes 192–5.

The Middle English text here agrees with *Ir* (pp. 16, 17) and *Tr* (p. 110, col. 1) in omitting additional observations that Charles founded a monastery at Sahagún (San Fagon) and that a thriving town grew up there (cf. Meredith-Jones, 109, xii–xiv).

317 'by an herewde': a practical detail left implicit in the standard Latin and *IrTrWPs-TANJohannes* (cf. Meredith-Jones, 109, xv).

319 'ore a thousonde ayenste a thousonde': the Middle English text is alone against the standard Latin and *IrTrWPs-TANJohannes* in omitting two final parameters: two against two or one against one (cf. Meredith-Jones, 109, xviii).

320–1 'alle Aigalondis knyʒttis, þat where Sarzyns': to judge from *Tr*, this awkward phrasing derives from an unusual reading in the Middle English translator's source; where the standard Latin reads *interfecti sunt Sarraceni* (109, xx), *Tr* has *interfecti sunt Sarraceni qui erant ex parte Aygolandi* (p. 110, col. 1).

322 'The þred tyme': this tally is not matched in the standard Latin or *IrTrWPs-TANJohannes* (cf. Meredith-Jones, 109, xxi).

323 '.ij. þowsonde ayenste .ij. þowsonde': according to the standard Latin and *IrTrWPs-TANJohannes*, before this escalation, two hundred were sent against two hundred, with the usual result (cf. Meredith-Jones, 109, xxi–xxiii); the Middle English omission could be the result of eyeskip.

325–6 'Aigalond profered plenare bataile': the standard Latin and *IrTrWPs-TANJohannes* cite Aigolandus's motivation for this decision, namely an understanding of how best to harm Charles which came to him upon his having cast secret lots of divination (cf. Meredith-Jones, 111, i–ii).

326 'and to þis agreed Charlis, on þe morne folowynge': i.e., Charles agreed to the proposed battle for the following morning; the Middle English renders a potentially confusing transposition of the clauses that end the corresponding sentence in the Latin: *Et madavit ei ut pugnam plenarium cum eo sequenti die faceret, si vellet; quæ ab utroque concessa est* (111, ii–iii).

327–8 'pyʒtte þeyere speris in þe grounde': before this *IrTrWPs-TAN-Johannes* mention that the troops assiduously prepared their arms for the next day (cf. Meredith-Jones, 111, iii–v).

329 'But what wonder whas þere?': the interjective rhetorical question is not matched in the standard Latin or *IrTrWPs-TANJohannes* (cf. Meredith-Jones, 111, vii).

330–1 'ryndyd, buddude, and grene': *corticibus et frondibus decoratas* (111, vii).

331–2 'on þe morne in þe vouwharde': the Middle English here agrees with *Tr* (*in acie proxima die*, p. 110, col. 1), *Ir* ('at the outset of the battle on the morrow', pp. 18, 19) in referring to the following day; cf. the Meredith Jones Latin, *in acie proxima* (111, viii); *WPs-T, yn y vydin gyntaf* (p. 9, ll. 26–7); *AN, devaunt la batayle* (l. 267); and *Johannes, en cele batail* (XVII, 1).

337 'But what?': another interjective rhetorical question not matched in the standard Latin or *IrTrWPs-TANJohannes* (cf. Meredith-Jones, 111, xiv).

337–8 'A grete wondurfulle þinge to see ore here—but þis whas ioye to alle soulis of them whos bodyes where martirid on þe morne!': the translation imitates the opening syntax of the Latin but mitigates its closing qualification—*Mira res, magnumque gaudium animabus, sed corporibus sit detrimentum*

(*Tr*, p. 110, col. 1; the standard Latin reading (111, ll. xiv–xv) is longer and more effusive; the Middle English would seem to be based on the simpler model).

340–1 'martirid for þe feythe and for þe loue of God': *occisi sunt* (111, xvii).

342–3 'Duke Milo, a worthi warrioure, a worthi Englysshe lorde, fadur of þat worshipfull knyȝt Rowlond': *dux Milo, Rotolandi genitor* (111, xvii–xviii). The variation from the Latin is further evidence of a determined (perhaps commissioned) revision of the source concerning Milo's identity; see Shepherd, 'Middle English *Pseudo-Turpin Chronicle*', 25–6; the n. to l. 264, above; and the Introduction, pp. l–lii.

344–5 'with fewȝ of þat Cristen hooste': *cum duobus milibus Christianorum* (111, xx–xxi; so *Ir* (pp. 18, 19) and *Tr* (p. 110, col. 2); *Johannes* has .*x*. *mile Crestiens* (XVII, 13); *AN* does not mention any number (ll. 277–80); *WPs-T* has *deu Gristawn* (p. 10, l. 12)). Perhaps the Middle English translator or his source read *militus* for *milibus*.

346 'his tristy swerde': *spatam suam* (111, xxi–xxii). The slight embellishment combines with 'manfully' later in the sentence (see the next n.) to enhance the impression of Charles's prowess.

'Caudiosa': *Gaudiosam* (111, xxii); *Joyouse* (*AN*, 279); *Joieuse* (*Johannes*, XVII, 15); *Gaudiosa* (*Ir*, pp. 18, 19); *Gawdios* (*WPs-T*, p. 10, l. 14).

347 'he slowȝ manfully': *trucidavit* (111, xxii). Cf. the addition of 'tristy' earlier in the sentence.

351 'wele-fytinge men': *virorum bellatorum* (111, xxvi); the term is also used at l. 489 and translates exactly the same Latin expression (123, viii–ix); however, cf. the use of the term at l. 1135. MED, s.v. 'wel', *adv.* 1b (b), equates the compound with 'wel-servinge'.

351–2 'þe gode Kynge Charlis': *Karolo* (111, xxv).

354–5 'This bataile morelisithe þe gode archebisshop Turpyne in þis manere': another awkwardly (and this time evidently unique) extra-narrative preface to a moralizing passage: cf. l. 304 and n. For the corresponding Latin, see Meredith-Jones 113, ii–iii.

355–6 'Alle Cristen me[n] . . . and þe deuyle': *In præfata acie fas est intelligi salutem pro Christo certantium*(113, ii–iii). In contrast to the generality of the Latin, the Middle English enters straight into the martial analogy to be elaborated upon in the rest of the passage.

358–9 'gostely enmyes and vicis': *vicia* (113, v).

362 'meke and besy': *assiduam* (113, ix).

362–3 'silence ayenste chydinge': beyond this point the Middle English agrees with *Tr* (p. 110, col. 2), *Ir* (p. 20, 21), *AN* (ll. 291–3), and *Johannes* (XVIII, 13–15) in omitting examples of poverty striving against wealth, and perseverance against inconstancy, found in the standard Latin (113, x–xi;). In addition to these, *AN* omits the examples of prayer against temptation and obedience against carnality. *WPs-T* omits the moral altogether (p. 10, l. 20), ending the chapter at the equivalent of Meredith-Jones 113, ii.

363–4 'ayenste alle the transgressions of oure Lordis commoundementis': there seems to be considerable variety in the treatment of this portion of the text: the standard Latin has *contra carnalem animum* (113, xii–xiii); *Tr* has *contra carnalem accidiam* (p. 110, col. 2); *Johannes* has *contre charnel corage* (XVIII, 15); *Ir* and *AN* omit (*WPs-T* omits the whole moralizing passage— see the previous note).

364–5 'þat is to sey, his gode dedis': only *AN* and *Johannes* have a comparable explication of the metaphor: *La lance, c'est l'ame . . . .* (*Johannes* XVIII, 16; cf. *AN*, l. 293 and n.).

365–6 'at þe day of his dethe.': after this sentence the Middle English agrees only with *Ir* (pp. 20, 21) in omitting two sentences, the first sustaining the imagery of the flowering lance to describe the righteous soul in heaven, the second recalling 2 Tim. 2:5 (cf. Meredith-Jones 113, xiv–xvi). *Tr* omits only the second sentence (p. 110, col 2).

368–9 'in heuene with aungelis and seyntis': *quatinus palmam de triumpho floridam habere mereamur in celesti regno* (113, xix–xx). The Middle English conclusion loses track of the prevailing figure of efflorescence.

374 'Xerephum': *Texephinum* (113, xxiii); but cf. *Tr*: *Zerephinum* (p. 110, col. 2).

376 'þe Kynge of Barbarie, the Kyng of Cordube': the Middle English list agrees with *Tr* (p. 111, col. 1) and *Ir* (pp. 22, 23) in omitting the names of four kings between those of the king of Barbary and the king of Cordoba (cf. Meredith-Jones 115, ii–iii). Like *Ir*, but unlike *Tr*, the Middle English also omits the personal names of the last four kings in its list.

376–7 'many oþer kyngis with Sarzyns, many withoute numbre': the first three words are matched in *Tr* (*et alios multos reges*, p. 111, col. 1) and *Ir* (*ocus righa imdha o sin amach*, 'and many other kings as well' (pp. 22, 23)), but the rest are not matched; the unmatched words may derive from a recapitulation of part of the opening sentence of the chapter which mentions *gentes innumeras, Sarracenos, Mauros . . .* (113, xxi) and which, with the recognition that 'Saracens' is a generic rather than a national name, is first translated in the Middle English as 'a grete numbure of Sarzyns—þat is to sey, Mauris . . . .'

381 'behotinge him moche golde and siluer': the Middle English agrees with *Tr* (p. 111, col. 1) and *Ir* (p. 22, 23) in omitting mention of nine horses which would carry this treasure (cf. Meredith-Jones, 115, vii; *Johannes* XIX, 14; *AN*, which has ten horses, l.306; *WPs-T* p. 11, l. 2).

383 'But why dude Aigalonde þis?': the question is not matched in the standard Latin or *IrTrWPs-TANJohannes*.

385 'þis foule pride and also þe tresoune': such vituperation is absent in *IrTrWPs-TANJohannes* and the standard Latin, which simply note that Charles understood Aigolandus's motives (cf. Meredith-Jones, 115, ix–x: *Karolus hæc animadvertens*). The same can be said of the use of 'treson' at l. 409.

386 'grete hooste': *cum duobus milibus fortiorum* (115, x).

389–90 'arayede him like a messengere': a pre-emptive clarification not matched in the standard Latin or *IrTrWPs-TANJohannes* (cf. Meredith-Jones, 115, xiv).

397–8 'to do the obeysance and serue þe and be þyne': *vult tibi militare et effici tuus homo* (115, xxi–xxii).

405–6 'toke gode hede of his kyngis strenkeþis': *et vidit reges* (117, iv).

407 'to þe hylle': the Middle English alone agrees with *Johannes* (XX, 21) in explicitly mentioning the hill again (cf. Meredith-Jones, 117, v: *rediit . . . quos retro reliquerat*).

407–8 'to his hooste': *ad duo milia* (117, vi).

409 'This treson': see n. to l. 385 (cf. Meredith-Jones 117, vii–viii).

413 'guwnus and engynes and alle oþer ordinaunce': *petrariis et mangarellis et toriis et arietibus ceterisque artificiis . . . et castellis ligneis* (117, xi–xiii). The crossing through of *O Gunneris* ahead of *engynes* just as a new column and page begins may signify a careless recollection of *guwnnis* at the end of the previous column, or two failed attempts at reading 'engynes' (the capital 'E' used in the manuscript could reflect the capitalization of the exemplar and could at a glance be confused with 'O' or 'G'). The change of form, however, from 'guns' to 'gunners,' might suggest the inadvertent copying of a trial translation of *petrariis* which had been subpuncted for excision in the translator's draft (*RMLWL*, s.v. *petr/a*, records 'gunner' as one sense of *petrarius*, c. 1440).

414–16 'Whanne Aigalond saw . . . to be take or be sley': all this is left implicit in the standard Latin (117, xiii) and *IrTrWPs-TANJohannes*.

429 'syned': *sero* (119, i). Cf. MED, s.v. 'signen' v. (2) (c): 'to ordain a battle'.

430 'departide in diuerse whardis': *castris et aciebus et turmis præparatis* (119, ii).

431 '[T]alabruge': *Talaburgus* (119, iii–iv). *AN*, *Johannes*, *Ir* and *Tr* all have the *T-* form (*WPs-T* omits); the spelling in *Turpines Story* is thus likely to have resulted from a misreading of a cursive *t* for *c* (cf. the n. to ll. 237–8).

432 'Tharantta': The reading of the standard Latin is *Charanta* (119, iv; so *AN* (l. 347) and *Johannes* (XXI, 8); *Wps-T* omits the name); in this case, however, the 'incorrect' Middle English *T-* form is allowed to stand, as it agrees with *Tr* (*Tharanta*, p. 111, col. 2) and *Ir* (*Taranta*, pp. 26, 27).

433-4 'grene-rynedide, flourynge, and buddynge': compare ll. 330–1. The wording of the corresponding phrases in the Latin is identical (*scorticibus et frondibus decoratas*; 111, vii–viii and 119, vi–vii). Perhaps the differences in the Middle English represent a slight attempt at elegant variation to embellish a patently unimaginative repetition. The strategy adopted by *AN* (l. 347–48) and *Johannes* (XXI, 10) of saying that the flourishing of the lances happened as it had done before reveals other translators' awareness of the utilitarian organization of the Latin.

436 'þey saw þis meruelouse tokyne, þey þankide God': the Middle English corresponds marginally more closely with *Tr*: *tanto Dei miraculo viso gavisi sunt valde* (p. 111, col. 2; cf. the standard Latin: *tanto Dei miraculo gavisi* (119, viii–ix; so *AN* (l. 350), *Johannes* (XXI, 12), *Tr* (p. 111 col. 2), *Ir* (pp. 26, 27), and *WPs-T* (p. 13, ll. 7–8)). The correspondence, however, is not strong, perhaps the result only of an implication the Middle English translator has drawn.

437-8 'By þe grete fyȝtte and at þe begynnynge': *insimul coadunati primitus in bello ferierunt* (119, ix–x).

439 'þe Sarzyns had þe ouer hande': the Latin is considerably more implicit and diplomatic, saying only that the Christian warriors *tandem martirio coronantur* (119, x–xi; so *Ir*, pp. 26, 27; *AN*, l. 354; *Johannes*, XXI, 14; *WPs-T*, p. 13, ll. 10–11).

441-2 'almoste steffelde amonge þe dede men': a substantial divergence from the other versions, which, if they mention it, agree with the Latin that Charles is oppressed by (implicitly) living *paganorum* (Meredith-Jones, 119, xiii (instead of *fortitudine paganorum*, *Tr* has *multitudine paganorum* (p. 111, col. 2); and *Ir* seems to follow this reading, pp. 26, 27); *AN*, ll. 355–57; and *WPs-T*, p. 13, ll. 13–14; *Johannes* omits).

442-4 'with alle his hert, with alle his myȝt, turned to God': an apparent mistranslation of *invocato omnipotentis* (119, xiii; between these two words *Tr* adds *dei*, p. 111, col. 2).

450 'Arabie': this reading is wrongly said in Shepherd, 'Middle English *Pseudo-Turpin Chronicle*', p. 23, to be found in *Johannes* at the corresponding point; *Johannes* does mention *li rois d'Arrabe* in a nearby chapter (XIX, 6), but at the proper point of correspondence (XXI, 21) *Johannes* agrees with the standard Latin (119, xx) in having *lo roi d'Agabe*. Thus, the Middle English here agrees among *IrTrWPs-TANJohannes* only with *Tr* (p. 111, col. 2), *Ir* (pp. 26, 27), and *AN* (l. 365). It is possible that the

'Arabian' readings represent the independent corrections of confused scribes.

457 'with grete besynes and charge': *cum summa cura* (121, iv).

458–9 'to gader strenketh ayenste þe enemyes of God': this reading is matched only in *Tr* (*preparatos ad bellandum contra talem hostem fidei Christiane venire præcepit*, p. 112, col. 1) and *Ir* (pp. 28, 29); it is an extension of the *C*-family variant recorded by Meredith-Jones: *præparatos ad bellum ad se venire mandavit* (121, iv, n.).

461–2 'fyȝtte ayenste þe paynenyms and þe enemys of God': again, a reading shared only with *Ir* (*conta inimicos fidei christiane dimicatiur*, p. 112, col. 2; cf. the standard Latin, 121, xi) and *Tr* (pp. 28, 29); see previous n.

464–5 'with þe condicioune forseid . . . into Spayne': the recapitulation is not matched in the standard Latin or *IrTrWPs-TANJohannes*.

468–70 'also, alle þicke . . . he acordide hem': this corresponds to a reduced form of Meredith-Jones 119, xvi–xix, but has been moved ahead of the comments on Charles's arming of those enlisted (119, xv–xvi). A similar transposition has occurred at ll. 471–3 below; see the next n. for further comment on both.

471–3 'And þus he . . . withoute numbure': this corresponds to Meredith-Jones 119, xxii–xxiii, but has been moved ahead of Turpin's assertion that he gave all those on campaign absolution, remission from their sins, and a benediction (119, xx–xxii). This and the transposition remarked in the previous note is not matched in *IrTrWPs-TANJohannes*. There appears to be a logical motivation for the changes; in both cases a more universal and contingent action (arming, absolution) is placed after a more particular or necessarily prior action (resolving personal discord, marshaling the whole army).

'.vj. skore thousand and .xxx.^{ti}': the number varies dramatically between versions; *AN* reports *quaraunte mile* (l. 388) and *Johannes* (XXII, 20) agrees with the 134,000 of the standard Latin (121, xxiii). *Tr* (p. 112, col. 2) and *Ir* (pp. 28, 29) have 130,000. *WPs-T* has 120,000 (p. 14, l. 21).

479–80 'The names of þe principal lordis þat were with King Charles': With the exception of *WPs-T* (p. 14, l. 25), this chapter break is not found in the standard Latin or *IrTrWPs-TANJohannes*.

483–96 'Turpynne . . . Rowlond . . . Olyuer . . . Arastanus . . . Engelerus . . . Gayferus . . . Candebaldus . . . Otgerus . . . Constantinus': *Turpines Story* agrees with *Ir* exactly in the names retained from what is a much longer list in the standard Latin (125, vi—127, i). *Tr* agrees with *Turpines Story* and *Ir*, but further omits mention of *Otgerius* (Ogier the Dane; p. 112, col. 2). *WPs-T* (p. 14, l. 26—p. 15, l. 30), *AN* (ll. 416–28) and *Johannes* (XXIV, 11–16) have longer lists.

485–6 'fowȝtte ayenste hem myn oune hondis': cf. Malory, *Morte Darthur*: 'Sir Gawayne . . . slew Kynge Pellynor hys owne hondis'(p. 77, ll. 20–2); 'he slew the erle Grype his owne handis' (p. 434, l. 14); 'I shall sle the myne owne hondis' (p. 610, l. 7), etc.

486–7 'lorde of Cunomanesis and Blauij . . . þe sonne of Milo, duke de Angloiris': *comes cenomannensis et Blavii dominus . . . filius ducis Milonis de Angleris* (123, vi–vii). Although the translator has not rendered vernacular equivalents for *Cunomanensis* (le Mans) and *Blavii* (Blaye), he has rendered *de Angleris* with an arguably French patois. There is no evidence in this of a detailed knowledge of France (Anglers would be the correct name, not Angloires), but the patois is enough to suggest that the translator knew full well that Milo was French. Consequently, the two other occasions in *Turpines Story* which make Milo English (ll. 264 and 342–3) could represent a scheme of deliberate renaming—where the current 'correct' example is a tell-tale oversight. For further consideration of the implications of this evidence, which may have a bearing on the patronage of the translation, see the Introduction, pp. l–lii and the n. to ll. 264.

488–9 'a grete man and a semely and douȝtty in armys': *vir magnissimus et summæ probitatis* (123, viii).

'wele-fyȝttinge men': see the n. to l. 351.

490 'moste eger in bataile': *bello doctissimus, brachio et mucrone potentissimus* (123, x–xi).

490–1 'þe Erle of Genebensis': the Middle English text here agrees with *Ir* (pp. 30, 31) and *Tr* (p. 112 cols. 1–2) in omitting the additional identification of Oliver as the son of Count Rainer (*AN*, (ll. 399–400), *Johannes* (XXIII, 9–10), and *WPs-T* (p. 15, l. 10) agree with the Meredith-Jones Latin, 123, xii).

493 'alle þese': a match with *Tr*, *Isti omnis* (p. 112, col. 2; so *Ir*, pp. 30, 31), against the simpler *Isti* of the standard Latin (123, xviii; so *AN*, l. 405; *Johannes* XXIII, 13; and *WPs-T*, p. 15, l. 16).

494–5 'Gayferus, kynge of Bedous, with .iij. þousonde': before 'Gayferus' and after 'þousonde' occur two lacunæ: *Ir* alone has the same lacunæ; *Tr* has the first but not the second, and *AN*, *Johannes*, and *WPs-T* have the second but not the first. For details and significance, see Shepherd, 'Middle English *Pseudo-Turpin Chronicle*', pp. 24–5. 'Bedous' is an unusual spelling, perhaps derived from an abbreviated form of the usual Latin B*urdegalensis* (125, iv; so *Tr* (p. 112, col. 2), *Ir* (pp. 30, 31), and *WPs-T* (p. 15, l. 22)); cf. *AN*'s reading *Bordles* (l. 416); and cf. the n. to ll. 490–1.

497–8 'many moo whos names ware vnknowen to me': the Middle English here agrees only with *Tr* and *Ir* in admitting to the omission of additional names, but in each case the reasons, and some other details, differ. *Ir* claims that 'many other kings and dukes and lords with their hosts . . . are not enumerated here' (pp. 30, 31). *Tr* reads *sed et nomina aliorum ducum cum numero suo exercituum pretermissi et hoc propter tedium nominum incognitorum* (p. 112, col. 2). *Turpines Story* alone evokes the impression that the names were, as a measure of the immensity of Charles's forces, unknown even at the time of the campaign.

499 'horsemen—but þe foottemen were none numbure': . . . *militum, sed et peditum numerus non erat* (127, ii).

499–500 'forsaid and forenamyd': *præfati* (127, iii).

500–1 '. . . famouse men of werre and redy to fyȝt and dyȝe for defence and mentenaunce of Cristis feythe': *viri famosi, heroes bellatores, potentum cosmi potentiores, forciorum forciores, Christi proceres christianam fidem in mundo propalantes* (127, ii–v; so *WPs-T*, p. 15, l. 32—p. 16, l. 4). The corresponding passages in *AN* (ll. 433–34), *Johannes* (XXIV, 18–19), *Ir* (pp. 30, 31), and *Tr* (p. 112, col. 2, quoted below) are all, like the Middle English, briefer than the standard Latin. Of these, *Ir* is closest to *Turpines Story*, but all contain substantial differences; the Middle English is the most ardent in its praise of the warriors. *Tr* reads, *viri famosi et bellatores fidei Christi* (p. 112, col. 2).

502 'and .iij. skore and .xij. disciplis': *duodecim apostolis et discipulis* (127, vi). The additional numbering of the Middle English is matched in Meredith-Jones's record by his B.3 text alone (see note to 127, vi; B.3 is Paris, Bibliotheque Nationale, *fonds latin* 5452, probably of French provenance, having revisions made by Geoffroi de Vigeois—see Meredith-Jones, p. 10). *IrTrWPs-TANJohannes* are consistent with the standard Latin, applying just the number twelve to the apostles and/or the disciples (*WPs-T* omits all numbering). The origin of the B.3 reading no doubt lies in recollection of the sequence of Christ's missions as described between (Vulgate) Luke 9:1–2—*convocatis autem duodecim apostolis . . . et misit illos prædicare regnum Dei* – and Luke 10:1— *post hæc autem designavit Dominus et alios septuaginta duos et misit illos binos ante faciem suam in omnem civitatem et locum quo erat ipse venturus*. Because of its biblical familiarity, it is conceivable that the reading could be introduced by any pious translator or copyist irrespective of the source manuscript family.

504–5 'to þe feythe': the phrase, here and at the end of the sentence, is not matched in *IrTrWPs-TANJohannes*, which generally agree with the standard Latin in attributing Charlemagne's deeds *ad decus nominis Dei* (127, vii–ix). The rhetorical advantage of the parallelism, moreover, does not obtain in the other versions, where God is mentioned only at the end of the sentence.

506–8 There is no chapter- or paragraph-break in *WPs-T* (p. 16, l. 9) or the standard Latin at this point (127, ix). *AN* begins a new paragraph (l. 439); *Johannes* (XXV), *Tr* (p. 112, col. 2), and *Ir* (pp. 30, 31) begin new chapters.

Like *Turpines Story*, *Tr* provides a title, though its content differs: *Qualiter conuenerunt exercitus Karoli in planicie de Burdens*. *Burdens*, however, appears to be matched by 'Burdeuce' in the subsequent sentence in *Turpines Story* (l. 508). This name for Bordeaux is otherwise represented in all Latin texts by forms of *Burdegalis*. Cf. n. to ll. 494–5.

509 'occupyed and `re'keuerid': *cooperiebant* (127, x). The scribal addition of (abbreviated) *re* to 'keuerid' creates a revision that renders the translation potentially more meaningful, if less literal. The notion of recovery of stolen territory was understood by crusade theologians as a legalistic justification for holy war: see Norman Daniel, 'The Legal and Political Theory of the Crusade,' in *A History of The Crusades*, ed. Kenneth M. Setton, 6 vols (Madison, Wisconsin, 1969–89), VI, 3–38 (pp. 6–7). 'Rekeuerid' translates the same Latin word several lines further on (l. 516; corresponding to Meredith-Jones 127, xix) and is so copied without need of correction. The earlier correction could suggest that the scribe was copying from the translator's draft, where, just as in the fair copy, a diminutive abbreviated *re*- had been added above or below the line.

512 'hauyne': *portus* (127, xiii). Neither MED nor OED record a sense of 'haven' as equivalent to 'gate' or 'pass,' and so it is possible that the translator mistakenly envisions a harbour instead of the mountain pass of Cize made famous in the *Chanson de Roland*; significantly, *Ir* refers to the location as a river (pp. 30, 31).

'de Belandam': both the standard Latin (127, ix) and *Tr* (p. 112, col. 2) have *de Bellanda*, and that is the form followed by the Middle English text in the other places where Arnold is mentioned (ll. 662, 669–70).

514–15 'Estultus . . . Charils': in the standard Latin (127, xv–xviii), *AN* (ll. 444–46), *Johannes* (XXV, 6–9), and *WPs-T* (p. 16, ll. 17–20), between the mention of Estultus and Charles, five other leaders of the Christian forces are named (in the Latin they are Arastagnus, Engelerus, Gandeboldus, Otgerius, and Constantinus, in that order). The Middle English agrees with *Ir* (pp. 32, 33) and *Tr* (p. 112, col. 2) in omitting these names.

519 'Aigalonde to Pampilioun': At this point the Middle English text agrees with *Ir* (pp. 32, 33), *Tr* (p. 112, col. 2), *Johannes* (XXV, 13–14), and *WPs-T* (p. 16, ll. 25–7), but not *AN* (l. 452) in omitting an account of Aigolandus's repairing of Pamplona as found in the standard Latin: *urbem quam rehedificaverat et rursum munierat* (129, ii–iii).

520–2 'come into þe felde . . . to come into þe felde': *exiret . . . exire* (129, iii–v).

523 'cowardly dyʒe': *turpe mori* (129, vi).

529–30 'How Charles and Aigelonde disputed þeire righte of Spaigne': the title agrees more closely with that of *Tr* than the standard Latin (129, heading to chapter XII) in mentioning that the disputation between Charles and Aigolandus concerns Spain: *Qualiter Aygolandus conuenit ad Karolus et disputacione eorum super terram Hyspanie* (p. 113, col. 1).

533 'fro Pampilioun': *ab urbe* (129, xi).

535 'to Kynge Charlis were he satte in his trone of astate': *ante Karoli tribunal* (129, xii). OED cites Hakluyt *Voy.* II. 62 (1599) as its earliest example of 'throne of estate' (i.e., throne of state; s.v. 'Estate' *sb.* 4.c); MED records only 'chair of estat', s.v. 'estat' *n.* 18(a), c. 1500 (?a.1437?).

'.ij.': *uno* (129, xiii); so *IrTrANJohannes* (*om. WPs-T*, p. 17, c. l. 6). The Middle English agrees with *Tr* (p. 113, col. 1) in failing to mention that the field was also six miles in width (cf. Meredith-Jones, 129, xv–xvi: *habens in longitudine et latitudine sex miliaria*). *Ir* seems to be dealing with a similar omission in its source when it mentions only that the distance between the two armies was six miles (pp. 32, 33).

540–1 'þou artte Aigalonde; þe whiche wrongefully þou haste take my londe fro me': the awkward use of prounouns represents a literal translation: *Tu es Aigolandus qui terram meam fraudulenter a me abstulisti* (129, xviii; *Tr* omits *a me*, p. 113, col. 1).

541–2 'þe whiche I gate by grete power': this reading agrees with *Tr, Ir, AN* and *Johannes* in being less ostentatious than the standard Latin's *brachio invincibili potentiæ Dei adquisivi* (129, xix—131, i). *Tr* has *quam ego cum potencia Dei acquisiui* (p. 113, col. 1; cf. *Ir* pp. 32, 33, *AN* l. 467, *Johannes* XXVI, 12, and *WPs-T*, p. 17, l. 11). The Middle English seems to be unique, however, in omitting mention of God.

543–4 'ware suggettis and tribunarius to me': *Tr* is closest in suggesting the content of the Middle English translator's source text: *meo imperio subieci* (p. 113, col. 1); Meredith-Jones has *meo imperio everti* (131, i–ii). OED only records 'tribunary' as an adjective (1612), and its obvious sense of pertaining to a tribune does not seem apposite in context; emendation to 'tributaries' might be defensible. MED, however, records 'tribunere' *n.*, 'a governor of a province' (?a. 1425).

545 'peruertid þese peple': *Dei Christianos . . . peremisti* (131, ii–iii); 'peruertid' may derive from confusion of the abbreviated *peremisti* with an abbreviated form of *peruertisti*.

550 'wen he went to scole': *Didiscerat . . . linguam sarracenicam . . . cum esset iuuenis* (131, vii–viii); cf. *WPs-T*, p. 17, ll. 22–23: *þan uuassei gynt yn ieuanc yno yn yscol*. As found in their oldest *Pseudo-Turpin* witnesses, this and the reference in chapter xxiii to Charles's service to Galafrius of Toledo (l. 1088–9) represent the earliest allusions to what became known as the *Meinet* tale among the *Enfances* legends of Charlemagne: see Smyser, *The Pseudo-Turpin*, p. 29, n. 2 and Meredith-Jones, p 303, n. to 130, viii. The reference to Charles's time in Toledo appears in the Latin in a separate sentence which follows the one which describes Aigolandus's pleasure at hearing his native tongue spoken by Charles (131, vii–ix; so *Tr* (p. 113, col. 1), *Ir* (pp. 34, 35), *AN* (l.473), and *WPs-T* (p. 17, ll. 21–3)). Like the Middle English, *Johannes* also rearranges the details, but in a different way (XXVI, 9–16).

551–2 'for so he my3t better denounce and declare his matris by hemselffe þan by anoþer interpretacioune': this is unmatched in the other versions and perhaps reflects the translator's own enthusiasms for translation. Later in the text, skill in translation again becomes a subject, and again the Middle English translator appears to indulge his enthusiasms by modifying the text; see the n. to ll. 792–4 and the Introduction, p. xlii–xliii.

553–4 'why ye toke awey': the Middle English agrees only with *Johannes* (XXVI, 18) in omitting Aigolandus's claim that it was from his people (*a nostra gente*, 131, xii) that Charles took away the territory (cf. *Ir*, pp. 34,35; *Tr*, p. 113, col. 2; *AN*, l. 476; *WPs-T*, p. 17, l. 27).

555 'title . . . bi eritaunce': *iure hereditario* (131, x).

559–61 'we shold labore to make alle peple Cristen, wherefore I labored and made alle Spayne for þe more partte—and þou haste made hem renegatis and false paynyms': *tuam gentem sarracenicam legi nostræ in quantum potui converti* (131, xvi–xvii; *Tr* replaces *converti* with *subiugaui*, p. 113, col. 2). *AN* (ll.481–2), *Ir* (pp. 34, 35), and *WPs-T* (p. 18, ll. 5–7) all agree with the Latin, while *Johannes* is somewhat closer to the more universalizing Middle English by describing those to be converted in the third person (*la gent paienime*; XXVI, 22–3). None of the other versions has quite the vituperative cadence of the Middle English; cf. the Introduction, p. xli.

561 'right a': for this word-order, cf. *The Canterbury Tales*, General Prologue, l. 857.

563–4 'god and . . . law3e': *lex* (131, xviii); evidently the English translator was concerned not simply to convey the sense of secular law.

565 'preceptis and comoundmentis': *præcepta* (131, xx).
'kepe and holde': here the Middle English appears to agree exclusively with *Tr*: *seruamus et tenemus* (p. 113, col. 2). The standard Latin has *tenemus* only (131, xx) and the other versions agree in having only one verb of possession (*Ir*, pp. 34, 35; *AN*, l. 485; *Johannes*, XXVII, 4; *WPs-T*, p. 18, l. 12). The Middle English could, however, simply be employing the familiar use of a tautological doublet to translate a single term.

568–70 'þou erriste in þat þou seiste þat youre law3e that Mawmethe yaffe to yow is more worthy þan oure': the standard Latin has simply *in hoc erras* (131, xxiii), but it is clear that the Middle English follows a version close to

Tr, which adds *cum dicis quam lex tua magis valeat quia Maumet precepta seruatis* (p. 113, col. 2; so *Ir*, pp. 34, 35).

571–2 'ye kepe þe lawȝe of a false veynyd dedely man þat is dampned in helle': a further example of vituperative expansion over the Latin (*vani hominis præcepta vana tenetis*; 131, xxiv—cf. the Introduction, p. xli).

573 'in oo godhede, in oo nature, in oo beynge': this triplet is not matched in other versions, nor is the third component of the subsequent phrase, 'and Him we serue,' added, perhaps, to establish a tripartite parallel (the Latin has *credimus et adoramus*; 131, xxv). The tripartite parallel comes, however, at the expense of an original bipartite parallel with the last two verbs of the next sentence ('leue and . . . worshipe': *creditis et adoratis*; 131, xxvi).

575 'ydolis þat beth deffeth and dome and veyne': the Middle English here is closest to *Tr*, *simulachris mutis et vanis* (p. 113, col. 2; *Ir* is close, with 'dumb and vain offerings,' pp. 34, 35). The standard Latin has only *simulachris vestris* (131, xxvi; so *Johannes*, XXVII, 9, *AN*, l. 491, and *WPs-T*, p. 18, ll. 21–2).

576 'þe feythe and þe lawȝe': *fidem* (133, i).

578–9 'for lacke of Cristen feythe': not matched in the other versions, all of which agree with the standard Latin *vestræ animæ ad Orcum proficisuntur* (133, ii–iii).

582–3 'but parte youre possessioune; youre lordship is with þe fendis': *sed prius vestra et possessio erit cum diablo* (133, iii, n.); the sense of 'parte' would seem to match MED 'parten', *v*. 2. (c) 'to disperse (something, a liquid or vapor); adjourn (an assembly); disrupt (an association of people)'. Perhaps, however, the English translator has misread *prius* as *privis*, in which case 'parte' may be used in the sense of OED *part*, *v*. II †8. *trans*. 'To depart from, go away from, take leave of, quit, forsake: = DEPART *v*. 8'.

585 'Cristen feythe and beleue': *babtismum accipe . . . et vive* (133, iv); the Middle English agrees with *Johannes* (XXVII, 16) in omitting the equivalent of *et vive*. *AN* (l. 498), *Tr* (pp. 36, 37), *Ir* (p. 113, col 2), and *WPs-T* (p. 19, l. 1) retain the reading.

594–5 'How þat Aigolondis peple were ouercome and he behyȝtte to be Cristen': There is no chapter break here in the standard Latin, *Tr*, *Ir*, *AN*, or *WPs-T*; but *Johannes* begins its 28th chapter at this point.

599 'isley eueryshone': after this point the Middle English here agrees alone with *AN* (ll. 504–7) in omitting a sortie of forty against forty (cf. 133, xvii–xviii).

603 'for drede of dethe': after this sentence and before the next, an extensive moralizing passage has been omitted (cf. 135, i–viii). *Tr* (p. 113, col. 2—p. 114, col. 1), *Ir* (pp. 36, 37—38, 39), *AN* (ll. 513–22), *Johannes* (XXVIII, 10–

14), and *WPs-T* (p. 19, l. 20—p. 20, l. 1) all retain some substantial version of the passage, which warns against the refusal to combat sin.

611 'and tolde hem': *Tr* (p. 114, col. 1), *Ir* (pp. 38, 39), *Johannes* (XVIII, 21–2), and *WPs-T* (p. 20, ll. 8–9) agree with the standard Latin that Aigolandus *dixit regibus et maioribus suis* (135, xv) rather than the whole army. However, the Middle English also adds 'kynges' to its next sentence where they are only implicit in the other versions.

614 'The ordre of Charles peple at mete and the pore men': in didactic texts of the later Middle Ages this, like chapter vii, is one of the most frequently abstracted of chapters from the *Pseudo-Turpin*, and it is rather conspicuously so abstracted in a number of Insular texts from the fourteenth and fifteenth centuries. As with chapter vii, the contemporary popularity of the episode may account for the confident ease of the Middle English translation at this point. Unlike chapter vii, the story of the thirteen poor men in its English renderings elicits opposing interpretations about the prerogatives of religion and class. For details, see the Introduction, pp. xxxiv–xxxvii, and the notes to this chapter below. The story may have been adopted by the original *Pseudo-Turpin* from an account of Charlemagne's crusade against the Saxon king Wittekind as reflected in Peter Damian's *De Eleemosyna*: see Smyser, *The Pseudo-Turpin*, p. 30, n. 3, and Meredith-Jones, who quotes the episode in Damien, pp. 303–4. The Middle English chapter title agrees with the first part of the title in *Tr*: *De ordinibus qui erant in convivio Karoli et de pauperibus unde Aygolandus scandalum sumpsit et renuit baptizari* (p. 114, col. 1; cf. Smyser, *The Pseudo-Turpin*, p. 71, n. to XVI, 1, and Meredith-Jones's A.6. text, p. 136).

616–17 'aboute nyne of þe day': *circa horam tertiam* (135, xviii).
'for to haue be cristenyde': *causa baptizandi* (137, i).

618–19 'at þe mette at a stattly borde beste besyȝe': *ad mensam prandentem* (137, ii). *IrTrWPs-TANJohannes*, like the Latin, do not comment on the splendour of the table. Insofar as the chapter is inherently concerned with the moral and material implications of rank and privilege, the Middle English presents an appropriate visual elaboration.

'diuerse ordis': here the Middle English uniquely omits a preliminary list of the kinds of people seated at the tables: knights, monks, canons, clerics (cf. Meredith-Jones, 137, iii–vi); the omission appears to have been made in the interests of efficiency, as, with the exception of knights, the other categories are named and sub-classified in the subsequent text.

622 'birris ore pulyons': *birris* (137, viii).

622–3 'bisshoppis, doctoris, and prestis of oure lawȝ þat techith vs oure lawȝe and expouneythe hit': *episcopi et sacerdotes nostræ legis . . . qui nobis legis præcepta exponunt* (137, viii–ix).

626–7 'feer shynnynge habitte': *habitu candido* (137, xiii).

628 'for alle Cristen peple': *pro nobis* (137, xiv; so *AN* (l. 548), *Johannes* (XXIX, 14), *WPs-T* (p. 21, l. 5)). The Irish versions, like the Middle English, offer unique variants in this sentence: *Ir* omits mention of the canons regular (pp. 38, 39) and *Tr* reads . . . *canonici regulares, et hii simili modo beneficiam Conditoris implorant, et missas et matutinas et horas canonicas decantant* (p. 114, col. 1).

629 'xiij': *Johannes* (XXIX, 16), *Ir* (pp. 40, 41) and *Tr* (p. 114, col.) agree against *WPs-TAN* in counting only twelve paupers (and cf. Meredith-Jones's list of alternative manuscript readings for 137, xvi). These are likely to be coincident rather than genetic variants.

630–1 'hauynge a litille mette': *parvo cibo et potu utentes* (137, xviii).

632 'þe messengeris of oure Lorde God': the standard Latin is periphrastic (*gens Dei, nuncii domini nostri* (137, xx; so *AN*, 554 and *WPs-T*, p. 21, ll. 12–13)). The briefer Middle English reading agrees with *Johannes* (XXIX, 18–19), *Ir* (pp. 40, 41), and *Tr* (p. 114, col. 2; *sunt Dei nuncii domini nostri*).

633 'for loue' perhaps represents the subsense of 'in estimation' available in the Latin *sub numero* (137, xx; so *Tr* p. 114, col. 2). *Ir* is more literal with *according to the number* (pp. 40, 41). *AN* has only *en soun noun* (l. 555), *WPs-T* has *yn enw* (p. 21, l. 15), and *Johannes* has *el non* (XXIX, 19–20).

633–4 'we fede and yeue mette': *pascimus* (139, ii).

634–5 'þese þat sitte aboute þe beth wele icloþide; þey ette gode metis and drinke gode drinkis': the Middle English account is unmatched by *IrTrWPs-TANJohannes* in omitting Aigolandus's general observation that Charles and those who sit with him *felices . . . sunt* (139, iii).

636–7 'fare euylle': *IrTrWPs-TANJohannes* agree with the standard Latin in describing the paupers' state of hunger (*fame pereunt*, 139, v). Perhaps the Middle English translator, seeing beforehand that the paupers had 'a litille mette,' felt that their case would be overstated.

'litille made of': *turpe tractantur* (139, vi; *Tr* has *turpiter tractantur*, p. 114, col. 2). The sentence which ends with this phrase is framed in the interrogative in the standard Latin (139, v–vi), *Tr* (p. 114, col. 2), *Ir* (pp. 40, 41), *WPs-T* (p. 21, ll. 20–4) and *AN* (ll. 557–61) (i.e., all take the form of 'why is it that those whom you call the Messengers of God endure . . . ?') The Middle English agrees with *Johannes* (XXIX, 20–5) in rendering a more direct (and bolder) statement.

637–40 'He seruythe . . . his meynye': cf. Matthew 25: 40.

638–9 'grete vnreuerence and shame': *Magnum verecundiam* (139, vii).

641 'þe contrary': an addition to the Latin source, *Legem tuam, quam dicebas esse bonam, nunc ostendis falsam* (139, xviii–ix). If the editorial insertion of 'gode' at the beginning of the sentence is correct (an alternative would be *trew*), then perhaps the addition of 'þe contrary' represents an effort to overcome a perceived lack of absolute rhetorical opposition with 'false.'

642–3 'gretly disklawnder how vngodely Charlis tretide Goddis messengeris': not matched in the standard Latin (139, x), *AN* (l. 565), *WPs-T* (p. 21, l. 28), or *Johannes* (XXIX, 28–29); 'gretly disklawnder', however, has a match in the Irish texts: *Tr* has *scandalizatur* (p. 114, col. 2) and *Ir* has *re scannuil* ('with scandal', pp. 40, 41).

644 'he refuside Cristyndome': the standard Latin (139, x–xi) and *IrTrWPs-TANJohannes* add that Aigolandus demanded battle the next day.

647 'sufficiently': this agrees with *sufficienter* in *Tr* (p. 114, col. 2) as opposed to *honorifice* in the standard Latin (139, xiv); *Ir* ('in plenty', pp. 40, 41) is consistent with *Tr*; *AN* has only *ben* (l. 569); *Johannes* (*honoreement*, XXX, 3) and *WPs-T* (*yn enrydedus*, p. 22, l. 2) agree with the standard Latin.

648 '. . . ry3t inow': an extensive moralizing passage essentially arguing that faith without good works is like a body without a soul has been removed from the end of this chapter (cf. Meredith-Jones, 139, xv—141, iii); the passage is present in *Ir* (pp. 40, 41 and 42, 43), *Tr* (p. 114, col. 2), *WPs-T* (p. 22, ll. 3–18), *AN* (ll. 571–90), and *Johannes* (XXX, 3–16). On possible contexts for the omission by the Middle English translator, see the Introduction, pp. xxxvi–xxxvii.

658 'Aigalonde': *IrTrWPs-TANJohannes* agree with the standard Latin (141, x–xi) that it was the Saracens generally who took heed of their losses, not Aigolandus alone.

662–5 Between its translations of *Arnaldus de Bellanda* and *Arastanus Rex*, the Middle English text omits mention of *Estultus comes cum suo exercitu* (141, xiv; so *Tr*, p. 115, col. 1); *IrWPs-TANJohannes* all retain the count's name in some form. The same is the case subsequently in the Middle English for *Constantinus romanus*, who normally appears after mention of *Otgerius Rex* (141, xvi). Like the Middle English, *WPs-T* (p. 23, ll. 5 ff.) omits Constantinus, but also omits Gandelboldus and Otgerius.

'his retynue . . . his peple . . . his feleship . . . his meyné': the Middle English renders some elegant variation in contrast to the rather pedestrian Latin '*suo exercitu . . . cum suo . . . cum suo . . . cum suo*' (141, xiv–xvii; *Ir* (pp. 42, 43), *WPs-T* (p. 23, ll. 3–5) and *AN* (ll. 601–8) are also pedestrian, but cf. *Johannes* XXXI, 8–13).

665 'Kynge Charlis with his grette hooste': at this point the Middle English text departs from the usual *C*-text reading *Karolus et principes exercituum* (141, xvii, n.; so *Ir* (pp. 42, 43), and *Johannes* (XXXI, 13); *AN* substitutes *principes* with the names of Turpin, Roland, and Oliver (l. 609—and see Short's note thereto); *WPs-T* does not mention Charles, but is otherwise consistent with the *C*-text reading (p. 23, ll. 6–9)). The Middle English reading seems to correspond more closely to that of the standard Latin, *Karolus cum innumeris exercitibus suis* (141, xvii); a peculiar reading in *Tr,* however, *Karolus vero et* princeps *exercituum* (p. 115, col. 1, emphasis added) suggests the possibility of a similar variant in the Middle English translator's source.

667–9 'Charlis lette crye and bad hem alle, in His name þat þey came fore, to fyȝte manfully ayenste þe enemyes of God and þe feyth': no doubt a deliberately personal and heroizing revision of the standard *C*-text reading, *in Domino confitentes alacriter amovebant* (141, xvi, n.), though it seems as likely that the revision began with the translator's misreading of an abbreviated *amovebant* as *amovebat*, which caused him to infer Charles as the singular subject.

679 'wadude': *natabant* (143, viii).

680 '. . . he slow': as with the previous two chapters, an extensive moralizing passage has been removed from the end of this chapter (see Meredith-Jones 143, x–xx); and as with the previous chapters, some version of the passage is present in *Ir* (pp. 44, 45), *Tr* (p. 115, coll. 1–2), *WPs-T* (p. 23, ll. 23–9—p. 24, ll. 1–6), *AN* (abbreviated, ll. 625–9), and *Johannes* (also abbreviated, XXXII, 2–6). The same omission is made in Meredith-Jones's A.1. text (142, n.). The passage omitted proclaims the transcendence of the Christian faith over all others and exhorts Christians to support their faith with good works.

681–2 'How þe Cristen men were slaye þat wente by niȝte to spoile þe ded Sarasins': the title is more fulsome than that given in the *Titulus* (ll. 44–5); there the title more accurately reflects the usual Latin formulation, *De Christianis qui ad illicita spolia redierunt* (143, heading to chapter XV).

689 'covnturwaytide': an obvious predicate to Altumaior's subsequent attack, but one left implicit in the standard Latin (145 ii–iv) and *IrTrWPs-TANJohannes*.

690 'on þe halkis of þe hylle': the standard Latin has *inter montes* (145, iii), but *Tr* has *inter colles* (p. 115, col. 2; cf. the 'glens' of *Ir*, pp. 46, 47).

690–1 'He went bytwex hem and þe citté': *IrTrWPs-TANJohannes* are not this specific, though *Tr, inrruens super eos, ipsos occidit* (p. 115, col. 2) is more suggestive of such a manoeuvre than the standard Latin *peremit illos omnes* (145, iv).

692 '. . . þere, aboute . . .': addition of 'was' between these two words would supply what might seem to be a missing verb, but the syntax of the Latin appears to be responsible for the formulation, where *erat* is separated at some distance from its object: *erat numerus illorum qui interfecti sunt circiter mille* (Tr., p. 115, col. 2)

'. . . aboute a þousonde.': as with the endings of the previous three chapters, an extensive moralizing passage has been omitted (corresponding to Meredith-Jones 145, v–xv); some version of the passage is present in *Tr* (p. 115, col. 2), *Ir* (pp. 46, 47), *AN* (ll. 641–649), and *Johannes* (XXXII, 15–24). The passage compares the slain Christians with those who return to sins earlier confessed and goes on to single out professional religious who, having turned away from the world, allow themselves to return to it and bring upon themselves eternal death. This omission, perhaps more than the earlier examples, avoids an overelaborate interpretation of the obvious. The same omission is made in *WPs-T* (p. 24, l. 15) and Meredith-Jones's B.3. text (145, n. to l. vi).

693 'How Charles faughte with Furre prince of Nauerne': Compare with the *Titulus* (l. 46); there the title more closely reflects the usual Latin title, *De Bello Furre* (145, heading to chapter XVI). *Tr* has *De bello contra Furre nomine conmisso* (p. 115, col. 2).

699–700 'yeue him ore shew him sume token': *ostenderet ei* (147, i).

704–5 'for compacioun þat he hade of hem': not matched in the Latin (see 147, iv–v). Of *IrTrWPs-TANJohannes*, only *Johannes* has a similar expansion: *qant il vit ce, si fu moult dolenz por la pitié de tanz prudomes* (XXXIII, 9–10).

706–8 'O, how meruelouse . . . bethe þe wey of God!': *Quam incomprehensibilia sunt iudicia Dei et investigabiles viæ eius!* (147, v–vi; the source is Romans 11:33).

709 'Nabarris that ware Sarzyns': this equation is matched only in *Tr* (p. 116, col. 1), which appears to have preserved a reading that erroneously omitted *et* from the standard Latin *Navarrorum scilicet et Sarracenorum* (147, viii).

711 'how holy': *sanctissima* (147, x).

715–16 'The bataille of Ferekot and the disputacion of good Rowlande': *De bello Ferracuti gigantis et de optima disputacione Rotolandi* (147, heading to chapter XVII). The Middle English translator's decision to see *optima* as describing 'good' Roland rather than Roland's argument suggests a perception of him more as the worthy hero of the romances and *chansons de geste* than the theological contestant the source *Pseudo-Turpin* would have him be at this point. The *Titulus* also has this unique reading, ll. 47–8.

718–19 'Admiraldus, kynge of Babilon': so *Tr* (*Admirandus rex Babilonis*, p. 116, col. 1), *Ir* ('Admirantus, that was the King of Babylon,' pp. 48, 49) and *WPs-T* (*Amilald vrenhin Babilon*, p. 25, l. 15); the standard Latin has *Babilonis Admirandus* (147, xvi; so *AN* (l. 673) and *Johannes* (XXXIII, 25)).

'Vageris': allowing the initial *V-* of the Middle English to be a misreading of initial (lombardic) *N-* , *Tr* and *Ir* are closest with, respectively, *Nageras*

(p. 116, col. 1) and forms of *Nagerus* (pp. 48, 49); the standard Latin has *Nageram* (147, xiv); *AN* has *Nazeres* (l. 671); *Johannes* has *Nadres* (XXXIII, 23); *WPs-T* has *Ager* (p. 25, l. 12) and *Nager* (p. 25, l. 19).

723 'had with him a þousonde and fourtty giauntis': the standard Latin instead describes the giant as having the strength of forty men: *vim quadraginta forcium possidebat* (so *WPs-T* (p. 25, l. 18), *AN* (ll. 675–6) and *Johannes* (XXXIII, 27); *Ir* omits (pp. 48, 49)). Only *Tr* matches the Middle English in the quantity and its use to number reinforcements: *mille et xl* forcium habebat (p. 116, col. 1). Just how the Middle English translator arrived at 'giauntis' is not clear; perhaps he assumed that a giant would surround himself with his own kind, 'of the kynrade of Golias'.

724–5 'þanne this giaunte Ferrakutte came to Charlis': *ut eius adventum Ferracutus agnovit, egressus ab urbe singulare certamen* (149, i–ii; so *Tr* (p. 116, col. 1), *Ir* (pp. 48–49), *WPs-T* (p. 25, ll. 20–21), *AN* (l. 677–8), *Johannes* (XXXIV, 1–2)).

730 'The lenkethe ore þe stature': *statura* (149, vii).

731 'he hadde a longe face': the Middle English here agrees with *Tr* (*facies eius oblonga valde*, p. 116, col. 1) and *Ir* (pp. 50, 51) against *WPs-TANJohannes* in not providing a cubit measure of the face or mentioning the length of the nose (cf. Meredith-Jones 149, viii–ix; *WPs-T*, p. 25, ll. 28–9; *AN* ll. 683–4; *Johannes* XXXIII, 28–9).

738 'alle þese he toke': *IrTrWPs-TANJohannes* agree with the standard Latin that these men were taken up (or deployed) *duo . . . insimul separatim* (149, xv; cf. *Ir* pp. 50, 51; *Tr* p. 116, col.2; *WPs-T*, p. 26, l. 9; *AN* l. 692; *Johannes* XXXIV, 13).

740–3 'Wan Rowlonde saw . . . þat none in alle þe hooste durste go to þis gyaunte, he commyttid him hoely to God with fulle truste in God': matched only in *Tr* (*quod nullus esset ausus contra gigantem accedere, in Domino confidens licet*, p. 116, col. 2) and *Ir* ('Roland . . . saw that fear did not permit any man to go against the giant. He having trust in his own God . . .', pp. 50, 51).

743–6 'he . . . seid þat he wolde fyȝtte with thicke Ferakutte, for, he seid, God was strenger þan man —"And for þe feythe of God and for þe defence þerof, I wolle asaye him"': a boldly pious excursus not directly matched in any of the other versions. However, *Tr* does add to the standard account of Roland's request (q.v. in the note following) that he made it *fide munitus* (p. 116, col. 2); *Tr* says that Roland advanced to battle (rather than made the request) 'being firm in the faith' (pp. 50, 51). *AN*, like the Middle English, frames Roland's request as direct speech, and, while it has some of the Middle English version's piety, has little of its boldness: *Beus uncles, lesset moy aler combatre a ço jeant pur le honur Deux acrestre* (ll. 695–6).

747–8 'by besy instaunce': *Rotolandus . . . vix impetrata* (149, xviii–xiv).

748–9 'Charlis preyd . . . þat He wolde helpe Rowlonde in fyȝtte with þis gyaunt as He halpe Dauyd aȝenste Golie, of whome þis giaunt came': apart from its otherwise unique recapitulation of the giant's lineage (see ll. 719–20), the passage is matched only in *Tr* (*Orabatque Dominus ut tanquam alteri Dauid eum de manibus Goliath gigantis eriperet et constantem contra talem inimicum reddieret*, p. 116, col. 2) and *Ir* (pp. 50, 51).

750–1 'in þe name of God': not matched in *IrTrWPs-TANJohannes*, and consistent with the changes remarked of Roland's appeal to Charles at ll. 740–6.

754–5 'Rowlonde confortide him in God and toke his herte to him and his strenkethe': matched most closely in *Tr* (*Rotholandus resumptsis viribus a Domino confortatus*, p. 116, col. 2) and *Ir* ('Roland receiving relief and help from God,' pp. 50, 51). Cf. Meredith-Jones: *Rotolandus, resumptis viribus suis, in Domino confisus* (151, ii).

759 'it blente': a practical detail left implicit in the standard Latin (151, vi–vii) and *IrTrWPs-TANJohannes*. The other texts, moreover, all agree against *Turpines Story* in the fantastical detail that the giant's horse was cut in half.

763 'he faylyd of Ferakut': *minime . . . lædit* (151, x–xi).

764 'þan was Ferakutte wroþe': an appropriate characterization matched only in *AN* (*Ferragu fu mout irrez*, ll. 711–12) among *IrTrWPs-TANJohannes*. Short (*AN*, p. 85, n. to ll. 711–12) suggests the reading is original to *AN*, but notes that it is 'also echoed in the *Grandes Chroniques:* 'qui trop fu correchiez' (ed. J. Viard (Paris, 1923), III, p. 43)'. It is also echoed in Caxton's *Charles the Grete*: 'Feragus, beyng euyl contente for hys hors that was dede . . .' (p. 222, ll. 27–8); Caxton's source, and that of the *Grandes Chroniques*, is the *Speculum Historiale* of Vincent de Beauvais. Apart from qualifying the claim of originality to *AN*, the correspondence in *Turpines Story* could be further evidence of a considerably more complex manuscript context than that which is represented by the surviving witnesses (for further observations on such evidence, see Shepherd, 'Middle English Pseudo-Turpin Chronicle', 22–5 and the Introduction, pp. xxxviii–xl).

765 'as God wold': not matched in the standard Latin or *IrTrWPs-TANJohannes*.

767 'truly a schrewide fyste and an heuy!': not matched in the other (clearly humourless) versions.

773 'grette': the size of the sword is not mentioned in the standard Latin or *IrTrWPs-TANJohannes*. However, some of the other texts do agree that Roland's counter-arm, a staff, is large (see the next note), and so the Middle English translator would here appear to have dramatized more concretely one of the reasons for the stalemate which Roland and the giant are about to experience.

774 'grete knabbit longe': *retortum et longum* (151, xxii); that the staff is 'grete' or in some way large in a dimension not mentioned by the Latin is also reported in *Ir* ('long, thick', pp. 52, 53), *AN* ('retors e gros e long', l. 721); *Johannes* does not mention size, but in seeing the staff as 'nouel' (XXXV, 12—'knotted'), comes closest to 'knabbit.'

775 'with the whiche he bare of Ferakuttes strokes': the tactical detail is not matched in the standard Latin or *IrTrWPs-TANJohannes.*

776 'but he hurte him noȝt': after this point the Middle English agrees with *Tr* (p. 117, col. 1) and *Ir* (pp. 52, 53) in omitting the equivalent of Meredith-Jones 153, i–iii: *Percussit etiam eum magnis et rotundis lapidibus qui in campo habundanter erant, usque ad meridiem, illo sæpe consenciente, et eum nullo modo lædere potuit. WPs-T* (p. 27, ll. 19–21), *AN* (ll. 723–4) and *Johannes* (XXXV, 13–15) retain the passage.

778 'But wat dude ientille Rowlonde? He toke a stone . . .': *Rotholandus, ut erat iuvenis alacer et nobilis animi tulit lapidem . . .* (153, n. to l. v). *Turpines Story* alone frames the passage as a question, with the effect of emphasizing the extraordinary and exemplary nature of Roland's gesture.

788 'neyþer swerde ne spere ne arow ne stone': there is considerable variation among *IrTrWPs-TANJohannes* in the composition of the list (the Middle English being the most ample). The standard Latin has *aut gladium, aut lapidem, aut baculum* (153, xiv); *Tr* omits *aut baculum* (p. 117, col. 1); *Johannes* generalizes with 'nule arme' (XXXVI, 3); *WPs-T* has *na gwæw, na chledf, na phrenn* ('neither spear nor sword nor staff,' p. 28, ll. 1– 2); *Ir* has *neither sword nor stone nor any other weapon* (pp. 52, 53); *AN*, suggesting some correspondence with *Ir*, has *launce ne espeye ne nule autre arme* (l. 737).

792–4 'the Spayennyshe speche, þe whiche þe giaunte went þat Rowlond vndurstode noȝt—but Roulonde vnderstode riȝt wele': *lingua yspanica quam Rotolandus satis intelligebat* (153, xv–xvi). Like the standard Latin, *IrTrWPs-TANJohannes* leave the giant's fatal assumption implicit. If the Middle English explication possesses any sophistication it surely lies in the sardonic cadence achieved in the *vndurstode noȝt . . . vnderstode riȝt wele* antistrophe. Cf. an earlier apparently unique passage in *Turpines Story* also declaring an enthusiasm for translation skills, ll. 551–2. See also the Introduction, p. xlii– xliii.

799 'and I am Roulonde': the repetition of this information from just two sentences before seems awkward and probably represents the translator's misunderstanding of syntax in the Latin (153, xx–xxi), *Francorum genere* *oriundus, inquit Rotolandus, sum* (i.e., it is as if the translator sees the final comma coming after *inquit*).

810 'ne "holy goste"': not matched in the standard Latin or *IrTrWPs-TANJohannes*.

813 'þere þou erriste': *in fide claudicas* (155, x).

815 'for þe Fadur is God, and þese .iij. parsonys bethe . . .': after 'God' the Middle English omits the equivalent of *filius est, spiritus sanctus est* (155, xi–xii); the omission is not matched in *IrTrWPs-TANJohannes* and disturbs the parallelism available in the next sentence.

819–20 'Here Roulande bringith ensaumple how there may be þre Persones and oon God': the manuscript designates this as *Capitulum xxj*, but, as the *Titulus* and the general tradition of chapter division in the *Pseudo-Turpin* indicates, this is not in content a separate chapter. The break might be æsthetic, dividing what is the longest chapter in the *Ps-T* into two roughly equal parts, and doing so at a moment of apostatic tension. This is, however, the only 'chapter' within the text to have a complete—if erroneous—decorated initial, and the chapter begins a new gathering; the implication is that the chapter break was inserted by the producers of the manuscript and its title devised by the rubricator. For the location of other complete initials, see the Introduction, pp. xvii–xviii. Hereafter, chapter numbers are corrected in the edition to match those given in the *Titulus*.

823 'coeternalle and coequale': *coæternæ . . . et coequales* (155, xvii).

825 'In þese parsonys is parsonel propurtté': *In personis est proprietas* (155, xviii). The sense of 'parsonel propurtté' would seem to be that of an individual distinctive quality or attribute; cf. MED 'Personalle' *adj.* 1.(a), 'pertaining to a person as an individual, individual, private' and 'Proprete' *n.* 4b. 'a quality, characteristic, an attribute; distinctive quality . . . (a) of a person, soul, God, angel, etc.'.
    '[in] þe godhede is vnité': *in essencia unitas* (155, xviii–xix).

826 'in þe maiesté is worshippid equalité': i.e., equality is worshipped in the majesty [of the godhead]; *in magestate adoratur æqualitas* (155, xix).

827 'oon in þree and þree in oone': *Trinum Deum et unum* (155, xix–xx).

829 'in creaturis': *per humanas creaturas* (155, xxii–xxiii). The more general translation probably represents the recognition that not all of Roland's analogies will be with man-made objects. Cf. *Ir*: 'in things and in human creatures' (pp. 56, 57).

831 'but oone in þe harpe ore in harpinge': *et una cithara est* (155, xxiv).

831–2 'So in God is Fadur, Sonne, and Holy Goste—in oo God': a rather anæmic translation of *sic in Deo tria sunt, pater et filius et spiritus sanctus, et unus est Deus* (155, xxiv–xxv).

836 '*candor, splendor,* and *calor*—shynynge, lemynge, and hetinge': *candor, splendor et calor* (157, ii). If 'calor' is to be distinguished from 'splendor' in Latin or English, it is in the signification in 'candor' of the whiteness or purity of the light emitted. Rather than drawing this distinction out in the parenthetical information, the translator has provided in 'shynynge' and 'lemynge' near-synonyms. Cf. the similar distinctions drawn from this common analogy in the *Ludus Coventriæ* play of Christ and the Doctors: 'In þe sunne consydyr ȝe thyngys thre / The splendure þe hete and þe lyght / as o thre partys but oo sunne be / Ryght so thre personys be oo god of myght' (*The N-Town Play: Cotton MS Vespasian D.8*, ed. Stephen Spector, 2 vols, EETS ss 11 (1991), vol. 1, p. 200, ll. 81–4; on the possible source of the analogy in Augustine, *de Trinitate*, see vol. 2, 482, n. to 21/81–4). Other features of the passage such as its debate format and discussion of the nature of the Virgin Birth present a broad parallel to the Roland-Ferracutus debate, but there is insufficient correspondence of detail to argue that the *Pseudo-Turpin* is a certain source.

837–8 'in a welle buthe þree þinggis—and yut is þe welle but oo thynge': the standard Latin goes on to name the three things, *medius, scilicet, brachia et circulis* (157, iii–iv); like *Turpines Story*, the Irish texts also possess the lacuna: *Tr* has *Et in rota plaustri tria sunt—et tamen vna rota est* (p. 117, col. 2); cf. *Ir*, pp. 56, 57). *WPs-TANJohannes* are complete. For further discussion of the implications of this lacuna, see Shepherd, 'Middle English *Pseudo-Turpin Chronicle*', 23–4.

846 'in his eternité': *ineffabiliter* (157, xii).

848 'how was he, þat God vnmade, imade man?': . . . *qualiter homo effectus est qui Deus erat* . . . (157, xiv). Cf. OED s.v. 'Unmade', *ppl.a.* 2.: '. . . uncreated but existent. c. 1350, *Athanasian Creed in MS Bodl. 425*, fol. 69ᵛ, *Bot on unmade and on mikel is he*'.

851 'his oune godly power': *spiramine sacro suo* (157, xvii). Cf. *Ir* with its at once more literal and more elaborate *consecrating breath of the Holy Spirit* (pp. 56–9).

852–3 'withoute feleship or werke of man': *sine humano semine* (157, xviii).

855–6 'gete of God þe fadur withoute man': *de Deo patre nascitur sine matre* (157, xxii); *Ir* agrees most closely with the Middle English reading: *begotten of God the Father without his having any human father* (pp. 58, 59). For *sine matre, Tr* has *sine homine matre* (p. 117, col. 2), perhaps pointing to the origin of the readings in *Turpines Story* and *Ir*, where *matre* has possibly been understood to signify the general sense of 'source'.

'gete and conceyuyde': *nascitur* (157, xxii).

857 'Such getinge and suche conceyuynge': *Talis enim* (157, xxiii).

860–2 'in a bene a gurgulione, a worme in many an herbe, fruȝtte, and trees

. . . and also many fysshis in þe see, and beis': the Middle English list of creatures is shorter than that of the standard Latin, which adds vultures and serpents, 157, xxv–xxvi. The Middle English list corresponds most closely to that found in *Tr*: . . . *fabe gurgulionem et arbori facit gignere vermes et multos pisces et apes . . .* (p. 118, col. 1; the list in *Ir* is practically the same, pp. 58, 59; *WPs-T* (p. 30, ll. 27–8) and *Johannes* (XXXVIII, 6–8) have different combinations; *AN* omits).

'or female': not matched in the other versions; possibly the result of a misreading of *sine masculino semine* (157, xxvi–xxvii) as *sine masculino femina*.

866 'withoute feleship of man': *sine masculino concubitu* (159, i; for *masculino*, *Tr* has *humano*, p. 118, col. 1; *Tr* has *without the seed of anyone else*, pp. 58, 59).

869 'þou graunttiste': *Bene . . . dixisti* (159, v–vi).

882–3 'reseyue after here deseruynge gode or euyll: peyne for synne and ioye for gode dedis': *accepturi meritorum suorum stipendia, prout gessit unusquisque sive bonum sive malum* (159, xvii–xix).

885 'a wete corne iburiede in þe erthe': though scientifically more accurate, the Middle English translation is not as apposite in context as the Latin, *granum frumenti mortuum in terra ac putrefactum* (159, xx–xxi).

887 'fleshe and body and soule': *carne et spiritu* (159, xxii).

887–8 'þe laste dredefulle day of dome': the Latin is less 'dreadful', *die novissimo* (159, xxii–xxiii). Cf. Malory, *Morte Darthur*: 'nevermore shall one se another off you before the dredefull day of doome' (p. 1013, l. 30).

892 'For why?': not matched in the standard Latin or *IrTrWPs-TANJo-hannes*.

895 'Criste þe fadurs Sonne of heuene': *ipse* (161, i); *Tr* adds *filius* (p. 118, coll. 1–2).

897 '. . . fro dethe to lyue': The standard Latin goes on: *et a morte nullatenus teneri potuit, ante cuius conspectum mors ipsa fugit, ad cuius vocem mortuorum phalans resurrexit* (161, ii–iv). *Tr* is more truncated than this but is still additive in comparison to the Middle English: *multi Magister ipse a mortuis potuit refugere* (p. 118, col. 2). *Ir* is conflated and garbled at this point: '. . . *as Elijah and Elisha easily awoke many dead, it was easier than that for God to waken his own son from the dead.' Said Feracutus, 'I well see . . .* (pp. 60, 61). *Johannes* (XXXIX, 14–16) and *WPs-T* (p. 32, ll. 4–8) are consistent with the standard Latin; *AN* at this point is in the midst of 'the most extensive interpolation introduced by William [de Briane] into his text' (p. 86, n. to ll. 794ff.).

899 'I can noȝt se it ne belyue it': *prorsus ignoro* (161, vi).

902–6 Between the examples of the millwheel and climbing a hill, the standard Latin has the example of a bird: *Avis volans in ære quantum descendit tantum ascendit* (161, xi–xii). As with the Middle English, that example is wanting in *AN* (ll. 817–19), *Johannes* (XL, 5–8), *Tr* (p. 118, col. 2) and *Ir* (pp. 60, 61); *WPs-T*, however, retains the example (p. 32, ll. 16–17).

906–7 'and ascende into þe Souþe': not matched in the standard Latin or *IrTrWPs-TANJohannes*.

908 'in suche maner wyse þe Sonne of God ascendiþe': *Unde ergo filius Dei venit, ibi rediit* (161, xv).

912–13 'in loude and presyinge': *laus et decus in ævum* (161, xix).

915–16 'grete knabbide staffe' is not matched in the Latin or *IrTrWPs-TANJohannes* (cf. Meredith-Jones 161, xx–xxi); and 'grete gresly swerde' is matched only with *spata* (161, xxi; so *IrTrWPs-TANJohannes*). Cf. the notes to ll. 773–5, where the same weapons are also more dramatically rendered.

917 'avoydude þat stroke': *saltavit ad lævam* (161, xxii).

919–20 'þe gode Roulonde': *Rotolandus* (161, xxv). On other similar additions, see the Introduction, p. xli.

920–1 'for he was so moche and so heuey': a practical detail left implicit in the standard Latin and *IrTrWPs-TANJohannes*.

921–2 'To god helpe he with his soule cried, to Criste Ihesu Mari Sonne, preyinge hem boþe': *coepit invocare in auxilium beatæ Mariæ virginis filium* (163, i–ii; so *IrTrWPs-TANJohannes*).

924 'turned him': i.e., Roland turned himself (*erexit se*; 163, ii).
'his swerde': i.e., the giant's sword (*mucronem eius*; 163, iv).

925 'But wat!': not matched in the standard Latin or *IrTrWPs-TANJohannes*.

929 'worthy Roulonde': *Rotolandus* (163, ix). Cf. the n. to ll. 919–20.

929–30 'came home to Kynge Charlis his vnkulle hole and sounde, withoute hurtte ore wounde': *vero suis incolumis redierat* (163, ix; so *IrTrWPs-TANJohannes*). The additional detail in *Turpines Story* is no doubt intended to accommodate the sentiments elaborated earlier in the account of Charles's concern over the welfare of his nephew (see ll. 740–51 and notes thereto).

932 'with grete crye and power': *ingenti impetu* (163, xi).

933 'þe townne [and] castelle': the manuscript reads 'þe townne of Castelle' (capitalization reflects that of the manuscript). The Latin reads *urbs et castrum* (163, xii). The seeming reference to Castille is more likely to be the error of a copyist than a translator.
'iyeldude': *capitur* (163, xii).

933–4 'Charlis prisoneris þat Ferakutte toke were delyuered': a personalizing revision of *pugnatores a carcere eripiuntur* (163, xiii).

937 'Kynge Charlis': *imperatori nostro* (163, xiv); so *AN* (*nostre empereres* (l. 848)), but the other texts all agree with the Middle English in omitting the possessive adjective (*Tr*, p. 119, col. 1; *Ir*, pp. 62, 63; *Johannes*, XLII, 1; *WPs-T*, p. 33, ll. 21–2). Several other such instances appear in this chapter and are especially, perhaps not surprisingly, consistent among the non-Francophone texts: see ll. 944, 946, 956–8, 959–60, 964 and notes thereto.

939–40 'þe kynges flew before fro þe bataile of Pampilioun': after the reminder that the two Saracen kings were at Pamplona, the standard Latin (163, xvii–xix), *AN* (ll. 851–3), and *Johannes* (XLII, 5–6) all add the names of between five and seven towns from which Saracen reinforcements presented themselves; *WPs-T* mentions *seith dinas* (p. 33, l. 25) but does not name them. *Turpines Story* agrees in its complete omission with *Tr* (p. 119, col. 1) and *Ir* (pp. 62, 63).

944 'þe Cristen men': *nostri* (165, iv); again *AN* retains the possessive form (*le nostre* (l. 856), as does *Johannes*, where it had not before (XLII, 10); *Tr* (p. 119, col. 1), *Ir* (pp. 62, 63), and *WPs-T* (p. 34, l. 4) agree with the Middle English in omitting the possessive form. Cf. the n. to l. 937.

946 'þe forewarde': *prima turma militum nostrorum* (165, viii–ix); again *AN* retains the plural possessive form (*nos gens* (l. 862)); *Johannes* omits the entire line (XLII, 13); again, *Tr* (*prima turma militum Christianorum*, p. 119, col. 1), *Ir* ('his people', pp. 64, 65) and *WPs-T* (p. 34, l. 13) agree with the Middle English in omitting the plural form. Cf. the n. to l. 937.

950–1 'But here may ye lerne a shrewde wyle of werre of þe Sarzyns, for thus þey hade disposide here forewarde': a piece of engaged analysis not matched in the standard Latin or *IrTrWPs-TANJohannes* (and, in the alliterative collocation 'wyle of werre,' the basis of a kind of analytical leitmotif emerges; see also ll. 962, 970–1 and notes thereto). The subsequent account of the appearance and effect of the Saracen strategy is also treated with an engagement not matched in the source; see the notes to ll. 955–6, 956–8, and 961–3. A similar addition to the source occurs in the alliterative *Siege of Jerusalem* (c. 1390–1400), where Vespasian sees through 'a wonder wyle' conceived by Josephus to trick the Romans into believing that the besieged Jews had plenty of water: 'No burne abasched be, þoȝ þey þis bost make: / Hit beþ bot wyles of werr for water hem fayleþ' (*The Siege of Jerusalem*, ed. Ralph Hanna and David Lawton, EETS 320 (2003), lines 786, 795–6). Perhaps the *Turpines Story* translator had read this text.

953 'a longe berdde, iharniyde like þe deuyllis hede': *larvas barbartas et cornutas dæmonibus consimiles* (165, xi, n.).

954 'a tympane ore a cymballe': *timpana* (165, xii).

955–6 'þey cried and smote theyere cymbalis and made a grete horible noyse': *manibus fortiter percuciebant* (165, xii–xiii).

956–8 'Wen þe horse of Charlis hooste harde þat horible noyse and saw3e þat cursyd sy3tte of þe visours . . .': *Quorum voces et sonitus equi Christianorum militum ut audierunt et terribiles similitudines ut viderunt . . .* (*Tr*, p. 119, col. 1; cf. Meredith-Jones 165, xiii–xiv). Apart from its emotional additions to the Latin, the Middle English again is consistent with *Tr* in omitting a second-person possessive reference to the Christian forces (*nostrorum militum*, 165, xiii; so *Ir*, pp. 64, 65); again *AN* (l. 867), *Johannes* (XLIII, 4), and *WPs-T* (p. 34, l. 13) follow the standard Latin. Cf. the n. to l. 937.

959–60 'þe secunde warde and þe þred warde': *aliæ duæ turmæ* (165, xvii).

'Charlis ooste': *nostrorum exercituum* (165, xvii–xviii); again *Johannes* (XLIII, 8) retains the second-person possessive form, though *AN* omits any mention of the warriors at this point (l. 869); again, *Tr* (p. 119, col. 1), *Ir* (pp. 64, 65) and *WPs-T* (p. 34, l. 17) agree with *Turpines Story* in omitting the second-person possessive. Cf. the n. to l. 937.

961–3 'Wan Charlis saw3 þis, he merueylide þerof whye his peple flew3e; but wen he herde of þat wyly turne of werre, he merueylid no3t': a lively rendering of the standard *C*-family addition, *Quo viso Karolus super modum miratus est donec cognovit quare ita fieret* (165, xix, n.); note the echo of 'wyle of werre' above, ll. 950–1.

'fayer and softe': *lento gradu* (165, xix).

964 'þe Cristen men': again the Middle English agrees with *Tr* (p. 119, col. 2), *Ir* (pp. 64, 65) and *WPs-T* (p. 34, l. 22), against the possessive forms of the standard Latin (*nos*, 165, xx) and *AN* (*nous*, l. 871); *Johannes* has only *les* (XLIII, 12). Cf. the n. to l. 937.

'Cordube': *urbe prefata* (*Tr*, p. 119, col. 2); the standard Latin has only *urbe* (165, xxi).

964–5 'to an hylle . . . were Charlis hooste lay': none of the other versions allow the possibility that Charles had an emplacement for a second army. However, where the standard Latin has *insecuti sunt nos, quosque ad quendam montem pervenimus* (165, xx), *Tr* has *persequti sunt Christianos quosque ad quidam montem exercitus Karoli pervenivit* (p. 119, col. 2) allowing for the (mis)inference that Charles had indeed placed a second army by the mount.

966 'for þere Charlis hade py3tte his tentes to rest alle ny3t': all the other versions agree with the Latin that the reason the Saracens turn back is that Charles's forces stand their ground ready to fight (165, xxii); only after the Saracens turn do the Christians put up their tents (165, xxii—167, i). The evident non-sequitur of the Middle English can be explained by the misreading of the Latin source suggested in the previous note.

969 'curside vysours': *larvas nefandorum* (167, iv).

970 'horible noyse and crye': *timpanorum sonitus* (167, vi); but cf. *Ir*, 'the dreadful noises of their tabors' (pp. 64–66, 65) and *WPs-T*, *y leisseu uffernawl* (p. 35, l. 1).

970–1 'Here was o wyle of werre ayenste here wyle!': *Ars mirabilis!* (167, vi, n.) Clearly the Middle English translator has departed from the model of the Latin to bring to a satisfactorily wry conclusion the sequence of 'wyle . . . of werre' leitmotifs he has introduced above (see ll. 950–1, 962 and notes thereto).

972 'frely and fouȝtte withoute eny fere': *confidenter as pugnam parvipendentes sonitus subdolos impiorum* (167, viii–ix).

973 'manly': *constanter* (167, ix).

974–8 The ultimate source of the Saracen battle cart probably lies in accounts, such as those found in the *Carmen de Frederico I* or Otto Morena's *De Rebus Laudensibus*, of the *carroccio* employed by the Milanese at the battle of Carcano against Frederick Barbarossa, 9 August, 1160. See Smyser, *The Pseudo-Turpin*, p. 35, n. 1.

978–9 'but wat dude he?': not matched in the standard Latin or *IrTrWPs-TANJohannes*. After the notice of Charles's recognition of the Saracen strategy, the Middle English agrees with *Ir* (pp. 66, 67), *Tr* (p. 119, col. 2), and *WPs-T* (p. 35, ll. 12–13) in omitting a description of Charles in his armour (cf. Meredith-Jones 167, xvi–xvii).

'tristinge and callinge after þe helpe of God': the reading is closer to that of *Tr*, *divina coroboratus virtute* (p. 119, col. 2; so *Ir*, pp. 66, 67), than that of the standard Latin *divina obumbratus virtute* (167, xvii).

983 'þey þat were lefte alyue': a remarkable statement of the obvious not matched in the other versions. Perhaps the intended sense is emphatic, suggesting those *few* who were left alive.

983–4 'þey made a grete crie': *Ilico facto utrorumque exercituum magno clamoreet impetu* (167, xxi–xxii).

988–9 'hilde of him as for chehoffe lorde': *de illo teneret* (169, iv). The English diction is essentially legal, a chief lord being 'the immediate lord of the fee, to whom the servants were directly and personally responsible' (John A. Alford, *Piers Plowman: A Glossary of Legal Diction* (Cambridge, 1988), p. 28).

994 'Pictis': *Pictavis* (169, x), i.e., Poitevins, though it is possible that the English translator understood the British Picts.

995 'Almeyns': *Theutonicis* (169, x); cf. *Ir: hAilmainechaibh* (p. 66).

995–7 'þe londe of Burdugalie to þe Danys; and þe Flemyngis þe londe of Galice for þe Frenshemen wold not inhabitte þat londe': *terram*

Portugallorum Dacis et Flandris dedit. Terram Galleciæ Franci inhabitare noluerunt (169, xi–xii). For *noluerunt*, *Tr* has *voluerunt* (p. 120, col. 1) and *Ir* agrees, with '[the Franks] thought it delightful' (pp. 68, 69), clearly succumbing to a misreading of *v* for *n* either in the copying of the Latin exemplar or in its translation.

1000–1 'How þat Charlis wente to Seinte Iames and made Compostilla a see': the standard Latin title is *De concilio Karoli* (169, heading to chapter XIX) to which *Tr* adds *et qualiter profectus est ad Sanctum Iacobum* (p. 120, col. 1); the title as given in *Tr* corresponds exactly to that given in the Middle English *Titulus*, ll. 50–1.

1005 'sherished hem and yaffe hem': *edificavit* (169, xvii).

1005–6 'were peruertide renegatis': *ad perfidiam Sarracenorum revertebantur* (169, xviii).

1008 'in citteis and cuntrayes': *per civitates* (169, xix).
'þey': *præsules et principes et reges Christiani* (169, xxi–xxii).

1009–11 'Sure': *Tr* has *Syriam* (p. 120, col. 1; cf. Meredith-Jones: *Yriam*, 171, ii—this is *Iria Flavia*, modern El Padrón).
'In Sure . . . to Compostle.' The translator or copyist has failed to preserve the reason for the decision about 'Sure': *pro urbe non reputavit* (171, ii–iii).

1017 'chargis': *servitute* (171, x).

1022–3 'here stauys and þeyere mytrus': *virgæ episcopales* (171, xiv).

1024–5 'by eny heresy ore erroure': *peccatis populorum exigentibus* (171, xvi).
'began to be hurte ore fayle': *defecerint* (171, xvii).

1031–2 'þe sees of Cristis herthely kynddomys': *procul dubio sedes* (171, xxiii).

1036–8 'Sey þou . . . þi kyngdome': like *Turpines Story*, *AN* (ll. 932–5) here alludes to Matt. 20:21. However, the standard Latin (171, xxv—173, i), *Tr* (p. 120, col. 2), *Ir* (pp. 70, 71), *WPs-T* (p. 37, ll. 12–14), and *Johannes* (XLVIII, 3–4) all allude to Mark 10:35–7. The differences could represent the independent substitutions of discriminating translators or copyists; cf. Walpole's note to the *Johannes* reference cited above (*Johannes*, p. 203), and Ian Short, 'A Note on the *Pseudo-Turpin* Translations of Nicolas de Senlis and William de Briane,' *Zeitschrift für romanische Philologie* 86 (1970), 525–32, 526.

1039 'Ephesum' [as opposed to the translation's usual 'Ephes(e)us']: *Ephesianam* (173, iv).

1040 'Criste [ordeynyd] .iij. apostolus for his principalle counceleris': *tres apostolos, Petrum videlicet, et Iacobum et Iohannem, præ omnibus apostolis Dominus instituit* (173, iv–vi). 'Ordeyned' is conjectured solely on the implied parallelism with the same word in the latter part of the sentence; the Latin, however, has *instituit . . . constituit* (173, vi–viii). Elsewhere in this chapter, the translator's response to forms of *instituere* is varied: see, e.g., 'ordeyned' (l. 967; cf. Meredith-Jones 169, xxi); 'put' (l. 1010 cf. 171, ii); and 'be stabylly ikeptte' (l. 1030; cf. 171, xxi). Cf. the n. to l. 1093.

1041 'shewyde his misterijs and priuiteis': *secreta ceteris plenius, ut in evangeliis patet* (173, vi–vii).

1042 '. . . aboue alle oþer sees': after this point the Middle English agrees with *Tr* (p. 120, col. 2), *Ir* (pp. 70, 71), and *AN* (l. 940) in omitting the following elaboration found in the standard Latin: *Et merito hæ sedes dicuntur principales, quia sicut hi tres apostoli dignitatis gratia ceteros præcesserunt apostolos, sic loca illa sacrosancta in quibus prædicaverunt, et sepulti fuere, dignitatis excellentia omnes totius orbis sedes iure præcedere debent* (173, viii–xii; so *WPs-T*, p. 37, ll. 17–23). *Johannes* (XLVIII, 10–11) offers a brief summary of the elaboration but does not omit it wholesale.

1046–50 'for riȝt as . . . by many miraculis': the Middle English here follows *Tr*, which offers a truncated version of Meredith-Jones 173, xvi–xxi: *quia beatus Iacobus qui inter ceteros apostolos precipua dignitate maior post Petrus extitit et tanta predicacione ecclesiam munivit et sepultura sua sacratissima consecravit et miraculis adhuc choruscare non cessat* (p. 120, col. 2; so *Ir*, pp. 70–1). *Johannes* (XLVIII, 14–17) offers what seems to be a further reduced version of this truncated account; *AN* (ll. 943–5) is even more truncated (perhaps independently so) and alters the order of precedence to Peter, John, then James. *WPs-T* (p. 37 ll. 28–31—p. 38, ll. 1–7) is consistent with the standard Latin.

1050–4 The concluding sentence follows *Tr*, which again offers a truncated version of the standard Latin (173, xxi–xxvii): *Tercia vero sedes rite Ephesus dicitur, quia beatus Iohannes evangelista in ea evangelium suum, scilicet In principio erat verbum, eructavit et concilia et miraculis et propria sepultra consecravit* (so *Ir*, pp. 70–3; *AN*, ll. 942–45; *Johannes*, XLVIII, 18–20). *WPs-T* follows the standard Latin (p. 38, ll. 6-12). Also like *Tr*, *Ir*, and *AN*, *Turpines Story* omits the final two sentences of the chapter as found in the standard Latin (173, xxvii—175, vi) which describe the definitive and just nature of judgements made in the three sees, and conclude that through the power of God and Saint James, with the aid of Charles, Spain has since remained Christian. In this instance, *WPs-T* (p. 38, ll. 12–21) and *Johannes* (XLVIII, 20-2) are consistent with the standard Latin.

1055 'The discripcion of King Charles persone': the title generally agrees with that of *Tr*: *De stata et condicionibus Karoli* (p. 120, col. 2; cf. the standard Latin, *De persona et fortitudine Karoli* (175, heading to chapter XX)). The title of this chapter as recorded in the *Titulus* (ll. 52–3) is, however, consistent with the standard Latin title. The contents of the chapter are loosely based on Einhard, Book III, §22 (for the relevant passage in translation, see Einhard, *The Life of Charlemagne*, in *Two Lives of Charlemagne*, ed. and trans. by Lewis Thorpe (London, 1969), pp. 76–7).

1058 'a fulle fayer lokynge': *visu efferus* (175, viii); cf. *Ir*, 'he was pleasant to look at' (pp. 72, 73).

1060 'and beste shappid': not matched in the standard Latin or *IrTrWPs-TANJohannes*.

1060–2 'and in alle . . . kny3ttehode and chyualrye': the syntax follows that of the Latin, *omnibus artubus fortissimus, certamine doctissimus, miles acerrimus* (175, xi–xii).

1062–4 'His foredde . . . a spanne longe.' *Turpines Story* agrees with *Tr* (p. 120, col. 2) and *Ir* (pp. 72, 73) in omitting the measurements of Charles's beard and nose (*et barba unum [palmum], et nasus circiter dimidium*, 175, xiii–xiv); *AN* (l. 954) *Johannes* (XLIX,10–11), and *WPs-T* (p. 39, ll. 1–3) all retain these measurements. Uniquely, *Tr* also omits the initial measurement of Charles's face.

'shynnynge eyen like a lyone ore a carebokulle': *similes occulis leonis scintillantes ut carbunculus* (175, xv–xvi).

'a spanne': the Middle English agrees exclusively with *Ir* (pp. 72, 73) in measuring a whole palm rather than a half (*dimidium palmum*, 175, xi).

1065–6 'gyrdulle þat gyrdude': *Cingulum . . . cingebatur* (175, xix–xx).

'to þe gyrdinge-stede': *præter illud quod dependebat* (175, xx—177, i).

1067–8 'a quarter of a shepe, ore .ij. hennus, a gose, a pestelle of porke': the list of animals is shorter than in the standard Latin and *IrTrWPs-TANJohannes*, and gives the impression of only two (herculean) dietary alternatives: the quarter of a sheep or the other animals altogether. *Ir* (pp. 72, 73) agrees with *Tr*'s *arietis . . . aut galinas . . . aut anserem . . . aut spatulam porincam . . . aut pavonem . . . aut leporem* (p. 121, col. 1; the list omits only *grugam* from that of the standard Latin (177, iii)). *AN* (ll. 960–61), *Johannes* (XLIX, 18–21) and *WPs-T* (p. 39, ll. 9–12) all have complete lists.

'He dranke wynne lymfatted soburly': *modicum vinum aqua limphatum sobrie bibebat* (*Tr*, p. 121, col. 1; the standard Latin has *et aquam limphatum* (177, iv, n.))

1070 'with his swerde þat was callide Caudiosa': the detail is matched only in *Johannes* (XLIX, 27), but the addition is more likely to be a recollection of the sword's name, given two chapters earlier (l. 982), than a reflection of the translator's source.

1071–6 'Furþermore . . . . Also . . . . Furþermore . . . . Also . . . .': the seemingly formalized adverb sequence is echoed uniquely in *Tr*, which has *Item . . . . Item . . . . Item . . . . Verum* (p.121, col. 2; cf. Meredith-Jones, 177, viii–xii).

1073 The double occurrence of 'ly3ttely' in the manuscript (see apparatus), though easily attributable to eyeskip, could also reflect the copying of both the original literal translation of *velociter elevabat* (177, x) and its more colloquial correction in the translator's draft. The usual practice in the Middle English text is to place the verb before the adverb.

1074 'to his brest': *ad caput* (177, x).

1074-5 'Furþermore, he was . . . domus and iugementtis': a reading usually omitted in *C*-family texts but common to *Tr, Ir,* and *WPs-T*; see Shepherd, 'Middle English *Pseudo-Turpin Chronicle*', pp. 22-3.

1076 'dyscrete in spechis': the standard Latin has *locutionibus luculentus* (177, xi; so *Ir* (pp. 72, 73)); *AN* (l. 968) and *Johannes* (XLIX, 30) omit, but the Middle English, like *WPs-T* (p. 39, l. 19), agrees with *Tr* (p. 121, col. 1): *locuconibus locupletus.*

1079-80 'And wan he . . . nakyde and idraw3e': *Ante eius tribunal spata nuda, more imperiali, ferebatur* (177, xv-xvi).

1083 '.xl. þe secunde parte and .xl. þe þred parte of þe ny3t': *IrTrWPs-TANJohannes,* like the standard Latin, place these details at the end of the account of Charles's sleeping arrangements (cf. Meredith-Jones 177, xxii-xxiv).

1088-9 'in exile at Tolowse': *in puericia exulatum . . . in palacio Toleti* (179, ii-iii; the Middle English translator appears to mistake Toledo for Toulouse). On the background of this allusion to Chalemagne's *Enfances* see the n. to l. 550.

'Galafrius Almiraldis': *Galaffrus, admirandus Toletæ* (179, i-ii; *Tr* has *Galfridus admiraldus toleti* (p. 121, col. 1); *Ir* has 'Galfridus Admiraldus, son of Toletus' (pp. 74, 75)). Below, l. 1091, the spelling changes to *Galafri* in agreement with the ablative of the Latin, *Galafri inimicum* (179, v).

1091 'Barmatum': the standard Latin has *Braimantum* (179, iv), but *Tr* matches, *Barmatum* (p. 121, col. 1); *Ir* has *Barmatus* (p. 74).

1092 'londdis, prouyns, citteis, and townnus': *diversas terras et urbes* (179, vi; *Tr* omits *diversas* (p. 121, col. 1)).

1093 '[he ordeyned]': *instituit* (179, viii). The choice of 'ordeyned' is conjectural, as the translator's response elsewhere to *instituit* in an ecclesiastical context is varied; perhaps, indeed, the translator found the Latin term problematic, as this is the second instance in the Middle English where a lacuna stands where the appropriate verb should be: see the n. to l. 1040.

1096 'now': matched only in *Tr* by *ad presens* (p. 121, col. 2; cf. Meredith-Jones, 179, xii).

1097 'in þis matere of cronykullynge': a naming of the task at hand not matched in the standard Latin or *IrTrWPs-TANJohannes* (cf. Meredith-Jones, 179, xii).

1101 'The treson of Ganalon and þe batail of Rounsivale': a shortened version of the chapter heading found in *Tr* (itself virtually the same as the heading in Meredith-Jones's A.6. text, p. 178): *De prodicione Ganaloni et de bello Runcieuallis et de passione pugnatorum forcium Karoli* (p. 121, col. 2); the extended title of the standard Latin is, however, matched in the Middle English *Titulus* (ll. 54–6). From this point on, *WPs-T* turns to a version of the *Chanson de Roland* for its account of Roncevaux; the standard edition is *Cân Rolant: The Medieval Welsh Version of the Song of Roland*, ed. Annalee C. Rejhon (Los Angeles, 1984).

1110 'but it was more [for] drede þan for loue': *sed in caritate ficta* (179, xxii). Cf. Malory, *Morte Darthur*: 'what for drede and for love, they helde their pece' (p. 56, l. 1).

1115 'þis false man': a touch of vituperative anticipation not matched in the standard Latin or *IrTrWPs-TANJohannes*.

1117 'þe myȝttieste': another slice of anticipation not matched in the other versions (see previous note).

1122 'þey toke þe wynne': *vinum solummodo . . . acceperunt, mulieres vero nullatenus* (181, xii–xiii).

1123 'to þeyer grete arme': the reading is approached only in *Tr* (*in dampnum suum* (p. 122, col. 1)) and *Ir* ('to the damage of their own souls,' pp. 78, 79); however, the Middle English remains less damning.

1124 'hauyn': probably a mistranslation of *portus* (181, xv); see n. to l. 512.

1127 'Roulonde and Olyuere': perhaps out of familiarity with these heroes as they appear in romances and *chansons de geste*, the Middle English translator removes the formalities of the Latin, *Rotolando nepoti suo, Cenomannensi et Blaviensi comiti, et Olivero Gebennensi comiti* (181, xvi–xvii). The pairing of these names without qualification was traditional and possibly proverbial; see the Introduction, p. xli, n. 95. Other examples occur at ll. 1133, 1140, and 1141.

1129–31 'þe nyȝt after þis many of þe hooste were dronke of þat wynne and toke many of þucke women and so were dede': *quia præcedentibus noctibus vino sarracenico ebrii quidam cum mulieribus paganis et christianis etiam feminis quas secum multi de Gallia adduxerant, fornicati sunt, mortem incurrerunt* (181, xxi–xxiv). For a discussion of the implications of the differences in this passage between *Turpines Story*, the standard Latin, and *IrTrWPs-TANJohannes*—differences which tend to diminish the moral outrage of the passage—see Shepherd, 'Middle English *Pseudo-Turpin Chronicle*', pp. 27–8; see also the Introduction, pp. xl–xli. An explanation of the inverted translation of *præcedentibus* to *after* is difficult; by placing the fatal debauchery after the separation of Charles's forces, the translator perhaps meant to leave open the possibility that only one of the branches of the army sinned—presumably that branch which did not include the finest and, in literary terms, most famous warriors, who did not partake of the women (cf. the translation's alterations as described in the previous note and the notes to ll. 1123 and 1153).

1133 'and [with] þicke few Rowlonde and Olyuere . . .': *et præfati* . . . (181, xxvi)). Cf. the n. to l. 1127.

1134–6 'by þe councelle of Ganalioun . . . by Ganoliones counselle and ordinaunce': the Latin matches only the final phrase, with *ubi consilio Ganaloni* (183, i). The repetition, if not copied in error, is perhaps meant to convey with vehemence the thoroughness of Ganalon's perfidy.

1135 'wele-fyȝtinge men': *Sarracenorum* (181, xxvii). Cf. the n. to l. 351.

1140 'Roulonde and Olyuere': *nostros* (183, iv–v). Cf. the n. to l. 1127.

1141–2 'oure feliship, Roulonde and Olyuere with here company': *nostri* (183, v). Cf. the n. to l. 1127.

1146–49 'But sum were sley with speris . . . and sume were honge on trees': the list follows that of the Latin but omits *alii securibus absciduntur* (183, xi) and *alii perticis verberando perimuntur* (183, xii).

1150–1 The inclusion of Ganalon and Turpin in this list is not as inept as it may seem; the sense is that all of the worthiest warriors in the world were now dead, except those listed.

'Baldwynne . . . . Baldwynus': the variation in inflection corresponds to that of the Latin, *Balduinum* . . . . *Balduinus* (183, xv–xvi).

1152–3 'Wen þis bataile was doo': the standard Latin has only *Tunc* (183, xvii), but *Tr* has *Post tantam victoriam* (p. 122, col. 2; so *Ir*, pp. 80, 81); the Middle English translator would seem to have had before him the same reading attested by the Irish texts, but decided to soften its estimation of the Saracens' action.

1153 'went abacke to here loggynge': evidently a mistranslation of *una leuga retro redierunt* (183, xvii–xviii). At this point in the text, *Tr* (p. 122, col. 2), *Ir* (pp. 80, 81), *AN* (ll. 1047–65), and *Johannes* (LIV) all retain a lengthy contemplation of why God permitted those who did not earlier sin with women also to die in this battle (see Meredith-Jones 183, xviii -185, xvi). Again, the omission of the passage in *Turpines Story* is consistent with other unique changes to the text which tend to highlight the heroism of the Christian warriors; see the Introduction, pp. xl–xli.

1154–5 'The paine of Rowlande and þe deþe of Marcerie and fliȝte of Bigalande': the title matches that of *Tr*: *De passione Rotholandi et de morte Marsiri et fuga Belligandi* (p. 122, col. 2; cf. the title of Meredith-Jones's A.6. text, which reads *morte* for *passione* (184, heading to chapter XXII).

1157–8 '. . . to aspye þe hooste of þe paynyms were þey were, and as he went . . .': . . . *causa explorandi adversus paganos, et adhuc ab eis distaret* . . . (185, xvii–xviii).

1159 'wery of fyȝttinge': the Latin adds *in nemore latentem* (185, xix–xx; so *Johannes* LV, 3; *AN* has him *demusaunt pur les cristiens*, ll. 168–69). For *latentem Tr* has *iacentem* (p. 122, col. 2; *so Ir*, pp. 82, 83). The somewhat awkward syntax of the Middle English here suggests that the scribe might have failed to copy a phrase corresponding to the Latin which describes the Saracen in the woods.

'bonde faste him': perhaps the syntax is influenced by the Latin, *nexum fortiter* (185, xx), but cf. similar placing of 'faste' at l. 795.

1162–3 'hyuery horne are a trompe': *tubam suam eburneam* (187, iii).

'as lowde as he myȝt': not matched in the Latin, which simply has *sonuit* (187, iii; *Tr* has *insonuit* (p. 122, col. 2)). The addition possibly reflects anticipation of Roland's later fatal sounding of the horn whereupon *venæ colli eius et nervi rupti fuisse feruntur* (193, xiv).

1168 'þou shalte haue þi lyue': *vivum te dimittam* (187, viii).

1171 'vpon a rede horse, and a rounde shylde': *cum equo ruffo et clipeo rotundo* (187, xi).

1172–3 'he callid to God to helpe him': the standard Latin (187, xii–xiii), *Tr* (*virtute Dei animatus* (p. 123, col. 1)), *Ir* (pp. 82, 83) and *AN* (ll. 1089–90) find Roland already encouraged by the power of God; *Johannes* omits mention of Roland's motivation (LV, 19–20).

'And anone . . .': the manuscript breaks off at this point. The best approximations to the missing text are likely to be represented by *Ir* and *Tr*, and the reader is directed to Hyde's edition of *Ir* for the most convenient presentation of matter which need not be repeated here. However, using the Middle English *Titulus* as a guide, chapter xxvii ('The Maneris and the liberaliteis of gode Rowlonde' (ll. 61–2), cf. Meredith-Jones 201, xv, ff.) is missing from *Ir*, as is material summarized by the last two clauses of the heading to chapter xxx ('how Roulonde was beried with oþer many; how sume were beried at Relaten', (ll. 69–70), cf. Meredith-Jones chapters XXVIII and XXIX). *Tr*, on the other hand, lacks the equivalent of the last chapter ('How the Nabarris where noȝt begete of a trew kynredde' (ll. 75–6); cf. Meredith-Jones Appendix C, p. 249 ff.). Like *Turpines Story*, *Tr* and *Ir* omit the equivalents of Latin chapters XXX (*De concilio quod ad Sanctum Dionisium Karolus fecit*) and XXXI (*De septem artibus*). Occasionally, the equivalent of chapter XXXI is omitted from *Pseudo-Turpin* manuscripts of different families (cf. Meredith-Jones, 221, n. to l. xv), and the equivalent of chapter XXX is sometimes abridged (see Meredith-Jones, 216, n. to l. xx), but there is no record that they are omitted together in *C*-family texts other than *Turpines Story*, *Tr*, and *Ir*.

GLOSSARY

The glossary lists mainly those words which are obsolete or whose spelling or sense may make them unfamiliar to modern readers. In instances where the use of a particular form includes both modern and pre-modern senses, for the most part only the pre-modern sense is glossed. Headwords are cited in the form in which they appear in the text. Plural forms of the headword in *-s*, *-is*, *-ys*, or *-es* are generally not cited unless they present a difference in sense, or if the text preserves only the plural form. *y* as a vowel is listed as for *i*. Initial 3 is listed as for *y;* *þ* follows *t*. The scribes typically use *u* medially and *v* initially for both the vowel and consonant; these are ordered in the glossary according to modern usage.

The infinitive is the usual entry form for verbs if the form appears in the text; in the absence of the infinitive all other inflected forms are usually listed; present tense is assumed if only the person and number are given. Past participles beginning with *i-* (representing the reflex of Old English *ge-*) are listed under the initial letter of the stem of the verb. A maximum of three occurrences of a particular form and sense are recorded by line number, and the existence of subsequent occurrences indicated by 'etc.' Parenthetical references to corresponding words in the Latin source cite page and line numbers from the Meredith-Jones edition. An '*n*' after a line reference draws attention to a note in the apparatus or Commentary. A '*t*' after a line reference indicates an occurence in the first manuscript title (top of fol. 326ra). An asterisk before a citation designates an emended form.

a, *v.* unstressed form of 'have' used as an auxiliary 919

a, *prep.* into 945

abacke, *adv.* in retreat 958

abbattis, *n. pl.* abbots 625

abey(3)e, *v.* render obedience 382; submit to 1009

abide *v.* wait, remain 456; **abydinge,** *pp.* waiting 939

aborne, *adj.* yellowish- or brownish-white in colour 1057

abou(3)t(te), *prep.* around 412, 634, 1081; around the number of 616, 692, 1164

acordide, *pa.t. pl.* brought to agreement 469; agreed 593, 770

adoune, *adv.* downward 154

aferd, *ppl.adj.* affected with fear 1170

aferre, *adv.* far off 637, 1171

afore, *prep.* in the presence of 881, 1080; in the time before 892, 896

afotte, *adv.* on foot 771

after, *prep.* according to 186, 470, 882, etc.; in accordance with 243, 285, 305, etc.

a3ene *see* **ayene**

a3enst(e) *see* **ayenste**

agone, *ppl.adj.* past 4

ayene, a3ene, *adv.* once more 263, 401, 407 etc.; in return, in reply 796

ayenste, a3enst(e), *prep.* in opposition to 318, 319, 320, etc.

ayenewarde, *adv.* back, in return 905

almy3tty, *adj.* all-powerful 566, 570

almus, *n. sg.* charitable bequest 25

alowyde, *pa.t. pl.* consecrated 1012

also, *adv.* just as 400

amyddemonge, *prep.* in the midst of 345, 974

amyddis, *prep.* in the middle of 660, 672

anone, *adv.* at once, presently 226, 392, 599, etc.; ~ *as* as soon as 236, 445, 597, etc.

aperith, *3 sg.* becomes visible 336; **apered, aperid(e), aperyd,** *pa.t. sg.* 18, 78, 111, etc.; **aperiste,** *pa.t. 2 sg.* 151

apoyntide, *pp.* agreed 597

apoyntment *see* **poynt(e)ment(e).**

Apostolica, *Lat. adj.* of apostolic origin 1018

arayede, *pa.t. sg. refl.* dressed 389

are, *conj.* or 1163

arise, *v. refl.* ressurect 897

aryse, *v.* rise up 878, 881, 890; **aryseth,** *3 sg.* 229

areside, *pa.t. sg.* resurrected 894, 895, 896

iar(y)myd(e), *pp.* equipped for battle 652, 1069

arme, *n.* injury 1123

armys, *n. pl.* feats of arms 489, 493, 1061, etc.

artte *see* be

as, *adv.* such as 98; ~ *for* having status of 988*n*

asaye, *v.* put to the test 746

ascryuyde, *pa.t. pl.* attributed 333

asoyled, asoylide, *pa.t. sg.* absolved 475, 484; asoylith *3. pl.* 624

aspye, *v.* scout out, watch 1157; *pp.* 965

astate, *n.* estate, rank; *trone of* ~, throne of state 535*n*

auctorité, *n.* authorization 475

auenturus, *adj.* perilous 97

avoydude, *pa.t. sg.* evaded 917

awture, *n.* altar 1013

atwo, *adv.* in two 347

atweyne, *adv.* in two 918

bad *pa.t. sg.* commanded 668

banashid *pp.* outlawed 463

banere *n.* battle standard 976, 978, 981

bare *pa.t. sg.* carried 729, 730, 737, etc.; ~ . . . *of*, deflected 775, 917

batail, batail(l)e, batale, batayle, *n.* hostile engagement 2*t*, 17, 26, etc.

be, bo, *v.* be, exist (as) 40, 283, 416, etc; 2 sg. 113; *3 sg.* 817, 913, 1030, etc.; *3 pl.* 817, 1031; *subj.* 125, 135, 137, etc.; *pp.* 286, 617, 990, etc.; artte, 2 *sg.* 540; ben, *pl.* *180, 548, 627; beth(e), buthe, *pl.* 11, 180, 185, etc.; w(h)as, *pa.t. sg.;* 140, 180, 257, etc.; w(h)ere, w(h)are, *pa.t. pl.* 29, 39, 67, etc.; beyinge, beynge, *pr. p.* 5, 9

be-avyside, *ppl. adj.* well-informed 1075

beet, *pa.t. pl.* defeated 203

begete, *pp.* descended 75

behedide, *pp.* decapitated 1147

behy3t(t)e, *pa.t. sg.* promised 40, 594; behy3ttiste *pa.t. sg.* 399

behyld(e), *pa.t. sg.* observed 403, 795

behotinge, *pr. p.* promising 381

beyinge, beynge, *see* be

beis *n. pl.* bees 862

belefadur *n.* great grandfather 555 (*abavus,* 131.xi)

bel(l)y(e), *n.* womb 850; abdomen 1059

bene, *n.* bean 860

berdde, *n.* beard 953

beride, beried, beryed, *pa.t. pl. & pp.* interred 69, 70, 91, etc.

iberyedde, *pp.* interred 1054

beriell, *n.* grave, tomb 130, 182

berynge, *vbl. n.* sepulchre, place of burial 1046

beris, *n. pl.* bears 294

berithe, *3 sg.* yields 184

beseche, *1 sg.* implore 553

besegid, besegitte, *pp.* laid siege to 145, 666

*beschope, *n.* bishop 1010

besy, bisye, *adj.* diligent, earnest 2, 747

besy3e, *pp.* equipped, dressed; *beste* ~ of most splendid appearance 619

besynes, *n.* diligence 457

ibete, *pp.* broken 413

betokeneth, *3 sg.* signifies 127; betokenyd *pa.t. sg.* 109

betuex, betwexe, bytuex, bytwex, *prep.* between 105, 253, 431, etc.

beuteus, *adj.* elegant in form 111

bi, *prep.* by 89, 90, 555, etc.

birris, *n. pl.* hats or caps of a kind worn by priests or doctors of divinity 622

bisye *see* besy

bytuex, bytwex *see* betuex

blente, *pa.t. sg.* deflected, dissipated 759

blode, *n.* blood 678, 679

blow, *pa.t. pl.* sounded 667

bo *see* be

bode, *pa.t. pl.* remained 94

bokys, *n. pl.* books 245

bonde, *pa.t. sg.* tied 1159, 1166

borde, *n.* table 618, 619 (*pl.*), *630

(i)bore, *pp.* given birth (as) 235, 487, 805, etc.

bounde, *adj.* obliged through vassalage 460

ibrande, *pp.* burned 1148

bredde, *pp.* raised, nurtured 998

brede, *n.*[1] breadth 510

brede, *n.*[2] bread 1066

brende, *pp.* burned 546; brennynge *pr. p.* 1086

breþinge, *n.* respiration 889

bride, *n.* bird 225

bringith, *3 sg.* presents 819

bryncke, brynke, *n.* river bank 328; shore 226

brode, *adj.* in dimension 227

broke, *pp.* breached 221

broute, *pa.t. sg.* conveyed, carried 101, 773

bushop(e) *n.* bishop 1012, 1020, 1021, etc.
buthe *see* **be**

callid, *pp.* translated, meant to indicate 216*n*, 217
calor, *n. Lat.* warmth, heat 836*n*
camyste, *pa.t.* 2 *sg.* came 545
candor, *n. Lat.* brightness, radiance 836*n*
canste, 2 *sg.* are able (to) 843, 872
capitulum, *n. Lat* chapter 18, 79, 144, *etc.*
carebokulle, *n.* rubious gemstone 1063
carynge, *pr. p.* conveying 753
certen, *adj.* determined, fixed 174
ceside, *pp.* stopped 101
chanonys, chanouns, *n. pl.* collegiate clerics 243, 627
charge, *n.* moral weight, importance 457
charged, *pa.t. pl. refl.* loaded 686
chargis, *n. pl.* liabilities 1017
charité, *n.* love 360
chehoffe, *adj.* principal; ~ *lorde*: *see Commentary for ll.* 988–9
chese, *pa.t. sg.* elected, decided 522; *imp. sg.* decide upon 584
chirche *see* **churche**
chircheyerdis, *n.pl.* churchyards 68
chydinge, *vbl. n.* quarrelling with angry words 363
chyne, *n.* chin 756
chyualrye, *n.* martial prowess 1062
churche, chirche *n.* church 239, 242, 244, etc.
citté, *n.* larger town 28, 29, 145, etc.
claryneris, *n. pl.* clarions 667
clerkis, *n. pl.* clerics in minor orders 275
cleue, *pa.t. sg.* cut asunder 346
climattis, *n. pl.* regions 96
closet *n.* private chamber, oratory 710
closid(e) *pa.t. sg.* confined 220; 705; encased, enshrined 1095
cloþe, *n.* table cloth 630; cloth 968
icloþide, *pp.* clothed, dressed 629, 635
coequale, *adj.* equal with each other 823
coeternalle, *adj.* equally eternal 823
comlynes, *n.* handsomeness 160
commoundementis, comoundmentis, *n. pl.* religious commandments 364, 565
commounddide, comoundide, *pa.t. sg.* commanded, ordered 949, 1126; **comoundynge, comoundinge,** *pr. p.* 426, 1111
compasside, compassyde, *pa.t. & pp.* surrounded 661, 666

conceyue, conseyue, *v.* conceive, originate 852, 859, 863; **conceyuyde,** *pp.* 856
conceyuynge, *vbl. n.* conception, origination 857
confortide, *pa.t. sg. refl.* took spiritual strength 754
connynge, *n.* (military) expertise 470
contré, *n.* region 186; **contrius,** *n.pl.* 97
conuenient, *adj.* suitable, appropriate 1029
conueyinge, *vbl. n.* guidance 90
conveyd, *pa.t. pl.* guided, led 166
cosyn, *n.* kinsman 273, 275, 277, etc.
coste, *n.* end 458; flank, outer edge 661
co(o)stis, *n.pl.* regions 96, 127, 350, etc.
coper, *n.* copper 231
corne, *n.* grain, seed 885
cornell, *n.* soft core of a nut 833
couenabily, *adj.* of a becoming appearance 1059 (?homeoarchic rendering of *conuenable* by anticipation of its referent, *bellye*)
couenaunde, *n.* agreement 1118
councel(l)e, counselle, *n.* deliberative assembly 50, 1007, 1011, etc; advice, direction 1125, 1134, 1137
covnturwaytide, *pa.t. sg.* guarded against 689 (*see* MED *cóuntre-* (*pref.*), sense 2)
crafte, *n.* art, skill 189, 830
creaturis, *n. pl.* created things 829
credens, *n. yaffe* ~ *to*: accepted as true 1123
crie, crye, *n.* lamentation 674, 928, 984, etc.; shouting 970
crie, crye, *v.* proclaim; *lete crie* caused to proclaim 459, 668; **cried,** *pa.t. sg.* implored (in prayer) 921, 926; *pa.t. pl.* shouted 955
crieynge, *pr. p.* shouting 295
Cristen, Crystyn, *adj.* Christian 40, 44, 101, etc.
cristen, *3 pl.* christen 624; **cristenyd(e)** *pp.* 155, 592, 612, etc.
cronykullynge, *vbl. n.* recording in a chronicle 1097
cubitus, *n. pl.* measurement between 18 and 22 inches 731, 732
cursid, *pa.t. sg.* anathematized 209
curside,cursyd, *ppl. adj.* damnable 957, 969
custum(e), *n.* convention 976, 978

dampned, *adj.* consigned to hell 572
darttis, *n. pl.* spears 1147

debate, *n.* dispute; *at* ~ involved in a dispute 467, 469

declaracioune, *n.* elucidation 140

declare, *subj. sg.* elucidate 551

dede, *n.* feat (of arms) 8, 97, 193, etc.; dedis *pl.* 10, 102, 280, etc.

ded(e), deed, *adj.* dead 25, 45, 67, etc.

dedely, *adj.* destructive to the soul 571

dedis, *n. gen.* of the dead 305

deed *see* ded(e)

deffeth, *adj.* deaf 575

degré, *n.* rank 470

deyde, *pa.t. pl.* died 366

delyuer, *v.* save, rescue, set free 124; delyuerest, *2 sg,* 121; delyuered, *pa.t. sg. & pp.* 7, 120, 934, etc.

dene, *n.* head of a cathedral chapter 3

denounce, *v.* declare, report 551

departid(e), *pa.t. sg. & pl.* separated 83, 771, 948, etc.

deseruynge, *vbl. n.* merit 882

deseueryde, *pa.t. sg.* separated, divided 539

desirith, *3 sg.* desires 1087

deuydude, *pa.t. 3 sg.* divided 989

dyed(e), dyeth(e) *see* dyȝe

dyȝe, *v.* perish 501, 523; *1 sg.* 928; *subj.* 271, 367, 586, etc.; dyeth(e) *3 sg.* 223, 868; dyed(e), dyȝed *pa.t. sg.* 276, 366, 806, etc.

dyscrete, *adj.* discerning, judicious 1076

disheretide, *pp.* deprived of inheritance 467

disklawnder, *ppl. a.* reproached by, scandalized by 642

disposyd(e), disposide, *pa.t. sg. & pl.* resolved 272, 698, 1124 (*refl.*); prepared 951

dispudid, *pa.t. pl.* contested 37

disputacion(e), *n.* formal attack and defence of a thesis 47, 715

do(o), *v.* perform, carry out, dispose of 135, 397; ~ *þe (to) wete* cause you to know 122, 287; doste, *2 sg.* 112; dothe, *3 sg. & pl.* 276, 391, 638, etc.; doynge, *pr. p.* causing 396; dud(e), *pa.t. sg & pl.* did, disposed of 11, 117, 195, etc.; (i)do(o), *pp.* completed, disposed of 276, 283, 534, etc.; downe, *pp.* 989

doctoris, *n. pl.* scholars, doctors of divinity 622

dome, *n.* judgement 888; domus, *pl.* 707, 1075

dome, *adj.* without speech 575

(i)doo *see* do(o)

doynge *see* do(o)

doste *see* do(o)

dothe *see* do(o)

douȝtty, *adj.* valiant 488; douȝttyeste, *superl.* 1061

downe, *v. see* do(o)

drade *see* drede *v.*

idrawe, idrawȝe *see* drew(ȝ)

drede, *imp. sg.* be afraid 135; drade, *pa.t sg.* feared 722, 788

drede, *n.* fear 603, 1110

dredefulle, *adj.* to be feared 888

drew(ȝ), *pa.t. sg. & pl.* moved (towards) 348, 349, 768, etc.; of a sword: pulled out of its sheath 345, 757, 761, etc.; idrawe, idrawȝe, *ppl. adj.* 1080, 1085

dronke, *adj.* inebriated 1130

dud(e) *see* do(o)

duelle, *v.* settle 991; duellid, *pa. t. sg.* 210; duellinge, *pr. p.* 242, 1106

duke, *n.* military leader 263, 310, 342, etc.

durste, *pa.t. sg. & pl.* had the courage to 740, 742, 780, etc.

eche, *adj.* each 952

eger, *adj.* fierce 490

eyen, *n. pl.* eyes 1063

eyere, *n.* sky 293

eke, *adv.* also, moreover 811, 871

ellis, *adv.* otherwise 585, 1168

empere, *n.* supreme dominion 382

endis, *n. pl.* as *sg.* termination, last things 881

engynes, *n. pl.* siege engines, catapults 413

enmyes, *n. pl.* adversaries 358

ensa(u)mple, example, *n.* exemplary lesson 25, 176, 265, etc.

eny, *adj.* any 222, 223, 225, etc.

equalité, *n.* equality, parity 826n

erat, *Lat. imperfect 3 sg.* was 1053

eritaunce *see* heretaunce

erle, *n.* nobleman ranking above a viscount and below a marquess 490, 514, 736

erriste, *2 sg.* go wrong 569, 813

erroure, *n.* false belief, transgression 1025

erthely, herth(e)ley, *adj.* of this world 123, 1031, 1034

est, *adj.* eastern 1027

Este, *n.* (the) East 906, 908

Ester, *n.* Easter 1078

eternité, *n.* timelessness 846

ette, *3 pl.* eat 635

euer, *adv.* always, constantly 157, 229, 880

euery, *adj.* (*quasi-pron.*) each 261, 458, 470, etc.

eueryshone, *pron.* each one 599, 1142

euylle, *n.* what is painful 882

euylle, *adj.* wretched 280, 586

euylle, *adv.* wretchedly, wrongfully 629, 636, 637, etc.

euyne, *adv.* straight, directly 106

euyne, *adj.* straight 1072

example *see* ensa(u)mple

examynyde, *pp.* inquired into 1026

expartte, *adj.* skilled 493

explicit, Lat. pr. 3 sg. (here) ends 15

expouneythe, *3 pl.* set forth in detail 623

faddur, fader, fadure, *n.* father 343, 554; God the Father 572, 805, 814, etc; fadris, fadurs, *n.gen.* father's, 554 God the Father's 895

fayer, *adv.* in phr. ~ *and softe* quietly 963*n*

faylid, faylyd, *pa.t. sg.* became exhausted 194; ~ *of:* missed 763, 766

false, *adj.* deceitful 265, 276, 277, etc.; faithless, of false belief 201, 347, 561, etc.; untrue 641

fare, *imp. sg.*, ~ *wele*, an expression of good wishes at parting 13; *3 pl.* feed, be entertained with food 636

faste, *adv.* near 538, 690; vigorously 775; closely 795; tightly 1159

fauȝt(t)e, fawȝtte, faughte, fauȝte *see* fyȝtte

febelest, *adj. superl.* weakest, most vulnerable 404

feer, feiere, feire, *adj.* splendid, beautiful 537, 626, 1114

felde, *n.* field of battle 444, 521, 522, etc.

fele, *1 sg.* comprehend 842

feleship, feliship, *n.* armed companions 291, 298, 381, etc.; (sexual) intercourse 852, 864, 866

fende, *n.* the Devil 574; fendis, *n. pl.* demons 294, 296, 583; *pl. gen.* devils' 306, 362

fere, *n.* dread 295, 958, 972

feride, feryd, *pa.t. sg.* dreaded 157, 1065

fest, *n.* feast-day 183; festis, *pl.* meals 41

fette, *n. pl.* feet 445, 1084

few, *a.* small, limited 381

few(ȝ), *n.* a small number 344, 677, 1133

feyer, feyre, *adj.* handsome, beautiful 111, 247, 312, etc.

fyȝtte, *n.* combat, battle 188, 437, 670, etc.

fyȝtte, fyȝt(e), *v.* engage in combat with 141, 149, 474, etc.; *subj.* 318, 461, 744, etc.; fauȝt(t)e, fawȝtte, faughte, fauȝte, fouȝtte, fowȝtte, *pa.t. sg. & pl.* 202, 672, 693, etc.

fyȝttinge, *ppl.a.* military 472, 945

fyȝttinge, *vbl. n.* combat 1144, 1159

fylle, fille, *pa.t. sg. & pl.* collapsed, succumbed 19, 110, 154, etc.; ~ *vpon*, ~ *on* attacked 675, 918; *pa.t. sg.* happened 298; ~ (*by*) *lot(te)*: see lot(te)

fyngris, *n. pl.* fingers 732

flessly, *adj.* carnal 361

flew, flewȝe, fley, flow(ȝ), *pa.t. sg. & pl.* fled, ran away 325, 353, 447, etc.

floure, *v.* blossom 365; flourynge *pr.p.* 434

folouynge, *ppl. adj.* subsequent 419, 449

foluere, *n.* servant 2

fonde, *pa.t. 3 sg.* located 214

foottemen, *see* fotteman

for, fore, *prep.* because, because of 12, 64, 125, etc.; ~ *to* to, in order to (*forming infinitive*) 40, 101, 124, etc.; *as* ~: *see* as

forasmoche, *adv.* ~ *as*, ~ *that* seeing that, in consideration that 10, 283, 580

foredde, *n.* forehead 1062

forenamyd, fornamed, *ppl. adj.* named before 493, 500

forewarde, *n.* vanguard 946, 949, 951, etc.

foreyeuenes, *n.* forgiveness 132

forme, *n. vndure this* ~; *in this* ~ in this fashion 103, 138, 317, etc.

forsaid, foreseid, forseid, *a.* before-mentioned 128, 464, 499, etc.

fort(e), *adv.* until 980, 1128

forth(e), forþe, *adv.* forward, onwards 310, 508, 726, etc.

foryaffe *pa.t. sg.* remitted from 284

fot(t)e, *n.* lowest part of the leg, below the ankles 344, 767; measurement of twelve inches 1058, 1062

fotteman, *n.* infantryman 952; fottemen, foottemen, *pl.* 499, *946, 954

fouȝtte *see* fyȝtte

foule, *adj* shameful 385

fowȝtte *see* fyȝtte

frely, *adv.* without constraint 972

fro, *prep.* from 8, 81, 100, etc.

fruȝtte, frute, *n.* fruit 184, 860, 886, etc.

full(e), *adv.* very 5, 111, 313, etc.; fully 688

fullid, *pp.* satisfied 1035

gadure, gader, *v.* assemble 458, 483; gaderid(e), gaderyd, gadered, *pa.t. sg. & pl. (refl.:* gathered unto) 141, 262, 372, etc.

gete, *v.*¹ capture, conquer 548; *subj.* 147, 192.; *pa.t. sg.* 176, 188, 209; *pp.* 415

gete, gate, *v.*² *pa.t. sg.* engendered 810, 842, 845, etc.; *pp.* 844; igette, *pp.* 811

getinge ,*vbl. n.* engendering 857

giaunt(t)(e), gyaunt(e), *n.* giant 719, 724, 730, etc.

gyrdinge-stede, *n.*point at which a belt is tied or buckled off 1066*n*

gyrdude, *pa.t. sg.* encircled 1065

gyrdulle, *n.sg.* belt 1065

gode, *n.*¹ that which is good or joyful 882

gode, *n.*² property or possessions 268

god(e), *a.* fine, worthy 48, 61, 90, etc.

godenes, *n.* moral excellence 153, 334

godhede, *n.* triune God 573, 825, 835, etc.

godis, godys, *n.pl.* property 283, 285, 305, etc.

goynge, *pr. p.* proceeding 105

gose, *n.* goose 1067

gostely, *a.* spiritual 358

goutis, *n.pl.* water channels, drains 417

grappud, *pa.t. 3. sg.* took up forcibly 728

graunted, *pa.t. 3.sg.* agreed 1117

graunttiste, *2. sg.* agree 869

grauyd, *ppl.a.* carved 228

grene, *adj.* green 308

gresly, *adj.* terrible 916

grete, grette, *adj.* large 128, 188, 197, etc.; pre-eminent 3, 7, 10, etc.; gret(e)ly, *adv.* very much 109, 140, 157, etc.

gretefolde, *a.* manifold 96*n*

gretinge, *vbl.n.* salutation 4

greyþed, *pa.t. pl. refl.* prepared, readied 597

gunneris, *n.pl.* operators of siege engines 413 (*crossed through: see Commentary*)

gurgulione, *n.* weevil 860

guwnus, *n.pl.* siege engines 413

habbeis, *n. pl.* abbeys 1093

habireiounys, *n.pl.* jackets of mail or scale armour 702

habitte, *n.* garment, gown 627; *pl.* 625

halkis, *n.pl.* recesses, hiding places 690

halouyde, halowyde, *pa.t. sg.* sanctified, made holy 1044, 1049

halpe, *pa.t. sg.* assisted 483, 750, 774

hande *see* hond(e)

hard(e), *pa.t. sg. & pl.* heard 156, 261, 352, etc.

hardy, *adj.* brave 787

iharniyde, *pp.* furnished with horns 953

hatte, *n.* hate 360

hauyne *n.* harbour (mistranslation of Lat. *portus: see* 512*n*): 512, 513, 519, etc.

hawntid, *pp.*engaged in 102

hede, *n.* careful attention 405

heed, *n.* head 1069

heette, *subj.* eat 1066

heyth, *n.* height 229

helthe, *n.* soul's health, salvation 4

hem, *pron. 3 pl.* them 83, 101, 161, *etc.*; hemself(f)e, themselves 20, 552, 1151

hennus, *n. pl.* hens 1067

her *see* here, *pron.*

herbe, *n.* plant 860

herde, *pa.t. sg. & pl.* heard (of) 698, 803, 940 etc.; *pp.* 511

here, *n.*¹ ear 791; heris *pl.* 969, 971

here, *n.*² hair 1057

here, her, *pron. gen. 3 pl.* their 122, 132, 162, etc.

here, *v.* hear 337, 970, 1087; ~ *sey* hear someone say 858

herely *see* herly

heretaunce, heritaunce, eritaunce, *n.* inheritance, heirship 468, 555, 582

hereto, *adv.* to this (arrangement) 593

herewde, *n.* messenger 317

heris *see* here, *n.*¹

herly, herely, *adv.* early 772, 1134

hert(e), *n.* courage 442, 755

herthe, *n.* earth 809

herth(e)ly *see* erthely

hesely, *adv.* easily 779

hethen, *adj.* pagan 180, 666

hetinge , *vbl.n.* warming 836*n*

hette, *pa.t. sg.* ate 1066

heuene, *n.* heaven 82, 104, 126, etc.

heu(e)y, *adj.* oppressive, of great weight 767, 921

hyȝe, *adj.* tall, lofty 228, 301, 881, etc.; ~ *wey* principal road 538; *in* ~ tall 885

hyȝedide, *pa.t. sg. refl.* hid 689

hyȝtte *see* behyȝt(t)e

hylde, hilde, *pa.t. sg. & pl.* held, retained 425, 762, 791; ~ *of* possessed from 988*n* hyndur(e), *adj.* rear 947; ?under 227*n*

his, *v.3 sg.* is 142, 177*n*, 229, etc.

hit, *pron.* it 147, 190, 192, etc.; used pleonastically after a *pl. n.* clause, for rhetorical emphasis 622, 625, 627

hyuery, *adj.* ivory 1162

*hocsyn, *n.pl.* oxen 975

hoely, *adv.* completely 742

holde, *v.* hold in belief 565, 577; convene 1021; *pp.* held 1080; ~ *of* hold in feudal possession from 1121

*holde, *a.* old 227

holdis, *n.pl.* strongholds 260

hole, *adj.* complete, sound 225, 651, 930, etc.; *make* ~ *wey* advance without obstruction 959

hond(e), hande *n.* *ouer* ~ superiority in battle 439; *mannes* ~ human power 192; *strong* ~ military force 128, 545

honestly, *adv.* decently 647

honge, *pa.t. pl.* hanged 1149

hooste, hoste, *n.* army 9, 34, 128, etc.; *with grete* ~ with great military force 258, 386

hoselyde, *pp.* given the Eucharist 272

hosholder, *n.* head of a household 1015

idus, *n.pl.* ides; ~ *Maii* May 15th 183

ientille, *adj.* noble 778

in, *prep.* on 109, 269, 279, etc.

inasmoche, *adv.* ~ *þat*; ~ as in view of the fact that 285, 1019

inconuenient, *n.* legally or morally improper act, offense 562 (*indignum*, 131, xvii)

inhabitte, *ppl. a.* uninhabited 210*n*

inow, *adv.* enough 648

*inperscrutable, *adj.* incapable of being sought out 707

inposible, *adj.* not able to be 878

insomoche, *adv.* to such an extent 340, 958

instaunce, *n.* entreaty 748*n*

into, *prep.* until 133, 138, 196, etc.; onto 905

iorney, iurnaye, *n.* military expedition 136; travel to a distant place 510

ioyed, *pa.t. sg.* experienced joy 550

is, *pron. gen.3 sg.* his 850, 865

iugementtis, *n. pl.* judicial decisions 1075

iurnaye *see* iorney

kalendus, *n. pl.* first day of the month 1013

ket(t)e, kytte, *v. pa.t. sg. & pl.* severed 334, 436, 918

keuer, *subj. pl.* cover 967; ikeuerede, *pp.* 971

kynddome, *n.* sovereignty 1034

kynred(d)e, kynrade, *n.* lineage, ancestry 76, 720, 797

kytte *see* ket(t)e

kny3ttehode, *n.* martial practice 1062

knabbide, knabbit, *adj.* ragged 774, 915

(i)lade, *pp.* loaded 688, 1115

largenes, *n.* generosity 360

lasse, *adj.* (*& quasi-n.*) (those) lower in rank 1122, 1145; *cf.* more

laste, *adj.* final 306, 514; *at þe* ~ finally 82, 439, 605, etc.

law3e, law3, *n.* religion 563, 564, 569, etc.

leffe, *v. imper.* live 13*n*

lekis, lekys, *n. pl.* distances of twenty miles 517, 943

lemynge, *vbl. n.* gleaming 836*n*

lengeste, *adj.* longest 1059

lenkethe, *n.* length 509, 538, 730

lernyd, *pa.t. sg.* mastered in school 550

let(t)e, *pa.t. sg.* caused, permitted; ~ *crye* caused to be proclaimed 459, 667; ~ *ordeyne* caused to be established 645; ~ *stoppe* (*subj. pl.*) cause to be plugged up 969

leue, *1 sg.* believe in 575, 874

leuynge *pr. p.* living 219*n*

leuynge, *pp.* depositing 390

ley *v.* set; ~ *on* assail 949

leyd(e), *v. pa.t. sg.* laid, set 191, 411, 412, etc.; ~ *at* leveled at, thrust 762, 916

leyft, *pa.t pl.* allowed to remain 206

liberaliteis, *n. pl.* generosities 61

liffe, *subj. pl.* live 367

ly3ttely, ly3tly, *adv.* easily 865, 894, 900, etc.

ly3tte, *adj.*[1] little 1066

ly3tte, *adj.*[2] quick 1068

ly3tte, *subj. sg.* alight 225

like, *adj.*: ~ *to* in the likeness of 219, 232

like, *adv.* likely 415

lymfatted, *ppl.adj.* watered down 1068*n*

lym(m)ys, *n. pl.* limbs 839, 1060

lynnyne, *n.* linen 968

litulle, *adj.* diminutive 884

lyue, *n.* life 82, 876, 878, etc.

loggide, *pp.* lodged, temporarily living 1105

loggynge, *n.* shelter 349, 771, 1153

lokynge, *vbl.n.* countenance, appearance 1058*n*

lond(e), *n.* land 7, 121, 149, etc.

lore, *n.* doctrine, teaching 116

losyde, *pa.t. sg.* freed 1166

lot(te), *n.* chance selection; *fylle (by)* ~ happened by chance selection 85, 1035

loude, *n.* praise; ~ *and preysinge* high commendation and praise 590, 912

lustus, *n.pl.* desires 361

magnifiynge, *vbl. n.* glorifying 150

maiesté, *n.* greatness and glory of God 826

maiste *see* **mayste**

maneris, *n. pl.* customary behaviours 61

man(n)es, manys, *n. gen. sg.* of man 192, 193, 851

manly, *adv.* valiantly 973

manlynes, *n.* valour 160

imannyd, *pp.* supplied with fighting men 147

markis, *n. pl.* marquises 350

matens, *n.pl.* morning prayers 628

mater(e), *n.* subject matter, business 468, 1097, 1098; **matris,** *pl.* 551

mayste, maiste *2 sg.* can 134, 902, 905

me, *pron. gen.* my 284

mede, *n.* meadow 313

mene, *n.* means, ability 192

merke, *n.* sign 704

merked, *pa.t. sg.* remarked, heard 792

merveile, *1. sg.* wonder 119; **merueylid(e),** *pa.t. sg. & pl.* 159, 740, 961, etc.; **merueylinge,** *pr. p.* 108, 333

mervelous, *n. pl.* wonders 133

metropolis, Lat. n. see of a metropolitan bishop 178

met(t)e, *n.* dinner, dining 614, 618, 620, etc.; food 279 (*pl.*), 631, 634, etc.

meuyd, *pa.t. 3 sg.* changed from one position to another 923, 1036

meyné, meynye *n.* (armed) followers 640, 665

myddis, *n.* middle 196

my3t(te)ly, my3ttly, *adv.* strongly 191, 672, 756, etc.

mylle, *n.* apparatus for grinding corn 903 (*cf. the Introduction, note* 121)

mysbeleuynge, *adj.* holding a false belief 119

mytrus, *n. pl.* bishops' mitres 1023

moche, *adj.*[1] much 381, 509, 579, etc.

moche, *adj.*[2] large 921

moche, *adv.* greatly 119

moder, modur, *n.* mother 1036; ~ *son(n)e* mother's son, man 261, 676

moo, *adj.* more 254, 497, 740

more, *adj.* greater, of senior rank: *Seynt Iame the* ~ 85; *quasi-n.* in phrase ~ *and lasse,* of all ranks 1145

morelisithe, *3 sg.* interprets allegorically 354

morow(e), *n.* morning, next day 290, 349, 651, etc.

morowtyde, *n.* morning 1134, 1140

mowthe, *n.* mouth; ~ *-by-* ~ face-to-face 527

musid, *pa.t. sg.* contemplated 109

nakyde, *adj.* unsheathed 1080, 1085

navile, navylle, *n.* navel 790, 925

ne, *cj.* nor 554, 580, 581, etc.

nede, *n.* constraint, difficulty 923

nedis, *adv.* necessarily 271

neue, neveye, *n.* nephew 487, 799

nyeth, *3 sg.* nears, approaches 222: **ny3ede** *pa.t. 3.sg.* 955

nigromanci, *n.* evil magic 220

nyne, *adj.* nine o'clock 616

no, *cj.* nor 193

no3t, nou3t(te), now3t, *adv.* not 11, 75, 121, etc.

none, *n.* noon 973, 1141

none, *pron.* no one; ~ *numbure* numberless 499*n*

nout, *n.* nothing 850

O, *interj.* oh 148, 151, 706, etc.

o *see* **oo**

obeysance, *n.* formal gesture of submission 398

obeythe, *2. pl.* submit to 802

odure, *adj.* other 245

off, *prep.* about, concerning 24, 28, 29, etc.

oftetymes, *adv.* frequently 485

on *see* **oo**

one, *n.* one; ~ *-for-* ~ one-on-one 725

onyd(e), *pa.t. sg. & pl. refl.* united 659, 974

onshercheable, *adj.* incapable of being sought out or seen 707

oo, oon(e), o, on, *numeral adj.* one 180, 391, 661, etc.

ooste, *n.* army 960

opyn, *adj.* clear, unobstructed 129

oratorye, *n.* private chapel 705

ordeyne, *v.* establish, decree 646; ordeynyd, ordeyned, ordynyd, *pa.t. sg. &
pp.* 283, 459, 1015 etc.

ordinaunce, *n.* provision, arrangement
269, 286, 781, etc.; military array 413,
414

ordis, *n. pl.* ranks 619

ordre, ordur, *n.* disposition 41, 614;
ordure, religious order 243

ore, *conj.* or 318, 337, 463, etc.

oþer, *adj.* additional 1012, 1127; next 695

oþer, *conj.* or 520

ouer, *adj.* upper 230; ~ *hande* see hond(e)

ouȝte, *adv.* out 720, 1136

oune, *adj.* own 485, 498, 673, etc,

ouris, *n. pl.* prayers for the canonical hours
of the day 628

outetake, *adv.* except for 189, 215, 1150

pallis, *n.* ecclesiastical vestments 245

parischeth, *3 sg.* ceases to exist 223

parsonel, *adj.*; ~ *propurtté* an individual
distinctive quality or attribute 825*n*

parsonys, *n. pl.* modes of the divine being
in the Godhead 811, 813, 815, etc.

parte, *subj. sg.* disperse, disrupt 582 (*see
Commentary for other possible senses*)

partte, *n.* portion; *for þe more* ~ as much as
possible 560

passynge, passinge, *adv.* very 185, 190

payn(n)ym(e), *n. & a.* pagan 129(*pl.*), 142
(*pl.*), 257, 347, etc.

penys, *n. pl.* torments 288

pere, *subj. pl.* present (themselves) 881;
peryd *pa.t. 3 sg.* 281

peruertid(e), *pp. & ppl. a.* turned aside to
a false religious belief 94, 545, 1006

pese, *n.; hylde his* ~ remained silent 791

pese(s)ably, *adv.* so as to avoid hostilities
161, 380, 399

pesid, *pa.t. sg.* brought peace to 467

pestelle, *n.* haunch 1067

pyȝtte, *pa.t. sg. & pl.* thrust in; 165, 327,
330, etc.; fixed and erected 966

playne, *adj.* open, level 537

playne, *adv.* flat, as if razed 154

plenare, *adj.* full 325

poynt(e)ment(e), *n.* agreed arrangement
610, 616, 773

pore, *adj.* needy, indigent 41, 275, 465, etc.

portis, *n. pl.* mountain pass 454

power, *n.* emotional force 932

Prefectus, Lat. n. Commander 496

preier, *n.* prayer 445

preshinge, *vbl.n.* delivery of sermons
1045, 1048

presoneris, *n. pl.* prisoners 169

prestis, *n. pl.* clergymen having authority
to administer the sacraments and administer absolution 274, 623, 1008

presyinge, *vbl.n.* commendation 590, 912;
cf. loude *n.*

preveis, *n.pl.* latrines 417

prickyde, *pa.t. sg.* stabbed 924

prier, *n.* prayer 362

principio, Lat. n. the beginning 1053

priuiteis, *n. pl.* divine secrets 1041

processe, *n.* narration, tale 187

profur, *v.* bring forth against 999

Prologus, Lat. n. foreword 15

propurly, *adv.* in the strictest sense 216

propurtté *see* parsonel

prouynce, prouyns, *n. pl.* principal divi-
sions of a kingdom 99, 990, 1092

pulyons, *n. pl.* hats or caps of a kind worn
by priests or doctors of divinity 622

quekyn, *subj. sg.* revive 889

quod, *pa.t. sg.* said 829, 851, 913

rayedde, *pp.* positioned for battle 949

raþur, rather, raþer, *adv.* (more) readily
523, 894, 896, etc.

rede, *3 pl.* utter aloud 628

rede, *adj.* red in colour 702, 1171

reder, *n.* one who reads 175

regnythe, *1. pl.* rule 568

regulere, *adj.* living according to monastic
rule 627

rekeuerid, *pa.t. pl.* regained possession of
509*n*, 516

remenaunte, *n.* remainder 325

renegatis, *n. pl.* apostates from the Christian faith 201, 561, 1006

repreue, *n.* shame 591; *in* ~ held in shame
912

rerewarde, *n.* rearguard of a military
column 1128, 1134

reseyue, *subj. pl.* accept 882; reseyuyd(e),
reseyued, *pa.t. sg. & pl.* 83, 161, 1117

resydew, *n.* remainder 246

rest, *pluperf.* have rested 102

resten, *3 pl.* lie in the grave 315

reuer, *n.* river 312, 418

reuyne, *n.* raven 229

rewle, *n.* regulations of a monastic order 243

reynnys, *n. pl.* loins 1059

richesse, *n. pl.* precious things, treasures 238, 466, 687

right(e), *n.* right of possession 38, 100, 529

riȝtfulle, *adj.* righteous, equitable 1075

riȝtwysely, *adv.* justly 281

rynde, *n.* husk 833

ryndyd, rynedide, *ppl. adj.* covered in bark 330, 434

rodye, *adj.* of a healthy redness 1057

Romanus, Lat. n. the Roman 497

rotis, *n. pl.* roots 334

salle, *1 sg.* shall 1098

sample, *n.* example 829

Sarzyn(e)s, *n. pl.* Muslims 8, 45, 66, etc.

sawȝ(e), *pa.t. sg. & pl.* perceived (with the eyes) 193, 629, 827, etc.

saydust *see* sey

schrewide, *adj.* of an evil nature, ill-conditioned 767

scole, *n.* a centre of higher education 550

se, *v.* perceive (with the eyes) 527; *pr.1 sg.* 899; *pr. 3 pl.* 237

Sedes, Lat. n. episcopal see 1018

see, *n.¹* sea 104, 127, 165, etc.

see, *n.²* episcopal see 1001, 1019, 1028, etc.

sege, *n.* beleaguering of a fortified town 146, 191, 411, etc.

sey, *v¹* relate in speech, specify 211, 365, 373, etc.; *imper.* 401; *subj. sg.* 1098; *to here* ~: *see* here, *v.*; seyste, seiste, seyest, *2 sg.* 569, 812, 813, etc.; seith *3 sg.* 304; saydust, seydiste, seyduste, *pa.t. 2 sg.* related in speech 152, 640, 868; seid(e), seyd *pa.t. 3 sg.* 112, 275, 282, etc.; seying(e) *pr. p.* 111, 926

sey, *v.²* *pa.t. 2 sg.* saw 126; *imper.* make sure that 1036

seid, *ppl. adj.* previously-mentioned 183, 386, 447, etc.

seke, *adj.* ill 5, 271

semelid(e), semelyd, *pa.t. sg. & pl.* gathered together, met 315, 437, 652, etc.

semely, *adj.* handsome 488, 1057

semelynes, *n.* handsomeness 160

send(e), *pa.t. sg. & pl.* despatch (a communication) 5, 116, 317, etc.

septoure, *n.* rod symbolic of imperial power 1077

sepulture, *n.* tomb, place of burial 1049

seruythe, *3 sg.* attends to 637

sewere, *adj.* secure 130

sewyd, *pa.t. sg.* pursued 450

ishape, *ppl. adj.* formed 1058

shappid, *ppl. adj.* formed 1060

sharppe, *adj.* harsh, severe 997

shaw, *n.;* *hade* ~ caused to be shown, obtained an opportunity to look upon 704

sheffe, *adj.* foremost in importance 1043

shelinges, shelingys, *n. pl.* units of money equivalent to one twentieth of a pound sterling 274, 278

shepe, *n.* sheep 730, 1067

sherished, *pa.t. sg.* cared for 1005

shold(e), shode, *pa.t. sg. & pl.* should 6, 167, 275, etc.

sholdoris, *n. pl.* shoulders 702

sholle, *1 pl.* shall 357

shosyn, *pp.* chosen 123

shoys, *n. pl.* shoes 1071

shoyse, *n.* choice; *yeuynge* ~ providing the choice 318

shrewde, *adj.* crafty, ill-natured 950

shryue, *pp.* confessed 272

shulle, *2 sg.* shall 581

shurche, *n.* church 178

shylde, *n.* shield 390, 1171

shyn(n)ynge, *ppl. adj.* gleaming 627, 836*n*, 1063

syned, *pp.* ordained, appointed 429*n*

synes, synys, *conj.* since, seeing that 119, 563

synyfye, *subj. sg.* mean symbolically 110

skale, *n.* shell 833

skape, *subj. sg.* avoid danger 592

skapide, *pa.t. 3 sg.* got away from 418

skore, *n.* group(s) of twenty 387, 388, 397, etc.

slawȝte, slawȝtre, *n.* mass killing 66, 340

slaye, *pp.* killed 680

slee, *subj. sg.* kill 1168

(i)sley(e), (i)sleyȝe, *v.* 781; *pp.* killed 322, 324, 409, etc.; sleyne, *pp.* killed 344, 919

slewȝ, *pa.t. pl.* killed 675

slow, slowe, slowȝ(e), *pa.t. sg. & pl.* killed 169, 203, 260, etc.

slyȝe, *adj.* skilful 189

smete, *pa.t. sg.* struck 441

ismytte, *subj. sg.* strike 1069

soburly, *adv.* in moderation 1068

socoure, *v.* render aid to 351, 443; *imper.* 927

softe, *adv.* calmly 727; *fayer and ~* ; *see* fayer

sone, *adv.* within a short time 93, 103, 134, etc.

sonne, sone, *n.*[1] son 112, 114, 487, etc; **sonnys,** *pl.* 845, 1035, 1037

sonne, *n.*[2] sun 65, 906

soo, *adv.* thus 330

soweth, *n.* south 232

sowȝtte, *pa.t. pl.* searched for 298

sownde, *adj.* unharmed 225

sowne, *n.* sounding 59

sownnythe, *3 sg.* produces sound 830

spanne, *n.* hand-span 1064, 1065

sparthe, *n.* battle-axe 1080

Spayennyshe, *adj.* Spanish 793

spake, *pa.t. sg.* spoke 403, 552

Spaynelis, *n. pl.* Spaniards 241

speche, *n.* language 793; **spechis** *pl.* public pronouncements 1076

spend(e), *pa.t. sg.* disbursed 268, 279

spendiste, *2 sg.* disburse 285

spiside, *adj.* embalmed 67

splendor, Lat. n. brilliant light, gleaming 836n

spoyle, spoile, *v.* loot 45, 682, 685

stattly, *adj.* majestic 618

stauys, croziers 1022

stede, *n. see* gyrdinge

steffelde, *adj.* suffocated 441

steringe, *vbl. n.* guidance 90

sterres, sterris, *n. pl.* stars 104, 110, 126

styede, *pa. t. sg.* ascended 82, 807, 898

stodyed, *pa.t. sg.* directed thoughts toward 110

stoppe, *v.* plug up 969; **istoppid,** *pp.* 972

storyd, *pa.t. 3 sg.* ornamented 244

strenger, *adj.* mightier 744; **streng(g)est, strenkeste,** *superl.* 123, 946, 1061

strenketh(e), strenkith, *n.* power, might 52, 222, 404, etc.

strenkethis, *n.*[1] *pl.* strongholds 238

strenkeþis *n.*[2] *pl.* military forces 406

strenkeþide *pa.t. sg.* fortified 1048

streyte, *pp.* extended 105

stronge, *adj.*; *~ honde: see* honde

stronge, *adv.* securely 146

strongue, *n.* armed force (*cf.* MED *streng(e,* (2.b)) 56

strynggis, *n. pl.* strings 830

suddewȝ, *v.* conquer 141, 236; **suddued,** *pa.t. sg.* 97

sudget *see* **sug(g)et**

sufficiently, *adv.* in adequate supply 647n

sug(g)et, sudget, *n.* one who owes alliegance to a sovereign 382, 1014, 1092; *pl.* 542, 543, 562, etc.

sumwat, *adv.* to some extent 1098

sunne *see* **sonne,** *n.*[2]

suster *n.* sister 488

take, *pp.* obtained, seized, 416, 532, 541, etc.

taried, *pa.t..* returned temporarily 425

thanne *see* **þan**

theyere *see* **þeyer(e)**

theyers, *pron. gen. pl.* of their (kin) 462

thereas *see* **þer(e)as**

thicke *see* **þicke**

thoo, *adv.* then, at that time 1110

tydynggis, *n. pl.* news 718

tympane, *n.* timbrel or tambourine 954

tymys, *n. pl.* occasions 1076

Tituli, Lat. n. pl. headings 77

Titulus, Lat. n. sg. heading list 16

to, *prep.* at 519

toke, *pa.t.* obtained control of, laid hold of 89, 296, 352, etc.

tonge, *n.* language 217, 549

too, *prep.* to 190

tortes, *n.* candle 1086

to-torne, *ppl. adj.* torn apart 302

toune, towne, *n.* town 99 (*pl.*), 152, 414, etc.

trauayle, *n.* effort 209

trauese, *n.; at . . . ~* in dispute 469

treis, *n. pl.* trees 336

tremelyd, *pa.t. sg.* shook in fear 290

treuse, trewse *see* **truse**

trew(e), *adj.* legitimate 76, 151, 910, etc.

tribunarius, *n. pl.* governors of provinces 544n

tristinge, *pr. p.* having faith in 979

tristy, *adj.* reliable 346

trompe, *n.* trumpet 1163; *pl.* 667

trone, *n.* throne 882, 1079; *~ of astate: see* astat

truse, treuse, trewse, *n.* agreed temporary cessation of armed hostilities 35, 506, 616, etc.

tulle , *prep.* until 671, 1087

tumbe, *n.* tomb 130

turne, *n.* stratagem 962

iturnyd, *pa.t. sg.* converted 200

þan, þanne, *adv.* then 523, 532, 552, etc.

þankeynge, *pr. p.* offering gratitude to 165

þat, *dem. pron.* those 127(2), 968(2), 1103; *cj.* so that 147, 221, 271, etc.; *with* ~ ~ provided that, on the condition that 382, 398

þe, *pron.* you 122, 123, 136, etc.

þedur, *prep.* to there 166

þei, *pron.* they 311, 631

þeyer(e), theyere, *pron. gen. pl.* their 757, 771, 1123 etc.

þens, *adv.* (from) there 93, 164, 169, etc.

þer(e)as, thereas, *conjunctive adv.* where 407, 780, 981

þerin(e), *adv.* in that place, in that matter 90, 243, 555

þereon, *prep.* thereupon 1072

þerto, *adv.* to that place, to that matter 411, 448, 613, etc.

þicke, þilke, þucke, thicke, *dem. adj. & pron.* that (same), those (same) 88, 128, 234, etc.

þyn(e), *gen. pron.* your(s) 135, 137, 398, etc.

þo(o), *dem. pron. pl.* those 155, 285, 315, etc.

þorow, *prep.* through 170, 1069, 1094

þou, þow, *pron. 2 sg.* you 112, 120, 121, etc.

þouȝtte, *pa.t. sg.* intended, 919

þow, *conj.* though 712, 729, 791, etc.

þred(e), þredde, *adj.* third 322, 807, 876, etc.

þretinge, *pr. p.* menacing 762

þucke *see* þicke

vndur(e), *prep.* according to 103, 138, 317, etc.; ~ *this forme: see* forme; beneath 474, 779

vngodely, *adv.* badly, poorly 642, 645

vnité, *adj.* indivisibility 825, 840

vnknowe, vnknowen, *ppl. adj.* not known 107, 118, 498

vnknowynge, *ppl. adj.* (*as quasi-adv.*) without acknowledgment 663

vnkulle, *n.* uncle 743, 930

vnmade, *ppl.a.* uncreated but existent 848*n*

vnrehersid, *ppl. adj.* withheld from mention 180*n*

vnreuerence, *n.* disrespect 639

vnto, *prep.* until 94

vpsodoune, *adv.* inverted 390

valyȝe, *n.* valley 905

verbum, *Lat. n.* the word 1053

verely, *adv.* truly 383

vertuus, *n. pl.* virtues 358, 367

veyne, *adj.* worthless 575

veynyd, *ppl. adj.* (*?nonce-word*) made worthless 571*n*

vicion(e), vicioune, *n.* supernatural manifestation 63, 139, 282

vicis, *n. pl.* vices 359, 367

visour(e)s, visours, *n. pl.* faceguards on helmets 49, 935, 958, etc.

vitailid, *ppl. adj.* provisioned 147

vouwarde, vouwharde *n.* vanguard of a military column 328, 332

wadude, *pa.t. pl.* waded, walked in a liquid 679

wakyd, *v.¹ pa.t. sg.* awoke 785

wakyde, *v.² pa.t. pl.* watched, guarded 1082, 1087; wakynge, *pr. p.* 1081

iwallid, *ppl. adj.* furnished with walls of fortification 146

walyȝe, *n.* valley 905

wan(ne), wen(ne), whan(e), whanne, *cj.* when 86, 88, 193, etc.

warde, *n.* division of an army 656, 657, 948, etc.; ward(d)is, whardis, *pl.* 430, 655, 656, etc.

ware, *n.* army 1129

ware, *see* be, *v.*

wat, what, *inter. pron.; But* ~ ? What more? What of it? 102, 193, 337, etc.

water, *n.* body of water 197; river 253, 329, 516

waxe, *subj. sg.* become 365; waxid(e), waxed, wexide, whaxe, *pa.t. sg. & pl.* 27, 307, 335, etc.

wayne, *n.* wagon 975, 976, 982

wayte, *v.* watch, spy upon 1160

wele, welle, *n.* wheel 837, 838, 902, etc.

wele, *adv.* without difficulty, satisfactorily 13, 14, 304, etc.

wele-fy(ȝ)t(t)inge, *adj.* proficient in arms, valiant 351*n*, 489, 1135

welpis, *n.* kittens 889

wen(ne) *see* wan(ne)

went, *pa. t.* believed 793

were, *adv.* where 26, 106, 318, etc.

weride, *pa.t. sg.* wore 1077

werke, *n.* literary or artistic production, 175, 228; intercourse 853; werkis *pl.* deeds 135

werre, *n.* war 135, 500, 951, etc.
wery, *adj.* tired 777, 798, 1144, etc.
westementis, *n. pl.* ceremonial clothes 245
wete, *n.* wheat 885
wete, whete, *v.* know; *do þe (to)* ~: *see* do(o)
wexide *see* waxid(e)
wey, whey, *n.* passage 104, 110, 126, etc.; *hole* ~: *see* hole, *adj.*
whan(e), whanne *see* wann(e)
whardis *see* warde
whare *see* be, *v.*
what *see* wat
whaxe *see* waxid(e)
where, *v. see* be, *v.*
whete *see* wete
whey *see* wey
wile, *n.* passage of time 4
wyle *n.* strategem 950, 970
wyly, *adj.* crafty, shrewd 962
wynne, *n.* wine 1068, 1113, 1122, etc.
wyse, wise, whise, *n.* way, manner 112, 148, 282, etc.
with þat þat, *see* þat
withhylde, *pa.t. sg.* held back 268, 285
wodis, *n. pl.* forest, woods 1136, 1151, 1164; wode, woode *sg.* 335, 1166
wold(e) *see* woll(e)
wolduste *see* woll(e)
wolffis, *n. pl.* wolves 295
woll(e), *1 & 3 sg.* will, wish 284, 359, 382, etc.; wolte, *2 sg.* 398, 1167; wolduste, *pa.t. 2 sg.* 152; wold(e), *pa.t. 3 sg. & pl.* 154, 167, 168, etc.

wolte *see* woll(e)
wondurly, *adv.* with awe and admiration 160
wood(d)e *see* wodis
woodde, *adj.* mad 958
worddis, *n. gen.* of the world 881
worship, *n.* honour, glory 138, 148, 417, etc.
worshipfull, *adj.* honorable 343
worshipfully, *adv.* with honour 161, 1013
write, *pp.* written 11
wronge, *pa.t. 3 sg.* clenched 764

yaffe, 3aue, *pa. t. sg. & pl.* gave 465, 476, 569 etc.
ydulle, *n.* idol 219
ydulle, *adj.* idle 877
ye, 3e, *pron. 2 sg. & pl.* you 5, 113, 267, etc.
yee, *adv.* yes 843
yeftis, *n. pl.* gifts 1074
yelde, *v.* 158; *subj. sg.* give up, hand over 426, 520, 1016; *pa.t. sg. & pl.* 987, 988
iyeldude, *pp.* handed over 933
3ere, yere, *n.* year 183, 234, 1077; *as pl.* 9, 242
yerely, *adv.* annually 1016
yeue, 3eue, *v.* give 444, 456, 523, etc.; *imper.* 150; *subj. sg. & pl.* 274, 398, 427, etc.; yeuynge, *pr. p.* 317
3onger, *adj.* younger 747
yow, *pron. 2 sg.* you 6, 553, 569
yut, yutte, yet *conjunctive adv.* nevertheless, notwithstanding 831, 834, 838, etc.

INDEX OF PROPER NAMES

Spellings given are those of the scribe and rubricator; variant spellings are cited in order of frequency, or, where equal in number, in alphabetical order. A maximum of three occurrences of a particular name are recorded by line number, and the existence of subsequent occurrences indicated by 'etc.' The Latin form of each name is cited in brackets; the Latin forms are taken from Meredith-Jones, except where *Tr* provides a form closer to the ME. If a form in the ME is derived from an inflected form in the Latin, the inflected form is cited. An '*n*' after a line reference draws attention to a note in the apparatus or Commentary. A '*t*' after a line reference indicates an occurence in the first manuscript title (top of fol. 326ra). An asterisk before a citation designates an emended form.

Accintina (*Accintina*) city of Guadix, Spain 181

Adam (*Adam*) the first man 843, 844, 853, etc.

Adama (*Adama*) legendary city of Spain cursed by Charles 211*n*

Admiraldus (*Admirandus*) Saracen king of Babilon 718*n*, 1108

Affrica (*Affrica*) North Africa 257

Affricanis (*Affricanis*) North African forces in the army of Aigalonde 373

Agabie (*Agabia*) island of Zerbi, Gulf of Tunis 376

Agelonde, Agalonde see **Aigalond(e)**

*Agenni, Agenny, *Aginni (*Agenni*) city of Agen, Gascony 28, 370, 379*n*

Aigalond(e), Aigolond(e), Aigelond(e), Agelonde, Agalond(e), Aigilond, Aygalond (*Aigolandus*) Saracen king from North Africa 24, 31, 35, etc.

Akune (*Aquisgranum*) Aachen/Aix-la-Chapelle 4, 247

Alandaluffe, Alandulphe (*Alandaluf, Alandaluph*) Alandalusia 215, 994

Alexandre (*Alexandria*) city of Alexandria, Egypt 375

Almayne (*Theutonica*) Germany 199; see also **Douchelonde**

Almeyns (*Theutonici*) Germans 995*n*

Almiraldus see **Galafrius Almiraldus**

Altimaior, Altumaior (*Altumaior*) Saracen king of Cordova 74, 677, 689, etc.

Ambices (*Arrabites*) exceptionally strong Saracen women of Bysertim 186*n*

Angloiris *see* **Milo**

Appuleis (*Apulei*) inhabitants of Apulia, southeastern Italy 993

Aquitanye (*Aquitania*) Aquitaine 492

Arabie, Arabia (*Arabie*) the Arabic-speaking world 217, 374, 450

Arastanus (*Arastagnus*) duke of Brittany 491, 663

Arnolde de Bellanda/de Belandam (*Arnaldus de Bellanda*) of Beaulande, France; leader in the army of Charlemagne 512, 662, 669

Arogone (*Aragonis*) Aragon 994

Axa (*Axa*) Dax, in Gascony 251

Babilon(e) see **Galafrius Almiraldus**

Bace (*terram Basclorum*) land of the Basques 991

Bakari (*Baioariam*) Bavaria 98

Baldwynne, Baldwynus (*Balduinus*) leader in the army of Charlemagne; brother of Roland 1150, 1151

Barbarie (*Barbarie*) Barbary, Saracen countries of the north coast of Africa 376

Barmatum (*Barmatum*) Saracen King slain by Charlemagne 1091

Bayoun (*Baiona*) town of Bayonne, France 270

Bedous (*Burdeus*) city of Bordeaux, France 494*n*

Belicandus, Beligandus, Bigalande, Biligande (*Beligandus*) Saracen leader; brother of Marseri 58, 1107, 1135, etc.

Bellanda, Bellandam see **Arnolde**

Berthe (*Berta*) sister of Charlemagne; mother of Roland 488

Bigalande see **Belicandus**

Biligande see **Belicandus**

Biterensis (*Biterensium*) town of Béziers, France 248